W9-AEQ-500

THE
AMAZING
DR. DARWIN

THE
AMAZING
DR. DARWIN

CHARLES SHEFFIELD

THE AMAZING DR. DARWIN

This is a work of fiction. All the characters and events portrayed in this book are fictional, and any resemblance to real people or incidents is purely coincidental.

A Baen Books Original

Baen Publishing Enterprises
P.O. Box 1403
Riverdale, NY 10471
www.baen.com

ISBN: 0-7434-3529-X

Cover art by Bob Eggleton

First printing, June 2002

Library of Congress Cataloging-in-Publication Data

Sheffield, Charles.
    The amazing Dr. Darwin / by Charles Sheffield.
        p. cm.
    "A Baen Books original"—T.p. verso.
    Contents: Introduciton — The devil of Malkirk — The heart of Ahura Mazda — The phantom of Dunwell Cove — The Lambeth immortal — The Solborne vampire — The treasure of Odirex — Appendix: Erasmus Darwin, fact and fiction.
    ISBN 0-7434-3529-X (HC)
    1. Darwin, Erasmus, 1731–1802—Fiction. 2. Adventure stories, American. 3. Science fiction, American. 4. Naturalists—Fiction. I. Title: Amazing Doctor Darwin. II. Title.

PS3569.H3953 A83 2002
813'.54—dc21   2002022328

Distributed by Simon & Schuster
1230 Avenue of the Americas
New York, NY 10020

Production by Windhaven Press, Auburn, NH
Printed in the United States of America

10 9 8 7 6 5 4 3 2 1

To Dutch, Sally, Patty, and Nancy—
where this began.

CONTENTS

A Note to the Reader: All the stories in this book have previously been printed in magazine form. Three of them also appeared in the early 1980s as the volume, *Erasmus Magister*. This is the first complete collection.

INTRODUCTION

In these degenerate times when lawyers rule the world, most works of fiction are preceded by a nervous disclaimer that runs roughly as follows: "All characters in this book are fictitious. Any resemblance to actual persons, living or dead, is purely coincidental."

That cannot be considered one of the more exciting parts of the plot, and most people probably do not read it. The statement is there to discourage libel and defamation suits. I doubt that it helps. Like garlic against vampires, the disclaimer sounds comforting, but it never works when you really need it.

In this book I faced a different problem. Erasmus Darwin was undeniably a living, breathing human being, but his accomplishments were so substantial and diverse that it is difficult to portray him in fiction without being accused of painting him larger than life.

I do not think I have done that. If anything, I have understated the man. In breadth of interests, inventiveness, acquaintances (from King George III to Coleridge

1

to James Watt to Ben Franklin), and human kindness, Darwin bestrode his age. He is arguably the greatest eighteenth century Englishman, a better candidate for that title than Chatham, Pitt the Younger, Pope, Sam Johnson, Marlborough, Priestley, Cavendish, or any other figure in the arts or sciences.

The claim is a large one. In an appendix to this book I have sought to support it, and at the same time drawn a dividing line between the facts and the fiction of each story. If you, like me, tend to read a book from the back forward, be warned: *Statements contained in the Appendix reveal plot elements of each story*.

On the other hand, if you are such a person, it is already too late. You will be reading this Introduction last of all. I hope that you enjoyed the stories.

—Charles Sheffield

THE DEVIL OF MALKIRK

The spring evening was warm and still, and the sound of conversation carried far along the path from the open window of the house. It was enough to make the man walking the gravel surface hesitate, then turn his steps onto the lawn. He walked silently across the well trimmed grass to the bay window, stooped, and peered through a gap in the curtains. A few moments more, and he returned to the path and entered the open door of the house.

Ignoring the servant waiting there, he turned left and went at once into the dining room. He looked steadily around him, while the conversation at the long table gradually died down.

"Dr. Darwin?" His voice was gruff and formal.

The eight men seated at dinner were silent for a moment, assessing the stranger. He was tall and gaunt, with a dark, sallow complexion. Long years of intense sunlight had stamped a permanent frown across his brow, and a slight, continuous trembling of his hands spoke of other legacies of foreign disease. He returned the stares in silence.

After a few seconds one of the seated men pushed his chair back from the table.

"I am Erasmus—Darwin." The slight hesitation as he pronounced his name suggested a stammer more than any kind of contrived pause. "Who are you, and what is your business here?"

The speaker had risen to his feet as he spoke. He stepped forward, and was revealed as grossly overweight, with heavy limbs and a fat, pockmarked face. He stood motionless, calmly awaiting the intruder's reply.

"Jacob Pole, at your service," said the stranger. Despite the warmth of the April evening he was wearing a grey scarf of knitted wool, which he tightened now around his neck. "Colonel Jacob Pole of Lichfield. You and I are far afield tonight, Dr. Darwin, but we are neighbors. My house is no more than two miles from yours. You provided medication once, to my wife and to my young daughter. As for my business, it is not of my choosing and I fear it may be a bad one. I am here to ask your urgent assistance on a medical matter at Bailey's Farm, not half a mile from this house."

There was a chorus of protesting voices from the table. A thin-faced man who wore no wig stood up and stepped closer.

"Colonel Pole, this is my house. I will forgive your entry to it uninvited and unannounced, since we understand that medical urgencies must banish formalities. But you interrupt more than a dinner among friends. I am Matthew Boulton, and tonight the Lunar Society meets here on serious matters. Mr. Priestley is visiting from Calne to tell of his latest researches on the new air. He is well begun, but by no means finished. Can your business wait an hour?"

Jacob Pole stood up straighter than ever. "If disease

could be made to wait, I would do the same. As it is . . ." He turned to Darwin again. "I am no more than a messenger here, one who happened to be dining with Will Bailey. I have come at the request of Dr. Monkton, to ask your immediate assistance."

There was another outcry from those still seated at the table. "Monkton! Monkton asking for assistance? Never heard of such a thing."

"Forget it, 'Rasmus! Sit back down and try this rhubarb pie."

"If it's Monkton," said a soberly dressed man on the right hand side of the table, "then the patient is as good as dead. He's no doctor, he's an executioner. Come on, Colonel Pole, take a glass of claret and sit down with us. We meet too infrequently to relish a disturbance."

Erasmus Darwin waved him to silence. "Steady, Josiah, I know your views of Dr. Monkton." He turned full face to Pole, to show a countenance where the front teeth had long been lost from the full mouth. The jaw was jowly and in need of a razor. Only the eyes belied the impression of coarseness and past disease. They were grey and patient, with a look of deep sagacity and profound power of observation.

"Forgive our jests," he said. "This is an old issue here. Dr. Monkton has not been one to ask my advice on disease, no matter what the circumstance. What does he want now?"

The outcry came again. "He's a pompous old windbag."

"Killer Monkton—don't let him lay a finger on you."

"I wouldn't let him touch you, not if you want to live."

Pole had been staring furiously about him while the men at the table mocked Monkton's medical skills. He ignored the glass held out toward him, and a scar across the left side of his forehead was showing a flush of red.

"I might share your opinion of Dr. Monkton," he said curtly. "However, I would extend that view to all doctors.

They kill far more than they cure. As for you gentlemen, and Dr. Darwin here, if you all prefer your eating and drinking to the saving of life, I cannot change those priorities."

He turned to glare at Darwin. "My message is simple. I will give it and leave. Dr. Monkton asks me to say three things: that he has a man at Bailey's Farm who is critically ill; that already the *facies* of death are showing; and that he would like *you*"—he leaned forward to make it a matter between him and Darwin alone—"to come and see that patient. If you will not do it, I will go back and so inform Dr. Monkton."

"No." Darwin sighed. "Colonel Pole, our rudeness to you was unforgivable, but there was a reason for it. These meetings of the Society are the high point of our month, and animal spirits sometimes drive us to exceed the proprieties. Give me a moment to call for my greatcoat and we will be on our way. My friends have told you their opinions of Dr. Monkton, and I must confess I am eager to see his patient. In my years of practice between here and Lichfield, Dr. Monkton and I have crossed paths many times—but never has he sought my advice on a medical matter. We are of very different schools, for both diagnosis and treatment."

He turned back to the group, silent now that their high spirits were damped. "Gentlemen, I am sorry to miss both the discussion and the companionship, but work calls." He moved to Pole's side. "Let us go. The last of the light is gone but the moon should be up. We will manage well without a lantern. If Death will not wait, then nor must we."

The road that led to Bailey's Farm was flanked by twin lines of hedgerow. It had been an early spring, and the moonlit white of flowering hawthorn set parallel lines to mark the road ahead. The two men walked side by side,

Darwin glancing across from time to time at the other's gloomy profile.

"You appear to have no great regard for the medical profession," he said at last. "Though you bear marks of illness yourself."

Jacob Pole shrugged his shoulders and did not speak.

"But yet you are a friend of Dr. Monkton?" continued Darwin.

Pole turned a frowning face toward him. "I most certainly am not. As I told you, I am no more than a messenger for him, one who happened to be at the farm." He hesitated. "If you press the point—as you seem determined to do—I will admit that I am no friend to any doctor. Men put more blind faith in witless surgeons than they do in the Lord Himself."

"And with more reason," said Darwin softly.

Pole did not seem to hear. "Blind faith," he went on. "And against all logic. When you pay a man money to cut off your arm, it's no surprise that he tells you an arm must come off to save your life. In twenty years of service to the country, I am appalled when I think how many limbs have come off for no reason more than a doctor's whim."

"And on that score, Colonel Pole," said Darwin tartly, "your twenty years of service must also have told you that it would take a thousand of the worst doctors to match the limb-lopping effects of even the least energetic of generals. Look to the ills of your own profession."

There was an angry silence and both men paced faster along the moonlit road.

The farm stood well back, a hundred yards from the main highway to Lichfield. The path to it was a gloomy avenue of tall elms and by the time they were halfway along it they could see a tall figure standing in the doorway and peering out toward them. As they came closer he leaned back inside to pick up a lantern and strode to meet them.

"Dr. Darwin, I fear you are none too soon." The speaker's voice was full and resonant, like that of a singer or a practiced clergyman, but there was no warmth or welcome in it.

Darwin nodded. "Colonel Pole tells me that the situation looks grave. I have my medical chest with me back at Matthew Boulton's house. If there are drugs or dressings needed, Dr. Monkton, they can be brought here in a few minutes."

"I think it may already be too late for that." They had reached the door, and Monkton paused there. He was broad shouldered, with a long neck and a red, bony face. His expression was dignified and severe. "By the time Colonel Pole left here, the man was already sunk to unconsciousness. Earlier this evening there was delirium, and utterances that were peculiar indeed. I have no great hopes for him."

"He is one of Bailey's farmworkers?"

"He is not. He is a stranger, taken ill on the road near here. The woman with him came for help to the farm. Fortunately I was already here, attending to Father Bailey's rheumatics." He shrugged. "That is a hopeless case, of course, in a man of his age."

"Mm. Perhaps." Darwin sounded unconvinced, but he did not press it. "It was curiously opportune that you were here. So tell me, Dr. Monkton, just what is this stranger's condition?"

"Desperate. You will see it for yourself," he went on at Darwin's audible grunt of dissatisfaction. "He lies on a cot at the back of the scullery."

"Alone? Surely not?"

"No. His companion is with him. I explained to her that his condition is grave, and she seemed to comprehend well enough for one of her station." He set the lantern on a side table in the entrance and took a great pinch of snuff from a decorated ivory box. "Neither one of them showed much sign of learning. They are poor workers from the North, on their way to London to seek employment. She seemed more afraid of me than worried about her man's condition."

"So I ask again, what is that condition?" Darwin's voice showed his exasperation. "It would be better for you to give me your assessment out of their hearing—though I gather that he is hearing little enough."

"He hears nothing, not if lightning were to strike this house. His condition, in summary: the eyes deep-set in the head, closed, the whites only showing in the ball; the countenance, dull and grey; skin, rough and dry to the touch; before he became delirious he complained that he was feeling bilious."

"There was vomiting?"

"No, but he spoke of the feeling. And of pain in the chest. His muscle tone was poor and I detected weakened irritability."

Darwin grunted skeptically, causing Monkton to look at him in a condescending way.

"Perhaps you are unfamiliar with von Haller's work on this, Dr. Darwin? I personally find it to be most convincing. At any rate, soon after I came to him the delirium began."

"And what of his pulse?" Darwin's face showed his concentration. "And was there fever?"

Monkton hesitated for a moment, as though unsure what to answer. "There was no fever," he said at last. "And I do not think that the pulse was elevated in rate."

"Huh." Darwin pursed his full lips. "No fever, no rapid pulse—and yet delirium." He turned to the other man. "Colonel Pole, did you also see this?"

"I did indeed." Pole nodded vigorously. "Look here, I know it may be the custom of the medical profession to talk about symptoms until the patient is past saving—but don't you think you should see the man for yourself, while he's alive?"

"I do." Darwin smiled, unperturbed by the other's gruff manner. "But first I wanted all the facts I can get. Facts are important, Colonel, the fulcrum of diagnosis. Would you prefer me to rush in and operate, another arm or leg gone? Or discuss the man's impending death in the presence of his wife or daughter? That is not a physician's role, the addition of new misery beyond disease itself. But lead the way, Dr. Monkton, I am ready now to see your patient."

Jacob Pole frowned as he followed the other two men back through the interior of the old farmhouse. His expression showed mingled irritation and respect. "You sawbones are all the same," he muttered. "You have an answer for everything except a man's illness."

The inside of the farmhouse was dimly lit. A single oil lamp stood in the middle of the long and chilly corridor that led to the scullery and kitchen. The floor was uneven stone flags and the high shelves carried preserved and wrinkled apples, their acid smell pleasant and surprising.

Monkton opened the door to the scullery, stepped inside, and grunted at the darkness there. "This is a nuisance. I told her to stay here with him, but she has gone off somewhere and allowed the lamp to go out. Colonel Pole, would you bring the lantern from the corridor?"

While Pole went back for it Darwin stood motionless in the doorway, sniffing the air in the dark room. When there was light Monkton looked around and gave a cry of astonishment.

"Why, he's not here. He was lying on that cot in the corner."

"Maybe he died, and they moved him?" suggested Pole.

"No, they wouldn't do that," said Monkton, but for the first time his voice was uncertain. "Surely they would not move him without my permission?"

"Looks as though they did, though," said Pole. "We can settle that easily enough."

He threw back his head. "Willy, where are you?"

The shout echoed through the whole house. After a few seconds there was an answering cry from upstairs.

"What's wrong, Jacob? Do you need help there?"

"No. Has anybody been down here from upstairs, Willy? While I was gone, I mean."

"No. I didn't want to risk the sickness."

"That sounds right," grunted Pole. "Brave old Willy, hiding upstairs with his pipe and flagon."

"Has anyone downstairs been using tobacco?" asked Darwin quietly.

"What?" Pole stared at him. "Tobacco?"

"Use your nose, man. Sniff the air in here." Darwin was prowling forward. "There's been a pipe alight here in the past quarter of an hour. Do you smell it now? I somehow doubt that it was the man's wife that was smoking it."

He walked forward to the cot itself and laid a plump hand flat upon it. "Quite cold. So here we are, but we find no dead man, and no dying man. Dr. Monkton, in your opinion how long did the stranger have to live?"

"Not long." Monkton cleared his throat uncomfortably. "Not more than an hour or two, I would judge."

"Within an hour of final sacrament, and then gone," grunted Darwin. He shook his head and sat on the edge of the cot. "So now what? I don't think we'll find him easily, and we have all three sacrificed an evening to this already. If you are willing to waste a few more minutes, I'd much like to hear what the patient said when he became delirious. What do you say, gentlemen? May we discuss it?"

Pole and Monkton looked at each other.

"If you wish, although I am very doubtful that it—"

began the physician, his rich voice raised a good half octave.

"All right," interrupted Pole. "Let's do it. But I don't propose to debate this here, in the scullery. Let's go upstairs. I'm sure Will Bailey can find us a comfortable place, and a glass as well if you want it—perhaps he can even find you an acceptable substitute for that rhubarb pie." He turned to the other physician. "As you know, Dr. Monkton, when you were tending to the man I did little more than watch. With your leave, maybe I should say what I saw, and you can correct me as you see fit. Agreed?"

"Well, now, I don't know. I'm not at all sure that I am willing to—"

"Splendid." Jacob Pole picked up the lamp and started back along the corridor, leaving the others the choice of following or being left behind in darkness.

"Colonel Pole!" Monkton lost his dignity and scuttled after him, leaving Darwin, smiling to himself, to bring up the rear. "Slower there, Colonel. D'you want to see a broken leg in the dark here?"

"No. With *two* doctors to attend it, a broken leg would more than likely prove fatal." But Pole slowed his steps and turned so that the lamp threw its beam back along the corridor. "What an evening. Will Bailey and I had just nicely settled in for a pipe of Virginia and a talk about old times—we were together at Pondicherry, and at the capture of Manila—when word came up from downstairs that Dr. Monkton needed another pair of hands to help."

"Why not Will Bailey?" asked Darwin from behind him. "It is his house."

"Aye, but Willy had shipped a few pints of porter, and I'd been running reasonable dry. I left him there to nod, and I came down." Pole sniffed. "I'm no physician—you may have guessed that already—but when I saw our man back there in the scullery I could tell he was halfway to the hereafter. He was mumbling to himself, mumbling and muttering. It took me a few minutes to get the hang of his accent—Scots, and thick enough to cut. And he was all the time shivering and shaking, and muttering, muttering . . .”

The woman had been standing by the side of the cot, holding the man's right hand in both of hers. As the hoarse voice grew louder and more distinct she leaned toward him.

“John, no. Don't talk that way.” Her voice was frightened, and for a brief moment the man's eyes seemed to flicker in their sunk pits, as though about to open. She looked nervously at Jacob Pole and at Dr. Monkton, who was preparing a poultice of kaolin and pressed herbs.

“His mind's not there. He—he doesna’ know whut he's sayin’. Hush, Johnnie, an’ lie quiet.”

“Inland from Handa Island, there by the Minch,” said the man suddenly, as though answering some unspoken question. “Aye, inside the loch. That's where ye'll find it.”

“Sh. Johnnie, now quiet ye.” She squeezed his hand gently, an attractive dark-haired woman bowed down with worry and work. “Try and sleep, John, ye need rest.”

The unshaven jaw was moving again, its dark bristles emphasizing the pale lips and waxen cheeks. Again the eyelids fluttered.

“Two hundred years,” he said in a creaking voice. “Two hundred years it lay there, an’ niver a mon suspected whut was in it. One o’ auld King Philip's ships, an’ crammed. Aye, an’ not one to ken it ’til a month back, wi’ all the guid gold.”

Jacob Pole started forward, his thin face startled. The woman saw him move and shook her head.

"Sir, pay him no mind. He's not wi' us, he's ramblin' in the head."

"Move back, then, and give me room," said Monkton. His manner was brisk. "And if you, sir"—he nodded at Pole—"will hold his shoulders while I apply this to his chest. And you, my good woman, go off to the kitchen and bring more hot water. Perhaps this will give him ease."

"I canna' leave him noo." The woman's voice was anguished. "There's no sayin' whut he'll come out with. He might—" Her voice trailed off under the doctor's glare and she picked up the big brass bowl and reluctantly crept out. Jacob Pole took the man firmly by the shoulders, leaning forward to assure his grip.

"Inland from Handa Island," said the man after a few seconds. His breath caught and rattled in his throat, but there seemed to be a tone of a confidence shared. "Aye, ye have it to rights, a wee bit north of Malkirk, at the entrance there of Loch Malkirk. A rare find. But we'll need equipment to take it, 'tis twenty feet down, an' bullion weighs heavy. An' there's the Devil to worrit about. Need help . . ."

His voice faded and he groaned as the hot poultice was applied to his bare chest. His hands twitched, flew feebly upwards toward his throat, and then flopped back to his sides.

"Hold him," said Monkton. "There's a new fit coming."

"I have him." Pole's voice was quiet and he was leaning close to the man, watching the pallid lips. "Easy, Johnnie."

The dark head was turning to and fro on the folded blanket, grunting with some inner turmoil. The thin hands began to clench and unclench.

"Go south for it." The words were little more than a whisper. "That's it, have to go south. Ye know the position here in the Highlands, but we'll have to have weapons. Ye canna' fight the Devil wi' just dirks and muskets, ye need a regular bombard. I've seen it—bigger than leviathan, taller than Foinaven, an' strong as Fingal. Five men killed, an' three more crippled, an' nothin' to show for it."

"It's coming," said Monkton suddenly. "He's stiffening in the limbs."

The breath was coming harder in the taut throat. "Go get the weapons . . . wi'out that we'll lose more o' the clansmen. Weapons, put by Loch Malkirk, an' raise the bullion . . . canna' fight the Devil . . . wi' just dirks. Aye, I'll do it . . . south, then. Need weapons . . . bigger than leviathan . . ."

As the voice faded, his thin hands moved up to clasp Pole's restraining hands and Pole winced as black fingernails dug deep into his wrists.

"Hold tight," said Monkton. "It's the final spasm."

But even as he spoke, the stranger's muscles began to lose their tension. The thin hands slid down to the chest and the harsh breathing eased. Jacob Pole stood looking down at the still face.

"Has he—gone?"

"No." Monkton looked puzzled. "He still breathes, and it somehow seems to have eased. I—I thought . . . Well, he's quiet now. Would you go and find the woman, and see where that hot water has got to? I would also like to cup him."

Pole was peering at the man's face. "He seems a lot better. He's not shaking the way he was. What will you do next?''

"Well, the cupping, he certainly needs to be bled." Monkton coughed. "Then I think another plaster, of mustard, Burgundy pitch, and pigeon dung. And perhaps an enema of antimony and rock salt, and possibly wormwood bitters."

"Sweet Christ." Pole shook his head and wiped his nose

on his sleeve. "Not for me. I'd rather be costive for a week. I'll go fetch his woman."

"And that was it?" Darwin was seated comfortably in front of the empty fireplace, a dish of dried plums and figs on his lap. Jacob Pole stood by the window, looking moodily out into the night and glancing occasionally at Will Bailey. The farmer was slumped back in an armchair, snoring and snorting and now and then jerking back for a few moments of consciousness.

"That's as I recall it—and I listened hard." Pole shrugged. "I don't know what happened after I left the room, of course, but Dr. Monkton says the man was peaceful and unconscious until he too left. The woman stayed."

Darwin picked up a fig and frowned at it. "I have no desire to further lower your opinion of my profession, but now that he is gone I must say that Dr. Monkton's powers of observation are not impressive to me. You looked close at that man's face, you say. And as a soldier you presumably have seen men die?"

"Aye. And women and children, sad to say." Pole looked at him morosely. "What's that to do with it?"

Darwin sighed. "Nothing, it seems, according to you and my colleague, Dr. Monkton. Think, sir, think of that room you were in. Think of the *smell* of it."

"The tobacco? You already remarked on that, and I recall no other."

"Exactly. So ask yourself of the smell that was *not* there. A man lies dying, eh? He displays the classic Hippocratic facies of death, as Dr. Monkton described it—displays them so exactly that it is as though they were copied from a text. So. But where was the smell of mortal disease? You know that smell?"

Pole turned suddenly. "There was none. Damme, I knew there was something odd about that room. I know that smell all too well—sweet, like the charnel house. Now why the blazes didn't Dr. Monkton remark it? He must encounter it all the time."

Darwin shrugged his heavy shoulders and chewed on another wrinkled plum. "Dr. Monkton has gone beyond the point in his profession where his reputation calls for exact observation. It comes to all of us at last. 'Man, proud man, drest in a little brief authority, most ignorant of what he's most assured.' Aye, there's some of that in all of us, you and me, too. But let us go, if you will, a little further. The man gripped your wrists and you held his shoulders. There was delirium, you have told me that, in his voice. But what was the *feel* of him?"

Pole paced back and forth along the room, his skinny frame stooped in concentration. He finally stopped and glared at Will Bailey. "Pity you've no potion to stop him snoring. I can't hear myself think. A man can't fix his mind around anything with that noise. Let's see now, what was the feel of him."

He held his hands out before him. "I held him so, and he gripped at my wrists thus. Dirty hands, with long black nails."

"And their warmth? Carry your mind back to them."

"No, not hot. He wasn't fevered, not at all. But not cold, either. But . . ." Pole paused and bit his lip. "Something else. The Dutch have my guts, his hands were *soft*. Black and dirty, but not rough, the way you'd expect for a farmer or a tinker. His hands didn't match his clothes at all."

"I conjectured it so." Darwin spat a plum stone into the empty fireplace. "Will you allow me to carry one step further?"

"More yet? Damme, to my mind we've enough mystery already. What now?"

"You have seen the world in your army service. You have been aboard a fighting ship and know its usual cargo. Did anything strike you as strange about our dying friend's story?"

"The ship, one of King Philip's galleons, sunk off the coast of Scotland two hundred years ago." Pole licked at his chapped lips and a new light filled his eyes. "With a load of bullion on board it."

"Exactly. A wreck in Loch Malkirk, we deduce, and bearing gold. Now, Colonel Pole, have you ever been involved in a search for treasure?"

Before Pole could answer there was a noise like a hissing wood fire from the other armchair. It was Will Bailey, awake again and shaking with laughter.

"Ever been involved in a hunt for treasure, Jacob! There's a good one for me to tell yer wife." He went into another fit of merriment. "Should I tell the Doctor, Jacob?"

He turned to Darwin. "There was never a man born under the sun who followed treasure harder. He had me at it, too—diving for pearls off Sarawak, and trawling for old silver off the Bermudas' reefs." He lay back, croaking with laughter. "Tell 'im, Jacob, you tell 'im all about it."

Pole peered at him in the dim light. "Will Bailey, you're a shapeless mass of pox-ridden pig's muck. Tell him about yourself, instead of talking about me. Who ate the poultice off the black dog's back, eh? Who married the chimney sweep, and who hanged the monkey?"

"So you have found treasure before?" interjected Darwin, and Pole turned his attention back to the doctor.

"Not a shillings-worth, though I've sought it hard enough, along with fat Will there. I've searched, aye, and I've even hunted bullion out on the Main, in sunk Spanish galleons; but I've never found enough to pay a minute's rent on a Turkish privy. What of it, then?"

"Consider our wrecked galleon, resting for two hundred years off the coast of Scotland. How would it have got there? Spanish galleons were not in the habit of sailing the Scottish coast—still less at a time when England and Spain were at war."

"The Armada!" said Bailey. "He's saying yon ship must have been part of the Spanish Armada, come to invade England."

"The Armada indeed. Defeated by Drake and the English fleet, afraid to face a straight journey home to Cadiz through the English Channel, eh? Driven to try for a run the long way, around the north coast of Scotland, with a creep down past Ireland. Many of the galleons tried that."

Pole nodded. "It fits. But—"

"Aye, speak your but." Darwin's eyes were alight with pleasure. "What is your but?"

"But a ship of the Armada had no reason to carry bullion. If anything, she'd have been stripped of valuables in case she went down in battle."

"Exactly!" Darwin slapped his fat thigh. "Yet against all logic we find sunk bullion in Loch Malkirk. One more factor, then I'll await your comment: you and I both live fifteen miles from here, and I at least am an infrequent visitor; yet I was called on to help Dr. Monkton—who has never before called me in for advice or comment on anything. *Ergo*, someone knew my whereabouts tonight, and someone persuaded Monkton to send for me. *Who*? Who asked you to fetch me from Matthew Boulton's house?"

Pole frowned. "Why, he did." He pointed at Will Bailey.

"Nay, but the woman told me you and Monkton asked for that." Bailey looked baffled. "Only she didn't know the way, and had to get on back in there with her man. That's when I asked you to do it—I thought you knew all about it."

Darwin was nodding in satisfaction. "Now we have the whole thing. And observe, at every turn we come back to the two strangers—long since disappeared, and I will wager we see no more of them."

"But what the devil's been going on?" said Pole. He scratched at his jaw and wiped his nose again on his sleeve. "A dying man, Spanish bullion, a leviathan in Loch Malkirk—how did we get into the middle of all this? I come here for a bite of free dinner and a quiet smoke with Willy, and before I know it I'm running over the countryside as confused as Lazarus' widow."

"What is really going on?" Darwin rubbed at his grey wig. "As to that, at the moment I could offer no more than rank conjecture. We lack tangible evidence. But for what it is worth, Colonel, I believe that you were involved largely accidentally. My instincts tell me that I was the primary target, and someone aimed their shafts at my curiosity or my cupidity."

"The bullion?" Pole's eyes sparkled. "Aye, where they tickled me, too. If you go, I'd like a chance to join you. I've done it before, and I know some of the difficulties. Rely on me."

Darwin shook his head. The plate of fruit had been emptied, and there was a dreamy look on his coarse features. "It is not the treasure, that can be yours, Colonel— if it proves to exist. No, sir, there's sweeter bait for me, something I can scent but not yet see. The Devil, and one thing more, must wait for us in Malkirk."

The pile in the courtyard of the stage inn had been growing steadily. An hour before, three leather bags had been delivered, then a square oak chest and a canvas-wrapped package. The coachman sat close to the wall of the inn, warming his boots at a little brazier and shielding his back against the unseasonably cold May wind. He was drinking from a tankard of small beer and looking doubtfully from the swelling heap of luggage to the roof of the coach.

Finally he looked over his shoulder, measured the angle of the sun with an experienced eye, and rose to his feet. As he did so there was a clatter of horses' hooves.

Two light pony traps came into view, approaching from opposite directions. They met by the big coach. Two passengers climbed down from them, looked first at the pile of luggage on the ground, then at the laden traps, and finally at each other. The brooding coachman was ignored completely.

The fat man shook his head.

"This is ridiculous, Colonel. When we agreed to share a coach for this enterprise it was with the understanding that I would take my medical chest and equipment with me. They are bulky, but I do not care to travel without them, for even a few miles from home. However, it did not occur to me that you would then choose to bring with you all your household possessions." He waved a brawny arm at the other trap. "We are *visiting* Scotland, not removing ourselves to it permanently."

The tall, scrawny man had moved to his light carriage and was struggling to take down from it a massive wooden box. Despite his best effort he was unable to lift it clear, and after a moment he gave up, grunted, and turned to face the other. He shook his head.

"A few miles from home is one thing, Dr. Darwin. Loch Malkirk is another. We will be far in the Highlands, beyond real civilization. I know that it has been thirty years since the Great Rebellion, but I'm told that the land is not quiet. It still seethes with revolt. We will need weapons—if not for the natives, then for the Devil."

Darwin had checked that his medical chest was safely aboard the coach. Now he came across to grasp one side of the box on the other trap, and between them they lowered it to the ground.

"You are quite mistaken," he said. "The Highlands are

unhappy but they are peaceful. Dr. Johnson fared well enough there, only three years ago. You will not need your weapons, though there is no denying that the people hold loyal to Prince Charles Edward—"

"The Young Pretender," grunted Pole. "The upstart blackguard who—"

"—who has what many would accept as a *legitimate* claim to the throne of Scotland, if not of England." Darwin was peering curiously into the wooden box, as Pole carefully raised the lid. "His loss in '46 was a disaster, but the clans are loyal in spite of his exile. Colonel Pole"—he had at last caught a glimpse of the inside of the box—"weapons are one thing, but I trust you are not proposing to take *that* with you to Malkirk."

"Certainly am." Jacob Pole crouched by the box and lovingly stroked the shining metal. "You'll never see a prettier cannon than Little Bess. Brass-bound, iron sheath on the bore, and fires a two-inch ball with black powder. Show me a devil or a leviathan in Loch Malkirk, and I'll show you something that's a good deal more docile when he's had one of these up his weasand." He held up a ball, lofting it an inch or two in the palm of his hand. "And if the natives run wild I'm sure it will do the same for them."

Darwin reached to open the lid wider. "Musket and shot, too. Where do you imagine that we are travelling, to the moon? You know the Highlanders are forbidden to carry weapons, and we have little enough room for *rational* appurtenances. The ragmatical collection you propose is too much."

"No more than your medical chests are too much." Pole straightened up. "I'll discard if you will, but not otherwise."

"Impossible. I have already winnowed to a minimum."

"And so have I."

The coachman stood up slowly and carried his empty

tankard back into the inn. Once inside he went over to the keg, placed his tankard next to it, and jerked his head back toward the door.

"Listen to that," he said gloomily. "Easy money, I thought it'd be, wi' just the two passengers. Now they're at each other before they've set foot in the coach, and I've contracted to carry them as far as Durham. Here, Alan, pour me another one in there before I go, and make it a big 'un."

The journey north was turning back the calendar, day by day and year by year. Beyond Durham the spring was noticeably less advanced, with the open apple blossom of Nottingham regressing by the time they reached Northumberland to tight pink buds a week away from bloom. The weather added to the effect with a return to the raw, biting cold of February, chilling fingers and toes through the thickest clothing.

At Otterburn they had changed coaches to an open dray that left them exposed to the gusts of a hard northeaster, and beyond Stirling the centuries themselves peeled away from the rugged land. The roads were unmetalled, mere stony scratches along the slopes of the mountains, and the mean houses of turf and rubble were dwarfed by the looming peaks.

At first Darwin had tried to write. He made notes in the thick volume of his Commonplace Book, balancing it on his knee. Worsening roads and persistent rain conspired to defeat him, and at last he gave up. He sat facing forward in the body of the dray, unshaven, swaddled in blankets and covered by a sheet of grey canvas with a hole cut in it for his head.

"Wild country, Colonel Pole." He gestured forward as they drove northwest along Loch Shin. "We are a long way from Lichfield. Look at that group."

He nodded ahead at a small band of laborers plodding

along the side of the track. Jacob Pole made a snorting noise that could have as well come from the horse. He was smoking a stubby pipe with a bowl like a cupped hand, and a jar of hot coals stood on the seat behind him.

"What of 'em?" he said. His pipe was newly charged with black tobacco scraped straight from the block, and he blew out a great cloud of blue-grey smoke. "I see nothing worth talking about. They're just dreary peasants."

"Ah, but they are pure Celt," said Darwin cheerfully. "Observe the shape of their heads, and the brachycephalic cranium. We'll see more of them as we go further north. It's been the way of it for three thousand years, the losers in the fight for good lands are pushed north and west. Scots and Celts and Picts, driven and crowded to the northern hills."

Jacob Pole peered at the group suspiciously as he tamped his pipe. "They may look like losers to you, but they look like tough fodder to me. Big and fierce. As for your idea that they don't carry weapons, take a look at those scythes and sickles, and then define a weapon for me." He patted his pocket under his leather cloak. "Ball and powder is what you need for savages. Mark my words, we'll be glad of these before we're done in Malkirk."

"I am not persuaded. The Rebellion was over thirty years ago."

"Aye, on the surface. But I've never yet heard of treasure being captured easy, there's always blood and trouble comes with it. It draws in violence, as sure as cow dung draws flies."

"I see. So you are suggesting that we should turn back?" Darwin's tone was sly.

"Did I say that?" Pole blew out an indignant cloud of smoke. "Never. We're almost there. If we can find boat and boatman, I'll be looking for that galleon before today's done, Devil or no Devil. I've never seen one in this world, and I hope I'll not see one in the next. But with your ideas on religion, I'm surprised you believe in devils at all."

"Devils?" Darwin's voice was quiet and reflective. "Certainly I am a believer in them, as much as the Pope himself; but I think he and I might disagree on the shapes they bear in the world. We should get our chance to find out soon enough." He lifted a brawny arm from under the canvas. "That has to be Malkirk, down the hill there. We have made better time from Lairg than I anticipated."

Jacob Pole scowled ahead. "And a miserable looking place it is, if that's all there is to it. But look close down there—maybe we're not the only visitors to these god-forsaken regions."

Half a mile in front of them two light carriages blocked the path that led through the middle of the village. The ill-clad cluster of people gathered around them turned as Pole drove the dray steadily forward and halted twenty yards from the nearer carriage.

He and Darwin stepped down, stretching joints stiffened by the long journey. As they did so three men came forward through the crowd. Darwin looked at them in surprise for a moment before nodding a greeting.

"I am Erasmus Darwin, and this is Colonel Jacob Pole. You received my message, I take it? We sent word ahead that we desire accommodation for a few days here in Malkirk."

He looked intently from one to the other. They formed a curiously ill-matched trio. The tallest of them was lean and dark, even thinner than Jacob Pole, and the possessor of bright, dark eyes that snapped from one scene to the next without ever remaining still. He had long-fingered hands, red cheeks that framed a hooked nose and a big chin, and he was dressed in a red tunic and green breeches covered by a patchwork cloak of blues and greys. His neighbor was of middle height and conventionally dressed—but his skin was coal-black and his prominent cheekbones wore deep patterns of old scars.

The third member stood slightly apart from the others. He was short and strongly built, with massive bare arms. His face was half hidden behind a growth of greying beard, and he seemed to crackle with excess energy. He had nodded vigorously as soon as Darwin asked about the message.

"Aye, aye, we got your message right enough. But I thought it came for these gentlemen." He jerked his head to the others at his side. "There was no word with it, ye see, saying who was comin', only a need for beds for two. But ye say ye're the Darwin as sent the note to me?"

"I am." Darwin looked rueful. "I should have said more with that message. It never occurred to me there might be two arrivals here in one day. Can you find room for us?"

The broad man shrugged. "I'll find ye a bed—but it will be one for the both of ye, I'll warn ye of that."

Jacob Pole stole a quick look at Darwin's bulky form.

"A good-sized bed," said the man, catching the glance. "In a middlin' sized room. An' clean, too, and that has Malcolm Maclaren's own word on it." He thumped at his thick chest. "An' that's good through the whole Highlands."

While Maclaren was speaking the tall, cloaked man had been sizing up Pole and Darwin, his look darting intensely from one to the other absorbing every detail of their appearance. "Our arrival has caused problems—not expected, we must solve." His voice was deep, with a clipped, jerky delivery and a strong touch of a foreign accent. "Apologies. Let me introduce—I am Doctor Philip Theophrastus von Hohenheim. At your service. This is my servant, Zumal. Yours to command."

The black man grinned, showing teeth that had been filed to sharp points. Darwin raised his eyebrows and looked quizzically at the tall stranger.

"I must congratulate you. You are looking remarkably well, Dr. Paracelsus von Hohenheim, for one who must soon be approaching his three hundredth year."

After a moment's startled pause the tall man laughed, showing even yellow teeth. Jacob Pole and Malcolm Maclaren looked on uncomprehendingly as Hohenheim reached out, took Darwin's hand, and shook it hard.

"Your knowledge is impressive, Dr. Darwin. Few people know my name these days—and fewer yet can place my date of birth so accurate. To make precise—I was born 1491, one year before Columbus of Genoa found the Americas." He bowed. "You also know my work?"

As Hohenheim was speaking, Darwin had frowned in sudden puzzlement and stood for a few moments in deep thought. Finally he nodded.

"In my youth, sir, your words impressed me more than any others. If I may quote you: 'I admonish you not to reject the method of experiment, but according as your power permits, to follow it without prejudice. For every experiment is like a weapon which must be used according to its own peculiar power.' Great words, Dr. Hohenheim." He looked at the other man coolly. "Throughout my career as a physician, I have tried to adhere to that precept. Perhaps you recall what you wrote immediately after that advice?"

Instead of replying, Hohenheim lifted his left hand clear of his cloak and waved it rapidly in a circle, the extended fingers pointing toward Jacob Pole. As he completed the circle he flicked his thumb swiftly across the palm of his hand and casually plucked a small green flask from the air close to Pole's head. While the villagers behind him gasped, he rolled the flask into the palm of his hand.

"Here." He held it out to Jacob Pole. "Your eyes tell

it—fluxes and fevers. Drink this. Condition will be improved, much improved. I guarantee. Also—more liquids, less strong drink. Better for you." He turned to Darwin. "And you, Doctor. Medicine has come a long way—great advances since I had to flee the *charlatans* of Basel. Let me offer you advice, also. Barley water, licorice, sweet almond, in the morning. White wine and anise—not too much—at night. To fortify mind and body."

Darwin nodded. He looked subdued. "I thank you for your thoughtful words. Perhaps I will seek to follow them. The ingredients, with the exception of wine, are already in my medical chest."

"Solution." Hohenheim snapped the fingers of his left hand in the air again, and again he held a flask. "White wine. To serve until other supply is at hand."

The villagers murmured in awe, and Hohenheim smiled. "Until tomorrow. I have other business now. Must be in Inverness tonight, meeting there was promised."

"Ye'll never do it, man," burst out Malcolm Maclaren. "Why, it's a full day's ride or more, south of here."

"I have methods." There was another quick smile, a bow toward Pole and Darwin, then Hohenheim had turned and was walking briskly away toward the west, where the sea showed less than a mile away. While Malcolm Maclaren and the villagers gazed after him in fascinated silence, Jacob Pole suddenly became aware of the flask that he was holding. He looked at it doubtfully.

"With your permission." Darwin reached out to take it. He removed the stopper, sniffed at it, and then placed it cautiously against his tongue.

"Here." Pole grabbed the flask back. "That's mine. You drink your own. Wasn't that amazing? I've seen a lot of doctors, but I've never seen one to match his speed for diagnosis—it's enough to make me change my mind about all pox-peddling physicians. Made you think, didn't it?"

"It did," said Darwin ironically. "It made me think most hard."

"And the way he drew drugs from thin air, did you see that? The man's a marvel. What were you saying about him being three hundred years old? That sounds impossible."

"For once we seem to be in agreement." Darwin looked at the flask he was holding. "As for his ability to conjure a prescription for me from the air itself, that surprises me less than you might think. It is a poor doctor who lacks access to all the ingredients for his own potions."

"But you were impressed," said Pole. He was looking pleased with himself. "Admit it, Dr. Darwin, you were impressed."

"I was—but not because of his drugs. That called for some powers of manipulation and manual dexterity, no more. But one of Hohenheim's acts impressed me mightily—and it was one performed without emphasis, as though it was so easy as to be undeserving of comment."

Pole rubbed at his nose and took a tentative sip from his open flask. He pulled a sour face. "Pfaugh. Essence of badger turd. But all his acts seemed beyond me. What are you referring to?"

"One power of the original Paracelsus, Theophrastus von Hohenheim, was to know all about a man on first meeting. I would normally discount that idea as mere historical gossip. But recall, if you will, Hohenheim's first mode of address to me. He called me *Doctor Darwin*."

"That's who you are."

"Aye. Except that I introduced myself here simply as *Erasmus* Darwin. My message to Maclaren was signed only as Darwin. So how did Hohenheim know to call me doctor?"

"From the man who carried your message here?"

"He knew me only as Mister Darwin."

"Maybe Hohenheim saw your medical chest."

"It is quite covered by the canvas—invisible to all."

"All right." Pole shrugged. "Damme, he must have heard of you before. You're a well-known doctor."

"Perhaps." Darwin's tone was grudging. "I like to believe that I have a growing reputation, and it calls for effort for any man to be skeptical of his own fame. Even so . . ."

He turned to Malcolm Maclaren, who was still watching Hohenheim and Zumal as they walked toward the sea. Darwin tugged gently at his leather jacket.

"Mr. Maclaren. Did you talk of my message to Dr. Hohenheim before we arrived?"

"Eh? Your message?" Maclaren rubbed a thick-nailed hand across his brow. "I was just startin' to mention something on it when the pair of ye arrived here. But did ye ever see a doctor like that. Did ye ever?"

Darwin tugged again at his jacket. "Did Hohenheim seem to be familiar with my name?"

"He did not." Maclaren turned to stare at Darwin and shook his jacket free. "He said he'd never before heard of ye."

"Indeed." Darwin stepped back and placed his ample rear on the step of the dray. He gazed for several minutes toward the dark mass of Foinaven in the northeast, and he did not move until Pole came bustling up to him.

"Unless you're of a mind to sit there all day in the rain, let's go along with Mr. Maclaren and see where we'll be housed. D'ye hear me?"

Darwin looked at him vacantly, his eyes innocent and almost childlike.

"Come on, wake up." Pole pointed at the blank-walled cottages, rough stone walls stuffed with sods of turf. "I hope it will be something better than this. Let's take a look at the bed, and hope we won't be sleeping sailor-style, two shifts in one bunk. And I'll wager my share of the bullion to a gnat's snuffbox that there's bugs in the bed, no matter what Malcolm Maclaren says. Well, no matter. I'll take those over Kuzestan scorpions if it comes to a nip or two on the bum. Let's away."

West of Malkirk the fall of the land to the sea was steep. The village had grown on a broad lip, the only level place between mountains and the rocky shore. Its stone houses ran in a ragged line north–south, straddling the rutted and broken road. Jacob Pole allowed the old horse to pick its own path as the dray followed Malcolm Maclaren. He was looking off to the left, to a line of breakers that marked the shore.

"A fierce prospect," remarked Darwin. He had followed the direction of Pole's gaze. "And no shore for a ship-wreck. See the second line of breakers out there, and the rocks of the reef. It is hard to imagine a ship holding together for one month after a wreck here, still less for two centuries."

"My thought exactly," said Pole gruffly. "Mr. Maclaren?"

"Aye, sir?" The stocky Highlander halted and turned at Pole's call, his frizzy mop of hair wild under the old bonnet.

"Is the whole coastline like this—I mean, rocky and reef-bound?"

"It is, sir, exceptin' only Loch Malkirk, a mile on from here. Ye can put a boat in there easy enough, if ye've a mind to do it. An' there's another wee bit landing south of here that some of the men use." He remained standing, arms across his chest. "Why'd ye be askin'? Will ye be wantin' a boat, same as Dr. Hohenheim?"

"Hohenheim wants a boat?" began Pole, but Darwin silenced him with a look and a hand laid on his arm.

"Not now," he said, as soon as Maclaren had turned to walk again along the path. "You already said it, the lure of gold will attract trouble. We could have guessed it. We are not the only ones who have heard word of a galleon."

"Aye. But *Hohenheim* . . ." Jacob Pole sank into an unquiet silence.

They were approaching the north end of the village, where three larger houses stood facing each other across a level sward. Maclaren waved his hand at the one nearest the shore, where a grey-haired woman stood at the door.

"I wish ye could have had a place in that, but Dr. Hohenheim has one room, and his servant, that heathen blackamoor, has the other. But we can gi' ye a room that's near as good in here." He turned to the middle and biggest house, and the woman started over to join them.

"Jeanie. Two gentlemen needs a room." He went into a quick gabble of Gaelic, then looked apologetically at Pole and Darwin. "I'm sorry, but she hasna' the English. I've told her the place has to be clean for ye, an' that ye'll be here for a few days at least. Anythin' else ye'll need while ye are here in Malkirk? Best if I tell her now."

"I think not," said Darwin. But he swung lightly to the ground from the seat of the dray and began to walk quickly across to the black-shuttered third house. He had seen the repeated looks that Malcolm Maclaren and the woman had cast in that direction.

"I don't suppose there is any chance of rooms in here?" he said, not slowing his pace at all. "It will be some inconvenience, sharing a room, and if there were a place in this house, even for one of us—"

"No, sir!" Maclaren's voice was high and urgent. "Not in that house, sir. There's no room there."

He came after Darwin, who had reached the half-open door and was peering inside.

"Ye see, there's no place for ye." Maclaren had moved around and blocked the entrance with a thick arm. "I mean, there's no furniture there, no way that ye could stay there, you or the Colonel."

Darwin was looking carefully around the large stone-floored room, with its massive single bed and empty fireplace. He frowned.

"That is a pity. It has no furnishings, true enough, but the bed is of ample size. Could you perhaps bring some other furniture over from another house, and make it—"

"No, sir." Maclaren pushed the door to firmly and began to shepherd Darwin back toward the other house. "Ye see, sir, that's my brother's house. He's been away inland these past two month, an' the house needs a cleanin' before he comes back. We expect him in a day or two—but ye see, that house isna' mine to offer ye. Come on this way, an' we'll make you comfortable, I swear it."

He went across to the dray, ripped away the canvas with a jerk, grunted, and lifted the box containing Little Bess clear with one colossal heave. The other two men watched in amazement as he braced his legs, then staggered off toward the center house with his burden.

Pole raised his eyebrows. "I won't argue the point with him. It took two of us to lift that. But what's over there that he's so worried about? Weapons maybe? Did you see guns or claymores?"

"There was a bed in there—nothing else." Darwin's intrigued tone was at odds with his words.

"You are sure?" Pole had caught the inflection in the other man's voice. "Nothing mysterious there?"

"I saw nothing mysterious." Darwin's voice was puzzled. He went over to the dray and took one of his bags down from it. His expression was thoughtful, his heavy head hunched forward on his shoulders. "You see, Colonel Pole, that is one of the curiosities of the English language. I saw nothing, and it was mysterious. A room two months empty and neglected, and I saw nothing there—no dust, no cobwebs, no mold. Less than I would expect to see in a house that had been cleaned three days ago. The room was *polished*." He rubbed at his chin.

"But what does that mean?"

Darwin shrugged. "Aye, that's the question." He looked at the dirty grey smoke rising from the house in front of them. "Well, we will find out in due course. Meanwhile, unless my nose is playing me tricks there's venison cooking inside. A good dish of collops would sit well after our long journey. Come on, Colonel, I feel we have more than earned an adequate dinner."

He went in, through a door scarcely wide enough to permit passage of his broad frame. Jacob Pole stared after him and scratched his head.

"Now what the devil was all *that* about? Him and his mysterious nothings. That's like a sawbones, to conceal more than they tell. I'll still bet there's weapons in that place, hidden away somewhere. I saw their looks."

He picked up a small case and followed into the house's dark interior, where he could now hear the rattle of plates and cups.

Jacob Pole awoke just before true dawn, at the first cock crow. He climbed out of bed, slipped on his boots, and picked up the greatcoat that lay on the chest of drawers. Despite his misgivings, the bed had been adequately large and reasonably clean. He looked to the other side of it. Darwin lay on his back, a great mound under the covers. He was snoring softly, his mouth open half an inch. Pole picked up his pipe and tobacco and went through to the other room to sit by the embers of the peat fire.

He had spent a restless night. Ever since dinner his thoughts had been all on the galleon, and he had been unable to get it out of his mind. Hohenheim was after the bullion, that was clear enough. Maclaren had made no secret of the galleon's presence, but it was also clear from the way that he shrugged the subject away with a move of his great shoulders that he knew nothing of anything valuable aboard it. He had seemed amazed that anyone, still less two parties, should be interested in it at all. The Devil, too, had been casually shrugged off.

Yes, surely it was there—had been there as long as anyone in the village could remember.

Its dimensions?

He had pondered for a while at Darwin's question. As large as a whale, some said—others said much larger. It lived near the galleon, but it was peaceful enough. It would merely be a man's fancy to say that the creature *guarded* anything in the loch.

The three men had played a curious game of three-way tag for a couple of hours. Pole had wanted to talk only of the galleon, while neither Darwin nor Maclaren seemed particularly interested. Darwin had concentrated his attention on the Devil, but again Maclaren had given only brief and uninformative answers to the questions. He had his own interests. He pushed Darwin to talk of English medicine, of new drugs and surgical procedures, of hopeless cases and miracle cures. He wanted to know if Hohenheim could do all the things that he hinted at— make the blind see, save the living, even raise the dead. When Darwin spoke Maclaren leaned forward unblinking, stroking his full beard and scratching in an irritated way at his breeches' legs, as though resenting the absence of the kilt.

Pole shook his head. It had been a long, unsatisfying evening, no doubt about it.

He picked up a glowing lump of peat, applied it to his pipe, and sucked in his first morning mouthful of smoke. He sighed with satisfaction, and went at once into a violent and lengthy fit of coughing. Eyes streaming, he finally had to stagger across and take a few gulps from the water jug before he could breathe again and stand there wheezing by the window.

"You missed your true vocation, Colonel," said a voice behind him. "If you were always available to wake the village, the cockerel would soon be out of work."

Darwin stood at the door in his stockinged feet. He was blinking and scratching his paunch with one hand, while the other held his nightcap on his head.

Pole glared at him and took another swig from the water jug. Then he looked out of the window next to him, stiffened, and snorted.

"Aye, and it's just as well that one of us gets up in the morning. Look across there. A light in that house, and that means Hohenheim is up already—and I wager he'll be on his way to Loch Malkirk while we're still scratching around here. He's ahead of us already, and with his powers I wouldn't put anything past him. We have to get moving ourselves, and over to the loch as soon as we can."

"But you heard Hohenheim last night, announcing his intention to be in Inverness. What makes you think that he is still in Malkirk?" Darwin nodded to the grey-haired woman, who had silently appeared to tend the fire and set a black cauldron of water on it. "He is probably not even here."

"He is, though." Pole nodded his head again toward the window. The door of the other house had opened, and two figures were emerging. It was too dark to make out their clothing, but there was no mistaking the tall, thin build, backed by a shorter form that seemed to be a part of the darkness itself.

"Hohenheim, and his blackamoor." Pole's voice held a gloomy satisfaction. "As I feared, and as I told you, we come to seek bullion, and we find we are obliged to compete with a man who can see the future, travel fast as the wind to any place that he chooses, and conjure powerful nostrums from thin air. That makes me feel most uneasy. By the way, did you take the draught that he provided for you?"

"I did not," said Darwin curtly. He sat down at the table and pulled a deep dish toward him. "I found one bowl of Malcolm Maclaren's lemon punch more than enough strange drink for me last night. My stomach still gurgles. Come, Colonel, sit down and curb your impatience. If we are to head for Loch Malkirk, we should not do so until we have food in us. The good woman is already making porridge, and I think there will be more herring and bowls of frothed milk. If we are to embark on rough water, at least let us do so well-bottomed."

Pole sat down bad-temperedly, glared at his offending pipe, and pecked halfheartedly at porridge, oatcake, and smoked fish. He watched while Darwin devoured all those along with goat's whey, a dish of tongue and ham, and a cup of chocolate. But it went rapidly, and in five minutes the plates were clear. Pole rose at once to his feet.

"One moment more," said Darwin. He went across to the woman, who had watched him eating with obvious approval. He pointed at a plate of oatcakes. She nodded, and he gave her an English shilling. As he loaded the cakes into a pocket of his coat, Jacob Pole nodded grudgingly.

"Aye, you're probably right to hold me there, Doctor. There'll likely be little hospitality for us at the loch."

Darwin raised his eyebrows at the sudden truce, then turned again to the woman. He pointed at the rising sun, then followed its path across the sky with his arm. He halted when he had reached a little past the vertical, and pointed at the cauldron and the haunch of dried beef hanging by the wall. The woman nodded, spoke a harsh-sounding sentence, laughed, and came forward to pat Darwin's ample stomach admiringly.

Darwin coughed. He had caught Pole's gleeful look.

"Come on. At least dinner is assured when we return."

"Aye. And more than that, from the look of it." Pole's voice was dry.

The path to Loch Malkirk was just as Maclaren had described it, running first seaward, then cutting back inland over a steep incline. The ground was still wet and slippery with a heavy dew that hung sparkling points of sunlight over the heather and dwarf juniper. By the time they had travelled fifty yards their boots and lower breeches were soaked. When the loch was visible beyond the brow of the hill, they could see the mist that still hung over the surface of the water.

Darwin paused at the top of the rise and laid his hand on Pole's arm. "One second, Colonel, before we head down. We could not find a better place than this to take a general view of how the land lies."

"More than that," said Pole softly. "We'll have a chance to see what Hohenheim is doing without him knowing it. See, he's down there, off to the left." The shape of the loch was like a long wine bottle, with the neck facing to the northwest. An island offshore stood like a cork, to leave narrow straits through which the tides raced in and out. Once in past the neck of the bottle, the water ran deeper and the shore plunged steeply into the loch. Hohenheim and Zumal stood at the head of the narrows, looking to the water.

Darwin squinted across at the other side, estimating angles and widths. He sucked his lips in over his gums. "What do you think, Colonel?"

"Eh? Think about what?"

"The depth, out in the middle there." Darwin followed Pole's gaze to where Hohenheim and his servant had moved to a small coble and were preparing to launch it.

"Aye, it seems they may be answering my question for me soon enough—that's a sounding line they're loading with the paddles. Steep sides and hard rock. It would not surprise me to find that the loch sounds to a thousand feet. There's depth sufficient to cover a galleon ten times over."

"Or hide a devil as big as you choose." Pole wriggled in irritation, and Darwin patted him on the arm.

"Hold your water, Colonel. Our friends there will not be raising any treasure ship today. They lack equipment. With luck they will do some of your work for you. Do not overestimate Hohenheim."

"You saw that he has great powers."

"Did I? I am less sure. Observe, he uses a boat, so at least he cannot walk upon the waters."

Their voices had been dropped to whispers, and while they spoke Zumal had pushed the boat off, Hohenheim sitting in the bow. He was in the same motley clothes, quite at ease and holding the sounding line in his lap. At his command Zumal paddled twenty yards offshore, then checked their forward motion. Hohenheim stood up, swung his right arm backward and forward a couple of times, and released the line. Darwin muttered to himself and leaned in concentration.

"What's wrong?" Pole had noticed Darwin's move from the corner of his eye.

"Nothing. Only a suspicion that Hohenheim . . ."

Darwin's voice trailed off as the weighted line unwound endlessly into the calm waters of the loch. Soon Hohenheim had paid out all that he held, still without touching bottom. He spoke to Zumal, gathered in the line, and sat quietly as the coble moved slowly off toward the mouth of the loch. He tried the line again, and as they moved farther the depth gradually decreased until it was less than twenty feet in the neck at the entrance.

Hohenheim nodded and said something to his

companion. They both had all their attention on the line. It was Jacob Pole, looking back along the length of the inlet, who noticed the swirling ripple spreading across its surface. It showed as a line of crosscurrent, superimposing itself on the pattern of wavelets that was now growing in response to the morning sea breeze. The forward edge of the moving ripple was running steadily toward the coble at the seaward end of the loch. Pole gripped Darwin's arm hard.

"See it there. Along the loch."

The ripple was still moving. Now its bow was less than fifty yards from where Hohenheim was reeling in his line. As the spreading wave came closer, there seemed to be a hint of lighter grey moving beneath the surface. The wave moved closer to the boat, thirty yards, then twenty. Pole's grip had unconsciously tightened on Darwin's arm until his knuckles showed white. At last, where the bed of the loch became sharply shallower, the moving wavefront veered away to the left. Another moment and it was gone. All that remained was a spreading pattern of ripples, lifting the coble gently up and down as the light craft was caught in their swell.

Hohenheim looked round as he felt the motion of the boat, but there was nothing to be seen. After a moment he turned his attention back to the line.

Pole released his hold on Darwin. "The Devil," he said softly. "We've seen the Devil."

Darwin's eyes were glittering. "Aye, and it's a Devil indeed. But what in the name of Linnaeus is it? That's a real test for your systems taxonomical. It is not a whale, or it would surface and sound for its breathing. It is not a great eel—not unless all our ideas on size are in preposterous error. And it cannot be fish or flesh in any bestiary I can construct."

"Be damned with the name we give it." The shaking in Pole's hands was more pronounced, from excitement and alarm. "It was *big*, to make a wave that size—and fast. You scoffed at me when I brought Little Bess, but I was right. We'll need protection when we're on the loch. I'll have to carry it here and set it up to train where we need—forget the muskets, they'll be no better than a peashooter with that monster."

"I am not sure that the cannon will serve any useful purpose. But meanwhile, we have a duty." Darwin started heavily down the hill toward the loch side.

"Here, what are you up to?" Pole hesitated, then bent to pick up his pipe and spyglass from the heather as Hohenheim and his servant turned to face the sudden sounds from the hillside.

"To give fair warning," called Darwin over his shoulder. Then he was down by the water's edge, waving at the two in the boat and calling them to look behind them.

Hohenheim turned, scanned the loch's calm surface, then spoke quietly to Zumal. The black man paddled the coble in close to the loch side, running it to within a few feet of Darwin.

"I see no monster," Hohenheim was saying as Jacob Pole hurried up to them. "Nor did Zumal—and we were near, on water. Not spying in secret from shade of heather."

"There is a creature in the loch," said Darwin flatly. "Big, and possibly dangerous. I called to you for your own protection."

"Ah." Hohenheim put his finger to his nose and looked at Darwin with dark, suspicious eyes. "Very kind. You did not want to drive us from loch, eh? If so, you need better story—much better."

He looked at Darwin slyly. "So we are here for same purpose as each other. You would argue with that? I think not."

"If you mean a sunken galleon, for my part I would certainly argue." As he spoke, Darwin continued to scan the surface of the loch, seeking any sign of a new disturbance there. "I came here for quite different reasons."

"But I didn't," said Pole. "Aye, I'll admit it—why not? It drew me here, three hundred miles, that galleon, just as it drew you. How did you hear of it?"

Hohenheim pulled his tattered cloak around him and stretched to his full height. "I have methods, secret methods. Accept that I heard, and do not question."

"All right, if that's what you want, but I would like to suggest an alliance. What do you say? There's a ship out yonder, and Dr. Darwin spoke the truth. There is something out in the loch that needs to be watched for. The people of Malkirk set no value on the galleon, but we do. What do you say? Work together, we and you, and we'd have the work done in half the time. Equal shares, you and us."

Pole stopped for breath. All his words had rushed out in one burst, while Hohenheim listened, his black eyebrows arched. Now he laughed aloud and shook his head.

"Never, my good Colonel. Never. If we were equal, then maybe. Maybe I would listen. But we are not equal. I am ahead of you—in everything. In knowledge, skills, tools. Do it, my friend, try and beat me. I have power you lack, eh? Knowledge you lack, eh? Equipment, you ask about? Yesterday I was in Inverness, buying tools for seeing loch. Tonight it comes, tomorrow we use. Here, see for self."

He snapped his fingers a few inches from Jacob Pole's chin. As usual his gesture seemed exaggerated, larger than life, and when he opened his hand he was holding a square of brown paper.

"Here is list. Read, see for self—you will need every item on it. And you will be forced to buy in Inverness, two days away for you. By time you ready to begin, we will be finished and away from here."

Pole's sallow face flushed at the tone in Hohenheim's

voice. He shook off Darwin's hand and stepped within inches of the tall doctor.

"Hohenheim, last night you impressed me mightily. And you did us both a favor giving us those potions. This morning Dr. Darwin did his best to return that favor, warning you of a danger out on the loch. Instead of thanking him you insult us, saying we made up a monster to keep you away. Well, go ahead, ignore the warning. But don't look for help from me if you get in trouble. And as for the galleon, we'll work without you." He stepped back. "Come on, Dr. Darwin. I see no reason to stay here longer."

He turned and began to stride back up the hillside. Hohenheim looked after him and waved one hand in a contemptuous gesture of dismissal. His laugh followed Pole up the hill, while Darwin stood silent, staring hard at the other's lean face and body. His own face was an intent mask of thought and dawning conviction.

"Dr. Hohenheim," he said at last. "You have mocked a well-meant and sincere warning; you have refused Colonel Pole's honest offer of cooperation; and you have dismissed my word when I told you I did not come to Malkirk for the galleon. Very well, that is your option. Let me say only this, then I will leave you to ponder it. The danger in the loch is real, I affirm again—more real than I would have believed an hour ago, more real than the treasure that you are so intent on seeking. But beyond that, Doctor Hohenheim, I think I know what you are, and how you came here. Bear that in mind, the next time that you seek to astonish Malcolm Maclaren and his simple villagers with your magic flights to Inverness, or your panaceas drawn from the air."

He snapped his fingers—clumsily, with none of Hohenheim's panache—turned, and began to stump after Jacob Pole up the hilly path that led to Malkirk. Hohenheim's jeering laugh sped his progress as he went.

"He's still there, with another crowd around him. Now he's taken a big knitting needle from one of the women. I wonder what he's going to do with it? I could give him a suggestion or two."

Jacob Pole stood upright, turning from the window where he had stooped to look at the open area between the houses.

"Here, Doctor, come over and look at this."

Darwin sighed, closed his Commonplace Book in which he was carefully recording observations of the local flora, and stood up.

"And with what new mystery are we now being regaled?" He looked out onto the dusk of a fine evening. On the green in front of them, Hohenheim had taken the knitting needle and waved it twice in a flashing circle. He grasped the blunt end in both hands, directed the bone point at his heart, and pushed inward. The needle went into his chest slowly, an inch, then another, until it was buried to more than half its length. He released his hold and as the villagers around him gasped a bead of crimson blood oozed out along the white bone and dripped onto his tunic.

Hohenheim let the needle remain for a few seconds, a white spike of bone deep in his chest. Then he slowly withdrew it, holding it cupped in his palms. When it was fully clear he ran the length between fingers and thumb, spun it in a flashing circle, and handed it to be passed among the villagers. They touched it gingerly. As it went from hand to hand he took a small round box from his cloak, dug out a nailful of black salve on his index finger, and rubbed it into the round hole in his shirt. He was smiling.

"What is that drug?" Pole had his nose flattened against the dirty glass. "To save him from a wound like that— I've never known anything like it."

"I think I have," said Darwin dryly, and went back to his seat. But Jacob Pole was no longer listening. He went to the door and out, to join the group watching Hohenheim. The latter nodded as he appeared.

"Good evening again, Colonel." His voice was friendly, as though the morning incident had never happened. "We'll have no sea monsters, eh? But you come at right time. Now I will show antidote, cure for all poisons. So far, I have used only for crowned heads of Europe. Great secret, of high value." He glanced toward the other house. "A pity that Dr. Darwin is not here, he might learn much—or maybe not."

He reached into the tall cabinet by his side and took out a slim container of oily fluid. The pitch stopper came out easily, and he sniffed at it for a moment.

"Very good. Here is phial, see? Now, pass it round, one to another. Smell it—but not taste it. Deadly poison. If you want, replace with other poison—makes no difference to my antidote. I have made this extract from yew leaves. Colonel, you take it."

Pole sniffed carefully at the bottle. "It's terrible."

"Pass on to next man." The villager next to Pole handled the bottle delicately, as though it might explode. It went from hand to hand, some sniffing, others content to look, and at last came back to Hohenheim.

"Good. Now watch close." He reached again into the cabinet beside him and took out a neatly made cage of iron spokes around a wooden frame. A grey rat ran from side to side within, nervously rearing up against the narrow bars and sniffing hungrily at the air. Hohenheim held the cage high for a few seconds, so that the villagers could observe the rat closely. He set the cage on the ground, poured a drop or two of liquid from the phial onto a fragment of oat bread, and slipped it deftly between the bars.

The rat paused for a few moments, while the circle of

villagers held their breath. At last the rat sidled forward, sniffed the bread, and devoured it.

"I will count now," said the tall doctor. "Fifty pulse beats, and you see result."

He put his left hand to his right wrist and began to count in a clear, deep voice. At thirty the rat hesitated in its movements around the floor of the cage, and reared up against the bars. Ten more beats and it slipped to its belly, paws scrabbling against the wood.

Hohenheim did not wait to complete the count. He lifted the phial to his lips and tossed the contents down his throat. As the villagers muttered to themselves he inverted the bottle, allowing a few last drops of viscous liquid to fall to the grass.

"Now—and quickly—the antidote."

He pulled a flask of green liquid from his cloak, drained it, and carefully replaced the stopper. Amid the excited hubbub of the watching group, talking to each other in Gaelic about what they had witnessed, Hohenheim turned to Malcolm Maclaren. He was quite calm and relaxed, with no trace of nervousness about the poison.

"There is a limited amount of this antidote. If any have desperate need—or want for future use—I can make arrangement. Normally I do not sell, but here where doctors are few I will make special case. You tell them, eh? While you do it"—he was looking at the southern road in the gathering dusk, nodding knowingly—"I think I have business to attend. See? I bought yesterday in Inverness, now it comes. If you will help unload, I can use tomorrow."

He pointed to the laden cart coming toward them, drawn easily down the hill by two dusty horses. "Those are my supplies for work here." He turned to Jacob Pole. "As I told you, we are well advanced in plans. We have located the wreck, we have equipment to look at it. Maybe you and Dr. Darwin stop wasting your time here, would like to make arrangements to go home to south? Galleon will be done before you begin to look, eh? So good night, Colonel, and sleep well."

He nodded to Pole, bowed again to the circle of villagers, and strolled away toward the arriving cart. It was heavily laden with boxes and packages, and most of the villagers followed him, openly inquisitive. Jacob Pole stood, biting at a fingernail and staring angrily after Hohenheim.

"Arrogant pox-hound!" he said to Zumal, who alone still stood by him. The black man ignored him. He was busy. He turned the dead rat out of the cage, replaced everything back in the tall cabinet, and carefully closed it. Placing it on a low trolley, he pushed it to the house and went inside. While Pole still stood there undecided, Malcolm Maclaren came back along the path toward him. The stocky Scotsman was looking worried, biting his lip and frowning.

"Colonel, I'm not wantin' to trouble ye now, but is Dr. Darwin inside an' available for a word?"

"He is inside." Pole still sounded angry. "But if you can keep him to one word you are a better man than I am."

He led the way to the house. Darwin was sitting in the same chair, still at work on his notes. A bottle of Athole brose stood untouched by his side and he had been forced to light the oil lamp, but otherwise everything was exactly as Pole had left it. Darwin looked up and nodded calmly to Maclaren.

"Another display of medical thaumaturgy, I have no doubt. What was the latest wonder? *Ex Hohenheim semper aliquid novi*, if you will permit me to paraphrase Pliny." His tone was cheerful as he laid down his pen and closed the book. "Well, Malcolm Maclaren, what can I do for you?"

The Scot fidgeted uneasily for a few seconds, his dark face working under the full growth of beard.

"I did not come to talk to ye of Hohenheim," he said at last. "No, nor of yon galleon that ye seek to raise. I'm askin' help. Ye may recall I spoke to ye about my brother, away inland these past two month. We had word come in today, rare bad news. He took an accident, out on the mountains. A fall."

Darwin puffed out his cheeks but did not speak. Malcolm Maclaren rubbed his big hands together, struggling for the right words.

"A bad fall," he said finally. "An' we hear of injury to his head. They're bringin' him on back here, an' I'm expectin' him tomorrow, before nightfall. I was thinkin' . . ." He paused, then the words came in one rush. "I was wonderin' if ye might be willin' to do some kind of examination on him an' see if there's any treatment that would help him to regain his health and strength—we have plenty of money, that's no problem, we'll pay your usual fee an' more."

"Aha," said Darwin, so softly that Jacob Pole had trouble catching his words. "At last I think we see it." He stood up. "Fee is not an issue, Malcolm Maclaren. I will examine him gladly, and give you my best opinion as to his condition. But I wonder a little that you are not consulting Dr. Hohenheim. He is the one who has been displaying prodigies of medical skill to the people of your village. Whereas I have done nothing here to show power as a physician."

Maclaren gloomily shook his grizzled head. "Don't say that. I've had argument enough this very day on that subject, from man and woman both. I saw what he can do. Yet there's somethin' I canna put a name to, that makes me . . ."

His voice trailed off and he and Darwin stood eye to eye for a long moment, until Darwin nodded.

"You're an observing man, Malcolm Maclaren, and a shrewd one. Those are rare qualities. If your evaluation of Dr. Hohenheim is not one that you can readily place on logical foundations, that is not necessarily sufficient reason to distrust it. Like the animals, humans communicate on many levels more basic than words."

He turned to Jacob Pole. "You heard the request, and I am sure you see the problem it creates for me. I promised to help you with your equipment. But if I am also to be here, awaiting the arrival of Maclaren's brother, I will be unable to do it. I know you will not wish to wait another day—"

"An' there's no reason for that," said Maclaren gruffly. "If it's another pair of hands ye need, I've twenty men ready to serve—even if I have to break heads to persuade them of it. When do ye need that help?"

"Tomorrow afternoon will do well enough." Jacob Pole sensed that Maclaren was in his most cooperative mood. "I'll want help to carry something to the loch. On that score, you know all about the Devil there. But have you ever seen it yourself, and is it dangerous?"

"Aye, I've seen it, but never close, and never more than a shape in the water. Others here have seen it better. But I've never heard word of harm that came to any man that left the beast to live in its own way." Maclaren sat down, raising his head to look at the others. "We've had trouble in these parts, plenty of it, but it was not from the beast in the loch. Men have lost their lives, these past years in the Highlands—an' their heritances. But it was not the Devil's doin' that left the women lonely an' took all of us down close to beggary. For that ye have to look closer to your own kind. Aye, but I'm runnin' loose an' sayin' more than I ought."

He shook his head, stood up, and abruptly left the room. Pole, following him to the door, could at first see no sign of him in the dusk. Then he made out a squat, dark figure, striding rapidly across to the house with the black shutters. For the first time since they arrived, a light was showing in the window there.

It was a problem, and one that he could have anticipated. Jacob Pole crouched by the box that held Little Bess, grumbled to himself, and frowned at the late afternoon sunlight that was turning the peaks to the east into soft purple.

Darwin had been adamant, and Maclaren had agreed with him. The villagers could help carry the box, but they must not see the cannon inside. With weapons forbidden since the Disarming Act, a Highlander risked fines and transportation if he knowingly so much as assisted in carrying arms. The responsibility for handling Little Bess at the loch had to remain with Jacob Pole alone.

Very well; but how in damnation was he supposed to manhandle two hundredweight of cannon so that it pointed correctly to cover the loch? He was no Malcolm Maclaren, barrel chest and bulging muscles.

Grunting and swearing, Pole lifted the one-pound balls out of the box and laid them on the canvas next to the bags of black powder. Thank God the weather was fine, so nothing would get wet (but better hurry, and be done before the dew fell). With powder and shot removed, the box and cannon was just light enough to be dragged around to face the right direction. But now the sides of the box made it impossible either to prime or fire. And the cannon was too heavy to lift clear.

Pole sighed and took the iron lever that he had used to pry open the top of the container. He began to remove the sides, one by one. It was a slow and tedious job, and by the time that the last pin had been loosed and the wooden frame laid to the ground, dusk was already well on its way.

At that point, he hesitated. He had intended to fire one test round, to make sure that range and angle were correct. But perhaps that should wait for the morning, when the light would be better and the travel of the ball more easily seen. After a few moments of thought, he loaded a bag of black powder and a ball, and placed the fuse all ready. Then he went across to a square of covering canvas, well away from the powder, and took out tobacco, pipe, flint and tinder. He sat down. His pipe was already charged and the flint in his hand when he looked down the hill to the surface of Loch Malkirk. He had been too absorbed in his own work to pay any attention there. Now he realized that two figures were busy by the loch's edge.

Hohenheim and Zumal were wheeling a handcart full of boxes and packages. At the flat-bottomed coble they halted and began to transfer cartons. As the breeze dropped, Hohenheim's words carried clearly up from the quiet water. Pole, crouched there in his brown cloak, was indistinguishable from the rocks and the heather.

He repressed his instinctive reaction, to call a greeting. As they finished loading and moved offshore he sat, pipe still unlit, and watched closely.

"Steady now, until I give the word." That was Hohenheim, leaning far forward in the boat's bow. With the sun almost on the horizon, the shadow of the boat was like a long, dark spear across the calm surface of the loch. Hohenheim was leaning over into the shadow, so that it was impossible for Jacob Pole to see what he was doing.

"Back-paddle, and slow us—now." The coble was stationary on the calm surface. The man in the bow reached down over the front of the boat, pulled up a loop of line from the water, and tied it to a ring in front of him.

"Looks good. I see no drift at all since yesterday." Hohenheim turned and nodded to Zumal. "Get ready now, and I will prepare the rest."

The black man laid down the paddle and began to strip

off his clothes. The setting sun was turning the surface of the loch into a single glassy glare in Jacob Pole's eyes, and Zumal was no more than a dark silhouette against the dazzling water. Pole raised a hand to shield his eyes and tried to get a closer look at Hohenheim's activities.

The scene suddenly changed. As he watched, the even surface of the loch seemed to tear, to split along a dark, central line, and to divide into two bright segments. Pole realized that he was seeing the effects of a moving ripple, a bow wave that tilted the water surface so that the sunlight no longer reflected directly to his eyes. Something big was moving along the loch. He dropped his pipe unheeded to the heather, and his heart began to beat faster.

The coble was close to the seaward end of the loch, where the shallow water lay. The moving wave was still more than a quarter of a mile away in the central deep. But it was moving steadily along toward the boat. Pole watched in fascination as it came within about forty yards, to where the bed of the loch began to rise. Then the wave veered left and turned back along the shore. The two men in the coble were too busy to notice. Hohenheim had now taken a small barrel from the bottom of the boat, removed its top, and was adjusting something inside it. He said a few soft words to Zumal, naked now in the stern, and laughed. Behind them the ripples still spread across the sweep of water.

"Ready?"

Pole heard the single word from Hohenheim as the sun finally dipped below the western horizon and everything took on the deeper tones of true twilight. Zumal's nod was barely visible in the gloom.

"As soon as I lower it, follow it down. It lasts only a short while, so act quickly."

Pole watched the flash of flint and metal that followed the last words. It sparked three times, then there was the glow of tinder. Hohenheim was holding a smoldering wad of cotton over the open end of the barrel.

"*Now.*"

A dazzling white light was shining from the barrel's mouth. Hohenheim lifted it out and dropped it over the side. The flare sank at once to the bottom, but instead of being extinguished by the water it seemed to burn brighter than ever, with a blue-white flame.

The bottom of the loch was suddenly visible as a rugged, shiny floor of rock and sand. Close to the coble, just a few feet from the underwater flare, Jacob Pole could see the outline of a long ship's hulk. As he crouched by his cannon, almost too excited to breathe, he saw the naked form of Zumal slip over the side of the coble, swim to the float, and move hand-over-hand down to the anchor that marked the wreck.

Shielding his eyes from the direct light, Pole peered at the shape of the hulk. After a few seconds he could make out details through the unfamiliar pattern of light and shadow on the bed of the loch. He gasped as he realized what he was seeing.

In the village, the fading light had been the signal for new activity. Darwin could sense the bustle of movement through the walls of the house and there was a constant clatter of footsteps in and out of the kitchen.

It was one of the few signs of a rising tension. After Jacob Pole left, Maclaren had dropped in every half hour, trying to appear casual, and spoken a few distracted words to Darwin before hurrying out again. At five o'clock Maclaren had made a final visit and departed with the woman who did the cooking, leaving Darwin to dine as best he might on cold goose, oat bread, chicken fricassee, and bread pudding, and to order his thoughts however he chose.

When Maclaren finally appeared again he looked like

a different person. His lowland garb was gone, and in its place were brogues, knee-length knitted socks, the kilt, and a black waistcoat with gold-thread buttons.

"Aye, I know," he said at Darwin's inquiring look. " 'Tis against the law yet to bear Highland dress. But I'll do no less to welcome my brother home, whatever the law says. An' there's talk of a change of the rule in a year or two, so what's the harm? Surely a man ought to be allowed to dress any which way he chooses. But would ye be all ready then?"

Darwin nodded. He stood, picked up the well-worn medical chest that had been his companion on a thousand journeys, and followed Maclaren outside into the warm spring night. The Highlander led the way at a stately pace to the stone house with the black shutters. In spite of the darkness, Darwin had the feeling that many eyes followed their progress from the shadows.

At the door Maclaren halted. "Dr. Darwin, I'm not one to want to deceive myself. It's a bad wound, that I know, and I'm a man that respects the truth. I'm not after lookin' for ill news, but will ye gi' me the word, that ye'll tell me honest if it's good news or bad?"

The light was spilling out into the quiet night. Darwin turned to look steadily into the other man's worried eyes.

"Unless there is good reason to do it, to save life or lessen suffering, it is my belief that a full and honest diagnosis is always best. You have my word. No matter where the truth may take us tonight, I will provide it as I see it. And in return I ask that what I say should not create ill feeling to me and to Colonel Pole."

"Ye have that word, an' it's my life that stands behind it." Maclaren pushed the door wide open and they went on in.

The room had not changed, but now lamps had been placed in eight or nine places around it. Everything was well lit and spotlessly clean. There were lamps on each side of the big bed, where a man lay covered to the chest by a tartan blanket.

Darwin stepped forward. For many seconds he was motionless, scrutinizing the man's chalk-white face and loose posture.

"What is his age?"

"Fifty-five." Maclaren's voice was a whisper.

Darwin stepped forward and turned the blanket back to the thighs. When he rolled back an eyelid under his thumb the man did not move. He opened the mouth, studying the decaying teeth, and grunted to himself thoughtfully.

"Here. Help me turn him to his side." Darwin's voice was neutral, giving no clue as to his thoughts. With Maclaren's help they moved the man to his right side, revealing the red cicatrix that ran all the way from the crown of his head down to above the left temple. Darwin bent close and moved his hand gently along it, feeling the shape of the bone beneath the scar. The wound was indented, a deep cleft in the skull, and no hair grew above it.

Darwin sucked in a deep breath. "Aye, a sore wound indeed. One cleavage, straight from the sphenoid wing to the top of the *calvaria*. It is a wonder to see any man living after such an injury."

He pulled the blanket back farther, to show the legs and feet covered in a white and gold robe. Then he was a long while silent, scowling down at the patient. He sniffed the man's breath, examined nose and ears, and finally lifted the arms and legs to palpate the joints and muscles. The palms of the hands and the short, well-trimmed nails came in for their own brief examination, and he felt the condition of the sinews in wrists and ankles.

"Lift him to a sitting position," he said at last. "Let me see his back."

The skin over the ribs was white and unmarked, free of all sores and blemishes. Darwin nodded, looked again at the white of the eye that showed beneath the lid, and sighed.

"You can let him lie back again. And you can tell some man or woman that I have never in my life seen an injured person better cared for. He has been fed, washed, exercised, and lovingly looked after. But his condition . . ."

"Tell me, Doctor." Maclaren's look was resolute. "Do not disguise it."

"I will not, though my medical opinion will bring bitter news for you. His wound will prove mortal, and his condition cannot be improved. It can only worsen, and you must not expect there will be any waking from unconsciousness."

Maclaren clenched his teeth, and the muscles stood out along his jaw. "Thank you, Doctor," he said in a whisper. "An' the end, how far away will it be?"

"I can answer that only if you will give me some information. How long has he been unconscious? It is apparent that this is not a recent wound, with the degree of healing that it now exhibits."

"Aye, ye speak true there." Maclaren's face was grim. "Near three year, it has been. He was hurt in the summer of '73, an' has not wakened after that. We've tended him since then."

"I am sorry to end your hopes." Darwin drew the sheet back over the man on the bed. "He will die within the year. You brought me a long way for this, Malcolm Maclaren. Your devotion deserves a better reward."

Maclaren looked swiftly to the door, then back again. "What do ye mean, Doctor?"

Darwin waved his arm to door and window. "Let them all come in, if you wish. They are as worried as you are, and it serves no purpose to have them hide and listen outside."

"Ye think . . ." Maclaren hesitated.

"Come on, man, and do it." Darwin leaned again to look at the figure on the bed. "If you worry still about my state of knowledge and discretion, I could offer you a tale. It is a story of loyalty and desperation. Of a man, who might be this very man here"—he touched the smooth brow of the unconscious patient—"returned after many years to his homeland. There was an accident. Let us put it that way, although a sword or axe could leave just such a wound. After the accident the man was lovingly cared for, and the doctors of these parts did all they could, but there was no progress in his condition. At last, despite daily exercise of muscles and the best food that could be found, he began to weaken, to show signs of worsening. More expert advice and medical attention seemed to be the only hope. But how to obtain it, without revealing all and risking the wrath of a still vengeful government?"

"Aye, how indeed?" said Maclaren. He sighed and walked over to the door. A few words of Gaelic, and a file of somber men and women came into the room. Each went to the bed, knelt there for a moment, then moved back to stand by the wall. When all had entered, Maclaren spoke to them again, a longer speech this time. While Darwin watched, the faces in front of him seemed to fold and crumple as all hope drained from them.

"I have told them," said Maclaren, as he turned back to the bed.

Darwin nodded. "I saw it."

"They are brave folk. They will bear it bravely, whatever I tell them. But to ye I have told nothin', not one word, an' yet ye seem to know all. How can that be?" Maclaren's voice was husky but he held his head up high. "How can ye know this, as well as I know it? Are ye what Hohenheim has claimed to be, a man who can divine all by magical methods?"

"I would never claim what I believe impossible for any human." Darwin had moved forward again to the bed and was gently turning the head of the unconscious man. "I proceed by much simpler methods, ones available to all. Let me, if you will, continue with my tale. This man needed help, if help could be found, from other physicians. It would be futile of me to plead excessive modesty, and to deny that in the past few years my reputation as a court of last resort for difficult medical cases has spread throughout England—aye, and through Europe, too, if my friends are to be believed. Let us suppose it is true, and that my name was known here. Perhaps I could help, or at least tell the worst. But the idea of a direct approach, with a patient who was perhaps an outlaw and an exile—not to add that he is one of royal blood—why, that would be unthinkable. A subterfuge of some kind was necessary, one that would allow an examination without revealing too much. And if the patient could not easily be carried for a long distance, the presence of the physician in the Highlands must somehow be assured."

He paused and looked up at Maclaren. "Who was it worked out the details of the plan?"

Maclaren was sitting on the stone floor, his chin resting on his cupped hands. "It was I," he said softly. "An' God knows, it came from desperation, not from choosin'. But I still do not see how ye could know any of this."

"I was suspicious before I left Lichfield. You followed the first rule of successful deception: build upon what is real, and invent as little as you must. But you went too far, with a double lure, of great treasure and of a fantastic animal. The beast in Loch Malkirk would have been sufficient to bring me here without further embroidery, but you could not have known that. So there was added the galleon, and the priceless treasure, all to be revealed to me by the words of a dying man."

Maclaren smiled ruefully. "It worked. Ye came here, an'

that was a surprise to me. So where was the error in it?"

"Your plan went astray not in outline, but in detail. You had hired good actors, that was necessary, and they were well grounded in their roles—enough to convince Dr. Monkton. You had also told them to beware my examination, I surmise, since I would surely see through the deception. But Colonel Pole was there, and he was an accurate reporter. How could a tinker have the hands of a gentleman, or a delirious man suffer no fever?"

"We were not careful enough in choosin'—but still ye came, an' I don't see why ye did."

"The mystery that you had never intended brought me, more than treasure or Devil. Before we left Lichfield, I was asking myself, what would make anyone try to draw me here, three hundred miles from home? That curiosity was *my* motive, but what could *their* motive be? From the moment that we set out I was vastly curious, and when I arrived here my perplexity was increased. For here was Hohenheim, and I could not readily see how he fitted the situation at all."

Maclaren glanced around him at the circle of grieving faces. He shrugged. "Dr. Darwin, I said that I will tell ye true, an' I will. But I swear by the man who lies there helpless before us—an' I know no higher oath than mine to Prince Charles Edward—I cannot tell why Hohenheim came. He was no part of my thoughts or plans, an' his arrival surprised me totally. I am sorry to disappoint ye."

"You do not," said Darwin. He had a satisfied look on his face. "What you have just told me fleshes out the picture, and I can tell you the answer myself. As to how Hohenheim knew at once that I was a doctor, upon my arrival, that is easy. You had told him, by referring without thinking to a 'Doctor Darwin' who was coming to Malkirk. Hohenheim thought of me that way from the time you did it—but when he first spoke that knowledge perturbed me mightily. As for the rest, Hohenheim has been the unintentional confusion factor, the place where your plan suffered an accidental complication. Look back to the instrument by which your scheme was carried out—the hired players—and you will see the rest. Hohenheim—"

The boom of a cannon sounded through the quiet night, shockingly loud and near. Darwin and Maclaren looked at each other in confusion. There was a rush to the door of the house as the echo carried back from the eastern hills.

It was not a Spanish galleon. Jacob Pole was sure of it, sure as soon as he saw the ship's lines by the light of the flare. Everything stood out clearly in that white and penetrating light, and even the crusting of silt and the deep corrosion of iron parts were not enough concealment. A man without naval experience might be fooled, because there were similarities enough to cause confusion; but Pole saw through those, and was stunned by the knowledge. He was looking at a coastal cargo ship, high in the stern and with three masts, and he had seen many like it in English and Irish waters. It was not—could not be—the galleon they were seeking. And Hohenheim and Zumal did not know it!

Pole squatted by Little Bess and frowned down at the scene below. Zumal was down on the wreck's listing deck, prying the forward hatch with a long iron bar. It was slowly opening and releasing a cloud of fine silt that fogged the water. Outside that cloud the bed of the loch showed as a dazzling confusion of white sand and black rock. Above, Hohenheim was busy in the coble, lowering other tools and preparing a second underwater flare.

They did not know enough about ships to realize that this was not a wreck likely to bear treasure of any kind. But if they had discovered and were exploring the wrong ship, so much the better. The galleon must be somewhere else in the loch.

Pole nodded to himself and looked back along the length of the inlet. If he had to search for another wreck, there could be no better time for it than now, when the floor of the loch was so brightly lit. The powerful light made every detail in the water visible for scores of yards. He could see schools of fish, flashing here and there in panic from the alien glare in the water. Away from the loch's entrance the whole underwater panorama was a frenzy of darting silver shapes. And a great shadow moved swiftly among them, scattering them wildly from its path.

The light allowed Jacob Pole to see what had been hidden from them the previous day. The Devil was speeding along, the crest of its back a couple of yards below the surface as it moved away from Zumal and the bright flare. Pole could see a small head and long neck leading a massive body and powerful tail. The back was grey, and as it rolled to make a turn there was a flash of pink on its sides, and a brief sight of a red underbelly. It was at least seventy feet from head to tip of tail, and its swift forward motion came from the powerful body and wing-like side fins.

The creature was flying blindly along the loch, seeking escape from the light. Its frenzied rush set up a big wave and brought the beast closer to the surface as it neared the inland end of the loch. The surface was foaming under the power of the lashing tail. As the Devil turned, the flare near the loch entrance began to fade. A moment more, and the bow wave was racing back along the loch, with the beast close enough to the surface for the smooth back to be revealed.

Hohenheim had the second flare ready and Zumal was hanging on the side of the coble, taking breath before he dived again. They were both looking uncertainly along the water, not sure what was causing the sudden pattern of choppy waves.

Pole stood up and waved. "Hohenheim! Look out— you're in danger."

Without waiting to see the effects of his shout, he bent over the cannon. It took a second or two to line Little Bess to fire along the loch, and another second to strike the spark and apply the match at the breech. His hands were trembling with tension, and he could not control them.

The beast in the loch was less than fifty yards from the coble, and both men below were now aware of its rapid approach. Zumal cried out and tried to hoist himself into the coble, while Hohenheim left the second flare to burn in the bow while he took up the paddle and tried to move the boat away toward the safety of the shore. They were going too slowly. Pole glanced up, and saw that the Devil's dash toward the sea would take it straight into the coble.

As he straightened to shout again the cannon beside him roared and leapt backwards in recoil. He was surrounded by black smoke and could scarcely see where the ball went. The direction was good, but the timing a little too late. Instead of hitting the Devil's body the ball grazed the long tail and spent its energy uselessly in the waters of the loch. The beast leapt forward even faster.

A second shot would take minutes to make ready. Pole watched helplessly as the Devil surged frantically for the loch entrance.

The second flare was still alight. At the impact it flew high in the air. Fragments of the coble went with it and Hohenheim's body spun away, the limbs loose and broken like a wrecked puppet. There was an agonized scream— Hohenheim or Zumal, Pole could not tell which—and a crash of splintered wood. Then the Devil's broad back was standing six feet above the surface of the water as the beast thrashed and wriggled its way through the shallows to the open sea. It headed west and plunged into the deep water beyond the reefs.

Jacob Pole did not wait to chart the course of the Devil's departure. He was running down the hill, with the cannon's blast and the human scream of final agony still loud in his ears.

The surface of the loch was calm again. There was nothing to be seen but the bobbing light of the flare and shattered remnants of the coble.

At the sound of the cannon shot Malcolm Maclaren's face turned white. He looked at the figure on the bed.

"If that is soldiers, an' him here . . ."

Already four or five of the men had run silently from the room. Maclaren gestured to the women, and they moved to lift the unconscious man from the bed and wrap him in blankets. Before they could reach him, Darwin stood in front of them, his hand raised.

"Hold this action, and your men, too. Maclaren, that came from the loch—from Colonel Pole. There may be trouble there, but it's no danger for you or for your prince. If you want to send men anywhere, send them to the loch. That's where help is needed."

Logic had spoken to Maclaren faster than Darwin could. He had recalled the cannon that Pole had brought with him and carried to the loch. He shouted a command to the men outside, then moved swiftly over to the figure on the bed. There was a new hopelessness in his expression, as though he was fully realizing for the first time the import of Darwin's pronouncements on the future. He bent to kiss the unconscious man's hand, then looked up at Darwin.

"Ye are right about Colonel Pole, an' my men will be at the loch in minutes. An' if ye are right about this other, he canna' be revived—ever. It makes no difference now if he is living or dead, if he remains like this it's over. Our fight's all over an' done." The despair in his voice was total. Darwin moved to his side and laid a gentle hand on his shoulder.

"Malcolm Maclaren, I am truly sorry. If it will ease your mind at all, be assured of this: Prince Charles Edward departed this world as a conscious, thinking human the moment that he took that injury. If you had found a way to transport me here to Scotland the very day that it happened, I could have done nothing for him."

"I hear ye." Maclaren rubbed a knuckle at his eyes. "The line is ended, an' now I must learn to bear it. But it comes hard, even though I've feared that word all these past three years. It is an end to all hope here."

"So help me to look to those who can still be assisted. Bring lamps, and let us go down to the loch." Darwin started for the door, then instinctively turned back to the bedside to pick up his medical case. Before he reached it there was a shout and commotion outside the house.

"Come on, Doctor," said Maclaren. "That's my men calling, something about Colonel Pole."

It took a few seconds to see anything after the bright lamps of the room. Darwin followed Maclaren and stood there blinking, peering up the hill to where the group outside was pointing. At last he could see a trio of Highlanders. In their midst and supported by two of them was a stumbling and panting Jacob Pole. He staggered up to Malcolm Maclaren and stood wheezing in front of him.

"Talk to your blasted men—I can't get them to understand plain English. Send 'em back to the loch."

"Why? Dr. Darwin was worried for your safety there, but here ye are, safe an' well."

"Hohenheim and Zumal." Pole held his side and

coughed. "At the loch, but I couldn't help. Both dead, in the water."

Maclaren barked a quick order to three of the villagers, and they left at a trot. While Pole leaned wearily on supporting arms, Darwin stood motionless.

"Are you sure?" he said at last. "Remember, there have been other examples where Hohenheim's actions were not what they appeared to be."

"I'm sure. Sure as I stand here. I saw the coble smashed to pieces with my own eyes. Saw Hohenheim broken, and both their bodies." He bent forward, rubbing at his balding head with a hand that still shook with fatigue. "The ship they were looking at was not the galleon! I saw it, an empty hold in an old wreck, that's what they died for. The wrong ship. That's their end."

"Aye, the end indeed," said Maclaren. He was watching as a silent procession of women carried an unconscious body out of the black-shuttered house and away toward the main village. "An' a bitter end for all. Hohenheim came here of his own wish, but it was no plan of mine that would make him die here." He began to walk with head lowered after the women.

"Not quite the end, Malcolm Maclaren." Darwin's somber tone halted the Scotsman. "There is one more duty for us tonight, and in some ways it is the most difficult and sorrowful of all. Give me ten more minutes of your time, then follow your lord."

"Nothing could be worse," said Maclaren. But he turned and came back to where Darwin and Pole stood facing each other. "What is left?"

"Hohenheim. He came here uninvited, and you asked why. You did not seek to bring him, and I certainly did not. He has been a mystery to all of us. Come with me, and we will resolve it now."

Followed by Pole and Maclaren, he led the way across the turf to the house where Hohenheim and his servant had stayed. The door was closed, and no light showed within.

Darwin stepped forward and banged hard on the dark wood. When no answer came he gestured to Maclaren to bring the lamp that he was holding nearer, and opened the door. The three men paused on the threshold.

"Who is there?" said a sleep-slurred voice from the darkness.

"Erasmus Darwin." He took the lamp from Maclaren, held it high, and walked forward to light up the interior.

"What do you want?" The man in the bed rolled over, pushed back the cover, and sat up. Jacob Pole looked at him, gave a superstitious groan of fear, and stepped backwards.

The man in front of them was Hohenheim. The tunic and patchwork cloak hung over a chair but there could be no mistaking the hooked nose, ruddy cheeks, and darting black eyes.

"It's impossible," said Pole. "Less than ten minutes ago, I saw him dead. It can't be, I saw—"

"It is all too possible," said Darwin softly. "And it is as I feared." He leaned toward the man in the bed, who was now more fully awake and beginning to scowl at the intruders. "The deception is over. Hohenheim—for want of a true name I must continue to use your old one— we bring terrible news. There was an accident at the loch. Your brother is dead."

The red cheeks paled and the man stood up suddenly from the bed. "You are lying. This is some trick, to try and trap me."

Darwin shook his head sadly. "It is no trick, and no trap. If I could find another way to say this, I would do so. Your brother and Zumal died tonight in Loch Malkirk."

The man in front of him stood for a second, then gave a wild shout and rushed past them.

"Stop him," cried Darwin, as Hohenheim plunged out of the door and into the night.

"Is he dangerous?" asked Maclaren.

"Only to himself. Send your men to follow and restrain him until we can reach him."

Maclaren moved to the door and shouted orders to the startled group of villagers who were still waiting near the black-shuttered house. Three of them set off up the hill in pursuit of Hohenheim's running figure. When Maclaren came back into the room Jacob Pole was slumped against the wall, his head bowed.

"Is he all right?" Maclaren said to Darwin.

"Give him time. He's over-tired and he's had a great shock."

"I'm fine." Pole sighed. "But I've no idea what's going on here. I never saw any brother, or any deception. Are you sure you have an explanation for all this?"

"I believe that I do." Darwin walked around the room, studying the cases and boxes stacked against the walls. He finally stopped at one of them and bent to open it.

"Why did these men come to Malkirk?" he said. "That is easily answered. They came to seek treasure and the galleon. But there is a better question: *How* did they come—how did they know a galleon was in the loch? There is only one possible answer to that. *They heard it from the actors hired to tempt me here.* And is it not obvious that we have also been dealing with stage players here? You saw them and heard them. Think of the gestures, all larger than life, and of the hands that drew materials from the air. Their magic spoke to me strongly of the strolling magician, the attraction at the fairs and festivals throughout the whole of England."

"But how did you know their feats were not genuine?"

"Colonel, that would lie outside the compass of my beliefs. It is much easier to believe in prestidigitation,

in the cunning of hand over eye. I reached that conclusion early but I was faced with one impossible
problem. How could a man be here today, and a few
hours later be in Inverness? No stage magic or trick-
ery would permit that. Accept that a man cannot be
in two places at once and you are driven to a simple
conclusion: there must be two men, able to pass as each
other. Think of the value of that for impossible stage
tricks, and think how practice would perfect the illu-
sion. Two brothers, and Zumal as the link that would
travel between them to protect it."

"But you had no possible proof," protested Pole. "I
mean, a suspicion is one thing, but to jump from that
to certainty—"

"Requires only that we use our eyes. You saw Hohenheim at the village. And the next day you saw him again,
at the loch. But in the village he favored his left hand,
constantly—recall for yourself his passes in the air, and
his seizing from nowhere of flasks and potions. Yet at
the loch he had suddenly become *right-handed*, for casting
lines, for working the boat, for everything. We were seeing
brothers, and like many twins they were one *dexter*, and
one *sinister*."

Maclaren was nodding to himself. "I saw it, but I had
not the wit to follow it. Now one of them is dead, and
the other . . ."

"Knows a grief that I find hard to imagine. We must
seek him now, and try to give him a reason for living.
He should not be left alone tonight. With your permission, I will stay here, and when he is brought from the
loch I will talk to him—alone."

"Very well, I will go now and see if they have him
safe." Maclaren walked quietly to the door.

"And here is your proof," said Darwin. He lifted from
the open chest in front of him a long cloak. "See the
hidden pockets, and the tube that can be used to carry

materials from them to the hands. No supernatural power; only skills of hand, and human greed."

Maclaren nodded. "I see it. An' when ye find the reason that makes him want to go on livin', ye can tell it to me."

He left, and Jacob Pole looked across at Darwin. "Does he mean that? Why would he think to stop living?"

"He has had a bad shock tonight, but for him I do not worry; Malcolm Maclaren is a brave man, and a strong one. When he recovers from his present sorrow, his life will begin again—better, I trust, than before."

Pole went across to the empty bed and sat down on it with a groan. "I'll be glad when tonight is over. I've had too much excitement for one day. Let tomorrow come, and I can go to the loch again and seek the real galleon." His eyes brightened. "If there's one thing to pull from this sorry mess, perhaps it will still be the bullion."

Darwin coughed. "I am afraid not. There is no treasure—no galleon, even. It was only a part of the tale that was used to draw us here."

"What!" Pole lifted his head. "Pox on it, are you telling me that after all our work we came three hundred miles for nothing? That there is no treasure?"

"There is no treasure. But we did not come for nothing." Now it was Darwin's eyes that showed a sparkle of excitement. "The Devil is still in the loch. Tomorrow we will go there and learn the true nature of the animal."

Jacob Pole coughed. "Aye, well, the Devil. You are determined to study it?"

"Indeed I am. For that I would travel far more than three hundred miles."

"Well, Doctor, that's something I was going to mention to you. You see, after I fired the cannon—"

He paused. Something in Pole's look told Darwin that the night's bad news was not yet complete.

THE HEART OF AHURA MAZDA

The young man in the expensive topcoat leaned casually against the tavern wall and sipped at a pint of dark ale. He was eavesdropping and trying to disguise the fact, although the three people sitting in the corner were too absorbed in their own conversation to care in the slightest if they were overheard.

They were an ill-assorted trio. The one leaning on the table was well into his sixties, and instead of a wig he wore a round fur hat to cover his domed bald head. Now and again he would illustrate a point he was making with a sharp rap of his nails on the smooth board, or a snap of fingers in the air. His energy and animation of manner suggested a man half his age.

His two companions presented a less attractive prospect. Jacob Pole was in his fifties, thin to the point of being gaunt. His sallow complexion gave him a look of slight but perpetual jaundice. He sat briskly upright, the set of his shoulders marking his long years of military service.

Erasmus Darwin was if anything even less prepossessing. He was in his early forties, but his corpulence, lack of front teeth, and jowly face marked by smallpox conspired to make him look much older. Only the eyes redeemed his coarse appearance. They were grey, patient, and sagacious, and they twinkled with appreciation of the humor of the conversation.

"She's very intelligent," the fur-capped man was saying, in an English accent that was hard to place. "Pretty, too. Any man would be proud to be seen with her on his arm. So think about it, Erasmus. You have been a widower too long, maybe it's time you took another wife."

"Easy for you to suggest—you are already married, even if your lady is living in another country." Darwin gestured at a waitress to bring another pot of beef tea and a plate of savories. "Marriage is a large step. Answer me this, Joseph, and Jacob can be a witness. If you were free, would you honestly wish to be bonded to young Mary? I talk not of *bedding* her, now, I talk of *marriage*. Think of it, Joseph. Within a month she'd have reorganized your whole life." The slight stammer in his speech showed that he was enjoying the banter.

"Preserve me from that. I'm on trial now, am I?" The older man glanced from one of his companions to the other. "I rely on you, Erasmus, and on you, Jacob, to let no word of this reach Mary. But at my age, a man is either organized or he will never tolerate organization. And Mary Rawlings is too young for me"—he held up a hand to forestall comment—"too young for me to *marry*. The years after fifty are like late-season hothouse fruit, their enjoyment must be carefully planned. We have so few of them, and they must rest on a suitable *dish*." He pulled out of his waistcoat pocket a curious pair of spectacles that were divided horizontally in each lens, and used them to peer at a tiny fob watch. "No more tea for me. Five minutes, and I must be off. As for Mary, I'm too old and fragile to keep up with her young blood."

The fat man's grey eyes took on a new look, and he sat for a moment with his head cocked to one side. "What think you of that, Jacob?"

"You're the doctor, 'Rasmus, but I'll do my best." Jacob Pole peered at the older man as though seeing him for the first time. "For my money, Joseph, I'd say that you appear unnaturally hale, hearty, and energetic."

"Ah, but neither you nor Dr. Darwin has made an examination of me." The fur-capped man was grinning. "If you could just see my ruined liver and poor withered body—"

"A competent physician does not need that. The evidence of health is written in your bearing and your countenance." Darwin swivelled in his chair, so that he could take in the whole room of the tavern. "Look around you, now, and read the Book of Nature. See what is stamped in each face and body. There, by the door, side by side, we at once find goiter and rickets."

"You need to do better than that, 'Rasmus," Jacob Pole said gruffly. "Why, dammit, I can see that much myself."

"Patience, both of you. We begin with the easiest. Look along the bar, now, and take the men in order. The first is again too simple: consumption, in its middle stages. The second is in good health. Take the next one, the ex-sailor in the ragged jacket with his back to us. What do you see?"

Joseph Faulkner adjusted the spectacles on his nose, and peered carefully. "Without seeing his face . . . Hm. At the least, we have the effects of strong drink."

"Bravo. The half pint of gin clutched in his hand might be considered a clue, but we certainly admit the harmful effects of an indulgence in strong drink. What else?"

"Palsy?"

"No." Darwin shook his bewigged head in satisfaction. "That is a symptom, not a cause. Regard the uncertain set of the heels on the floor, and the way that the arm moves to reach the glass. You are viewing third-stage syphilis."

"You are sure?" Faulkner regarded the ex-sailor with a new eye.

"I am positive. He is far gone. If you could see his face, the ravages would become clear. But both of you, consider the man farther along, in the plum-colored fustian, looking this way and getting ready to leave. What of him, Colonel?"

Jacob Pole shrugged. "Ruddy face, clear eyes, a strong, square build. Thick black hair."

"True enough. But look below the surface. Well, Joseph? What do you say?"

"He ought to be healthy as a horse. But . . ." Faulkner paused.

"Aha! State your but. Your instincts are sound, Joseph, but you lack the detailed knowledge to support them. My friends, we must go beyond the *superficies* of hair and frame, if we are to achieve valid diagnosis." The stammer vanished from Darwin's voice when the subject was medicine. "Look rather at the color of the lips—is there not a purple tinge to them? Look at the veins in the temples, look at the posture, look at the cheeks, with a suggestion of grey. Look at the strain in his walk. Look at the clubbed fingertips. He suffers from severe and degenerative heart disease."

The other two men stared again as the black-haired stranger walked out of the tavern. Joseph Faulkner shook his head and took off his glasses. "Bedaddle. You are serious, are you not?"

"Completely. That man has perhaps a year to live."

"Scampages! If I did not know you to be a recent visitor

to London, I would swear those people all must be your patients." He turned. "Unless you, Colonel Pole? . . ."

"Not guilty." Pole shook his head. "I never set eyes on any one of them before."

"Then you are lucky, Erasmus, that we live in the Age of Reason. Two centuries ago you would have surely been burned for wizardry. When you sense such quick mortality, do you not feel the urge to speak to men and women of their diseases?"

"I do. But then I ask myself, to what end? If that man were my patient in Lichfield, and wealthy, I would certainly discuss his ailment and suggest a change of style in his life. But the unfortunate who left has no such opportunities. He is poor—you saw his shoes?—with no money for medications. Better to allow him to live as happy as he may. With or without my bad news, he will be gone by year's end."

Faulkner stood up. "As I must be gone now. I have a meeting across the river in Southwark. Until tonight, gentlemen, at seven?"

"And the renewed pleasure of your company." Darwin nodded, but he did not rise as their companion buttoned his heavy coat and strode out into the gloom and chill of a February fog. He poured more beef tea, for himself and Jacob Pole.

"Are you suggesting," Pole said gloomily, "that if I were sick, you would not tell me about it?"

"You mean, if I could not help you? Then I would say nothing." Darwin was absentmindedly eating his way through the whole tray of cheese and pork savories. "What happiness would it bring you, to know you were victim of some incurable disease?"

"Hmph. Well—"

Pole's reply was interrupted. The young man who had been hovering by the tavern wall stepped forward to the table.

Darwin did not seem in the least surprised. He merely nodded, and said with a full mouth, "I wondered which of the three of us was the focus of your interest. I am merely surprised that it is I, since I am more of a stranger to this city."

"I know that, sir." The other man nodded politely to Darwin and Pole but he was clearly uneasy, shifting from foot to foot. He was bareheaded, blond, and clean shaven, with a blooming fresh-skinned face that scarce needed a razor. "But it is nonetheless you with whom I wish to speak." He glanced again at Jacob Pole, this time unhappily.

Darwin gazed up at the earnest face. The youth was well dressed and healthy, but there was a certain stolidity of manner and dullness to his eye. "You may speak before Colonel Pole as you would before me. His discretion is absolute. It is, I assume, a medical problem that you suffer?"

"Oh, no sir." The young man was startled. "Or at least, sir, it is, but not my own. It is the problem of a—a friend of mine."

"Very well." Darwin pursed his full lips and gestured to the seat vacated by Joseph Faulkner. "Help yourself to beef tea, and tell me about your friend. Tell all, root and branch. Detail is at the heart of diagnosis."

"Yes, sir." The man sat down. He cleared his throat. "My name is Jamie Murchison. I am from Scotland. I came here to study medicine with Doctor Warren."

"A wise choice. The best doctor in London. You selected him as your teacher?"

"No, sir. My father chose him for me."

"I see. But if Warren cannot help with your problem, I am convinced that I will do no better."

"Sir, Doctor Warren's own health has not been good. Furthermore, he says that you are his superior, especially in matters of diagnosis. But in any case, I did not consult him for other, more personal reasons. You see, the lady with the problem—"

"Lady!"

"Yes, sir." Murchison paused uncertainly. "Is that bad?"

"No. But I owe you an apology. Nine out of ten who so begin, saying that they have a friend with a medical condition, are actually describing their own problem. I assumed it to be true in your case. Pray continue."

"Yes, sir. The lady is Florence Trustrum. She is nineteen years old and a second cousin to Dr. Warren. I met her through him. She hails from the Isle of Man, and is now in service at the house of your friend, Mr. Faulkner. That is the other reason why I preferred to entrust this matter to you. Mr. Faulkner does not know me well. Florence and I met each other socially, four months ago. We have become good friends. Two weeks ago, she came to me and confided a strange physical symptom."

"To wit?"

"In certain circumstances, she feels a crawling sensation on the skin of her face and arms."

"And that is all?"

"No, sir. At the same time she feels her hair stand on end, as though she has seen a ghost."

"Hair standing on end. For which a suitable medical term would be? Since you are a medical student, we may as well exploit that fact for the enlightenment of Colonel Pole."

Murchison frowned and shook his head. "I don't recall."

"It is known as *horripilation*. Remember that."

"Yes, sir. But it is not horra—horri-pil-ation, as I have read of it. Florence does not *see* gooseflesh, nor feel any sense of cold or terror when it happens. She says it may occur equally when she is cheerful, or relaxed, or thinking of something else entirely. And so I wondered, sir. In your great experience have you ever encountered any disease with such symptoms?"

"Never," said Darwin promptly. He rubbed at his jaw, which was in bad need of a razor. "Have you been present when it happens? Or has anyone else?"

"Not I. She said that Mr. Faulkner was with her on one occasion, and Richard Crosse, who lodges with Mr. Faulkner, on another; but neither man saw or felt anything."

"And the times and places?"

"The times, all different ones. The place, in her own room on the ground floor of Mr. Faulkner's home in Saint Mary-le-Bow. I have been there myself. I felt nothing, nor did I see anything unusual."

"But you did not think to consult your teacher, Dr. Warren."

"I thought of it, yes. But you see, if Dr. Warren were to think that Florence were ill, he will also feel it is his responsibility to inform her parents. And they will insist that she return home at once for treatment—they do not understand what a fine doctor she has here. And if she goes to the Isle of Man, while I must stay . . ."

"I understand perfectly. But as to my possible role?"

"Sir, I am only a student. There are many ailments outside my experience. And Florence told me that you will be visiting Mr. Faulkner's house tonight. You will see her. I thought, perhaps you will find a symptom in her invisible to me. If you would just take a look at her . . ."

"I will certainly look." Darwin smiled ruefully. "Before my friend Colonel Pole makes the point for me, I must admit to my own weakness. Even without your adjuration, I could not help but look. Diagnosis is so ingrained in me, it is a way of life."

"Thank you, sir." Murchison relaxed visibly. "You see, she does not *seem* ill. Is there anything else that you can think of to explain her condition?"

"Nothing." Darwin shook his head decisively. "I know no disease that provides such symptoms. But that is certainly not conclusive. In our knowledge of the human body, the best of us are no better than fumbling children. You may take comfort from this: *feeling well* is the best evidence I know of good health. If Florence continues to show no other symptoms than those that you describe, she should not worry. But I confess, I would certainly like to see—"

He was interrupted. An unshaven man carrying a lantern and dressed despite the cold only in dirty trousers and a thin blue shirt had come running into the inn. "Dr. Darwin!" he shouted to the room at large. "Is there a Dr. Darwin here?"

"There is." Darwin began to stand up, groping under the table for his heavy walking stick. "Damn it, Jacob, can you get that for me? I'm not built for bending." Then, to the man with the lantern. "I am Dr. Darwin. What do you want?"

"Emergency, sir." The man was gasping for breath. "At the Exhibition by the Custom House. They sends me to look for you, and ask you to go there."

Darwin looked quickly to Jamie Murchison, who shook his head. "No doing of mine, sir."

"Then come with me. Perhaps you will have opportunity to add to your store of medical knowledge." Darwin addressed the panting messenger. "I assume that someone at the Exhibition is ill?"

"No sir." The ill-clad man was heading rapidly for the door, but he turned to show a somber face. "Someone is dead."

Darwin and Murchison followed. Jacob Pole suddenly found himself alone at the table.

"Well, damn me," he said. And then, to the whole room, "You see the way of it? They sit here, they talk and talk and eat and eat, enough for a dozen normal folk.

I sit and listen." He fished into his pocket and threw coins onto an empty platter. "Then they run and run—and guess who's left alone at the end to pay the bill? Never trust a philosopher, my friends—he'll pick your pocket fast as any magsman, and then explain how you're lucky still to have your trousers."

"Gout," said Darwin, as they followed the lantern-bearing messenger through the fog-shrouded London streets.

The long, wan twilight of early February was near its end, and lamps were already burning in every house. It had snowed the day before, but the streets had been well cleared so that only grey mounds of slush remained. Now the yellow lamplight, bleeding out from tall, narrow windows, fell on the dull snow heaps and did more to emphasize their rounded shadows than to illuminate the pavement and road beyond.

Darwin banged his walking stick hard on the wet cobblestones. "Damnable gout, and damnable weather. Physician, heal thyself—but I have been unable to do so. I diagnose my condition, and I treat it well enough with cupping and with willow bark infusions, but I cannot cure it. Temperance helps, but this creeping cold brings it to life again. How much farther?"

"A few hundred yards." Jamie Murchison resisted the urge to help Darwin. The other man was considerably overweight, and a little lame, but he was stumping along cheerfully and energetically. "We must walk along Eastcheap and Great Tower Street, sir, then south to the river. Half a mile at the most. Have you not visited the Exhibition yourself, Dr. Darwin? It has been the talk of London for these ten days."

"I have not. Colonel Pole is your man for that—he plans a visit tomorrow. For my part, when someone tells of priceless jewels, and Persian demons, and Zoroastrian mysteries, I assume that it is merely an attempt to make a mumchance of the whole city."

"But this is different, sir. The ruby is protected by a curse—and now it seems that the curse has shown its power."

"We shall see. In a town full of calculating pigs, and dancing bears, and fire-eaters, and sword-swallowers, and purveyors of everything from Cathay aphrodisiacs to Indian opiates to French purges, anything may be claimed. For in my experience, London draws the charlatans of England, as a boil draws to it the body's poisonous humors. Have you visited this Exhibition yourself, Mr. Murchison?"

"Yes, sir. Twice." Murchison looked away to hide his embarrassment. "I went with Florence."

"Then tell me what you saw. I am setting a bad example by my skepticism. In life, as in the examination of a new patient, one should keep the mind forever open for novelty of impression. Tell me all."

"You will see it for yourself in another minute—we are almost there. But it is simple enough. Two weeks ago, the hall where the Exhibition resides was rented by a Persian, Daryush Sharani, for the purpose of displaying a magnificent ruby of vast age and religious significance. It is known as the Heart of Ahura Mazda, and it is huge—the size of a big man's fist. But the thing that makes the Exhibition unique, and attracts so much public attention, is that although Sharani stays always with the gem, he disdains other guards. He insists that the Heart carries with it its own protection, in the form of a curse within the stone. The curse of Ahura Mazda invokes a demon, who binds and makes helpless anyone who touches the jewel. If that demon is not quickly banished by Daryush Sharani, the would-be thief will die."

"Easy enough to *say*. Did anyone test the Persian's claims?"

"They did, when the Exhibition began. With a hundred or more people watching, four men tried to take the jewel while Sharani stood by smiling. As soon as each one touched the stone, he was bound rigid until Sharani reached over the Heart of Ahura Mazda and whispered the invocation that controls the demon. Then the men were released. They looked dizzy, and in discomfort; but they moved freely enough."

Murchison heard Darwin's skeptical grunt. "I felt as perhaps you are feeling, sir," he went on, "that it is easy enough to pay a poor man to stand still for a few minutes, and have him say that he was frozen by the curse. But one of the four was a nobleman, the Earl of Marbury, who is far beyond bribery and above corruption. He swore that as he tried to lift the Heart of Ahura Mazda he was seized by the demon, and unable to move a muscle until Sharani invoked the words of release. He also says that the demon's grip is pure torment, unlike any pain that he had ever felt before."

They had reached the hall, a rectangular building of grey limestone fifty yards from the river. The double entrance doors were iron-bound oak, open now but carrying two heavy padlocks. On the left-hand door was pinned an announcement that the Heart of Ahura Mazda would be on display from January 30th to April 25th. The right-hand door showed the admission price, of twopence per person per visit.

Within, half a dozen oil lamps lit an oblong sanded floor, in the center of which stood a large metal plate. Upon the plate was a silver pedestal, and on top of that an empty cushion of black velvet within a hemisphere of glass.

The messenger and Murchison hurried on at once toward the far wall, where a motionless human form lay surrounded by a small group of men. But Darwin stood just two steps inside the door, wrinkling his nose in perplexity and sniffing the air. It was ten more seconds before he walked forward, moving to study the pedestal and its empty cover. Finally he banged his walking stick hard on the stone floor, to produce a hollow boom that echoed around the hall. He walked forward to join the others.

The body lay supine, blue eyes open and arms thrown wide. Darwin knelt down beside it, and grunted in astonishment. The man was the black-haired stranger from the Boar's Head Tavern.

"And who are you, sir?" asked one of the men standing by the body. He was well dressed in a heavy woollen coat, leather boots, and gaiters, and he wore clerical garb. "The magistrate has already been called."

"I am Erasmus Darwin, a physician." Darwin did not look up. "But I fear I can do nothing for this poor fellow. Does anyone here know him?"

"I do, sir." It was a watchman, carrying a staff and a shielded lantern. "He's been regular in these parts these two year, an' often 'anging around when jewlery an' plate goes a-missin'. But nuffin's been proved, not near enuff for a dance at Tyburn."

"You sent for me when you found him?"

"No, sir. Not I."

"Then which of you did send for me?"

There was a silence. Darwin turned to the messenger, who shook his greasy head firmly. "None of these gentlemen, sir. I was given a florin in Lower Thames Street, by a man I never seed before. He said there was somebody a-dying in the Exhibition Hall, and I was to go to the Boar's Head an' bring Dr. Erasmus Darwin."

"I saw this man alive, in that same tavern, less than an hour ago." Darwin bent to grasp the man's wrist, and to touch him on temple, mouth, and at the hollow of his neck. He loosened the fustian jacket, and made a rapid examination of chest and abdomen. Then he stood up. "He has been dead less than thirty minutes. Who found him?"

"Me it was." The grubby watchman lifted his staff. "On me first round. I sees a window open at the back, so I come to the front an' let meself in." He held up a heavy bunch of keys. "With these. An' there he was. Dead as mutton. An' the jewel—gone."

"He is just where you found him?"

"Yessir. I think he staggers back here, see, tryin' to reach the winder, but 'e dies 'fore he gets to it."

Darwin shook his head and pointed to the sanded floor. In the lantern light, a pair of wavy lines ran from the metal plate and pedestal to the wet, battered shoes of the dead man. "He was *dragged* this way. You are sure that no one here pulled him?"

"Positive, sir." The clergyman spoke again. "I was passing by, and I came in straight on the watchman's heels. When we entered the man was exactly as you see him."

"Just as the demon left him," said a ragged man softly. The little group of people stirred and looked nervously around the shadowed hall.

"Now then, we'll have no blasphemies here," said the clergyman mildly. "When a man dies, there is no need to call for demons. I'm sure the doctor can tell us the natural cause of death."

The men around the body turned to Darwin expectantly. He hunched his shoulders, and shook his head in irritation. "The obvious diagnosis is a massive heart failure, but it is not a reply I can offer in good conscience. I saw this man earlier today, and observed him closely. He was not at the point of death. And I am sure that this was not present."

Darwin stooped, and lifted the limp right arm of the dead man. As he turned it, an ugly heart-shaped cicatrix about an inch and a half across was revealed on the palm of the hand. The middle was white, the edge a lurid blood-red.

"The Mark of the Beast!" Everyone except Darwin and Murchison took a pace back.

"Nonsense." The clergyman's voice sounded less confident than his words. "It is a simple wound—a burn. Is that not so, sir?"

"It is not." Darwin gestured at Murchison, who had sunk to his knees to study the mark more closely. "No medical student would admit such a conclusion were I to draw it. But as to what it is . . ." He fell silent, then looked up. "I would like a chance to examine the body more fully. I have seen nothing like this in twenty years as a physician."

He straightened, and walked across to the pedestal. He lifted it, in spite of Jamie Murchison's cry, "Be careful!"

"Careful of what?" Darwin peered at the empty setting of black velvet, then at the silvered sides of the pedestal. "If there is no demon who guards the Heart of Ahura Mazda, then surely I am in no danger. And if there is a demon who accompanies the ruby, since the ruby is not here, again I am safe."

"So you truly believe that we have a—a—" The clergyman had followed Darwin, but he could not bring himself to say 'demon.' "A great mystery," he concluded.

"No, sir." Darwin's fat face had tightened with powerful curiosity. "We do not have a mystery. We have at least five of them. How did that man die? Who or what killed him? Where is the Heart of Ahura Mazda now? Where is its faithful guardian, Daryush Sharani, and why did he run away? And finally—least perhaps, but also perhaps strangest of all—*who summoned me here to serve a dead man*—when I am a servant of the living?"

Dinner at Joseph Faulkner's house had taken a curious turn. The half-dozen guests had been drawn there at least partly by the promise of rare scientific and literary conversation from the eminent visiting physician and inventor from the Midlands. Instead they found a Darwin who was thoughtful and preoccupied. He ate his share and more of beef, parsnips, Yorkshire pudding, and horseradish sauce, but he allowed others to carry the full social burden until brandied plums and cream had appeared on the table and been disposed of. At that point he roused himself, poked with his finger for a fragment of meat lodged in his back teeth, and said, "Gentlemen—and ladies, too. If you will indulge me, I have a mind to play a game. I would like to propose a puzzle, a matter concerning which your thoughts and opinions would be most valued."

"At last!" Joseph Faulkner waved a hand around the table. "Speak on, Erasmus. Now I will confess it, I was worried by your silence tonight. The rest of us have said quite enough. My friends all came here to hear you."

The guests nodded, all but an aged aunt of Jacob Pole. She was very hard of hearing, but with wine at hand she seemed quite content and didn't mind missing the conversation.

"Anyone who came to hear me will be disappointed," Darwin said. "For I have no answers, only questions." He glanced around the room, well lit by wall candelabra and ceiling chandeliers, and found every eye on him. "Let me narrate the events that befell me this afternoon."

He told it carefully, summarizing everything from the arrival of the messenger at the Boar's Head Tavern to his own departure from the Exhibition Hall for Faulkner's house. As he spoke, he studied the others around the table.

It was a curious and curiously varied group. Joseph Faulkner kept an unusually egalitarian household, with a suitably unconventional seating arrangement for both guests and servants. Darwin was at one end of the table. At the far end was the host, and on Faulkner's left sat Mary Rawlings, a thirty-year-old redhead with milky skin and a determined look in her blue eyes. She had her hand often and possessively on Faulkner's arm. Darwin had shrugged mentally. His own views were liberal. Mary must know that Faulkner had a wife across the Atlantic, and she was surely old enough to make her own decisions.

In midtable there was an empty chair, intended for a manufacturer of agricultural equipment who had been detained by business in Norwich. He had sent his apologies, and into the vacant place Jamie Murchison's heartache, brown-haired and blue-eyed Florence Trustrum, had slipped at the end of the meal. She quietly helped herself to preserved plums and coffee. Joseph Faulkner had no respect for the traditional class separations, and her switch from servant to diner excited no comment.

Darwin had made his own evaluation of Florence as she supervised the serving of dinner, and decided that she was as healthy, vigorous, and straightforward a specimen of womanhood as he was likely to find in London. Imaginary ailments were as far from her life as the surface of the moon, and that made Jamie Murchison's remarks all the less credible.

Across from Florence sat Richard Crosse, who according to Murchison had visited her room but seen and heard nothing out of place. Seated between Colonel Pole and his deaf aunt, Crosse was a thin and intense young man in his middle twenties, slightly crookbacked and with one shoulder higher than the other. Somewhere in status between a paying lodger and a guest, he had kept his attention on his plate right through dinner. Only now did he turn dark, intelligent eyes toward Darwin.

At the end of the recital of the afternoon's events there was a respectful silence. "So you see," Darwin concluded, "there are five mysteries, with five questions to be answered. What thoughts do you have on any of this?"

There was another long silence. "Come now," Faulkner

said. "Theories. What about you, Richard? You are always full of wild ideas, and the only time you pulled your nose out of your studies this week, it was to tell me how excited you were about Dr. Darwin's visit. You must have something to offer."

Crosse shook his head, and turned beseechingly from Faulkner to Darwin. "I—I'm afraid that I—"

"No one is *obliged* to provide comment." Darwin came to the rescue. "I told you, Joseph, that all I have to offer is questions. It would be no surprise if others find themselves in the same position."

At the end of the table, Mary Rawlings was frowning and scratching the end of her snub nose with her forefinger. "Would you entertain the idea not of an answer, but perhaps of a sixth mystery?"

"Gladly. Consideration of new questions often allows us to answer old ones."

"You never visited the exhibition, did you, and never saw the Heart of Ahura Mazda?"

Darwin shook his head.

"So you have been assuming that Daryush Sharani escaped from the locked hall in the same way as the would-be thief entered it, through an open window."

"That is true." Darwin was frowning. "It was my assumption, but it seems a reasonable one. On the evidence of witnesses he was certainly present at the exhibition when it closed, at three o'clock, and certainly absent when the watchman opened the doors."

"It would be a good assumption—if Daryush Sharani resembled other men in his appearance. But he did not!" Mary Rawlings looked around the table for confirmation, and others nodded agreement. "He wore the most ornate and elaborate robes of scarlet and purple, and a tall red headdress. He also had a huge beard, big and black and bushy. There is no way that he could appear on the streets of London, even for two minutes, without being seen and remarked on by a score of people. Unless perhaps his clothes were found in the hall?"

"They were not." Darwin was looking at Mary Rawlings in admiration. "Young lady, *rem acu tetigisti*. You have put your finger on an absolutely crucial point. No clothes were found, nor the great ruby, the Heart of Ahura Mazda. Nor, for that matter, the day's takings from the Exhibition, which were supposedly in excess of five pounds."

"So this man Sharani became *disembodied*," said Jacob Pole at last. "Hm. Went up into thin air. I've seen a trick like that once or twice in India, but I never thought to see it in London."

"Nor will you." Darwin roused himself and snapped his fingers. "Rather the opposite. Ah, what a fool I am! I did not have the sense to observe the results of my own actions." He turned to his host. "Joseph, do you have a carriage available?"

"Of course. But why? You cannot be leaving already, when it's not yet nine o'clock."

"I must." Darwin stood up. "I must go back to the Exhibition, to demonstrate to myself that I am indeed an imbecile—and would have remained one, but for the valuable assistance of this company. And anyone who cares to come with me will observe the evidence of my folly."

The afternoon's foggy damp had been succeeded by a hushed and relentless rain, enough to keep anyone indoors with no urgent reason to be abroad. The interior of the coach was drafty and wet, but Darwin was in high spirits.

"The true disgrace is that I *noticed* it!" he said, as they clattered through empty streets toward the Thames. "And yet I did not apprehend its significance. When I was in the hall, I banged my stick on the stone floor, and remarked even then that the sound was strange. There was a boom to it, like an echo. I thought to myself, 'Rafters,' but the timbre was wrong. The echo was—*under* the floor!'"

Five of them were riding the coach. Joseph Faulkner had not asked who else might be going with Darwin—he was, and that was the main thing. Mary Rawlings had shown as much determination, grabbing Faulkner's arm so that he could not move without towing her along. The fourth in the coach was Jacob Pole. Scenting an adventure, with perhaps a priceless ruby at the end of it, he had arranged for his aunt to be taken home without him. She seemed puzzled, but made no objection. Last came Richard Crosse. He had swung aboard uninvited, sitting up next to the coachman in the pouring rain and as jittery as ever. He leaned over to look inside the coach, seemed on the point of a flood of speech, then as suddenly sat upright again.

The rapid night ride took less than five minutes, and at the hall Darwin bustled on ahead of the others. He stood before the great double doors, lantern in hand, and cursed mildly.

"Ahriman's ghost! Padlocked again—when now there is nothing to steal." He turned to Richard Crosse. "You are more limber than I. The back window, then, and unbolt the side door."

Crosse melted away into the darkness without a word. Thirty seconds later there was a rattle of bolts, and Darwin could stride inside. He walked five paces, wiped his forehead with his sleeve, and held the lantern high. "Do you see it? What we seek, of course, is some way down through a solid stone floor."

It was Mary Rawlings who found it, over in one dark corner of the hall. The hinged wooden trapdoor had been painted grey and sanded over, so that it resembled stone flags. When it was lifted she hung back, nervous for the first time, but Darwin unhesitatingly swung the panel full open and peered down. He listened intently. A moment later he had laid the lantern on the floor and was descending into blackness.

"Pass the light down to me." His voice came back hollow and distant, added to a nearby sound of trickling water. "Then come yourselves."

Joseph Faulkner went first, with a caution appropriate to his age. The others followed, with Jacob Pole firmly in tailguard position.

"Guarding the rear," he muttered.

"Aye, Jacob." Darwin's voice boomed from the darkness ahead. "Your own, no doubt."

They were emerging to stand on a long wet ledge about five yards wide. Beyond it, black and restless, flowed a stream of twice the width.

"It's a river," Mary said. "A real underground river."

"It is." Darwin was staring around him with vast satisfaction. "And it should be no surprise to us. London is ancient. We tend to forget the obvious, but this city, too, was once no more than woods and meadows. Most of the old streams run now below the surface, invisible and out of mind. And this must be one of them."

"You know, 'Rasmus, you're quite right." Jacob Pole was leaning over and staring at the water, his mouth open. "And me a Londoner, native born. I ought to be ashamed of myself. I knew this from my childhood. There were four old rivers on the north shore, the Walbrook, the Fleet, the Tyburn, and the Westbourne. Unless my old schooling serves me false, this must be a spur of the old Walbrook. The main river rises in Finsbury, and runs close by the Mansion House. It joins the Thames by Dowgate—or used to; but I've heard no mention of it for years and years."

"But what are you seeking here?" Mary stepped close

to the lip of the stream, peering over the worn stone edge at the water. "Is it that?"

She was pointing down. In the moving water, firmly supported by metal braces from the stony edge, sat a new structure. It was a waterwheel, and it was turning steadily under the pressure of the flow.

"That will do excellently well for a beginning." Darwin hunched low, and examined the wheel's construction. "Skillfully made," he said after a moment. "And recently set in place. There is a natural steady flow from the river, but I think temporal variation comes mostly from tidal change. Now then. Here, things become more interesting." He was moving with the lantern, following a pair of long black lines that ran from the wheel's center, into a complex tangle of broken gears and wheels, then finally appeared again to run across and up the slippery wall. He bent low, and scraped at the surface of one of the lines with his thumb nail. There was a glint of metal beneath.

"Where do they lead?" Faulkner asked. Mary Rawlings was holding his arm, in real or simulated nervousness, and the older man was enjoying the whole experience. "What's above there? It must be part of the hall itself."

"It is." Darwin followed the lines up with the lantern's beam, until they disappeared into the ceiling. "We are exactly beneath the pedestal. If it were present, the Heart of Ahura Mazda would stand right above us."

"But where's the Guardian?" Mary asked. "Weren't you expecting to see Sharani here?"

"I was *hoping* to do so. I was not *expecting* it." Darwin ventured along the stony side of the underground stream, leading the way quietly through dark and filthy culverts. Water dripped steadily onto their heads from dark wooden beams and brick arches, the latter furred over with mildew and patches of grey fungus. All the while, the rain-fed stream murmured along no more than a yard from their feet.

"Aha." Darwin paused, half a dozen paces ahead of the rest. "Something new. Bring the other light, Joseph, and let's take a close look."

He had reached a forlorn heap of garments, bright scarlets and purples dulled by lantern light. Beyond them, the stream branched into three smaller tributaries.

Darwin lifted a glittering robe and turban. "The servant of Ahura Mazda. Vanished into thin air, as Colonel Pole suggested, at this very point." As he spoke, a cold air blew through the tunnel, rippling the cloth in his hand.

Pole gave a little grunt and retreated a step. "Disembodied. Then we can follow him no farther with human agents?" His voice hovered between hope and disappointment.

"We cannot," said Darwin cheerfully. "However, that does not mean he cannot be followed by inhuman ones. Friend Daryush Sharani has made a most serious mistake. He should have thrown his outer garments into the river, rather than leaving them here. Don't touch the rest of these clothes." He turned to Faulkner. "Joseph, we require assistance. Can you find me a pair of bloodhounds?"

"At this hour? Erasmus, you certainly ask a lot of me." But Faulkner sounded delighted, and after a moment he turned to Crosse. "Richard, you know Tom Triddler's place, up past the Mansion House. Would you go there, and ask him for a pair of his best tracking hounds? Tell him it is for me. You'll have to bang on his door, because he's half deaf. But keep hammering. He'll come."

Crosse hesitated, turning his head to one side and opening and closing his mouth. Finally he nodded and hurried away into the darkness without speaking.

"I just don't know what's got into Richard tonight," Faulkner said. "He's behaving very odd. So witless and confused, you'd think he was in love."

"He is certainly that," said Darwin. "With Miss Florence Trustrum. Is it not obvious to you? He regards her with the hopeless yearning of a mortal for a goddess. Knowing your own fascination for such things, I am only astonished that you did not observe it long since."

He walked slowly back along the tunnel to the place where they had entered, and squatted down on the wet stone. And there, as unconcerned as though he sat in Faulkner's warm parlor, he began to examine in detail the mass of gears, wheels, wires, and pulleys that sat directly beneath the pedestal in the Exhibition Hall.

"Broken," he said after a few minutes. He held up a handful of components. "Quite deliberately, and beyond repair. I conjecture that several elements have also been removed. Without hints from its maker, its purpose is hard to divine."

"Never mind that old junk." Jacob Pole had been wandering moodily around, staring down now and again at the dark water. "I was hoping for excitement and treasure, not standing around in a smelly damp sewer. Are you really expecting a dog to be able to track down here, in the cold and dark? Tracking dogs need light and air."

"Not at all, Jacob. That is an old wives' tale." Darwin raised himself laboriously to his feet. "A good tracking dog will follow a scent as well at night as during the day, as well for a nonliving scent as for a living spoor, and as well underground as on the surface. If we are looking for a mystery tonight, we will find none greater than a hound's nose. It possesses subtleties for distinction of odors that we can scarcely imagine. How many centuries will it be, think you, before mankind will produce a machine to rival the nose of a dog for sensitivity and discernment?"

"Well." Pole sniffed. "I'm not persuaded. We'll see, soon

enough. But I'd always been told that if you took a tracking hound into a dark, airless place—"

He was interrupted by a cry from above, and a sound of clattering footsteps overhead.

"Here they come," Darwin said. "And now perhaps we can observe one of the wonders of Nature."

Richard Crosse came down the ladder first, carrying a mournful-looking black hound with jowls and ears that hung below its lower jaw. After him came a rumpled man carrying a second dog.

"Late work, Tom Triddler," said Faulkner cheerfully. He rubbed his hands. "No matter, I'll see you're well rewarded for it. Good trackers, are they?"

"Best I have, sir." Triddler put the dog down and swept off his cap, to reveal a totally bald head. He put the cap on again hurriedly. "Cold down here."

"But that will not interfere with the hounds?" Darwin asked.

"No sir. Nothing does. Not cold, not dark, not nothing."

Darwin nodded to Pole. "There, Jacob. You will see that your fears are groundless." He turned to Tom Triddler. "Are we ready to begin?"

"I am, and the dogs are." Triddler stared around him. "What an 'ole. Wouldn't like to come courting down 'ere. Got a scent for the dogs, 'ave yer? Old sock, somethin' like that."

"This way." Darwin led them to the heap of discarded clothing. "Any one of these should do it."

"Aye. Perfec'." Triddler drew the two hounds to the pile and pointed down. The dogs snuffled and wagged their tails furiously, while all the people clustered round them. "They've got it now—an' off we go. Go on, now, Blister. An' you, Billy, on yer way."

He was holding the two leashes lightly, while the dogs sniffed and snuffled. "Go on, now," he repeated. "We're waitin'. We don't 'ave all night."

His second urging was very necessary. The two dogs had turned around once, then settled on their bellies on the floor, tails wagging happily. But when Tom Triddler shouted them again into action they sank to rest, their jaws on the cold stone. Their tails drooped, and they stared at him with mournful eyes.

After another few attempts to spur them on, he shook his head. "I've never seen nothin' like it, Mr. Faulkner. They won't budge. Not an inch. Seems they don't like it 'ere underground."

"What did I tell you?" Pole gave Darwin a superior nod, and began to retreat toward the ladder. "I think the dogs have the right idea. It's damn cold down here, and it stinks. As you said, 'Rasmus, dogs have powers that we lack. They know we'll find nothing more. I'm ready to go home."

"Powers that we have *lost*," Darwin muttered, but his tone lacked its usual conviction. In his disconsolate manner, he was a good match for the two bloodhounds. "I was quite convinced. . . . But maybe you are right, Jacob. We will accomplish nothing more tonight. We might as well to bed."

He limped after Pole toward the ladder, so rumpled and so woebegone that Joseph Faulkner called after him: "Come now, Erasmus. There's always tomorrow."

"Aye," came the testy reply over Darwin's shoulder. "Another day to make a fool of myself."

"Ah," Faulkner said softly to Mary Rawlings. "That's not our Dr. Darwin, founder of the Lunar Society and Europe's leading physician. That's gout speaking. Come along, my dear, let's be out of here. There are more pleasant nighttime pursuits than underground sewer wandering. And in the morning you will see a new Erasmus."

But the morning came to a city immobilized. During the night, the rain had frozen and then turned to snow.

A deadly sheath lay on every flat surface, from east of the Tower to a mile past Westminster. A few hardy (or foolhardy) merchants had ventured forth, their draft horses skidding and shivering on treacherous roads, and after a hundred yards retreated. By ten-thirty the whole city was again shrouded and quiet.

Darwin sat in the parlor at Faulkner's house. He and Jacob Pole had been persuaded to stay over, but now he was chafing with impatience. The revelation had come to him during breakfast. There *was* a way to trace Daryush Sharani, and a sure one—if only Darwin could pursue it. But his weight and his gout together conspired against him.

Finally he went to Florence Trustrum's room on the ground floor, and asked her if she would deliver a letter to Jamie Murchison. She muffled herself in a wool head shawl, thick overcoat, and ugly leather boots, and set out into the still, white wilderness. Darwin sat at the window, counted the seagulls perched on the gable roof, and wondered at the instinct that sent them flying far inland when the northeasters blew in with the winter storms.

Florence returned breathless in little more than half an hour. "Jamie will do it this morning," she said.

"You are upset." Darwin took her by the hand. "What happened?"

"It was . . . nothing." She gave him a direct glance from bright blue eyes. "Oh, why not. I will tell you. Jamie— he asked me to marry him."

"Ah. And you replied?"

"I told him—that I did not know. But I think I do." She was gone, leaving the smell of warm wet wool behind her. Darwin nodded to himself, and went back to watching seagulls.

It was after noon when Murchison arrived. Joseph Faulkner, Jacob Pole, Florence Trustrum and Darwin were again in the dining room, enjoying a quiet lunch of cold pork, applesauce, sage and onion stuffing, and hot boiled carrots. Darwin had left instructions to the staff and Murchison was shown in at once, snowy boots and all. He hesitated on the threshold.

"You have it?" said Darwin eagerly, through a mouthful of pork crackling.

"I do. I went to the chandlers as soon as I received your message."

"And you found an address?"

"I did."

"And it is?"

Murchison looked at Joseph Faulkner, gulped, and stammered: "They gave me an address for the delivery of just the goods that you listed. But it was *here*!—this very house!"

"What!" Darwin stared at Faulkner, who shook his head.

"No good looking at me, Erasmus. I have not the faintest idea what you two are talking about."

"This house." Darwin subsided into his chair. After a few seconds of open-mouthed gaping at his empty plate, he closed his eyes and breathed a vast sigh. "It is so. And at last I see a whole picture." He stood up. "Come on. All of you."

With the other four trailing along behind, Darwin headed for the ground floor and the rear of the house. At a closed door he knocked and went straight in.

"But this is Richard's room!" protested Florence.

"Aye. Mr. Crosse is fortunately *in absentia* at the moment. So let us see—what we shall see." Darwin had moved to the writing desk by the window and was coolly opening drawers and examining their contents.

"Erasmus, this is a little too much." Faulkner moved to Darwin's side. "Richard is from an old Somerset family that I well respect, and I think of him as my guest. To see his room commandeered in such a way, and his private belongings despoiled—"

He paused. Darwin had reached deep into a left-hand drawer of the escritoire and pulled out a large, glittering stone.

"The Heart of Ahura Mazda." He brought it close to his face, turning it to allow its facets to catch the light from the window. "Hm. Jacob, what do you think? This is more your department than mine."

Pole took the gem and examined it for no more than two seconds. He sniffed and handed it back. "What a letdown, after such a chase. That's no ruby, priceless or otherwise. It's nothing more than high-quality glass. Cunningly cut, I'll admit that. I'd give you a shilling for it."

Darwin plunged his hand again into the drawer. "And now we have a part of the Guardian himself. His beard." In his hand was a tangle of hair, thick and black and bushy. "And as for the rest of Daryush Sharani . . ."

Darwin looked past Faulkner and the others. "Come in, sir, and claim your possessions. My behavior here leaves much to be excused."

In the doorway, face ashen, stood Richard Crosse. The dusting of snow on the shoulders of his black coat matched his countenance. At Darwin's gesture he moved forward and sank down to sit on a narrow window seat.

Darwin stared at him for a moment, and his expression changed. "When did you last have food and drink?"

Crosse shook his head. "Last night? This morning? Sir, I am not sure."

"This must not be." Darwin went to Crosse and gestured to Jacob Pole to support him on the other side. "We will go to the dining room, sir, and you will eat and drink. I will advance hypotheses, and you will correct me as you choose. Silence, now—I neither need nor expect an answer yet. Speak if you must, but above all, you must eat. Remember the natural law of the world, Mr. Crosse. Eat, or be eaten!"

It was an odd little procession. Joseph Faulkner and Florence Trustrum led the way, he looking back over his shoulder all the time. Next came Darwin and Pole, supporting Crosse between them. He walked like a zombie, without either volition or resistance. Last came Jamie Murchison, stolid young face scowling in puzzlement. At the door to the dining room, Crosse at last lifted his head and stared straight at Darwin.

"How did you *know*? How could you possibly know?"

"I know only part. I conjecture much. And on one central element, I am so ignorant that I scarce know what to ask you." Darwin steered Crosse to the table and nodded at Florence to fill a plate with roast pork and carrots and a glass with a mixture of beer and brandy. "But I do know where to begin. It is to assure you, Richard Crosse, that I know of no law that you have broken. You are as innocent as I, or the colonel who sits at your side."

Pole's audible sniff suggested that might be no great reassurance, but Darwin went on, "In a *legal* sense, you are blameless. But in a *moral* sense, Mr. Crosse, things are more complex. You sought to obtain assistance for a dying man, when many would have thought only of flight. That was commendable. But you were guilty of one universal failing—something that we all do, all too often. We wish to prove our own cleverness and importance to the whole world."

Crosse bowed his head in assent. After another unhappy look at Darwin he picked up a fork and at last began to eat.

"I am as guilty of that as anyone," went on Darwin. "Do you know where my own thoughts began on this matter? In as self-centered and introspective a place as one could dream of. I asked myself, who knew that I,

Erasmus Darwin, was at the Boar's Head Tavern yesterday afternoon? For only someone with that knowledge could seek to summon me to the Exhibition."

Florence Trustrum, showing excellent instinct, placed another piled plate of food in front of Darwin. He began to eat with his fingers, his eyes never leaving Richard Crosse.

"Let us define that small group of people. Joseph Faulkner and Jacob Pole certainly knew, since they were there with me. Mary Rawlings also presumably knew. Jamie Murchison knew, but since like Colonel Pole he was there with me when the message came, that struck him from the list of candidates. Who else? It seemed that there might be several others, but they must all be people *close to Jacob Pole or Joseph Faulkner*. Only they could know that we were meeting at the Boar's Head during the afternoon. So. The possible universe was circumscribed. But I could go no further with logic alone, to point a finger at one man or woman. Something new was needed. That something was what I hoped to find when we returned to the Exhibition Hall last night. At first, I thought that I had discovered it. The garments of Daryush Sharani were my guide, and they would allow us to follow him. But the hounds proved useless. I returned to this house, as baffled as I have ever been in my life." Darwin shook a finger at Pole. "You, Jacob, had already been planting doubts in my mind, suggesting that the hounds would prove useless at night and underground."

Pole shrugged. "I was right. They were useless, 'Rasmus. They told us nothing."

"Only because we asked them the wrong question. A dog can answer only in a dog's terms. Remember when Tom Triddler released the hounds? They sniffed at the clothing, and wagged their tails, and were all excitement. It was only when he shouted at them again, and told them to hunt for the scent, that they lost all enthusiasm.

As well they might! They had done their job, and they knew it. They did not deserve harsh words from their master. The source of the scent of the garments was right there—in person." Darwin pointed to Richard Crosse. "The hounds knew it, and they told us all that they could tell. Was it their fault that we were unable to read the message?"

"But *why*?" Jacob Pole scowled at Darwin across the table. "I don't know about all this dog's mind reading, but what is the point of all this? False rubies, and curses, and fancy dress, and deception. But 'Rasmus, say what you will, a man *died* at the Exhibition. You seem to be forgetting that."

"Not at all. We come to it now." Darwin licked his fingers, and nodded across the table at Richard Crosse. "Sir, I could make my estimate of the whole course of events. But at this point, I think you ought to make your statement. Remember, I am not the magistrate, nor is Mr. Faulkner. But a magistrate will be here, if we find it necessary to call for him. Forget your reticence, and speak. Let me preface you with only this: after I examined the contrivance in the river vault beneath the Exhibition, I suspected that the unusual materials for its construction would have been purchased from a local chandler. We have confirmation of that; your own name is I suspect to be found on the receipts."

Richard Crosse laid down knife and fork and stared in turn at each person seated around the table. He bit his lip. "I will tell. But after yesterday's disastrous events, I pledged my own soul to make no public revelation of one element of this affair. For all the rest, Dr. Darwin has said it for me. I wanted to prove my own cleverness, by a successful hoax on the whole world. You see, I had the means to do it—a method of my own devising, that would hold a grown man helpless. And it would do no damage."

"To a *well* man," said Darwin. "But for a man already suffering from degenerative heart disease, like the would-be thief . . ."

"I know that now—too late." Crosse rubbed at his gaunt jaw. "I thought that I had a harmless hoax. I would fool all this great city with the Heart of Ahura Mazda, and with the great exhibition of the power of the jewel. And then Daryush Sharani would disappear forever. I never intended to boast of my success, or to tell of the hoax. But I was the fool."

"And you were taking people's money," Florence Trustrum said.

He nodded at her. "I was. But never with thought of personal gain. The takings were a small amount, far less than the cost to me, and people seemed well pleased with what they saw. My family is well-to-do. If the weather had not turned so foul today, I would be on my way home to Fyne Court, in Somerset. I intended to say no more to you and Mr. Faulkner than that I was tired of life in London, and preferred the quiet of the Quantock Hills."

"Which would be a pity," Florence said softly.

"But the Earl of Marbury!" Joseph Faulkner, at the end of the table, broke into the conversation for the first time. "And all the other men made helpless by your 'demon.' What of them? I can accept the facts of your imposture, and even your disguise as Daryush Sharani. There is nothing new in elaborate robes and false beards. But you have said nothing to explain the true mysteries: how the Earl was persuaded to cooperate with you, or how the man died yesterday when he attempted to touch the Heart of Ahura Mazda. That is what we need to hear."

Richard Crosse stared down at the tablecloth and shook his head. "I have promised myself that I will never speak of that. If I were able to forget it myself, I would do so."

"Then we'll have the magistrate in, and the devil with it!" Faulkner slammed his hand down on the table. "Without the rest, what you have said is no explanation at all."

Crosse did not look up. "So be it," he said at last. "So be it."

Darwin held up a hand greasy with pork fat. "One moment, Joseph, before we rush to the law and the clumsy clutch of official justice. Mr. Crosse, I do not ask you to go beyond your own conscience. But I do ask you to come with me and listen to what I have to say. Colonel Pole and Mr. Faulkner will accompany us, under condition that they promise to remain silent on what they hear."

"You are my guest, Erasmus, and you would swear me to silence in my own house!" But Faulkner was already on his feet. He led the way out, turning as he left to say, "Florence, this is the day for hot chocolate. Order for yourselves, would you, and have a pot brought through to us." He glanced at Darwin. "A big one."

The panelled study across the entrance hall was unheated, and cold enough for frost patterns to sit on the inside of the window panes. Faulkner shivered, gestured to the armchairs, and sat down hard himself on a stuffed ottoman. "Should I have the fire lit in here, Erasmus?"

"I think not. This will be brief."

Faulkner rubbed his hands together. "Speak, then, before we all freeze."

"Without delay." Darwin turned to Richard Crosse. "I begin with a statement that might be considered more as personal opinion than fact. To men of inquiring minds, few elements of today's natural philosophy excite so much interest as the experiments of van Musschenbroek of Leyden, von Kleist of Pomerania, Benjamin Franklin of Philadelphia, and of our own Jesse Ramsden. Would you not agree?"

"You know all!" Crosse's face went even paler, and his dark eyes widened.

"Far from it. I know a little, and I guess a great deal. But let me imagine a tale for you. Suppose that we have a young man, one of feverish imagination and genuine inventive powers, who reads of the findings that I mentioned, and becomes fascinated with the whole field of *electricity*. He reads Mr. Franklin's great work, *Experiments and Observations*, and Mr. Joseph Priestley's encyclopedic *History of Electricity*. And his own imagination is, to employ an appropriate term, sparked. He has original ideas. He himself begins to experiment—but secretly, because he is still unsure of where his own notions will lead him."

"Dr. Darwin, you are a wizard! How can you know these things?"

"He's right, 'Rasmus," Pole added. "How the devil *do* you know?"

"I do not *know*. But events in this house gave sufficient reason for conjecture. Observe." Darwin leaned across to the desk and picked up an amber paperweight. He rubbed it hard against his own rough jacket, then held it out toward one of Joseph Faulkner's fur caps, perched on the arm of a chair. "See how the fur moves, to set each of its hairs separate from its neighbors. It is the oldest electric effect, already well known to the old Greeks—our very word, *electricity*, derives from their word for amber. When I heard that Florence Trustrum had reported her own hair standing separate on arms and legs, and odd sensations on her skin, within this very house, my thoughts turned idly to Leyden jars, and to electric sparkings. But I dismissed the idea as an irrelevance, and my musings went no further. Then last night I saw the underground vault, and within it the diverse but mysterious *apparati* of some electrical experimenter, copper wires and bars of iron and plates of lead. Yet still I made no connection! Only today, with the chandler's report of materials delivered to this very place, did my brain offer its synthesis. I recalled the smell of Exhibition Hall when I arrived there—the very air itself held the whiff of electrical discharge. And, at last, I could offer a rational explanation of the hounds' failure—or rather, to be fair to them, of their success. But who would have suspected it, that Daryush Sharani was last night one of our own company."

"You would." Richard Crosse had somewhat recovered his composure. With his secret revealed, a more thoughtful, fatalistic man emerged. "Your every suggestion is precisely right. So now I ask, knowing all, what do you want of me?"

"Knowing all?" Darwin started up in his chair. "Why, man, I know nothing of the most fascinating part of this whole business: what is your machine, that could render a would-be thief totally helpless, and how does it work? That's what I want to know, not the details of glass rubies, stage magic, or deception."

Crosse averted his eyes. "That I have sworn to myself I will never reveal. It has done enough damage already. If it were ever to be broadcast . . ."

"It would not be." Darwin was wriggling in his seat with excitement. "Not by me, or Jacob, or Joseph. I swear that what you tell us will go no further. On that you have my word as a physician and a human."

"What of the others?"

"Well, I suppose." Faulkner glared at Darwin. "Damn it, Erasmus, don't you think that Jacob and I ought to be allowed to make up our own minds? I know that to find out what's going on here, you'd be quite happy to pawn our souls." He turned to Pole. "What do you say, Jacob? I will go along with this, if you will."

"Right." Pole nodded to Richard Crosse. "Be assured of our silence, and speak on. Anything you say to us will never be breathed to another mortal. Though so far as I'm concerned, I'm as sure as a pig's tail curls that I'll not understand more than two words of your explanation."

"I wish that were true. But it is elementary, at the same time as it is mysterious." Crosse went to the desk and took out paper, pen, and inkwell. "I have results, but no sound basis for a scientific explanation. A turning wheel, like the waterwheel that you looked at last night, bearing magnets both fixed and moving, will produce a flow of electricity in loops of wire—the long copper lines, that you saw beneath the Exhibition Hall. And that flow, passed through other coils that I took out of the machine and threw into the river, becomes a force strong enough to bind a man immobile. I attached one wire to the metal plate around the pedestal holding the Heart of Ahura Mazda, and one to the metal rim of the protecting glass case, in such a way that I could disconnect it from the side of the pedestal itself without others seeing my action. It was connected thus." He sketched a series of simple diagrams in black ink, labeling each one as he did so. His trembling hands grew steady as he worked. "I assure you, I had tested this machine a hundred times on myself. It freezes the subject, with an indescribable feeling both pleasant and unpleasant at once. Free movement is impossible, but when the flow ceases there are no harmful aftereffects, merely a continued tingling like pins and needles."

"And that is what you did to the Earl of Marbury?" Darwin was peering at the sheet, his eyes alight.

"Exactly that—with no ill result afterwards, to him or to anyone else who tried the same. It seemed a perfect device for protecting the Heart of Ahura Mazda, the word of which would quickly spread all around London and assure the total success of the hoax. As soon as that game was over, I intended to explore the electrical effects that I had discovered until I had plumbed their deepest meaning. But after the death of the thief yesterday . . ." The face of Richard Crosse had filled with life and energy when he talked of his work. Now it clouded.

"I cannot explain why it proved fatal," Darwin said softly. "But I can suggest several avenues of thought that should be followed. First, the thief was wearing shoes that were broken and wet. As you and I both know, damp increases electric flow. More important, I suspect, was the swollen and thaw-fed condition of the underground river. If the rate at which the waterwheel turns dictates the level of the charge received by the pedestal, our wretched thief could have received an impulse many times that of your earlier experiments. Enough to blister his hand, and enough to provide a fatal jolt to an already weakened heart."

"Your suggestions are ingenious. But they will not be the basis for future experiment. Never again will I pursue such reckless follies." Crosse fell silent and hung his head as Florence Trustrum came into the room carrying cups, saucers, and a large silver pot of hot chocolate. He looked up only to give her a quick smile of thanks as she placed the tray at his side.

"What are you going to do with me?" he asked, after she had left the room. "You are right. I did not check sufficiently the natural variations in the electric force. A man is dead who should be alive."

Darwin raised his eyebrows and glanced at Pole. "Jacob?"

"Me?" Pole favored Darwin and Crosse equally with his scowl. "Why, damn it, I'm not going to do anything at all. If a thief and a rogue is dead who should have been arrested, I say, good riddance. It's time saved for the hangman."

"Very well. Joseph?"

"I agree with Jacob. And it's no concern of mine if the honorable citizens of London Town flock to see a hoax. From what Florence said, she and the rest more than got their money's worth. I don't want any more thaumaturgical exploits in this house—even if you call it science, Richard. But for the rest, my opinion of you has not changed. You are still welcome to stay here with me."

"Thank you, sir, but I must go back to Somerset." Crosse gave the closed door a long and unhappy look. "I should go at once."

"Go if you must, if that is your decision," Darwin said. "But if you others will permit it I would like one private word with Mr. Crosse. Alone. And it is nothing, I assure you, to do with electricity."

"And thank the Lord for that." Jacob Pole stood up and moved toward the door. "I said I wouldn't understand all your technical talk, and I was right. *Electricity*. What a waste of time and effort."

"Agreed." Faulkner was following Pole through the doorway. "Does *anybody* understand this thing called electricity?"

Darwin and Crosse looked at each other. In unison, they shook their heads.

"We do not, Joseph." Darwin smiled. "Not yet. For it is as your great countryman, Mr. Franklin, puts it so well in one of his letters: 'If there is no other purpose for the electricity than this, it may serve to make a vain man humble.'"

Jacob Pole paused, the door knob in his hand. "Then you should get Mr. Crosse's machine, 'Rasmus, and take a double charge for yourself."

He closed the door before a response could be offered. Darwin shook his head and tried not to grin. "Pardon me, Mr. Crosse. I have known Colonel Pole for a long time. If I may again become more serious, my previous inquiries of you were motivated by scientific curiosity. What I say now has no such origin. You may choose to

regard it as an unwarranted and unconscionable intru-
sion in your private affairs."

Crosse had been quietly tearing to pieces the diagrams
he had drawn of his equipment. "Continue," he said. "I
have at least been provided with fair warning."

"Very well. The subject is Florence Trustrum. You look
on her with favor?"

"Is it so obvious?" Richard Crosse's voice was bitter.
"I try to hide it. I look on her with favor, and more than
favor. But as you see, I am not made to—to 'court an
amorous looking glass.'" His hand went to his left shoulder.

Darwin snorted. "And yet your namesake, Richard, that
you now choose to quote, ascended to the throne of
England and wed the woman of his choice. Stop your
self-pity. You are as whole as any man in this house, if
you but think yourself so."

"I cannot entertain that thought. I will be returning to
Somerset as soon as the weather permits—if I am free
to do so."

"You are free. But I urge you not to go. You should
stay here, and determine if Florence feels an equal warmth
for you."

"She has no need of me. A new suitor is already here.
You saw him."

"I did. I suggest that he is no threat to you in Florence's eyes. Mr. Murchison is a pleasant young man, and
probably an honest and an honorable one. I wish him
no hurt, and I should not be taking sides. But let me
say this: the world is full of pleasant, handsome men,
as harmless and as simple-minded as Jamie Murchison.
You are different. You have that rarest gift, the one that
marks our transition to a higher being. You have *creativity*;
an inspired inventiveness coupled with true scientific
instinct."

"A creativity that kills. Dr. Darwin, I am flattered, I

cannot deny it. But there are others far more ingenious than I."

"No, sir." Darwin spoke with great authority. "Trust me in this. There are all too few such, in any time and place. London today does not contain five such men and women. If you do not pursue the great problems that you alone can see, who will pursue them? Mr. Faulkner, or Miss Rawlings, or Colonel Pole? Never. We may have the desire, but we lack the divine touch. Perhaps you think that your own children will do what you will not? Maybe. But only if they *exist*. You, and people like you, have a duty to the world: you must marry, and love, and propagate."

Richard Crosse removed his hand from his left shoulder and stared quizzically at Darwin. "Yet you are single, sir."

The older man paused. It was many seconds before he answered. "Aye. For now, but not I think forever. And I have children already, from a former marriage. However, you make an excellent point. I should be truer to my own principles. I will remember that."

Darwin stood up, patted Crosse's shoulder, and walked across to the door. On the threshold, he turned. "I am going to join the others now. Florence Trustrum will be back here in a few minutes, to collect the cups and the chocolate. She is fond of you. Say to her what you will. But say it."

"Sir, one moment." Crosse hurried to Darwin at the door, his pale face suddenly resolute. "I will try, surely I will try. But you should know that I have no gift for honeyed words. I have tried ten times to tell Florence how I feel, and each time I have failed."

"Then, Richard, you must try an eleventh time." Darwin smiled his gap-toothed smile. "Courage, man. Nature leaves no space in the world for failures. You can win. See here." Darwin reached into his pocket, and pulled out a glittering chunk of red glass. "Here is your own creation, the Heart of Ahura Mazda. Look on it when you speak to her. Surely the man who could conceive this can win a heart to replace it."

Crosse nodded, and took the jewel. Darwin finally closed the door, turned, and headed toward the rear of the house. He walked without noticing where he was going, absorbed by a new and intriguing thought. If Richard Crosse did not try again and did not win, why then, that very failure made him unfit to sire descendants. And the same idea could be applied to every field of activity, for animals as much as for men. A grand principle was at work, Nature forming what it needed for future generations, by an inevitable and continuous weeding of the present. It was happening now, and it had happened always.

Erasmus Darwin walked on, right past the room where the others were waiting for him. The smell of fresh-baked bread drew him by instinct toward the kitchen, while his mind strayed far away. Already he was wondering how his new thoughts could be framed in their most general form.

THE PHANTOM OF
DUNWELL COVE

"Salt ham, bread, *sauerkraut* cabbage, and near two pints of beer to slake the thirst. So what, then, would you expect?"

Erasmus Darwin seemed to be addressing the question to his own big toe. His bare right foot and broad calf were propped up on a wooden stool in front of him, while he stooped forward to examine the reddened and swollen toe joint. It was no easy task. He was grossly overweight, with an ample belly that hindered bending. The face that frowned down at the offending foot was fat and pockmarked, redeemed only by its good-natured expression and bright grey eyes.

"You would expect exactly what I got," he went on. He was dabbing ether onto the joint, preparatory to covering it with a waiting square of oiled silk. "For have I not told you, Jacob, that the surest way to induce an

113

attack of gout is through the consumption of ill-chosen food and drink? Salt is bad. Beer is bad. Claret and port are pure poison."

Jacob Pole took no notice whatsoever. He was prowling between the fireplace, where a good coal fire showed an orange heart, and the narrow shuttered window. He paused to peer out of the crack in the shutter as another gust of wind hit the house, banging on the thick door like a gloved hand.

"Damnable," he muttered. "Down the Pennines, and before that straight from the North Pole. And it's snowing again. We ought to be in warmth and sunshine. What man in his right mind would live in a place like this, when he could head south and enjoy the sun by day, and be lulled to sleep by warm breezes at night?"

"Aye. The south, where an Army colonel could develop malaria, to leave him shaking and shivering three or four times a year, regardless of weather." The square of silk was in position, and Darwin was carefully pulling on over it a woollen stocking. "I have Jesuit-bark in my chest, Jacob, if you need it. It is my professional opinion that you do."

"Later, maybe." Pole touched his hand to his jacket pocket, then returned to lean on the mantelpiece. "A slight case of trembles, but I'm in fair shape provided that I don't catch a chill. Better shape than you, from the look of it. Salt ham and beer! What prompted you, 'Rasmus, after all your lecturings to me?"

Darwin pulled on his soft boot, wincing for a moment as the sore toe felt the touch of leather. "Hunger, Jacob, pure hunger. What else? I was on the road early this morning, in anticipation of the bad weather that you now see. I knew of the childbirth problem at Burntwood, but the case of blood poisoning at Chasetown was a surprise and the supplies of food that I had taken with me in the sulky were gone by midday. Salt ham and beer were all that were available; yet a working man needs fuel. He cannot afford to starve."

"Be a while before that happens to you." Jacob Pole nodded at Darwin's belly. "And you were right about the weather. It's absolutely foul outside, and it's not even dark yet. I'm wondering."

"Wondering what?" Darwin was smiling knowingly to himself.

"Wondering how I'll ever get home tonight. There's more snow in the sky, and the road to Radburn Hall was hard going even early in the day."

"You should not even think of it." Darwin stood up, pressing his right foot tentatively on the rug. "What sort of host would I be, if I sent a friend out to freeze on a night like this? Moreover, Elizabeth will surely not expect you. Do one thing for me, Jacob, as a favor to my sore toe. Go and tell Miss Parker to set an extra place for dinner."

Another buffet of wind hit the stone walls of the house, but Jacob Pole had lost his gloomy expression when he hurried away toward the kitchen. He was back in just a few seconds.

"Erasmus, she said you already told her that I would be staying to dinner, and that just the two of us should be present."

"And was I wrong?"

"No. But how did you know?"

Darwin was grinning, a friendly grin even without front teeth. "You arrive at my home while I am away on my rounds. That is unusual, but not unprecedented. You await my return. Very well. But when I come here accompanied by Dr. Withering, you say scarce a word to either of us. And when he goes, you stay. Add to that your touching of your jacket pocket, not once but half a dozen times. Is it not obvious that you have something that you wish to show to me, and say to me, and that it is something calling for privacy?"

"I do, and it does."

"And it is not the delicate matter of a medical opinion."

"How the devil can you know that?"

"Because if it were, you would have spoken long since. You share my high opinion of Dr. Withering."

"Blast it, do you know everything?"

"Very little—until I am told." Darwin led the way through to the dining room. Earlier there had been a noise of small children, but now the room was empty. Two places were set, facing each other across the broad oak table. In the middle sat earthenware tureens of parsnips, potatoes, and Brussels sprouts, with between them a gigantic steaming pie, twenty inches across and already cut into ten slices. Jugs filled with milk and water stood at the end of the table, along with a concession to the visitor in the form of a pitcher of dark beer.

Jacob Pole sniffed the air. "Squab pie? My favorite."

"With apples, onions, *and* cloves. But before you assign me powers beyond the natural, I will admit that this was to be my dinner long before I knew you would be here to share it."

Pole pulled an envelope out of his jacket pocket and sat down at the table. "A pie that size. What would you have done if it were just you at table?"

"My v-very best." Darwin's voice took on the slight stammer that came often when he was joking. He had already lifted a mammoth portion of pie onto his plate and was reaching for the tureens. "Now, we are better equipped for conversation. At your service, Jacob."

But the gaunt colonel shook his head. "If you don't mind, I'd like to read a letter aloud to you before I say anything else. The only thing you must know before I begin is that the writer, Millicent Meredith, is my cousin. Milly is a widow, and four years ago I helped her with a family problem. Although we have always been regular correspondents, it is so long since we last met."

Darwin, his mouth already full of pie, reached out for the envelope. It had been opened, sliced cleanly at the top with a sharp letter opener. He slid out four pages of thick ivory-white paper, written on both sides in purple ink.

He handed the pages to Pole but kept the envelope, examining it carefully before placing it on the table to the left of his plate.

Pole, after a preliminary clearing of his throat, began to read.

> *Dear Cousin, You have often in the past urged me to follow the advice of your esteemed friend, Dr. Darwin, and to discard supernatural explanations for any event, regardless of appearances—*

"She has my ear and sympathy already."
"Aye. I thought that would catch you."

> *So it is for this reason that I am writing to you now, when my own rational faculties no longer seem able to operate.*
>
> *First, let me say that the plans for Kathleen's marriage have been proceeding apace, and I trust that you have received already the official invitation. Since Brandon Dunwell is eager for the ceremony to follow tradition, and to take place like all Dunwell family marriages at Dunwell Hall, Kathleen and I have decided to remain here in Dunwell Cove until the wedding. Brandon's family, who have already begun to arrive in anticipation of the event, are of course staying at the Hall, but I judge that inappropriate for the bride and her mother.*

Kathleen, you will be glad to hear, is in good health, although rather thoughtful in spirits. I hope that this is in contemplation of the major change which is soon to occur in her life, rather than to the events here which so perturb me.

Lest you accuse me of wandering, let me move at once to those events. The coach ride from St. Austell to Dunwell Cove is about seven miles, Dunwell Hall being on the direct route to the cove and less than one mile away from it. The coach runs regularly, but only twice a week, and it stops at the Hall as necessary to pick up or discharge passengers. As I understand it, the service has been this way for many years.

Ten days ago, a party of three of Brandon Dunwell's relatives arrived from Bristol. They boarded the coach at St. Austell, and rode in it to Dunwell Hall. When they arrived, they found that each of them had been robbed of their personal valuables, which since they carried jewellery appropriate to a wedding exceeded ten thousand pounds in value. This loss took place in spite of the fact that each of the travellers insists that the coach did not stop anywhere on the journey, nor did anyone enter or alight. The coachman confirms this. Also, since even here in Cornwall the January evenings are often chilly, the coach doors were closed and the window openings all muffled.

That was mystery enough. However, six days ago the episode was repeated identically with the arrival of another couple of Brandon's relatives. The loss in their case included golden brooches and diamond bracelets, removed from the chests and hands of their wearers and of great value. Again, both travellers insist that the coach did not stop, nor did anyone enter or leave the coach, and again this is confirmed by the coachman's own account. It was then that I heard the first whispers around the village of Dunwell Cove: That the phantom who robbed the coach is none other than Brandon's dead brother, Richard, whose spirit haunts Dunwell Hall and the road outside it.

Naturally, any muttering of such a nature is profoundly distressing to Kathleen, who I am sure by now has heard it. The rumors continue to grow, since only last night a third party of travellers was robbed by the phantom. They were travelling as before from St. Austell to Dunwell Hall, and again they were friends and relatives of Brandon Dunwell.

That is the situation as it obtains today. Brandon is sullen and furious, claiming that someone is seeking to ruin the celebration of his marriage. His relatives are equally angry, in their case at the material loss. But if I am honest, the only one for whom I care is Kathleen, and illogical as it seems, she has somehow taken onto herself the blame for the appearance of the phantom. Yet she swears, and she has never yet lied to me, that she has no idea what can be happening.

And so, dear cousin, I am casting my net blind over the ocean of my relatives. I am writing to you, and to certain others whom I trust and who are of wide experience, to ask if you can offer any explanation as to what has been happening on the coach ride between St. Austell and Dunwell Hall. Despite your urge that I remain always skeptical of events beyond Nature, the invisible phantom who haunts the coach appears able to perform acts so inexplicable, and yet so tangible, that it is tempting to invoke thaumaturgic causes.

I might add that I myself rode the same coach, four weeks ago when we first came to Dunwell Cove, and again last week when I had need to travel to St. Austell for the purchase of personal materials related to the wedding. Kathleen was not with me, but I was accompanied by a woman cousin of Brandon who is staying at the Hall. Talk of the phantom had made both of us nervous, but we neither saw nor heard anything unusual, either coming or going.

My question, cousin, is simple to ask but difficult to answer: What should I do? My instinct is to postpone the wedding, but on the face of it that is ridiculous. I have not lost one penny because of the phantom's actions. Nor, in fact, have the Dunwell family relatives, since Brandon is insisting on providing to them new articles of jewellery at least as valuable as those that have been lost. Brandon himself is rich enough that such compensation offers no hardship to him whatsoever.

Yet my heart remains troubled and uneasy. My instincts tell me that the phantom must be connected to the wedding, but in some way that I cannot conjecture. As you well know, dear Kathleen is my only daughter. She appears about to make an excellent marriage, to a man who is the sole owner of Dunwell Hall and of all its extensive lands and properties. And yet . . . and yet I know not what.

You once helped me greatly, and I have no right to presume again upon your time and good nature. But any suggestions, or any thoughtful advice that you may be able to offer will be gratefully received by—your loving cousin, Milly.

Pole laid down the final sheet. Across from him his companion did not seem to have moved, but almost half the pie had vanished and the vegetable tureens were much diminished.

Darwin sniffed and shook his bewigged head. "A mystery, sure enough. And a clear cry for help. But I heard nothing that could not have been read aloud in the presence of Dr. Withering."

"True enough. But there is more. And it is more personal to the family." Jacob Pole tapped the letter. "Milly didn't spell it out to me, because she knew I know all about it, but she has other worries on Kathleen's behalf. You see, two years ago Kathleen was engaged to another Dunwell. That was Richard, Brandon's elder brother. But he stabbed a man to the heart, was tried for it, and sentenced to death. The day before he was due to be executed he broke out of his cell and escaped along the cliffs east of Dunwell Cove. When he was cornered he jumped into the sea rather than be recaptured. Three days later his drowned body was found at low tide, trapped in the rocks and the tidal ponds. Kathleen was of course heartbroken by the murder, the trial, the verdict, and then the suicide. So now, when there's talk of a phantom, and people say it's the ghost of dead Richard . . . you can see how poor Milly's thoughts are running."

"She wonders about a ghost, which I can believe in no more than I am persuaded of the existence of a phantom who performs so mundane a function as the robbing of coaches."

"Perhaps." Pole was at last helping himself to food, while conscientiously avoiding Darwin's eye. "But if it's no ghost, then we need another explanation."

"Which in the circumstances is quite impossible to

provide." Darwin reached far along the table, to slide within easy reach a round of soft cheese and a bowl of dried plums and candied peel. "Jacob, I love a good mystery as much as the next man, and perhaps a deal more. But if you have heard me say it once, you have heard me say it a hundred times: In medical analysis, there is no substitute for personal presence. For if medication and surgery form the lever of medicine, examination provides the fulcrum of diagnosis which allows them to act. One must observe at first hand: the jaundiced eyeball, the purple or livid lips, the sweet or necrotic breath. One must examine the stools and the urine, and palpate the cool or fevered skin. Without that direct evidence, a doctor has nothing but hearsay. And in many ways, the curious events involving your cousin and her daughter are little different. So what, to continue the medical analogy, are the *facies* of the situation? I can list a dozen facts which may be important, and concerning which we know nothing. Without facts to sink them, a thousand ideas can be safely launched. Yet you would propose that we sit here in Lichfield, and conjure an order of events in west Cornwall? I say, that cannot be done with any shred of plausibility."

Pole nodded gloomily. "I suppose you're right." He said nothing more, but went on quietly eating. After a few seconds Darwin reached across to pick up the letter and began reading it over.

"When is the wedding?" His words were hardly intelligible through a mouthful of Caerphilly cheese and plums.

"February 12th—ten days from now."

"Hmph. Do you know the bridegroom?"

"Neither him, nor his dead elder brother. In truth, the whole Dunwell family are strangers to me."

"And your niece, Kathleen?"

"I was present at her birth. She deserves the best husband in the world."

"And finally, your cousin Milly. Would you describe her as an imaginative woman, one with an active fancy?"

"Quite the opposite. She's direct and straightforward, with a bottom of good sense."

"Hmph." The silence this time went on for much longer, until at last Darwin stood up and walked over to the window. He peered out, looking up at the sky. "Ten days, eh? And it is sixteen days to the full moon."

"That's right." Pole was suddenly smiling. "Ample time. It would be four days each way, six at very worst. We would be there and back, and you'd not miss a single meeting of your precious Lunar Society."

"That is as well. Our group is overdue for a meeting with Mr. Priestley, reporting on his latest experiences with dephlogisticated air. All right." Darwin was absentmindedly wiping greasy hands on the tablecloth. Once the decision had been made he moved at once to practical details. "Let us assume that Dr. Small and Dr. Withering will serve as *locum tenens* in my absence. It will take at least four days to reach Dunwell Cove, but such a timetable presumes that we will be able to obtain a coach to take us to the service running south from Stafford. In such weather, that may not be easy."

"Ah—well, as it happens that's already taken care of. I arranged for a two-horse dray to collect me here, first thing in the morning. It has ample room for two."

"Indeed." Darwin raised his thin eyebrows. "And what of your necessary baggage?"

"It's all with me. You see, I thought that I—"

"Say no more." Darwin raised a plump hand, and leaned far back in his chair. "I now wish to ruminate on the fact that my actions are apparently so easily dictated." He waved at the table, where half the pie remained untouched. "And you must eat, instead of pecking like a sparrow. Come, Jacob, no protests. You know the rule of nature: *Eat or be eaten*. I do not relish the thought of a winter travelling companion who is weakened by lack of nourishment."

He scanned the table top, a frown on his face. "And while you do your share, I will inquire as to the status of our hot dessert. Ginger pudding was promised."

The contrast was striking. As far west as Launceston, winter ruled. The road surface was iron-hard and stable, the crust of snow breaking barely enough to give firm support to a horse's hooves. Hedgerows, formed from black tangles of leafless hawthorn, marked the converging lines of highway across the white and rolling landscape of the Bridetown Hills. Finches, robins, and starlings, perched within the hedges, were fluffed out to grey and brown balls of feathers. They did not move as the coach passed by. Within the vehicle the passengers sat just as unmoving, swaddled from toes to ears. The interior, no matter how much the occupants might struggle to block each crack and chink of door and window with rags and clothing, remained ice-cold.

But beyond Launceston, the road skirted left of the brooding, craggy mass of Dartmoor. The way to the south lay open. Within a few miles, the snow cover melted magically away, while at the same time, as by coincidence, the sun broke through and began to disperse a long-held low overcast. The road surface softened as the coach proceeded, and at last at the foot of the hedges the snowdrops and first yellow crocuses stood in open bloom. Beyond the boundary hedgerows, birds and rabbits busied themselves in the soggy fields.

"By the grace of the great Gulf Stream." Darwin had abandoned the broad hat that had protected his head since leaving Lichfield, and for the past few miles he had been peering out through the coach window at the rapidly changing scenery. "The Stream laps the whole of the western peninsula, to the point where winter in Cornwall and Devon never approaches the severity of our inland experience. A few more miles south, and I swear we will see full Spring. But even in Lichfield, we still have reason to be grateful for the Stream's existence. Were it not for that benign presence, all England would be colder than Iceland."

Jacob Pole did no more than grunt. For three days he had said little and eaten less, contenting himself with making the atmosphere in the closed coach hideous with strong tobacco, that he first cut in thin slices from a purple-brown solid block, rubbed well between his hands to shred and flake it, and stuffed into a curved meerschaum pipe so well-used over the years that its golden exterior had turned almost black. He lit his pipe with the aid of a small oil lamp, constantly burning for just that purpose. Smoke rose up in pungent blue-white spirals to fill the closed coach. Darwin, as confined in movement as his companion, had grumbled about the nauseating stink as he scribbled both verse and prose in his bulky Commonplace Book, but between rhymed couplets and engineering ideas he had eaten and drunk enough for two from the hamper that sat next to him on the seat. His precious medical chest, too bulky to travel within, was lashed to the coach's flat top.

"And because it is never true winter in the extreme southwest," Darwin went on, "the native flora must surely contain members of the vegetable kingdom not encountered farther north and east. Think of it, Jacob. I may return home with the basis for a whole new pharmacopeia, derived from plants that I have never seen before."

Another grunt was Pole's main reaction, until at last he removed the pipe from his mouth.

"Blast it, Erasmus, I don't have your spare padding. If you're planning to keep up the geography and medical lectures, you might at least do it with the window closed."

"So that you can once more asphyxiate me with your fumes? You are fortunate that there are no other passengers, less patient and long-suffering than I. Also, the day will come when you regret your emaciation." Darwin patted his belly in a satisfied way. "This is not mere padding. It is valuable reserves, against the possible vicissitudes of Nature."

But he pushed the window to, as tightly as it would go, and leaned back in his seat. "Five more minutes, Jacob, and it will be time to dot your pipe and light your brain. That last milepost shows us to be only one mile short of St. Austell."

"I'm aware of that. Why d'ye think I've been sitting here steaming, the past half-day?"

"Are you afraid that your cousin may have alerted others to our impending arrival? I thought that you in your letter were to warn her against such action."

"I did. And I rely on Milly completely. So far as anyone in Dunwell knows we are no more than guests for the wedding party on the bride's side."

"So why the long face?"

"Her reply created that." Pole patted his chest, but made no move to draw a letter from within his quilted and buttoned overcoat. "Too much gratitude, in advance of results. She seems to think we're gods—especially you."

"And why not? We are as much gods as any that exist."

"You don't want to go talking like that around the people at Dunwell Hall. Especially Brandon Dunwell. According to Milly he's a very pious, God-fearing man— a bit too much, I suspect, for her taste."

"And therefore far too much for mine."

"No doubt. But the real problem is, I'm afraid Milly is hoping for a lot more than we can deliver. I can tell from her letter, she's thinking we'll arrive at Dunwell Cove with a full explanation. And you told me yourself, you have absolutely no ideas about the phantom."

Darwin's full mouth pursed. "I said no such thing. If you will but recall our conversation on that first evening, I said that I had a thousand ideas. That is still true. But until we arrive at Dunwell I have no sieve, no way to retain truth and riddle away plausible nonsense. But that will change. In fact, it is already changing."

While they were talking, the rhythm of the wheels was taking on a different cadence. The rumble of movement over town cobblestones replaced the crunch of gravel of a well-kept country road.

The coach was arriving, a few minutes earlier than the driver's estimate, at the St. Austell coach house. The wheels were still turning when Darwin opened the door. He swung himself to the ground, lightly for a man of his size, and stared around with eyes gleaming.

They had arrived on a private vehicle, not a regular service, and the only person waiting at the coach house was a straw-haired boy nine or ten years old. Seated on a bench, he was enjoying the new-found sun and staring at Darwin with open curiosity.

"A bad start." Pole, climbing out more slowly and gesturing to the driver to unload their cases and the medical chest, glared at the lad. "Nothing here. I was hoping we'd learn something in St. Austell and have a suggestion to offer Milly."

"And so we may. Make no mistake, Jacob, as a witness a young boy is far to be preferred to a grown man or woman. He has fewer *preconceptions* as to what he believes he should see."

Darwin walked across to the lad, who was still gawping at the new arrivals. He reached into his pocket, and fished out a shilling.

"Roight, sir." The voice was full of the singing tone of the far West Country, and at the sight of the coin the boy had come to his feet at once. "You'll be wanting me to handle the cases, sir?"

"No. Just answer one or two questions." Darwin sat down on the bench and gestured for the lad to do the same. "What's your name?"

"Georgie, sir."

"Well, Georgie, we will be taking the coach from here to Dunwell Cove. Will it be arriving soon?"

"Yes, sir. He be here any time now."

"Is it always the same coach that is used for Dunwell Cove, or are there several?"

"There's only the one. Same coach, and mostly same horses."

"And it is always driven by the same coachman?"

"Yes, sir. Always the same man, it be, for a long time now."

"What is his name?"

"Jack Trelawney." Conflicting expressions ran across the boy's open face. "Stinkin' Jack, some around here be callin' him."

"But it is not a fair name?"

"No, sir. He were once powerful smelly, a while back. But not now."

"I see. You like Jack, don't you?"

"Yes, sir, that I do." Georgie blushed, a fiery scarlet like a sunburst. "He never thrazzes me for nothing, not like some as drive the coaches." He looked down, then turned to glance up at Darwin through thick eyelashes that any girl might have envied. "He's not being in trouble, is he?"

"No trouble at all, so far as I know. But would you point him out to me when he comes in?" Darwin stood up, dropped the coin into a grubby hand, and was rewarded with a shy smile.

"Yes, sir. I'll point 'im out. Thank'ee, sir."

Pole had watched and listened from over by the coach, which had already been turned and provided with fresh horses in preparation for its journey back to Taunton. "A good shilling down the drain," he grumbled, as Darwin returned to his side. "And we've not been in St. Austell above five minutes."

"But *my* shilling, to spend as I chose." Darwin's voice took on a more thoughtful tone, and he went on, "A shilling spent, not wasted. You see, Jacob, there is a hidden calculus, not recognized yet by our philosophers but perceived instinctively by many financiers. Knowledge is a close relative to money, just as money is related to knowledge."

Pole flopped down to sit on his travelling chest. "Damn it, 'Rasmus, you're getting too deep for me. Money leads to knowledge, eh? So what knowledge did your shilling just buy from yon lad?"

"I do not yet know." Darwin shrugged his heavy shoulders. "As I said, it is not a recognized calculus, and its working rules have still to be established."

"Then for the moment I'll hang on to my shilling." Pole nodded toward the bench, where Georgie was gesturing urgently to Darwin and pointing along the road. "Here's what you got for yours."

Approaching the coach house on foot was a dark-clad figure holding a leather gun case. His long overcoat was marked in front with pale brown stains, and he wore a round hat with a rim pulled low to shield his single eye from the bright sun. A black patch covered the other eye, and bushy brows and a full black beard emphasized rather than concealed thick lips, red and glistening. The man's complexion was very dark, adding credence to the idea that the remnants of the defeated Armada had two centuries earlier discharged their exhausted Spanish crews onto the Cornish coast. The coachman took in Darwin, Pole, and luggage with one swift glance, nodded a greeting at the boy, and strode on through into the coach house.

Two minutes later he was back from behind the building, driving a two-horse cabriolet with a modified wooden body. He held the reins lightly and the team was fresh and frisky, but the coach wheeled smartly around to stop precisely at the pile of luggage.

He jumped down from the driver's seat and grinned at his passengers with a rapid gleam of white teeth. "Jack Trelawney, at your service. Dunwell Cove or Lacksworth, sirs? Or are you for Dunwell Hall?"

The voice, like the man's actions, was quick and economical, lacking the Cornwall burr. The brown eye scanned the two men, head to toe. Without waiting for an answer he bent to hoist the medical chest to the rear of the coach.

"Dunwell Cove. The Anchor Inn." Darwin had done his own share of rapid observation. Jack Trelawney was of medium height and build, but he had lofted the heavy chest with no sign of effort. The tendons on the backs of his work-hardened brown hands stood out as he lifted, showing in white contrast to fingers and nails yellow-stained on their end joints as by heavy and prolonged use of tobacco.

"Very well." Trelawney had just as rapidly loaded the other luggage. "We have a light load today, and you are the only passengers. Payment before we start, if you do not mind. Thank you, sirs." He pocketed the money without seeming to look at it and gestured them to board.

"I think maybe a ride in front, with the weather so improved." Darwin moved to stand close to Jack Trelawney, then paused and frowned. "What do you say, Jacob?"

"Not for me. I'm still thawing out."

"Oh, very well. Then I'll keep you company." Darwin swung open the door of the coach and led the way inside. He waited until the door was closed. Trelawney had climbed up front in the driver's seat, and the two-wheeled cabriolet was on the move. Then he was out of his place again.

"Devil take it, Erasmus, can't you sit still for a second?" Pole, in the act of taking out pipe and tobacco, was forced to stop, because Darwin was leaning right over him, examining doors and windows. "What are you up to?"

"Looking for a way for the phantom to enter." Grunting with effort, Darwin progressed from ceiling to floor, and was soon on hands and knees peering under the seats.

"For God's sake! If you think the phantom hides away under there, and pops out when nobody's looking . . ."

"I do not." Darwin, hands and sleeves filthy with cobwebs and old dust, finally climbed back to his feet and dropped into his seat facing Pole. "A modification to the original vehicle, with well-fitting doors and windows. It would please my friend Richard Edgeworth, because it is not of conventional design. But it is soundly made. Be silent for a moment, Jacob. I wish to listen."

Jacob Pole sat, straining his own ears. "I don't hear a thing."

"You do. Listen. That is the squeak of coach bodywork. And all the time there is the clatter of the wheels over hard surface. That snort was one of the horses, hard-breathing."

"Of course I hear *those*. But they are just noises. I mean, there's nothing to *listen to*."

He had lost his audience, because Darwin was up again, this time opening a window. He stuck his head out, peering in all directions.

"The coast road, of course." His bulk filled the opening and his voice sounded muffled. "Typical Cornwall, granite, slate and feldspar. But St. Austell has reason to be glad of that, for without decomposed feldspar there would be no treasure house of china clay. Furze, broom, and scabgrass. Poor soil. And I note lapwings, terns, and an abundance of gulls. Forty yards from road to cliffs, and beyond them a drop to the sea. Very good. And now for the other side." He was across the coach in two steps, to open the window there.

"Are you all right, sir?"

Jack Trelawney's voice, calling from the front of the coach, showed that he had noticed the activity within.

"Perfectly well. Enjoying the scenery and the weather." Darwin stayed for half a minute, then closed the window and slid back to his seat. "Rising ground to the right, we're on the edge of a little moor. More granite, of course, and no sign of people. I doubt that the ground here is very fertile."

"I'll take your word for it." Pole sniffed, and continued stuffing his pipe. "I didn't know you were thinking of setting up farming here, or planting a flower garden. And I'm wondering what you are proposing to tell Milly and Kathleen. They have as little interest as I do in a catalog of local muds and rocks, and still less in the Cornish bestiary."

"I am not proposing, initially, to *tell* anything. It would be premature. I intend first to ask questions. As for an inspection of the surroundings and setting of Dunwell Hall and Dunwell Cove, we are seeking to explain a strange event. And any event, no matter how strange, inhabits a natural environment, which must itself reside within limits set by the physically possible. Therefore, we must first establish those bounding conditions."

"Aye. And after that?"

"After that we will meet the phantom; and, as Shakespeare puts it, 'give to airy nothing a local habitation and a name.'"

Darwin's tone was cheerful and confident, but Jacob Pole merely shook his head. The rest of the ride went in silence, one man smoking and the other deep in thought, until the motion of the coach slowed. Jack Trelawney rapped hard on the front of the partition.

"Dunwell Cove. What about the luggage, sir?"

"Place it all inside the inn."

"Aye, aye, sir." In less than a minute Trelawney had bags and medical chest down and within the door of the inn. "Be by tomorrow, about eight of the morning," he said. And then, before Darwin and Pole had time to turn, he was back up onto the footboard of the coach and rolling away down the road.

"Not one for wasting time," said Pole gruffly. But there was no further chance to comment on Jack Trelawney's departure, because the inn door was opening again, and a woman emerged.

"Cousin!" She ran forward and gave Pole a hearty hug, then turned to his companion. "And here is the great Dr. Darwin. Exactly as I imagined you from Jacob's descriptions, but much more handsome."

"And you, madam, are much more beautiful." Darwin offered his hand, at the same time as he gave Pole an accusing side-glance. "I have seldom seen so fair a complexion or so engaging a smile. Indeed, were it not for the color of your hair, I would mistake you for your own daughter, Kathleen."

"Now, sir!" Milly Meredith was fair, short, and plump, with red cheeks and lively blue eyes. She dimpled at the compliment, then shook her head. "Although neither Kathleen nor I is able to smile much at the moment. If you will come inside, I have something new that I must show you."

She led the way. The interior of the Anchor Inn was dim-lit, since the glazed windows were small and the frugal innkeeper would offer no oil lights until darkness forced it. But the table was set, and at Milly's nod a stout woman in a flowered skirt headed at once for the kitchen.

Milly sat by the window and invited the two men to take seats across from her at the long bench. "Your room is ready upstairs, but I thought that after your long journey you might welcome a meal. I hope that travel has not spoiled your appetite."

"Not in the least." Darwin placed himself opposite Milly. "I am famished, and look forward to dinner with the liveliest anticipation."

"I fear that it will be fare less fancy than you are accustomed to. Only Cornish pasties, with potatoes, leeks, pickled onions, and pickled cauliflowers."

"It sounds excellent—and I will not inquire as to what form of meat may be in the pasty. There is an old Cornish saying, madam: 'The Devil will not come into Cornwall, for fear of being made into a pie.' "

Milly Meredith laughed, but Darwin sensed the undercurrent of anxiety within the sound and went on, "Perhaps we can dispose of serious concerns before dinner, ma'am. First, you mentioned that there is something new?"

Milly glanced around before she answered. "New, and most disturbing." She reached into the waistband of her skirt, pulled out a folded piece of yellow paper, and handed it across the table to Darwin. "Two days ago, I discovered this within my sewing kit."

He opened it and read aloud, while Pole leaned across to see the paper. " 'Kathleen must on no account marry Brandon Dunwell. If you value your daughter's health and happiness, make sure the wedding does not take place.' That is all? No other message, no envelope?"

"Nothing."

"And Kathleen?"

"Knows nothing of this. She returns in the morning." Milly drew in a deep breath, and her lips trembled. "I have been so tormented, wondering if she should be told."

"Not unless some purpose is served by doing so. I deem it premature to burden her with this. In fact, if it is possible to avoid any involvement of Kathleen in my actions, I will do so." Darwin looked again at the note,

and his face became perplexed. "Before this note I had
been pursuing a certain line of thinking, which must now
perhaps be abandoned. May I keep this?"

"Of course. But Dr. Darwin, what should I *do*? The
wedding is in five days, the guests are arriving, the plans
proceeding. Brandon is arriving later today, to discuss
more arrangements with me."

"What time do you expect him?"

"Soon." She glanced out of the window. "Before dark.
He has an aversion to the night. But before he comes,
may we talk? Dr. Darwin, I am desperate, and desperately worried. Jacob assures me that you are the most
learned man in the whole of Europe, and the wisest. Tell
me what I must do, and I promise that I will follow your
advice."

"Until I have had the opportunity for more thought concerning this new missive, I am not sure that I am equipped
to offer advice. But let me hold for the moment to my
original idea. Let us consider the phantom. I realize that
you were not visited by that phenomenon in your own
journeys from St. Austell, but I would like you to think
hard, and to recall the circumstances in which the robberies took place. What can you tell me of each, beyond
what you described to Jacob in your letter?"

"I will try." Milly sat for a moment, her rounded forehead broken by frown lines. "January 15th, the first occasion. The coach left St. Austell about five, just as dark
came on, and reached Dunwell Hall a little before seven.
The evening was clear and cold, and we had been
wondering if it would snow, which it did not. But the
second and third times were very different. On January
23rd we had an absolute deluge of rain, and the coach
arrived in mid-afternoon with all the luggage soaked. The
passengers also complained of being slightly wet, but their
main concern was with the loss of their valuables. And
on January 28th, the last appearance of the phantom, the

weather was a cold, ugly fog, and the day hardly seemed to become light from morning to night. The coach again arrived at Dunwell Hall in mid-afternoon. And its occupants had again been robbed."

"Strange indeed. Do you know, had they enjoyed a meal while on the coach? Or perhaps shortly before leaving St. Austell."

"I am sure that the last group at least did not. When they arrived here they were in high good humor, except that they pronounced themselves famished to the point where hunger was making them positively queasy."

"Indeed?" Darwin raised his eyebrows and shook his head. "No food or drink. Then I must think again, and set another notion in train. Is there any other circumstance that you deem worthy of mention?"

"Not really. I was not actually present on those coach journeys, you see, and everything was related to me *secundus* rather than *primus*. But all agree, the coach did not stop. Nor did anyone enter it. I am sorry, but that is all I can tell you."

"Sorry? For what?" Darwin was anything but displeased. "If only my patients described their symptoms with such brevity and clarity, the practice of medicine would be a good deal easier."

The food was at last arriving, and Darwin halted his questioning while it was being served. Jacob Pole and Milly Meredith chatted, catching up on family matters, while Darwin ate heartily, stared at nothing, and from time to time looked again at the note in front of him.

"Health and happiness," he muttered at last. "No food or drink. Happiness *and* health. How strange. Mrs. Meredith, I would very much like to meet Brandon Dunwell, even if only for a few moments. Could you perhaps introduce me, as a friend of yours?"

"Dr. Darwin, Jacob has told me so much of you, I consider you as such a friend."

"Then you must call me Erasmus, not Dr. Darwin. And you should begin doing so at once. It must appear natural by the time that Brandon Dunwell arrives."

"Very well. Erasmus." Milly glanced from him to Jacob Pole and back. Her cheeks turned a brighter pink. "There is one problem. You are not on the list of guests for the wedding. Brandon would accept your presence the more readily if he thought—if we were to somehow suggest—that you were here for other reasons. That you had come, perhaps, because you and I—"

"Say no more. He will learn that I am interested in Millicent Meredith, as any sensible man would be interested."

"And you must call me Milly."

"I already think of you that way." Darwin bowed gallantly, as far as his girth and the table top permitted. "Milly, if it will not disturb your meal, I would like to ask a question or two concerning friend Brandon. He seems to keep curious hours. Do you happen to know why he pursues activities only in the daytime?"

"I have no idea, but it was not always so. Brandon today is sober, quiet, and serious. Years ago, from what I have heard, it was very different. He indulged in gambling, and drinking, and hard living, and was out to all hours."

"But you are sure that he has abandoned that style of living?"

"Quite sure. I would not normally have mentioned his earlier actions at all, since they are so inconsistent with his behavior today."

"You were right to do so. I compliment you. It is a rare intelligence, Milly, who answers what a man *means*, rather than what he asks." Darwin cocked his head at a sound from outside. "Is that a horse?"

"Brandon, for a certainty. I recognize the harness bells." Milly stared about her. "Doctor—Erasmus—I hope

I do not betray your interests. I am new to deception."

Darwin reached across and gripped her hand in his. "It is like sin, Milly. Improvement comes rapidly with practice." He deliberately held on, until the door opened and a newcomer stood at the threshold, a brown basset hound at his side. The dog sniffed at Darwin's luggage, still standing just inside the entrance, and wagged its tail.

"Sit, Harvey." The man waited until the dog sank to its belly, then propelled himself into the room with an almost spasmodic surge of energy. His heels clattered on the floor, as though he was deliberately stamping them. Milly Meredith sprang to her feet with a matching urgency.

"Brandon, this is my friend, Erasmus Darwin." Her blush could have come equally well from embarrassment or knowledge of deception. "He will be staying here for a few days."

But Brandon Dunwell showed little interest in Darwin. He nodded a greeting, blinking pale, tired eyes, and moved at once to the window. He leaned forward toward Milly, gripping the edge of the table.

"Kathleen has not yet returned?"

"Tomorrow morning."

"Good. For her sake, I would like to discuss certain financial arrangements for the wedding without her presence." He paused, and stared pointedly at Darwin and Pole.

Darwin nodded reassuringly at Milly Meredith. "Our journey here was a long one. If you will excuse us, Milly, Jacob and I will retire. We need rest."

He led the way, off up the curving wooden staircase. He and Pole were sharing a room under the eaves with two beds. Between them stood a dresser bearing a large bowl and a jug of water. Darwin went across and drank directly from the pitcher, then sat heavily on one of the beds. He pulled out the yellow paper and stared at it.

"Pox on this, 'Rasmus." Jacob Pole was over by the window, prowling the bare boards. "I'm sorry. I bring you here for one mystery, and Milly hits you with another before you're halfway in the front door."

"This, you mean?" Darwin tapped the paper. "It will help, Jacob, not hinder. There is surely only one mystery underlying all events, and a concatenation of strange events reduces the possibilities."

"You mean you know what this is all about?"

But Darwin merely sniffed and puffed out his cheeks. He was silent for a long time, until finally Pole said, "Well, if you're going to sit in a stupor I'd better have the cases brought up."

He was absent for maybe five minutes, and returned with two servants from the inn. Between them they were carrying the bags and medical chest, and Milly Meredith followed close behind.

"He's gone," she said, "if you want to come down."

Darwin shook his head. "I was not deceiving Brandon Dunwell when I said I was in need of rest. Also, I must have time to think. Before that, however, I would like to ask you a few more questions. Please bear with me. Some you may feel are tedious and pointless, and some will be extremely personal."

"Personal?" Milly blushed, but her gaze did not waver. "Ask me anything. And I will tell you everything I can."

"Then I will not stand on ceremony. Do you like Brandon Dunwell?"

Milly looked miserably at Jacob Pole, who shook his head. "The truth, Milly. No weasel words. You can trust Erasmus as you would me."

She drew in a shuddering breath. "I know. Dr. Darwin—Erasmus—I dislike him. And yet I dislike *myself* for disliking him. He has been so good to Kathleen, and he is so clearly fond of her. Perhaps too fond, to the point of obsession."

"And she?"

"That is much more difficult. She says nothing. But sometimes I wonder if she is marrying him for my sake."

"I gather that he is extremely wealthy. While your own situation is—what?"

"You shame me. I am of good family, but Kathleen and I are poor. As you may have deduced, Brandon will bear the bulk of the wedding costs, even though by tradition that falls to the family of the bride. You see, by every rational standard this is a most excellent marriage for Kathleen."

"Do not despise yourself for that. There is no virtue in poverty. But now I must proceed to an even more delicate matter."

"I cannot imagine one. But I will answer whatever I can."

Darwin turned to Pole. "I wish to warn you, too, Jacob, before you respond with outrage to my question. But this is vital information. Milly, is it possible that Kathleen and Brandon Dunwell have in certain matters anticipated their marriage vows?"

Jacob Pole grunted, while Milly Meredith turned fiery red. "I understand." She looked down at the wooden boards. "Even a mother cannot be completely sure. But unless Kathleen is lying to me, and unless my own instincts are also totally wrong—she and Brandon have not."

"And anyone else? Is Kathleen *virgo intacta*?"

"That is my belief."

"Thank you." Darwin nodded in satisfaction. "Kathleen is lucky to have you for her mother. Let me move on to what I trust will be less delicate ground. Since you have known him, has Brandon Dunwell ever been away for an extended period?"

"About a year ago, he was absent from Dunwell Hall for several weeks."

"Do you know where he went?"

"I understood that it was to London."

"The great center of everything—including disease. That makes excellent sense, though it proves little. By that time, of course, his brother Richard had been arrested."

"Arrested for the murder of Walter Fowler, convicted, and dead, over a year before."

"And you knew Richard, also?"

"Very well." Milly sat down abruptly on one of the beds.

"And did you like him?"

She stared hard at Darwin. "I have never before said this to anyone, and I beg you not to repeat it—particularly to Kathleen. But until I learned that Richard was a murderer, I far preferred him to Brandon. Even though he was deemed odd by the staff at Dunwell Hall."

"Define, if you can, that oddity."

"They say that in spite of his family's wealth, he had no interest in managing the estate. He was trained as a physician, but chose not to practice. He spent many hours alone, engaged in strange pastimes. He had eccentric friends and visitors, many of them from the Continent, who with Richard dabbled in what the servants at Dunwell Hall judged to be black arts."

"I gather you do not agree with their assessment?"

"No. It is his brother, Brandon, who believes in portents, demons, and magical effects. Richard was a skeptic. But at the same time he was rash and impractical, and except for his odd friends he seemed to prefer animals to people."

"And yet he wooed and won your daughter."

Milly smiled sadly. "Say, rather, that she wooed him. I remember, they met at the Bodmin Goose Fair, and that night Kathleen would talk of nothing else. She said she had looked into Richard's eyes, and seen his soul. His

arrest and then his death, only three months later, broke
her heart."

"A true tragedy. For everyone." Darwin spoke softly, and
placed his hand on Milly Meredith's arm. "One more
question, if you will permit it, and then I will cease. I
can see that this memory distresses you."

"I will not deny it. But you came here to help me, and
I must do my part. Ask on."

"Richard Dunwell killed a man, Walter Fowler. It seems
out of character with what you have said of him."

"Certain events would drive him to anger, almost to
madness. The man had apparently been beating a lame
dog. It was later discovered dying, and its master, Walter
Fowler, dead."

"But surely, if Dunwell had explained the sequence of
events . . ."

"He attempted concealment. Fowler's body had been
dragged away and hidden in the gorse bushes. Richard's
monogrammed knife, marked with blood, was buried close
by." Milly swallowed. "A servant found Richard's clothes,
also stained with blood, in his rooms at the hall. Erasmus,
if you please—"

"I understand. You have been more than helpful, and
we will talk of this no more." Darwin sank onto the bed,
his fat face thoughtful and his eyes suddenly far away.
"You have given me enough to think about. More than
enough. With your leave, I will turn this over in my
mind. And then we will see what tomorrow may bring.
I would appreciate one other thing before you retire: a
general map of Dunwell Hall."

"The interior?"

"That, if you are able to provide it. But most important, I need the location of the kennels."

The next morning was brisk, with a damp and gusting west wind. When dawn broke, Darwin was already

fully dressed and standing at the window. Behind him Jacob Pole was sitting up in bed, coughing and spitting.

"Damn it, Erasmus, to wake a man in the middle of the night, when his blood's as thin as water and his guts are—"

"There is hot tea on the dresser. I permitted you to sleep as long as possible."

"Aye. And woke me when I was in the middle of the best dream I've had in a twelvemonth, me in my uniform and Middletown aflame—"

"I need your help, Jacob. Urgently. I have a pony and trap ready, and in five minutes I must be on my way."

Pole was out of bed at once, nightshirt flapping around his thin legs. "Where the devil are my clothes? Are you after the phantom? Do you want me to come with you?"

"Not on my first trip, which will be a short one. But when I return, half an hour from now, I would greatly value your presence."

"I'll be ready. So will your breakfast."

It was closer to an hour when the pony came clip-clopping back to the Anchor Inn. Jacob Pole, standing outside with his overcoat on and his head muffled by a scarf, stared at what was sitting next to Darwin.

"Christ. Is that what's-its-name?"

"Harvey."

"You stole Dunwell's dog!"

"Borrowed him. Come aboard, Jacob."

"Hold on a second. The food hamper. It's keeping warm." Pole hurried inside, reappeared in a few seconds, and climbed into the trap next to the dog, which sniffed at the laden wicker basket and wagged its tail. "Get your nose out of that! Erasmus, you're going to have competition."

"He's entitled to a share. If I am right, he has as much a task to perform as we do."

"Well, he may know what you're up to, but I don't. Come on, man. I'm damned if I'll be more in the dark than a dog."

"If you would but be quiet for a few moments, Jacob, all will be made clear." Darwin shook the reins, and the trap started forward. "Listen . . ."

The ride from Dunwell Cove to St. Austell took less than forty-five minutes. By the end of that time the hamper was nearly empty, the basset hound was gnawing on a meaty ham bone, and Jacob Pole was shaking his head dubiously.

"I don't know. You've added two and two and made twenty."

"No. I have subtracted two and two, and made zero. There is no other possible explanation that fits all we know and have heard."

"And if you're wrong?"

"We will think again. At the very least, this experiment can do no harm."

They were approaching the coach house. It stood even quieter than the previous afternoon.

"There's nobody here."

"Patience, Jacob. There will be, very shortly, if Jack Trelawney is to make good on his word and be at Dunwell Cove by eight. You stay in the trap, and call him this way when he appears." Darwin climbed down holding the dog by its leather collar. He stood so that they were shielded from the road by the trap itself. The only sound was the panting of the basset hound.

"Coming now," said Pole in a gruff whisper, after another five minutes had passed. And then, at full voice, "Mr. Trelawney! Will you be making the run to Dunwell Cove this morning?"

"Aye, sir. If you can wait ten minutes. You'll be going?"

Darwin stood motionless, as the sound of booted feet

came steadily closer. Finally he released his hold on the dog, and stepped around the trap.

The basset hound was already moving. It raced across to Trelawney and gambolled around him, tail wagging back and forth like a flail. Trelawney, after the first futile effort to push the dog away, allowed it to jump up and push its nose at his face.

"You see, Mr. Trelawney," Darwin said quietly, "a man can stain his complexion to a darker hue. He can disguise his eyes with false eyebrows and a patch. He can redden and thicken his lips with cochineal, or other coloring matter. He can even change his stance and his voice. But it is as hard for a man to change his *smell*, as it is to persuade a dog to adopt a new name."

Trelawney stood perfectly still. The single brown eye beneath its bushy brow stared at Darwin for a moment, then looked away along the road.

"Flee, if you will." Darwin gestured to Pole. "Neither my companion nor I is in any condition to catch you. But do you wish to spend your whole life running?"

"I may not run. Not so long as Kathleen Meredith plans to marry Brandon Dunwell." The dark face twisted in anguish. "It is no matter of jealousy, sir, or of simple envy. It is a matter of—I cannot say what."

"Of your loyalty to Brandon? But you do not need to say it, sir, for I can give you your second opinion *statim*. I saw it the moment that he made his entrance to the Anchor Inn."

"You know!"

"The stamping on the ground, as though his feet are padded and cannot feel it beneath them. The loss of balance in the darkness, which forces him to shun unlit rooms and go out only during daylight. The need to grip an object whenever possible, so as to remain steady. These are the clear symptoms of *tabes dorsalis*. Brandon Dunwell is paying a high price for his wild early years.

He is suffering from syphilis, in its advanced state of *locomotor ataxia*."

"And Kathleen . . ."

"Is healthy. He must not marry her, or any woman. And I will make sure of that."

The other man sighed, and the muscles of his face relaxed. "Then that is all I care about. For the rest, I am in your hands. How much do you know?"

"I know little, but I suspect a great deal and wish to propose even more. For instance, I guessed last night that this must have been your basset hound. Who but a student of medicine, as you were, would name his dog *Harvey*, after the immortal William Harvey, discoverer of the circulation of the blood? Your brother might take your dog, but he could not change its name. And who but a student of medicine might have ready access to a corpse, when one was needed to inhibit further pursuit? Even before that, I wondered at an incongruity. You were known, I was told, as *Stinking Jack*. But I deliberately moved close to you yesterday, and detected no odor."

"When I had reason to go to Dunwell Hall, I did my best to offer Harvey a false scent. I succeeded, but apparently at some slight cost in reputation." Trelawney pushed the eye patch up onto his forehead. His brown eyes were clear and resigned. "Very well. I admit it. I am Richard Dunwell. Although you are apparently a perceptive physician, you are not a magistrate. Do you intend to arrest me? If not, what do you propose?"

"I have definite plans. How permanent is the stain of your skin?"

"It can be removed with turpentine. The glued eyebrows may be more difficult."

"But scissors would reduce them. The three of us must join in serious discussion—inside the coach house. I do not wish to be observed."

Before marrying a woman, look at her mother.

But the maxim worked poorly with Kathleen and Milly Meredith. Standing together outside the Anchor Inn in the pale light of a cold, overcast noon, the two women formed a study in contrasts: Milly fair, short, and dimpled, with the peaches-and-cream complexion of a milkmaid; her daughter tall and stately as a galleon in light airs, high cheekboned, gypsy-dark, and with flashing black eyes.

And yet, Darwin thought, admiring them from his hiding place, perhaps the old rule was not so wrong after all. Both women would be very easy to fall in love with. Certainly there was no mistaking the adoration on Brandon Dunwell's face, as he helped Kathleen to board the coach and climbed in after her. The two sat side by side, and Kathleen waved to her mother before Milly went back into the inn. Kathleen closed the window. The cabriolet, with Jacob Pole driving, rolled off at a moderate pace along the road to St. Austell.

One minute later Darwin was inside the inn stable and climbing up on horseback. He did not look too comfortable there. As the cabriolet vanished from view, a second man holding a horse by the reins ran toward him from the rear of the stable.

His thin-featured face had the unnatural pallor of a man who has just shaved off a dense beard. Brown eyes beneath cropped black eyebrows seemed worried and perplexed.

The transformed Richard Dunwell swung quickly up into the saddle. "We must hurry!"

Darwin did not release the reins of the other horse. "On the contrary, we must not."

"But Colonel Pole—"

"Knows exactly what he has to do, and is thoroughly reliable. We will follow, but cautiously. If we were to be observed by Kathleen, or by your brother, our plans would become worthless."

He started his horse along the deserted road that led toward St. Austell.

"Kathleen still knows nothing?" Richard Dunwell came forward to ride two abreast.

"Nothing. I wish that it had been possible to take her and Milly into my confidence, but I fear their inability to dissemble. Patience, my friend. Play your part correctly, and soon all need for dissimulation will vanish."

"God grant." Richard Dunwell rode on, his face grim. As they rounded every turn, or breasted a hill, his eyes were constantly scanning the road ahead. At last he gave a little cry and urged his horse to a gallop. The cabriolet was visible a quarter of a mile in front of them, with Jacob Pole dismounted from the driver's seat and standing in the road beside the coach.

Darwin followed at a more leisurely pace. When he came to the cabriolet a door was already open. Richard Dunwell, with infinite tenderness, was lifting from within the coach the unconscious body of Kathleen Meredith. He sank to his knees, holding her and staring hungrily at her silent face.

"Not now, man." Darwin swung himself off the horse's back. "You have other duties to perform. Fulfill them well, and you will have a whole lifetime to gaze upon that countenance. But hurry!"

Richard Dunwell nodded and laid Kathleen gently on the ground, with Darwin supporting her head. "You will explain?"

"Everything, as soon as she wakens." Darwin passed across to Richard a gallon jar. "Seawater, with a little wormwood and *asafoetida* mixed in. Disgusting, but necessary. Now—go! Jacob is waiting, and you have little time to prepare."

The other man nodded, but he received scarcely a glance as he headed for the waiting coach. When it rumbled away Darwin's attention was all on Kathleen. Soon he detected a change in her breathing.

Just in time! The creak of coach wheels was still audible when her eyelids trembled. He held the *sal volatile* vial of ammoniac water under her nose, and leaned close as her eyes fluttered open to show their whites.

"Do not be afraid, Kathleen." He spoke slowly and clearly. "I am a good friend of your mother and of your uncle, Jacob Pole. You are in no danger."

Her lustrous dark eyes rolled down, to focus on the fat, amiable face close to hers.

"Who are you?" The words were hardly a whisper.

"I am Erasmus Darwin. I am a physician."

"Brandon—"

"Is not here."

"But just a second ago he was holding my hand— in the coach—" She lifted her head and her gaze roamed over the coast road and deserted cliff. "And now—"

"I know." Darwin lifted her to her feet and watched to make sure that she stood steady. "That is very good. I have much to tell you, and I believe that you will find it all welcome news. But first, as soon as you are clear-headed, one other unpleasant act must be completed. When you are ready, you and I will ride a little way together. The horses are waiting."

Even at noon the air was chilly, made more so by a cutting wind from the sea. Brandon Dunwell had closed the windows tight, but still he felt chilled. He held Kathleen's hand, yawned, and shivered a little. Someone was walking on his grave. Even the hand gripped in his suddenly felt damp and clammy.

He turned to look at her, and flinched back in horror. Kathleen had vanished. Instead he was holding the hand of a *man*, a pale-faced figure whose damp hair flopped

lank on his forehead and whose dark, wet clothes clung
to his body like cerements.

The man gave him a death's-head smile that showed
blackened teeth. "Greetings, brother."

Brandon gasped. "Richard!" He dropped the cold hand
and shrank back against the side of the coach.

"Richard, indeed. But a condemned murderer. Even in
the grave I cannot rest." The apparition inched a little
closer. "Neither I nor you will ever find rest, brother—
unless you confess."

"No! I did nothing. Don't touch me!" A pale hand was
lifting clawlike fingers toward Brandon's face. Wafting from
it came a dank, rotting odor that made him want to
vomit.

"Nothing?" The hand paused, inches from Brandon's
cheek. Water dripped from the loose sleeve. "You call the
murder of Walter Fowler nothing? I bring you his greetings
. . . and his accusation."

"It was not my doing." Brandon's breath came in great,
sobbing gasps. "I mean, it happened but it was not my
fault. Ask Fowler. It was an accident—an argument. I
didn't mean him to die." His voice rose to a scream.
"Please, for God's sake, don't touch me!"

"One embrace, Brandon. Surely you would not deny
that, to a loving brother, when we have been separated for so long? Except that where I dwell now, there
is neither time nor place." The sodden figure squelched
closer along the coach seat. "Come, one kiss of memo-
ries. Even if you refuse to confess, you are still the
little brother of whom I was always so fond and pro-
tective."

Richard Dunwell lifted his arms and opened them wide.
Brandon gave a squeak of terror and wriggled away. He
opened the door of the moving coach and tumbled out
headfirst. But he did not seem to be hurt, and in another
moment he was on his feet and heading at a blind,

staggering run away from the road toward a dip in the cliffs on the seaward side.

Richard Dunwell waited for the coach to stop before he stepped down. Almost as unsteady on his feet as Brandon, he moved around to where Jacob Pole sat in the driver's seat. "You heard?"

"Every word." Pole's voice was gruff. "His admission is partial, but more than enough."

"He says it was an accident." Dunwell's tone showed how much he wanted to believe that, but Pole shook his head.

"Think what came after. Your knife, marked with blood. Bloodstained clothes in your rooms at Dunwell Hall. That speaks of preparation, not accident. And afterwards, silence from Brandon. Even when his own brother stood at the gallows' foot."

Richard shivered, and it was more than wind cutting through wet clothes. "You force me to accept what I would rather deny. But he is still my brother. I would not see him hanged. What now?"

Pole nodded to the two horses approaching the coach. "I cannot say. However, Dr. Darwin is never without one plan—or a dozen."

Those plans had to wait a few moments longer. Richard Dunwell helped Kathleen to dismount from her horse, then the pair stood stock-still and hesitant in the biting sea breeze. Neither seemed able to speak. Finally she wrinkled her nose in disgust.

"Ah, I should have mentioned that," said Darwin. He at least seemed cheerful. "That stench is by deliberate design—and temporary."

The trance was broken. Kathleen shook her head and smiled. "I don't care if he smells like the grave." And she added, in a low tone intended for Richard alone, "So long as you are not in it."

"And will not be, I trust, for a long time." Darwin came forward, forcing them apart.

"But *how*?" Kathleen glanced from Richard to the coach. "The murder and confession I understand, but the thefts—"

"Patience, Miss Kathleen. There will be time enough for answers—in a little while." Darwin faced Richard Dunwell. "He has to be followed, and at once. You, or I?"

"It should be me." Dunwell glanced away along the deserted cliffs, following the line that his brother had taken. "But I must know one thing before I go. Was it pure avarice, the simple desire to assume the family estate, that made Brandon act so?"

"It was not." Darwin took Richard Dunwell's hand in his. "And the very fact that you feel obliged to ask that question tells me that you cannot be the person to pursue him, lest you stand a second time accused of murder—and this one no forgery of jealousy. Brandon is to be pitied, yet it is not a pity that you can be expected to feel. He coveted something that you had; a thing to be found in a lady's eyes, not measured in gold or rubies or family holdings." He lifted Kathleen's hand, and joined it to Richard's. "Go back to the inn with Jacob. Leave the horses here. If I do not return within two hours, you may assume that I am . . . in need of assistance."

Darwin set out along the cliff. He did not look back, but he scanned the grey skyline and every bare rock and tufted mound ahead. Bad weather was on its way. The low cloud layer had descended farther, and a patchy sea-rack was blowing ashore with the wind. The shore at the foot of the cliffs was a jumble of white waves, black slate outcroppings and tidal pools, among which wandered forlorn seabirds. Even Darwin's rational eye could easily populate that desolate scene with the unquiet ghosts of drowned mariners. To Brandon Dunwell's superstitious mind, the sudden appearance of his brother close to the point where he had jumped to his death must have been sheer horror.

Brandon's physical condition had not allowed him to run far. Darwin came across him slumped on a shelf of rock at the very edge of the cliff. He was leaning far forward with his head in his hands and his eyes covered. He did not hear Darwin's approach, and gave a great shuddering jerk when a hand gripped his shoulder.

"Courage, man." Darwin spoke softly. Brandon seemed too terrified to look around. "What you saw in the coach was no apparition from beyond the veil. Your brother Richard is alive. He presented himself so only to force confession—which you gave."

Brandon lifted his head and shook it wearily. But he was beyond denial, and after a few seconds he slumped back to his original position. "Richard is alive. Then I am dead." And his toneless voice was that of a dead man.

"Only if you choose it so." Darwin became brisk and businesslike. "You are a very sick man. But although you cannot be cured, you can be treated. And if I cannot offer you health, I can offer you hope."

"Hope." Dunwell glared up at Darwin, and his tired, red-rimmed eyes showed his despair and exhaustion. "Hope to live long enough to dance on air. Better to go here, and now."

"That is your choice." But Darwin took a firm grasp of the back of Dunwell's jacket as he sat down next to him on the cliff-edge shelf of black rock. "You should know, however, that your brother is not a man to seek vengeance."

"Walter Fowler—"

"Is in his grave. He will not come forth from it, no matter what we do. Naturally, Richard must assume his estate again, and establish his innocence. But a signed letter from you, before your 'escape' and departure forever from these parts—"

"Sick and penniless."

"You know your brother better than I do. Would he send you forth even now, after all that you have done to him, to wither and die a pauper?"

Brandon said nothing, but he shook his head and stared into the blowing fog.

Darwin nodded. "You have money on your person? Then take one of the horses waiting along the road, and go to the Posthouse Inn at St. Austell. I will plead on your behalf with Richard, and come to you tomorrow. With writing materials."

Brandon Dunwell nodded. He took a deep breath and stood up. Darwin watched him closely until he had backed well away from the cliff and was turning to face inland.

"I will do as you say." Dunwell's pale eyes stared into Darwin's bright grey ones. "But one thing I cannot understand. Why are you willing to do this for me? I am a murderer, and worse."

"Because I too looked once upon a woman's face, and was lost." Darwin's eyes took on their own emptiness. "I believe I would have done anything—*anything*, no matter how terrible—to win her."

"She went to another?"

"At last. But I was fortunate. I won Mary, and was saved from my worst self. Seven years ago, she died." Darwin gave a strange shiver and a shrug of his heavy shoulders. "Seven years. But at last I learned that life went on. As yours will go on."

A fine rain had begun to fall. Neither man spoke as they walked slowly, side by side, toward the waiting horses.

It might have been a time for celebration, but the evening mood at the Anchor Inn was far from boisterous.

Milly Meredith and her guests, at Darwin's request, had been permitted the use of a private room at the rear of the building. The loud, cheerful voices from the front parlor and the clatter of dishes in the kitchen only added to the feeling of restraint at the long table.

Richard Dunwell sat by the wall across from Kathleen. He had thoroughly bathed, so that no trace of graveyard stench clung to him, and he had scrubbed his blackened teeth to their usual white. Borrowed trousers and jacket from Jacob Pole were a little too long, covering his hands beyond the wrist. He seemed in no mood for food or speech, but sat with the basset hound Harvey at his feet, following Kathleen's every move.

Darwin was next to him, facing Milly, with Jacob Pole beside Darwin at the end of the table and providing the principal interface with the kitchen. A steady supply of food and drink appeared according to Pole's command, the bulk of it despatched by Darwin alone, who had recovered his spirits and seemed exempt from the subdued, uneasy air that possessed the others.

"I saw, but did not understand," he said. "When 'Jack Trelawney' appeared on the scene I noticed at once his yellow fingertips and nails. I assumed they were stained from habitual use of tobacco. But there was never a sign of a pipe, and he neither smoked nor chewed." He turned to Dunwell. "According to the servants at Dunwell Hall, you spent many hours alone engaged in strange pastimes. You had eccentric friends and visitors from the Continent, and dabbled in 'black arts.' Now what, to a servant, is blacker art than alchemy? Those are acid stains on your fingers, are they not?—the result of alchemic experiments."

Richard Dunwell nodded. "Performed also during my time in France, and again here. Contact with muriatic acid, and slow to fade."

"I have seen them a dozen times on the fingers of our friend, Mr. Priestley." Darwin shook his head in self-criticism.

"They should have told me everything. But instead of using my brain to explain the phantom, I went off along a false scent of drugged food and drink."

Millicent Meredith had been gazing at Darwin admiringly, but now she caught Jacob Pole's eye. He grinned at her in an irritating way. "I know, Milly. I've been through it myself with Erasmus a hundred times." He turned to Darwin. "I'm sure that you and Richard think you are being as clear as day, but I have to tell you that for people like Milly and me, it's all a darkness. Short words and simple, 'Rasmus, and quick. I did exactly what I was told to do when I was driving the coach, so I know *who* was the phantom—it was Richard— but for the life of me I still don't know *how* was the phantom."

Milly nodded vigorously. "That's my question. How could he walk through the walls of a coach, and never once be seen?"

Darwin raised an eyebrow at Richard Dunwell, who nodded. "Not *walk*, but *float*. For the phantom was no more than thin air. In Paris, the celebrated Monsieur Lavoisier showed it to me: a gas, simply prepared, with a faint, sweet smell, which at first renders a person cheerful, and then quickly insensible. That is what you released into the cabriolet, Colonel Pole, when Brandon and Kathleen were within it. I had experimented—on myself—and learned that it is safe to use for short periods. Once the occupants of the coach were asleep, anyone had a good five minutes after opening the door before the fresh air awakened the passengers."

"And again, I had evidence placed before my face— and ignored it." Darwin scowled, placed a whole brandied plum in his mouth, and struggled to speak around it. "Second robbery—downpour of rain. Passengers *wet*. But coach not leaky—saw that for myself. So someone been inside. If passengers don't see, they must be asleep."

"But why *robberies*?" Milly seemed as confused as ever. "Surely, Richard, you didn't come all the way from France to rob your own relatives? Suppose you had been caught?"

"Caught, stealing that which was in justice already his?" Kathleen spoke for the first time, color touching her high cheekbones. "He had every right to take—"

"No, Katie." Richard Dunwell squeezed her hand, and at the pressure and his look she fell silent. "I did in truth steal, simply because I needed money to stay. When I came here I had intended a brief visit, only to look at you once again and confirm that all was well. Your face told me that it was not. And when I saw Brandon, and watched his walk, I knew at that point I could not leave."

"Brandon's *walk*?" Milly Meredith gave Darwin one startled look of comprehension. "Happiness *and* health—"

He nodded his head gravely. "Kathleen is doubly lucky—triply lucky. She has avoided a disastrous union, and will marry a healthy and an honest man."

"Honest enough." Pole snapped his fingers and turned to Richard Dunwell. "But not *totally* honest. Come on, Richard, admit it. You persuaded young Georgie at the coach house to lie for you. He said that you had been driving the coach from St. Austell to Dunwell Cove for a long time, which convinced me that you at least could not be the phantom."

Dunwell frowned back at him. "Georgie said that? I cannot explain his statement. I told you, I came to England little more than two months ago, when I heard word of a possible wedding. And I said nothing to Georgie."

"You mean that *he* was lying?"

"Not so, Jacob." Darwin had eaten everything in sight. Now he was sitting back contentedly and ogling Milly Meredith, not at all to her displeasure. "For a while I was as puzzled as you by Georgie's duplicity. Then I realized that he was not lying. He was telling the exact truth—as he perceived it."

Darwin pointed down below the table, to where the basset hound was blissfully licking Richard Dunwell's hand. "For to a ten-year-old boy, or to a dog—are not two months an eternity?"

THE LAMBETH IMMORTAL

The morning had threatened rain and it was finally arriving. At the first warm drops the old horse whinnied protestingly and distended her nostrils. She lowered her head and walked on steadily through the darkened summer morning, pulling the sulky easily behind her.

"I told you, Erasmus." Jacob Pole turned and looked at his companion triumphantly. "I knew in my guts we'd have rain after that east wind last night."

Darwin, squeezed in beside him, pulled a brass-bound instrument from the side box of the coach and looked at it gloomily. "This still shows a setting for fair."

"Aye, and it will, while we get soaked. I'll back my old bones over that fancy new contrivance of yours every day of the week."

"I begin to think you may be right." Darwin looked up at the clouds, pouted his full lips, and shook his head. "Yet my barometer is based on sound scientific principles, whereas the behavior of your joints remains one of life's mysteries. I am wondering now if the lessons I learned at Lichfield must be studied anew in East Anglia. Perhaps this must be somehow reset to local values."

He poked at the barometer thoughtfully with a stubby finger, ignoring the rivulet of water that was beginning to stream from his broad-brimmed felt hat. Jacob Pole looked at it skeptically.

"I wish you could reset me along with it. Rain brings me the same aches and pains whether I am in Lichfield or Calcutta. If we had waited at the inn for an hour or two, as I suggested, we'd be snug and dry now and tapping a bottle of good port wine."

"And tonight we'd have gout to make your present aches seem nothing," retorted Darwin.

His companion pulled his leather cloak about him and hunched down in his seat, looking moodily at the road ahead. Its chalky surface ran, arrow-straight, off into the distance, paralleling the canal and earthen dike on their left.

"Three miles to Lambeth, at the last stone," said Jacob Pole, his thin face gloomy. "And not so much as a barn in sight to shelter in. We'll be soaked through before we are halfway there."

"No doubt we will." Darwin sounded undismayed at the prospect. "And if we are, Jacob, I will be obliged to remind you that it was at your urging that we took this detour from our original plan."

His friend looked slyly at Darwin's calm profile. "It was my idea to go to Stiffkey, that I admit. You'll agree with me when you taste the Blues—the best cockles on the East Coast. But it was no idea of mine to come to Lambeth. Ancient ruins hold no fascination for me, unless there's something like this inside them."

He pulled a snuffbox of chased gold from a pocket inside his cloak, opened it, and sniffed a substantial pinch.

"And it was no idea of mine to go to Norwich in the first place," he continued. "I could be back home now, with Elizabeth and my young Emily. You were the one invited to inspect the new hospital. I had a miserable time. I've bargained with men and women across the face of the globe, and I tell you, there's no slyer, sharper dealer than a Norfolk tradesman."

"That must tell something about you, Jacob, I'm afraid, since it was only last night that you were boasting about the low price you paid for the Norwich boots you are wearing. But I doubt that you'll find opportunity to haggle in Lambeth. I expect to find flint pits there, not shopkeepers. Do you realize those diggings were old before the Romans set foot in Anglia? Some of the flints were used to build the Legion's Fort at Brancaster, and even those were from the newer site."

As he spoke, the old mare was plodding patiently on. The rain was warm, and not unpleasant. The surface of the canal, reflecting a steel-grey sky, was a broken pattern of small ripples as the heavy drops spattered the still waters. The line of poplar trees along the bank marched steadily away in front of them, shrinking to green dots on the far horizon.

"Ledyard said he will meet with us at the Lambeth Inn," went on Darwin. "But I fear he may not have received our message from Norwich. The coach deliveries have been worse and worse. He warned me in his last letter that the inn offers bad food and worse beds. I hesitate to go to his home uninvited, until a personal meeting can supplement our correspondence." He looked ahead, shielding his eyes from the driving rain with his free hand. "Take a look there, Jacob, and tell me if I am seeing true. Is that the Lambeth church ahead? If it is, then that will be Alderton Manor, on the rising ground behind the village, with Alderton Mill next to it. The flint pit should be just west of the mill."

Jacob Pole peered far ahead, his eyes seeming to pierce

the mist of raindrops. After a few seconds he nodded vigorously.

"I see all three. If that's Alderton Manor, it's big. I can count three wings, maybe four. But did you notice the horseman ahead of us? He's coming this way, hugging the edge of the dike. See him, there between the water and the trees?"

The rain was easing a little. Darwin frowned into the thinning drops. "I'm not sure. You know that your sight is better than mine for distances. Do you think that it might be Ledyard?"

Pole had pulled a small spyglass from the leather travelling bag between his feet. He put it to his eye, cursing the movement of the sulky on the rough road surface.

"I think not," he said after a few moments. "Unless your friend Ledyard has taken to riding sidesaddle. Whoever it is, she's riding fast. Must be on an emergency errand."

The two men watched in silence as the mounted figure approached. The woman rode a black stallion, at least seventeen hands high, controlling the big animal with no sign of effort. She pulled up quickly beside them on the roadside, with a clatter of hooves on the chalky surface.

"Dr. Darwin?" she said, leaning far over in the saddle. They looked at her in surprise. As she reined in the animal she had swept back the hood of her riding cloak, to reveal an unruly mass of blond-red hair tightly curling about her head. Darwin recalled the Viking forays into East Anglia a thousand years earlier. Some evidence of their invasions remained. The woman was in her late twenties, with blue-grey eyes and a fair complexion. The set of her jaw removed any suggestion of the china doll hinted at by her other features.

"I am he," replied Darwin at last. "But you have the advantage of me, madam, since I find it hard to believe that you are James Ledyard, my only acquaintance in Lambeth."

"Thank God for that," replied the blond woman mysteriously. "I am Alice Milner. Dr. Ledyard is busy on an urgent case at Alderton Manor."

"And he asked you to come and meet us for him?" asked Pole.

"No. He told me not to," the woman replied, shaking down her curls. "He told me to go and lie down and get some sleep. I had to sneak out of the back of the manor and saddle Samson myself."

"This is Colonel Pole," said Darwin. He had caught the unspoken question in her look when Pole spoke to her. "We are travelling together. See now, if James Ledyard told you not to meet us, and suggested rest, then why are you here?"

Alice Milner had turned her horse and was walking it alongside the sulky. The old mare, ignoring both the new arrival and the conversation, was proceeding at her own steady pace toward Lambeth. The woman shook the stallion's reins.

"Can you not go faster?" she asked, impatient at the plodding horse.

Darwin regarded her shrewdly. "No," he replied. He paused, waiting for her response. "At least, not without some reason."

The woman looked quickly back at the sulky. "You are Erasmus Darwin." It was a statement, not a question. "According to Dr. Ledyard, you are perhaps the premier physician of Europe. Will it hasten your pace if I tell you that my fiancé, Philip Alderton, suffered a serious accident last night, and remains now in a grave condition at the manor?"

Darwin and Pole exchanged a swift glance. "It would indeed," said Darwin, "were it not clear from your manner that there is more than a simple accident involved in this.

If it is my medical prowess that you seek, why did not Dr. Ledyard ask for it?"

Behind them the sun was breaking through a rift in the rain clouds. It shone on the woman's head, picking out the red-gold glints in her hair. She bit at her lower lip and stared straight ahead along the road to Lambeth.

"He does not want a second opinion," she said at last. "But it is more than that. James Ledyard told me that you are opposed to all superstitions and religious dogmas, heathen or Christian. I rode here to implore you to apply that philosophy to Alderton Manor, and to the village of Lambeth. I cannot persuade them from their pre-Christian mysteries. The simplest accident will lead to a month of talk about the Alderton Pit."

Darwin had watched her closely as she spoke, noting the frown on her forehead and the hesitation when she mentioned Alderton. He shook the rein he was holding, and the old mare picked up her speed a fraction.

"If I am to help you," he said. "I will need the full story—not the fragments that you are throwing to us. Give all to us, root and branch. For instance, you lack the Norfolk accent, and I would place you from the West Country. Devon, perhaps, or Cornwall. Yet there is Dane in your appearance, not Celt. How do you come to be here in Lambeth, and what is the accident you spoke of? Remember, I cannot resolve a mystery without *facts*. I am no magician."

His manner was abrupt, and there was a slight stammer on some of his consonants. Yet his manner was friendly, with a sunny smile—slightly lessened in effectiveness by the lack of front teeth. Alice Milner smiled in return, and nodded her head ruefully.

"I hope for miracles," she said. "But I have no right to expect them. Let me begin at the very beginning."

She pulled her hood forward to protect her from the rain, which was coming again in another heavy shower.

"You are quite right, I was born in Norfolk but not raised here. My parents live now in Plymouth, but we have our roots in East Anglia. Three years ago, I left the West Country and went to study the Asian cultures in London." She grimaced. "From Papa's reaction, one might think I had gone to sell my body to some of London's gambling bucks. He became inured to the idea after a year or two, the more so when I met and was wooed by Philip Alderton. My parents in their usual fashion checked Philip's family background when I wrote about him, and were much relieved to learn that the Aldertons have lived in Lambeth with mill and manor since the Conquest. Had father checked more than stability and prosperity, he might have been less sanguine."

"I have heard nothing of Philip Alderton," said Darwin. "As Ledyard has described it to me in his letters, Charles Alderton is the head of the house, and the flint pit is on Alderton land. Is Philip his son?"

"His nephew. Charles Alderton died two months ago, without issue, and Philip inherited this estate as the closest living relative. That death has added to the superstitions in Lambeth. Uncle Charles died alone, in Alderton Pit. James Ledyard says it was a normal enough death, of some kind of seizure, but the villagers rumor otherwise. The landlord of the Lambeth Inn—you will meet him shortly—is full of a strange tale of the Alderton's family doom, that goes back for more than a hundred years. The innkeeper claims that Charles Alderton is merely the latest victim."

"Every old family has its tales of disaster," said Darwin. "It is no more than a consequence of record-keeping. Misfortunes will befall any line in ten generations, and you should be surprised if there were no family skeletons. So Philip came here to claim his inheritance, did he, and you came with him. What do your parents think of that?"

"They do not approve. They think me forward and

imprudent. But I arrived here only last week. Philip's departure from London on the occasion of Charles Alderton's death was sudden. I stayed on at Dowgate Stairs and continued my studies, until Philip sent me a letter urging my presence here."

They were approaching the village, a huddle of poor houses standing around a common. A handsome old church and a Tudor inn stood opposite each other in the center, the sacred facing the profane. Past the village, the ground rose gently in a low hill. At its crest stood the manor, and slightly to the north of it on a second slope the sweeps of the mill turned slowly in the northern breeze. Alice Milner stared ahead at the peaceful prospect. Her nose wrinkled in disgust.

"I must say the life of a Lambeth rustic has little appeal to me—although Philip has been extolling the virtues of his position as lord of the manor since my arrival. He insists that my interest in antiquities should imply an interest in Alderton, since the manor, mill and flint pit are all of great age. The heating of the manor certainly bears him out. It is a drafty icebox."

Her tone was light, but there was a thin tremble in her voice that made Darwin look hard at her hands and face.

"Perhaps you should be riding in the coach, madam. Jacob or I can take the stallion. I believe that you are much in need of food and rest."

Alice Milner took a deep breath and sat up straighter in the saddle. "No, I can manage well enough until we reach the inn." She looked at Darwin with new interest. "As you surmise, I am not feeling well. There was little sleep for me last night because of worry, and no food yet this morning. Even so, I would have sworn that my fatigue was well concealed."

Jacob Pole gave a harsh bark of laughter. He lifted his head clear of the leather cloak. "From me, my dear, and from most people. But don't hope to hide anything from Erasmus. He can spot disease where any other would see nothing. He will see it in the way that you walk or eat or speak—or in nothing at all, if you are merely sitting. I remember the case of the Countess of Northesk, when she came this year desperately ill to Lichfield—"

"Now, Jacob," interrupted Darwin. "This is no time for your cock-and-bull stories of medical practice. Miss Milner has yet to tell us of her fiancé's accident, and we will soon be at the inn." He turned to her. "If you are not too weary, my dear, pray continue with your account. I doubt that there will be privacy for discussion in the public rooms of the inn."

She nodded. "Especially in Lambeth. The Alderton's family business is everyone's business here. Let me continue.

"As you will see if you ride the countryside, the mill ahead of us is the only one for a good distance. Since this is mainly wheat country, the wheels are very busy, and several villages come to this estate for their grinding. Just before I arrived here, Philip had asked Bretherton—he is the chief servant at the manor—why the mill is worked only to sunset. I should add that although Philip was born at the manor, he has not lived there since he was a small child, and he is not familiar with local habits. Bretherton told him that no one from the village will work the mill after dark. They fear the place."

"Do they, indeed." Darwin clicked his tongue softly, making the old mare prick up her ears. "Now you intrigue me. It must be a strong superstition, if it will stand between a Norfolk villager and his pocketbook. Is this a new fancy, acquired with the death of Charles Alderton near the mill?"

"Not at all. It goes back many years—many generations, if Bretherton and the villagers can be believed. As a result of it, Philip had to turn away grain from a big farm in

Blakeney, just two days ago. Without night work, there was no way the mill could grind the corn by the time it was needed. The mill produces good revenues for the manor. As you might imagine, Philip became very angry. Yesterday, he declared that he would run the mill at night himself, to prove that the fears of the villagers were ridiculous. I didn't care for his idea, but he scoffed at my worries. There happened to be a good easterly wind, and the mill is perfectly placed to catch one. At sunset, he went down to the mill with one of the newer servants from the manor, Tom Barton. Philip offered him a guinea for the night's work. Barton had not been long enough at the manor to be steeped in the tales of the mill and the pit, and he had a reputation for greed."

"*Had* a reputation?" Darwin reacted to the odd choice of tense.

Their companion was silent for a moment, looking away from them across the canal. The rain was moving north, to the sea beyond the gentle hill slopes ahead, and the summer air was wonderfully clear. Ripples of wind moved across the ripe wheat, field after field shaking the droplets from their laden heads.

"Yes," she said at last. "Tom Barton and Philip were found this morning in the Alderton Pit, by the villagers arriving for work at the mill. Barton was dead. Philip was badly injured and unconscious from loss of blood. Both men had terrible wounds."

The flowering poppies showed like specks of venous blood in the gold of the corn fields. The air was suddenly colder as the sun went behind a lingering rain cloud.

"Old Hezekiah Prescott was in the group that found them," said Alice. "He went back to spread the word around the village. The Lambeth Immortal has come back."

They had come to the mean houses that marked the edge of the village. Young children ran to meet the coach, and followed it at a respectful distance as Alice led the way to the courtyard of the inn and dismounted.

Darwin swung down from the sulky with an agility surprising for his bulk and looked about him keenly. The Lambeth Inn had retained its basic Tudor beams and plaster, but some rash hand had added a styleless scullery and washhouse to the rear, marring the whole structure. Across the common, the church loomed surprisingly large. In the Norfolk pattern, it was built of fragments of hard flint imbedded in grey mortar. Farther up the hill stood Alderton Manor, as big as all the houses of the village together, and behind it Alderton Mill.

"They must be a religious lot," remarked Jacob Pole. "That church would hold everybody in the village ten times over."

Darwin nodded. "It would. All the villages along this part of the coast had many more people when the ports were open. The silting has closed all of them over the past century. Good for the cockles, maybe, but bad for most businesses."

"That's true for the mill, too," added Alice Milner. "Philip says they would never have built a post mill the size of that one, for a village the size of this." She handed the stallion's reins to the ostler and led the way inside the inn. "I expect we'll be eating lunch here. May I suggest that you let me order for you? I know what to avoid."

The main room was dominated by the huge fireplace at the far end, empty now for the summer, and by the line of serving hatches leading through to the kitchen. The landlord stood on the opposite side, by the long oak table. He was red-cheeked and at least as fat as Darwin.

"Now then, Willy," Alice said to him in a determined voice. "We'd like lunch, and we don't want any swill, like the pie you offered me two days ago. We'll have coddled eggs, fresh bread, cold pork and beer—and I want to see the joint and carve it myself."

The landlord was not at all put out by the hard words. "I'll have it for you presently, Miss Milner," he said cheerfully, and went back into the kitchen.

Jacob Pole looked at Willy's waddling form as the innkeeper went through the doorway. "There can't be much wrong with the cooking, if he can get to that size. He'd hold you in a tug-of-war, Erasmus, and there aren't many that can."

"You should see his wife," said Alice. "She would make two of him."

"Pity we're not in Persia, or Araby," said Pole absently. He seemed to be lost in thought, but his eye was on Alice. "I could have sold her for a fortune there. The fatter the better, as far as your Arabs are concerned."

"And since when are women chattels," began Alice angrily. "I admit, it was once that way here, but now—"

"Don't get excited, my dear," interrupted Darwin. "And you, Jacob, stop it. This is not the time. It's just Jacob's idea of a joke," he explained, turning to Alice. "He has a lie for every country of the globe. Now, can we hear more of the events at Alderton Manor, or do you prefer not to discuss them here?"

"Willy Lister has the longest tongue in the village, and the biggest ears. Best wait," she said, as the landlord returned carrying a huge tray on which stood a loin of pork, warm fresh bread, and a stone pitcher of beer.

"Eggs'll be a minute or two. Have to be goose eggs, if you don't mind," he said. "Hens haven't been laying for the past couple of days, something's upset 'em." He seemed ready to say more, then looked at Alice, ducked his head to avoid meeting her eyes, and hurried back to the kitchen.

"See what I told you?" she said angrily, while he was

still in earshot. "Mindless, superstitious rubbish, and he's one of the worst for spreading it."

"But it's not to be dismissed completely on that account," said a voice from the door. The man who entered and walked forward to the table was in his middle thirties, short and slightly built. His legs were slightly bowed, and Darwin's practiced eye discerned a slight limp, well disguised.

The newcomer swept off his woollen cap and held out his hand to Darwin.

"Welcome to Lambeth. I'm honored to meet you and sorry I was not here when you arrived. And this must be Colonel Pole. James Ledyard, at your service."

"How did you know which one was I, sir?" asked Pole curiously.

"He watched me, watching his walk," said Darwin, with an appreciative nod. "Correct, Dr. Ledyard?"

The other's appearance was slightly sinister. He was wigless, and wore his grey-streaked black hair long and swept back, revealing a pale, bony forehead. The mouth was full and red, with canines that extended beyond the incisors. His smile was friendly, but oddly disquieting.

"And what did you decide about me, Dr. Darwin?" he asked.

"Little enough." Darwin shrugged. "You suffered from rickets as a child, but not too badly. You are experienced in weapons-handling—in the Seven Years' War, perhaps, although you must have been a mere child for most of it. At some time in your life you suffered a broken patella—as I did myself. Very painful, was it not?"

The other nodded. "The worst pain of my life." His look turned to Alice. "Miss Milner, I had hoped that you would have had sense enough to remain at the manor, after the recent events there. I hope you will now return to your fiancé's side."

Alice stared back at him coldly. "I will—if Dr. Darwin will accompany me."

Ledyard hesitated, then shook his head. "Dr. Darwin came here at my invitation to examine the flint pit and the ancient monuments, not to become involved in local medicine." His manner was embarrassed and uneasy.

"But you are the one, a week ago, who told me that he is unmatched in the medical field," said Alice. She was beginning to look angry, and her jaw was jutting forward. "If that is true, I would expect you to welcome his help, even if you deem it bold to ask for it."

Ledyard's embarrassment seemed to grow. "Of course, I would welcome his help, although it would indeed be an imposition to request it. But there are reasons . . ." He paused, clearly uncomfortable. "I will compromise," he said at last. "If you will go now to the manor, we will—with Dr. Darwin's approval—follow you later."

Darwin had caught something in Ledyard's look. "That is perfectly agreeable to me and to Colonel Pole," he said quickly. He turned to the door, where the innkeeper was standing holding a tray of coddled eggs, unashamedly following the whole conversation. "Landlord, if you will bring those over here, we are ready to consume them. And is there a table out behind the inn, where we can eat in the open air?"

"I suppose so," said the fat innkeeper grudgingly. "There'll still be damp on that bench, though. Straight out the back door, on past the trough." He put down the laden tray and left reluctantly.

"You need food too, my dear," said Darwin to Alice. "Why not carve something now from the loin, to eat on the way back to the manor? Help yourself also to bread and eggs."

Alice gave them a puzzled look, as though she was not sure how she had been made to follow Ledyard's suggestions. There was a hint of future reprisals in her expression, until she picked up the carver and savagely began to cut thick slices of pork.

"I assume that Philip Alderton's condition has improved," said Darwin, "since you are not afraid to leave him without physician."

"I think his situation is stable." Ledyard picked up a slice of pork that Alice had cut and began to chew on it thoughtfully. "He lost a lot of blood, but most of the wounds are not as deep as I feared. And he has a remarkable constitution."

"But he lost enough blood to make him lose consciousness?"

Ledyard hesitated again. "I am not sure of that. I would have said no, but I could find no head blow or other wound that could account for it, and loss of blood is the obvious explanation."

He paused and looked at Alice.

"Miss Milner, you have now cut enough pork to feed the Tribes of Israel. Not an ideal choice of metaphor, I suppose." He smiled to himself, and suddenly appeared a younger and more attractive man. "At any event, are you now ready to return to the manor? I wish to have a private conversation with the doctor." Alice gave him a poisoned look. She seemed ready to argue, but Jacob Pole had stood up and walked across to the table.

"I may as well go with you," he said. "I know from experience that we ordinary mortals get nothing from the conversation when a few bloodletters get together."

He began to place pork and bread in a square of yellow cheesecloth. He winked at James Ledyard, who was looking at him gratefully, and turned back to Alice.

"I remember a conversation between three witch doctors, when I was looking for fire opals in Malagasy." He began trying to ease Alice toward the door. "I had just been stung by the Great Madagascar Hornet, in an uncomfortable place that I prefer not to mention. Those potion-peddlers were jabbering away in their *cuclapi* dialect, discussing ways of removing the sting that would leave me enough to sit on. I lay there on my belly, warding off mosquitoes the size of bumble-bees . . ."

"Colonel Pole," interrupted Alice. "We have no Great Madagascar Hornet in these parts, but"—she smiled—"if our local fishermen are to be believed, we have pike in our streams big enough to swallow a swan in one mouthful. You should get along well with them. I will come with you, but from choice, not from subterfuge."

Darwin's eyes remained on James Ledyard as the latter watched Alice leave the room with Jacob Pole. "A remarkable young lady," he remarked.

"Very much so," replied Ledyard fervently. He picked up the tray of pork and bread and gestured to Darwin to bring the eggs and beer. The two men went outside and settled themselves at a ramshackle table out of earshot of the inn kitchen.

Darwin began to attack the food with gusto. "I assume that there are aspects of Philip Alderton's attack that are too unpleasant to mention in front of his fiancée," he said, through a mouthful of warm bread and goose-egg yolk. "What were his injuries?"

"As I described them," replied Ledyard. "That was not the main reason for my reticence." He was looking on with some surprise at the energy with which Darwin was demolishing the contents of the tray.

"Come on, man, eat up," said Darwin, catching the look. "It's the law of the world, you know. Eat or be eaten. Try some of these eggs. You can't beat a goose egg for flavor."

Ledyard shook his head. "Let me talk while you eat." He settled back in the sun and put his knitted cap back on his head. "I was over in Moston last night, delivering a child. Stillborn, sad to say. I came back to Lambeth late, and was just settling into my bed when I was roused to go over to the manor and look to Philip Alderton. On my way, I went past the flint pit. Did Alice mention to you that Alderton and Barton were found actually in the pit?"

Darwin nodded.

"Then you may know that there is a particular story about it in the village. The pit is old—that's why we were both interested in it. I estimate it was there thousands of years before the Romans, and as I told you in my letters it must be from the very dawn of our civilization. Now, did you ever hear of Black Shuck?"

Darwin leaned back and stopped chewing. His eyes were thoughtful. "Aye, I've read of it, but not recently. And not near Lambeth, either. It's a legend by Cromer, forty miles along the coast. The black hound, big as a calf, that runs down travellers. What of it?"

"I'll come to it. Lambeth has its own legend of a monster. The Lambeth Immortal. It has been here, the word goes, for hundreds of years, and it lives in the Alderton Pit. You'll not get a villager there at night, and it's hard enough during the day."

"And the monster resembles Black Shuck?"

"In effect, if not in appearance. It rends its victim, as Barton and Philip Alderton were savaged."

"But not Charles Alderton. Alice said he died of a seizure."

"Of a stroke of some kind, an attack of apoplexy. Great excitement—or great fear—would produce that effect. Charles' health in his final years was not good. But he had no wounds on his body."

James Ledyard blinked his dark eyes in the bright sun. There was a restless and secretive air to him when he spoke of the Aldertons. Although Alice Milner had been raised in the West Country, it was Ledyard, with his broad, dark skull, who looked the Celt. He rubbed his unshaven chin and pulled his cap lower over his eyes.

"There is more," he said. "Even Black Shuck could not account for last night's attacks. Alice does not know it yet, but Barton had taken two of the hounds from the manor with them to the pit last night. Cambyses and Berengaria, each over five stone in weight, each of them young and strong. Their bodies were also found in the Pit. When I add that Tom Barton is a hefty young man, and that Philip Alderton has perhaps the strongest build of anyone I have ever examined, you will begin to see the problem. There is something in the flint pit that could kill two powerful and well-trained dogs and a strong man, and very nearly kill another with the muscles and build of a Hercules. Do you now see my dilemma? I am loath to add to village mutterings about the return of a monster, but I can offer no rational explanation of my own. It is a mystery."

Darwin was sitting hunched on the bench, his double chin cupped in his hands, his elbows on the table in front of him. His grey eyes were thoughtful, alight with their usual burning curiosity.

"No," he said at last. "It is not a mystery. It is three mysteries. What was it that killed Charles Alderton, that induced his apoplexy? What was it that killed the hounds and Tom Barton, and nearly killed Philip Alderton? And the final question: why were they all in the flint pit, at night? There must be a single answer that will explain all these things."

He placed his hands on the table and pushed himself to his feet. "I do not think we will find answers here. With your permission, I would like to examine Philip Alderton, and inspect his wounds for myself. Also, I would like to see the body of Tom Barton. I too do not care for superstition. We must give the airy nothing of the Lambeth Immortal a local habitation and a name, and our efforts to do that must begin at Alderton Manor."

❦   ❦   ❦

"Why were we in the flint pit? I must say that was my doing entirely." Philip Alderton's bedroom was in the north wing of the manor, facing out to the distant sea. Alderton, weak but fully awake, lay propped up on pillows in the ornate four-poster bed. Darwin was seated by the bedside, and Jacob Pole stood by the window, watching the clouds sail up like great galleons over the northern horizon.

"Three days ago," went on Alderton, his chest and arms bare, "I was going through some of Uncle Charles' possessions in the old study in the west wing. As you can see from the style of this building, the manor is well over two hundred years old, and I wanted to find the master plan with an eye to a few changes to the buildings. There were old books and papers scattered everywhere, in odd chests and bookcases. I found all sorts of things, but not the plans I wanted. Late in the afternoon, I found the book that is over there on the mantelpiece. Colonel Pole, would you bring it over here and show it to Dr. Darwin."

While Alderton was speaking, Darwin had been gently inspecting his wounds and his general physique. There were deep lacerations on the chest and arms, and one on Alderton's cheek near his left eye. Ledyard's description of him as a Hercules had been no exaggeration, although it occurred to Darwin that the likeness was drawn from the wrong mythology. With his pale blue eyes, straw-colored hair, great muscled arms, and huge rib cage, Alderton was a Norse god, a Thor who would have no trouble swinging a hundred pounds of double-bladed war axe at the enemy.

"You are fortunate," said Darwin. "Your constitution is remarkable. Most men with these wounds would be too weak to talk. I assume that you have always been unusually strong physically? No sickness as a child?"

"None to speak of." Alderton sounded casual. "I could

always perform the usual fairground tricks—straighten horseshoes, or bend six-inch nails. At the moment I feel as weak as a primrose." He nodded at Pole, who was looking curiously at the book he was holding. "Colonel, would you please open that and give the parchment in it to Dr. Darwin. I found it in Uncle Charles' daily workbook, just as you now see it."

Darwin took the yellowed page. It was singly folded and about five inches square. The writing was crabbed and spidery, and the ink had aged to a rusty red-brown, much faded. Darwin carried it over to the window to get a better light.

"Aloud, if you would," said Philip Alderton. "Then let me explain it to you."

Pole thought there was a condescending tone in Alderton's voice, and looked quickly over at Darwin. The latter didn't seem to have noticed, as he frowned at the paper in his hand,

"*Moon full on the Hill,*" he read, "*Wind strong on the Mill, No cloud to the East. Pit send forth the Beast.*"

He paused, frowning. "Go on," said Alderton.

"*Howl through the tombed brain,*" Darwin continued. "*God-Mercy on my Pain.*"

"That was in Uncle Charles' daybook, on the page two days before his death," said Alderton. "The last entry in that book declared his intention to 'resolve the mystery in the Pit' as soon as the weather conditions were right. On the night of his death the moon was full, and the weather was clear and windy."

Darwin was still peering closely at the yellowed paper. "This is old, well over a hundred years. See the texture of the sheet, and the writing style. Has the mill stood in its present position for such a time?"

"And longer. It is one of the oldest post mills in East Anglia. The Aldertons ground corn there for the Plantagenets. Now, if you will, take a look at my uncle's diary.

You will find it describes the origin of the note you are holding. Uncle Charles found it in the lockbox of another of my ancestors, Gerald Alderton. He quit the manor in 1655, and devoted his life to religious works. After his death, his belongings were returned here. They were meager enough, just the lockbox and a Bible."

"But that means the monster has been in the Pit for at least a hundred and thirty years," said Pole. "No creature lives that long. Am I not right, Erasmus?"

Darwin did not answer. He had walked to the window and was looking out across the land, north to the distant salt flats. Flowering sea-lavender, pink and purple, extended from the nearer shore to the long spit of sand that was still building to remove Lambeth further from the sea. He looked again at the paper he was holding.

"But Gerald Alderton survived the monster," he said, ignoring Pole's question. "And you have survived. What is your interpretation of this message?"

"Part of it is clear enough." Alderton moved his great shoulders on the pillows. "When the moon is close to full, and there is a strong wind and a cloudless night, a Beast appears in the flint pit. That much, I decided when I first saw the paper. The rest of it, even after my experience there, remains a mystery to me. Last night the conditions were fitting. I had offered Barton a guinea to go to the mill with me and work it at night. When I saw the weather was suitable, I decided to go to the pit also. I offered Barton another guinea to go there with me, and see what we could find. He would not agree at first, but his greed drove him."

"And he paid for that greed with his life," said Darwin quietly.

Philip Alderton shrugged. "He was paid for his work, and I had no reason to think there would be real danger to him in the pit. Legends are not facts. It was unfortunate that he died, but my own conscience is clear."

"Aye." Darwin caught Pole's look, and shook his head a fraction. "For Tom Barton, it was indeed unfortunate. But you insist that you thought there was no danger, despite the village superstitions?"

"I believed there was something in the pit, that I admit. The legend of the Lambeth Immortal is too clearly established for me to dismiss it entirely as a folk tale. I will go no further than that. Surely that is your view also, as a rational man."

"I prefer to defer judgment," said Darwin quietly, "until I have had the chance to examine the body of Tom Barton, and those of the two hounds."

Philip Alderton showed his first sign of emotion. "The hounds are a loss; they were fine beasts, and valuable ones."

"What I do not understand," replied Darwin, "is your own position. You were in the pit, you were attacked by the Beast, and presumably you defended yourself against it. But you have said nothing of this. Did you see the Beast? What was its size, its shape, its method of attack. Have you no recollection?"

"Nothing. I remember that Barton and I were looking about us when we got to the bottom of the pit. I had just remarked that I could see nothing unusual. The moon had risen enough to give us a good view of the walls of the pit, and just to the east of us we could see the mill. It had been left free to turn at sunset, and with the strong east wind the sweeps were moving at a fine pace. I was thinking again about the waste of money in failing to operate the mill at night. After that I recall nothing until I woke here in this bed. I saw no Beast, nor do I know how or when it came to the Pit."

"I doubt you will be operating the mill at night, after last night's events," said Darwin. "I think the best thing for you to do now is rest. I want to see the bodies.

Then, I think that a walk over to the mill may be in order."

Alderton leaned back. "It irritates me to lie idle like this. I wish that I felt strong enough to come with you."

Darwin picked up his broad-brimmed hat from the foot of the bed. "Not yet. You'll be back on your feet in a few days, but give it time. One encounter with the Lambeth Immortal is more than enough. Let Colonel Pole and me make the visit."

"Here, Erasmus," said Pole, as soon as they had left the room and were out of earshot of Alderton. "I'll face danger as well as the next man, you know that. But I'm not sure I like this at all. What do you hope to see in the Pit, anyway, in broad daylight?"

Darwin's mind seemed far away. "Daylight?" he said absently. "Did I mention daylight? We'll be going there tonight, when the moon is up—and we must hope for a clear sky, and another strong wind. The Immortal is a finicky beast, it seems, when it comes to a personal appearance."

"And the Pyramids," said Jacob Pole. He put down his glass. "There's nothing in the world the least bit like them. Armies of slaves, generations of effort—they were the burial place for kings, with all their gold and their jewels." He shook his head. "Picked clean long ago," he added regretfully.

"But just to see them and study them." Alice Milner had been hanging on Pole's words as though they were a new gospel. "I'd give half my life to visit the places you have been talking about tonight."

"Well, I gave half mine, and there's little enough to show for it. Some unlucky devils have given a good deal more than that. You know, they put a pretty trap in some of the Pyramids, just to discourage thievery. They placed a stone at the entrance to the inner tomb. As soon as it was moved, the stones above it fell in all along the tunnel. I've seen crushed skeletons that must have been two thousand years old."

"It would be worth the risk," said Alice. Her blue eyes were blazing with excitement. "That's how I want to spend my life, not sitting like a stuffed monkey as the *grande dame* of some ha'penny estate, surrounded by peasants who'll sell their mother for a shilling. Lady Montagu roamed the East, why couldn't I do it?"

"Mary Montagu was an amazing woman," said Darwin, helping himself to a large slice of gooseberry tart. "But even she could not have travelled as she did without her husband."

"Then I'll marry, and take my husband with me," cried Alice.

"But first," said James Ledyard quietly, "you will have to get Philip Alderton to accept that idea. I do not think it is the role that he sees for you. He wants a mistress for Alderton Manor, to help him rule the roost. A high position is a new experience for Philip."

His tone was bitter. The four of them were sitting at the table in the great dining room of the east wing of the manor. The remains of two stuffed capons had been removed to a side table and Bretherton, the chief house-keeper and butler, stood to answer calls for desserts. Despite his self-effacing manner, he had been unable to resist a slight nod of agreement at Ledyard's final words.

"In any case," went on the young doctor. "I do not understand your interest in only foreign antiquities. The Sphinx is fascinating, I do not deny it. I would welcome a chance to visit it, should opportunity arise. But what about the flint pits, not half a mile from here? They are the relics of a civilization as old as Egypt. Dr. Darwin made a visit to Lambeth, just to see them. But you, Alice, cannot be persuaded to look at them."

There was a pleading note in his voice. Darwin rose

to his feet and went to the window. "You should see them, my dear. But I suggest that you continue to ignore them, at least for tonight. The moon is rising, and there is again an east wind. Colonel Pole and I have it in mind to take a walk over to the mill. Ready, Jacob?"

"Let me get a coat. It's less warm tonight." Pole looked across the table, where James Ledyard was regarding Alice with hungry eyes. "And I think I'll take a brace of pistols, too. I never found an Immortal yet that would relish a couple of bullets through the brisket."

"Mister Charles was carrying a pistol." Bretherton, mournful and angular, spoke for the first time. "It did nothing to save him."

Pole looked at the black-clad servant in surprise, but said nothing until he and Darwin had left the room. "There's a cheerful pox-hound," he said when they were in the hall. "First time he speaks, it's to tell me that my powder and ball won't work. I hope he's wrong."

"But he's right, Jacob," said Darwin cheerfully. "Weapons did nothing to help Charles Alderton—and did you know that Philip Alderton was carrying a pistol, too? It seems that he had no opportunity to use it. All the same, I support your idea. Iron will master flesh, be it of Beast or Man."

His manner was animated, as though he was looking forward to their exploration. They took a filled lantern from the rack in the halls. As they moved toward the door, James Ledyard came limping rapidly after them.

"Dr. Darwin, would you permit a third man to come with you?"

Darwin hesitated. "Normally, I would be happy to agree," he said after a moment's thought. "But I am not keen to leave Philip Alderton without medical care. I would rather that you stay here, in case any crisis should arise."

Ledyard stepped back. "If you really think it necessary,

I will not argue that view." He looked at Darwin, who did not seem disposed to speak further, and moved slowly back to the dining room.

"He'll be as happy there with Alice," said Pole. "He hides it well, but I've seen it too often to miss it. He's hot for her. I wonder what Philip Alderton thinks of that?"

"I doubt if he notices it at all," replied Darwin. "Ledyard is not wealthy, nor of good family. Rickets is not a disease of the rich, you will recall. He will be deemed below the Alderton scale of evaluation, by Philip at least. I would just as well have Ledyard in the house, if we are to be exploring the flint pit. Come on, Jacob. Get well muffled up. We may be out there for a couple of hours. Bretherton has instructions to organize a search if we are not back in four—though I imagine he would not find it easy to obtain volunteers for that."

"Four hours." Pole sniffed. "Christ, Erasmus, if we're not back in four hours, I fancy we'll have seen a lot more of the Immortal than we care to. Bretherton will be coming out to pick up our pieces. He'll be able to use our guts for garters, for all the need we'll have for them. Lead on; and I'll keep my hands on the pistols."

The air outside was chilly. With the red-brick bulk of the manor behind them, they walked steadily uphill toward the dark mill. It stood at the brow of the hill, north and a little west of them. The moon was close to full, and they could pick their way easily enough without need of the lantern. Ahead of them, the great sweeps of the mill were turning rapidly in the gusty east wind, and as they drew closer they could hear the groaning of the wind-shaft and toothed head-wheel, eerie across the silvered landscape.

Darwin walked to the east side of the mill and looked closely at the turning sails, black in the moonlight.

"It's an odd design, Jacob," he said at last. "See the

lattice pattern on the sweeps? And they are an unusual width. I don't know how efficient that is, and they don't use that style much any more. Alderton is right, this mill is an old one, but it's still in good working order."

He stood for several minutes longer in silence, watching the regular sweep of the great mill-sails.

"Do you realize, Jacob, that we may be looking at a dying industry? When Newcomen's engines are perfected, and those of our friend Jamie Watt, the days of these mills will be over. Wind power is too fickle and too variable. In another hundred years, steam mills will be grinding our corn over the length and breadth of England."

Pole stirred restlessly behind him. "Maybe. Not in our lifetime, Erasmus, and I must say I'm glad of that. You can keep your damned steam. I'll take the old mill here any time, over a hot fart from one of Jamie's iron boilers. Think of the Beasts that may walk out of *them*. Let's get on down to the pit. We won't track the Immortal this way."

Darwin did not move. "I want to examine all the pieces of Gerald Alderton's poetic message. '*Moon full on the Hill,*' he says. Well, we have that, certainly. And we are not lacking for his '*Wind strong on the Mill,*' either." He turned and looked behind them, where a low bank of thin cloud lay on the eastern horizon. "That's not so good. '*No cloud to the East,*' we need, and that's undeniably cloud—but it's not covering the moon. I wonder how much cloud the message permits. So, let's go to the next step. '*Pit send forth the Beast.*' It hasn't managed to do that tonight. Let's go along and have a look inside it."

He took a last look at the sweeps turning above them, then walked round the mill. The flint pit of Alderton was less than forty yards from there, a deep depression cut into the soft chalk on the west side of the hill. The steps leading down into it were broad and shallow, winding in a spiral around the outer edge. Twenty feet down, the pit floor was lumpy and uneven, still showing the marks where the flints had been pried from the soft chalk.

"Five thousand years," breathed Darwin softly. "This has been here that long." They were standing at the very edge, looking down into the pit. A faint current of colder air seemed to rise from the depths, like a breath from five thousand winters. It was easy to imagine faint darker shapes crouched close to the moon-shadowed eastern edge.

Pole and Darwin began to walk cautiously down the wide steps, looking about them with every pace they took. The white walls of the pit reflected the moonlight, making the lantern unnecessary until they were close to the bottom.

On the final steps, Darwin unshuttered the lamp and swung it to illuminate the shadowed areas of the pit. The dark shapes seemed to flee before its beam. There was nothing to be seen, and no sound but the creaking of the mill sweeps and gears, and the soft whistle of the wind through the wooden lattice. The usual night noises were silent, cut off by the damp chalk walls.

Jacob Pole eased his pistols from their case, primed them, and quietly laid the case on the floor of the pit. The two men stepped cautiously across the uneven surface, exploring the dark clefts and overhangs where the moonlight never penetrated. On the side farthest from the mill, the chalk floor had a smooth, level area, like an oval table top. After a few minutes of fruitless search, they paused there together to decide their next actions.

The moonlight reached this part of the pit, with the moon standing almost exactly behind the mill. The latticed sweeps of the mill sails broke the beams to a pattern of rapidly moving black bars across the pit floor. Darwin watched the sweeps as they turned rapidly against the backdrop of the rising moon. His manner had become tense and silent.

"Well, 'Rasmus," said Pole at last. He was reluctant to speak above a whisper. "What now? There's no sign of the Beast. It will soon be midnight, by my guess, but where's the Immortal? Did Gerald Alderton's message tell us how long we have to wait to have it appear?"

Darwin did not answer. His eyes had fixed on the moon, as it flickered into sight through the turning mill-sweeps. His countenance was set in a frown, as though he was groping for something that was just beyond his recall. At last he nodded. He began to mutter to himself, as though counting, his left index finger firmly set on the pulse in his right wrist.

After a minute or two, he seemed to have come to some decision.

"All right, Jacob," he said, "I don't think we'll be seeing the Immortal here tonight. Or tomorrow night, either. We may as well make our way back to the manor, before Bretherton begins to wonder about us." His manner had become relaxed and yet resolved. "Could we get over to Kings Lynn, do you think, and back here again in three days?"

"Easily." Pole drew a deep breath, and began to unload his pistols and put them in their case. "But I must say, Erasmus, this is a bit of a letdown. Where's the Immortal? And why Kings Lynn? I thought we'd be stopping off at Stiffkey next. Is there a Beast, or isn't there? Only yesterday, you were saying that no beast could be immortal, by its nature."

"I'll explain about Kings Lynn later. As for the other, I said only that no beast could ever advance the place of its species in the world, unless it would yield to its own offspring." Darwin was beginning to retrace their steps back to the manor. "I did not say that a beast could not be immortal, in theory; only that any natural beast would at last die, as an individual, by accident or by sickness. So it must propagate its kind, if its race is to survive; and once propagation is admitted as a necessity, immortality or very long life must then appear as a disadvantage, since it reduces the rate at which the race has scope for improvement. *Ergo*, the Lambeth Immortal, regarded as an immortal being that has been living in the Alderton Pit for hundreds of years, must be revealed as a most improbable animal."

Jacob Pole snorted, and jerked his thumb back in the direction of the pit. "Are you denying that Tom Barton was killed there? Do you dispute the reality of his death, or of Philip Alderton's wounds?"

"Not at all." They had reached the side door of the manor. "That death was very real, and the wounds fully tangible. That does not change my argument. Ghosts, if they exist—and as you know I am skeptical—cannot inflict real, corporeal wounds when they are themselves nonmaterial. And conversely, real beasts, for the reasons I have given you, cannot be immortal. Our problem, to my mind, consists only in providing the compatible link between immortality and the reality of those injuries sustained by Barton and Alderton. I prefer not to discuss this once we are again within Alderton Manor. We can go into chapter and verse on the road to Kings Lynn. I would like to leave early tomorrow morning. For now, that is enough philosophizing."

Pole had followed most of Darwin's comments with a look of incomprehension. "First time I've ever heard *you* call for less talk, 'Rasmus," he grunted, as they opened the door.

The other man puffed out his pudgy cheeks thoughtfully, and turned back to look again at the dark and silent pit. "There's good reason, Jacob, that I assure you. If ghosts were anywhere, I would have expected to meet them in that excavation. Couldn't you almost see it, in your inner eye? The crouching figures, there in the dark, freeing the flint from the chalk, chipping away at the stone." He shook his heavy head. "And I am not a man of a neurasthenic temperament. Well, let us defer speculation. I feel sure that no one in the manor has yet retired for the night. They are hoping or fearing a second appearance of the Immortal. I would like to have ten minutes of conversation with Alice, Alderton and James Ledyard. And I suppose we should have Bretherton present, too. Get rid of your pistols, prop your eyes open for another hour, and let us see what we can arrange."

The coach was stuck. Despite their mightiest efforts, it would not budge from the mire that three days of rain had made of the carriage road. Darwin, cloaked against the brisk wind, looked apprehensively at the eastern sky. Far out over the metallic grey of the sea, the cloud was beginning to break.

"It's clearing," he said gloomily. "And the rain is over. Tonight it will be fair again, if the barometer is any guide."

Jacob Pole looked up briefly from the side of the coach, where he was directing four local farm laborers, hastily recruited, in placing a heavy baulk of timber beneath the left side axle.

"We stayed over-long in Kings Lynn," he said. "My fault. I had no idea that this road would become so bad with the rain. The chalk surface drains well, but there must be clay beneath. Give me two more hours, and we may be on our way again. If we hold closer to the dike for the rest of the trip I think we'll not be mired a second time."

Darwin had walked over to the side of the coach and was looking ruefully at the heavy clockwork instrument that lay there, carefully swaddled in gunnysacks and oilskin.

"Not your fault, Jacob. Mine. I needed to remain there until they had this ready for me. Were it not for this, I would favor going the rest of the way on foot. We cannot be above six miles from Alderton Manor. But having borne it these many miles, I reject the idea that we should leave the instrument behind."

"Is it so all-important that we be there tonight? You told them there would be nothing of interest in the pit until we got back. Surely they will avoid it until then."

"Not so, Jacob." Darwin shook his head. "I wish that I had been so precise. I told them there would be nothing there for three days—which was true. But I was confident that we would be back before then. Now I regret that I did not speak more of what was on my mind. I wished to avoid starting a hare that might prove to be no more than my imagination working to excess. That would serve no purpose."

The left timber was in place, and the right side was already similarly buttressed. Two other stout logs had been placed to serve as twin fulcrums. With the old mare pulling hard ahead, the men began to bear down on the levers that the long timbers provided.

"Come on, Erasmus," said Pole, when Darwin, still looking east and deep in thought, showed no signs of action. "This was your idea, and you're twice my weight. Get that arse on the end of the beam here, and see if we can't have a little lift of the sulky. Use your heft."

"You perceive at last the virtue of substance," said Darwin, settling his ample rear at the very end of the beam. The sulky at once rose several inches in the mud. "A pity that you yourself are so much of skin and bone. 'Let me have men about me that are fat'—an excellent philosophy for our present plight."

"Hmph!" Pole grunted, heaving away on the same timber. From his spreadeagled position on the beam he could see little more than the expanse of blue cloth that covered

Darwin's broad buttocks, a few inches from his face. "Erasmus, you're all mouth and britches. If you had been my size, we wouldn't have bogged down at all." He raised his voice. "Come on, lads. When I call to heave, bear down all together on the other side."

"We must get to the manor before moonrise," said Darwin. "If not, I am much afraid that blood will be on my head."

"I think not." Pole's voice came as a series of grunts between concerted heaves at the timbers. "I still don't see anyone going to the pit tonight, unless we are there too."

Darwin was bouncing energetically on the beam, and the sulky gradually lifted free of the grip of the clinging mud. "Ledyard and Alderton may stay in the manor. The one that I am worried about is Alice. We know she is headstrong. She wanted to go to the pit even before we left, and I am sure that she is even keener to do so now. When that young lady makes up her mind about something, I am not sure that Philip Alderton, or James Ledyard, or even Cicero himself, has the persuasive power to change it.

"Aha!" The wheels had lifted suddenly, spilling Darwin from his position at the end of the beam full-length onto the gluey Norfolk mud. The mare, slipping as she went, managed to keep moving and haul the sulky free of the quag.

Darwin scrambled to his feet and cast an anxious look at the western sky. "An hour to sunset, at most. And feel that breeze. It's freshening from the east. We have to get back and keep them out of that pit at moonrise."

Pole was hurriedly handing out silver to their four helpers, then checking the wheels and axles of the sulky. "We'll never do it. We'll have to slow our pace when twilight comes on us, and Rebecca has had a hard time getting us clear of the muck. She won't be able to make her best pace without an hour or two of rest."

Darwin picked up the reins and grunted his disgust. "It's scarcely credible. Twenty places between here and Kings Lynn where we could have had a change of horse, and now we find there is none to be had before Lambeth. Come on, Jacob, Rebecca must forget her age for tonight."

The old horse pricked up her ears at the mention of her name, and pulled willingly south through the deepening dusk. As they drove, the cloud cover broke and dispersed before the freshening wind. The moon shone through the remaining wisps, the sun's rim dipped below the horizon, and the first stars appeared.

By the time they were finally within sight of the lights of the manor, full dark was upon them. The old mare slowed her pace and stepped gingerly through the gloom, wisely ignoring Darwin's encouraging words and Pole's blistering curses.

At last they were in the grounds of the manor. They turned the coach in along the private road, through the landscaped garden with its formal topiary, and on to the servants' wing, nearest to the west entrance. Pole thrust the reins of the sulky into the hands of a startled footman, who had stepped outside to empty a pail of peelings and kitchen scraps into the poultry run. The two men rushed together through the great house to the east wing dining room.

Bretherton was alone there, sitting at the side table and enjoying a surreptitious glass of wine. He stood up quickly, confused and embarrassed by their sudden entry. Darwin waved away his stammered explanation.

"Where are Mister Philip and Miss Alice?"

"Gone down to the mill, sir, and I fear to the pit also. Miss Alice said that she was going tonight since you had said the Beast might appear, and you had not returned. Mister Alderton said he would go with her for her protection, because he was afraid she would come to harm alone."

"And Dr. Ledyard?"

"He followed them down, not five minutes ago. He had been out on a case, and he got here after they had left."

Darwin swore. "Come on, Jacob. And you too Bretherton. Get down to the pit, as fast as you can go. You both have the legs of me. I'll explain this later."

Pole at least did not stay to question. He had heard that tone in Darwin's voice only once before. He grabbed the startled Bretherton by the arm and dragged him off on the double. Darwin followed as fast as his age and weight would permit, but he quickly realized the folly of a headlong rush over unfamiliar ground. He slowed, and was soon far behind.

The full moon had risen in a clear sky, and lit the hill ahead. On its brow Darwin could see the sweeps of the mill turning rapidly in the easterly wind, the latticed arms black and silver in the moonlight. A little closer to him lay the dark opening of the flint pit.

He could see no sign of the others, but as he came closer he heard a loud outcry from the depths of the pit. Hurrying to the edge of it, he looked down. Alice Milner was easily visible in her long, white dress. Next to her, one arm still held in a sling, stood Philip Alderton. They were both watching a group of struggling figures, rolling around the chalky floor. It took some time for Darwin's eyes to adjust to the deeper darkness below. When they did so, he could see that Pole and Bretherton were holding the struggling figure of James Ledyard firmly between them.

"Hurry up, Erasmus, and give us a hand," cried Pole, as soon as Darwin called down to them. "He was attacking Alderton, just as we arrived. It's a good thing Philip has the use of one arm now, or he might have been badly hurt before we could get Ledyard off him."

Darwin, puffing and gasping for breath after his exertions, did not descend into the pit. Instead, he sat down heavily on the first of the chalk steps, and leaned his broad back against the pit wall.

"I'm not coming down there," he wheezed, after another few moments to recover his wind. "Get out of the pit. All of you. Quick as you can, unless you want a close look at the Lambeth Immortal. Go on back to the house. I'll follow you, as soon as I have my breath back. Then I believe I can show you something about this whole business. Go to it!"

His tone was urgent. Still holding Ledyard tightly, the others began to scramble up the chalk steps and move back toward the comforting lights of the manor.

The mysterious clockwork device had been freed of its sacking cover. It stood now on the dining-room table, an intricate assembly of gears and escapements. A shuttered lantern had been placed behind it. At the opposite end of the table sat the somber figure of James Ledyard, his dark clothes scuffed and whitened with chalk marks from the floor of the pit. Pole and Bretherton flanked him, also seated. Their expressions were wary and watchful. A little behind them sat Alice Milner and Alderton. Darwin alone was at the other end of the table, fiddling with the mechanism. The others watched him closely, with looks that ranged from impatience in Alderton to tight-lipped tension in Ledyard.

"How much longer, Dr. Darwin?" Alderton's voice was exasperated. "We are putting up with your fiddling and posturing from deference to your reputation. But is it not clear from tonight's events that Ledyard is no more than a common assassin? He was responsible for my injuries and for Barton's death. Why do we wait here, when we ought to be delivering him to justice?"

"One moment longer," said Darwin. "I wish to be sure this instrument is exactly set before I use it." He exchanged a strange look with Ledyard, then bent and made a small adjustment to the brass fan that was fixed to the front of the device above the long pendulum. He squinted along the line of sight, moved the lantern a fraction, and at last seemed satisfied. He straightened up.

"I ask five minutes of your time. Then, if you wish, Dr. Ledyard will be dealt with as Mr. Alderton has suggested. I want to use this device to explain the events at the pit. It was made for us, at my specification, by Harrison the clock maker at Kings Lynn."

"And at monstrous cost," grumbled Pole. "It should be made of gold for the price he charged."

"Hold your fire, Jacob," said Darwin. "You will see that it is worth the investment we made. Before I engage the gears, let me ask, what did each of you see tonight, when you were down there in the pit?"

There was a moment's silence. "Dr. Ledyard was attacking Mr. Alderton," said Pole gruffly. Bretherton nodded his agreement.

"Right. And before that. What did you see, Alice?"

She looked puzzled, and glanced at Philip Alderton next to her before she answered. "Before the attack? Philip and I were alone there at first. There was really nothing to see. Just the walls of the pit, and the sky. Was it not so, Philip?"

Alderton shrugged and looked bored. "No Immortal, if that's what you're trying to get to, even though the conditions were supposed to be perfect for its appearance. I had gone there to tell Alice to stop that nonsense, and to return to the manor. I knew from personal experience that there are dangers in that pit. That was my main interest—not sight-seeing down there. Get to the point, and we can all end the evening."

Darwin looked finally at Ledyard, who first seemed ready to speak, then bowed his head and remained silent.

Darwin shrugged. "I am sure that you all believe that you are telling me the truth," he said. "It is easy to prove that none of you is telling me the *whole* truth. The pit is deep, as we all know. But it is not so deep as a well.

From where you were standing, you could all clearly see two other things: the moon, and the mill."

Alice nodded. "Of course." She turned to Alderton. "Remember, Philip, I said that I could distinguish the small flints in the pit walls, even without the need of a lantern."

"And of what possible importance is that?" said Alderton.

"Most important," replied Darwin. "For if you could see the moon, then you could also see the mill, outlined against the moon. That will always be the arrangement when the full moon first rises. As it comes high enough in the sky to be seen from the bottom of the pit, the mill stands so that the sweeps of the mill intercept its light. Now recall, if you can, the words of Gerald Alderton's warning—for that is what his message was intended to be. Who can remember it?"

"I do," said Alice softly. *"Moon full on the hill."*

"As it was tonight," said Darwin. "And next?"

"Wind strong on the mill."

"So that, had the sweeps been left free to turn, they would be moving round at a good pace. If you watch them closely, you will find that their speed depends little on the force of the wind, provided that it is beyond a certain strength. The sweeps turn at a rate that is close to constant. What is our next condition?"

"No cloud to the East," whispered Alice.

"And why is that so important?" said Darwin. "Why, for the obvious reason. The moon would not otherwise be visible. So we had Gerald Alderton's conditions. A moon, shining into the pit through the sweeps of the mill. Are these enough to call forth the Beast of the Pit, to rend and to kill? Are they sufficient, or is some other factor needed also? Well, that is what I propose to test, with the aid of this instrument." He pointed to the iron and brass clockwork assembly in front of him.

The others were looking at him skeptically, except for James Ledyard who was shaking his head in vehement objection.

"Don't do it," he said. "For God's sake, Dr. Darwin, no sane man will seek to conjure demons, no matter where they dwell."

Darwin hesitated, weighing Ledyard's words. "That is quite true," he said at last. "Unless we raise them to exorcise them, once and for ever. It must be done. All of you, watch closely now, keep your eyes fixed on the lantern beam."

He unshuttered the lamp, and the beam shone out the length of the room, behind Darwin's mechanism. At a signal from him, Pole stood up and quietly snuffed the candles in their ornate mounts along the walls. He closed the heavy curtains. The room was silent, lit only by the single lantern.

Darwin bent over the instrument in front of the lamp, and released a metal catch on its side. There was a steady whirring noise and the metal fan in front began a slow revolution. Darwin hurried back along the table, paying out a length of line that was attached to the side of the mechanism. He drew it taut and took up a position standing behind the others. The fan blades intercepted the lantern beam, throwing a flickering pattern of light and dark across the interior of the room.

Darwin increased the tension on the line he was holding, and the moving blades turned faster, black bars across the bright beam. He was making delicate adjustments, seeking a particular speed of rotation. Another sound began to grow in the room. Above the steady whir of the machinery there was growing a labored, tortured breathing. It was a strangled growl, deep in the throat.

Alice had turned her head away from the beam. She gave a scream of terror. By her side, Philip Alderton, the veins in his neck and head congested with blood, began to lurch to his feet. The wooden arms of his chair splintered like dry twigs in the grip of his powerful hands. He began to turn toward Alice, huge in the flickering light of the lantern beam.

Darwin released the line. Before Alderton had fully risen, he leaned over him from behind. The doctor's hands, strong and precise, pressed firmly on Alderton's carotid arteries. Grunting in his throat, Alderton tried to bring his hands up to free himself from Darwin's grip. After a few seconds, he swayed forward and fell unconscious to the thick carpet.

Darwin released him as he fell. "Let's have lights, and quickly," he said. He took a deep breath, as though he had been starved of air for several minutes. "You, Bretherton, bring servants here and have your Master carried up to his bed. I judge that he will be unconscious at least five minutes. Give him nothing but water when he wakens, and tend him closely until Dr. Ledyard or I have the opportunity to examine him."

He went over to the clockwork machine and halted the whirling fan. Pole lit a spill from the lantern on the table and applied it to the candles in their wall brackets. As the room grew light again, James Ledyard gave a long sigh. He shook his head as four servants helped Bretherton to lift Alderton's great body and bear it from the room.

"That is what my mind refused to accept," he said. "I feared it, but it went against all my training and my innermost beliefs. I told myself that such a thing was impossible. But I was wrong."

"Not wholly wrong, I think." Darwin looked sympathetically at the young doctor. "Wrong in detail, but not in essence. Your instinct told the man, but not the method." He went over to the curtains and opened them wide. The full moon was still visible, now high in the sky.

"Well past midnight, I would judge," he said. "We must remain awake until Philip Alderton revives. Miss Alice, will you see Bretherton and ask for food to be brought here. Cold roast and a pie will suffice." He turned again to Ledyard. "And what suspicions had you developed about Philip Alderton? I can perhaps guess some of them, from your behavior when first we met. You will recall your reluctance to involve me in treating his wounds."

Ledyard pulled his chair closer to the table. He looked sidelong at Alice, as she slipped back into the room and sat down without speaking by the long window. "I had suspicions. I have always denied the supernatural, as inconsistent with a rational view of the world. Yet tonight we saw it with our own eyes, the conclusion that my mind had thought of, but rejected. Philip Alderton is a *loup-garou*, a lycanthrope. We saw the beginning of the change. If you had not rendered him insensible, he would have killed Alice, and perhaps all of us. Even in his weakened condition Philip Alderton was stronger than any of us. In wolf form he would have been irresistible."

"He would," said Darwin. He seated himself opposite Ledyard, and rested his chin on his cupped hands. "But that is not relevant. Your confusion arises from a mistaken belief that the wonderful and the supernatural are the same thing. A mother's feelings when she sees her baby's first smile are not beyond the natural. They can be explained well enough by simple laws, that derive from animal urges to perpetuate the species. They are certainly not *supernatural*. But I would be the last person to assert that her feelings are not *wonderful*. That distinction is crucial, if we wish to understand the events at Alderton Manor in the last week—and in the past two hundred years."

Jacob Pole had been standing listening to Darwin, a lit spill still in his hand ready to light his pipe. He swore

as the heat reached his fingers, and dropped the spill hurriedly to the floor.

"Pox on it, Erasmus. I suppose you think you are making sense, but it's all gibberish to me. What the devil
has Philip Alderton's change to a bestial form got to do
with smiling babies? We've not seen one baby since we
came to the manor."

"Jacob, have you never heard of *analogy*?" Darwin
sighed. "So much for simile. Well, we have time to spare
until Philip Alderton wakes. A full explanation will be
of interest to everyone."

He turned to Bretherton, who had quietly entered carrying a board laden with meat pies, cold roast beef, and
cheeses. "Is your Master comfortable?"

"Yes, sir. Two men are at his bedside. We will know
as soon as he stirs."

"He may be nauseated when he wakens. Cutting off
the supply of blood to the brain, as I did, may produce
that effect. You should be prepared for that possibility."

"Yes, sir." Bretherton turned, but he hesitated before
going to the door. "Doctor, the men are afraid of Mister Alderton. They heard what happened here. Are they
safe with him, or might he change again?"

"Heard it from you, I suppose," said Darwin. "Tell them
that they are perfectly safe."

"But are they?" asked Alice, as soon as Bretherton had
left the room. "If Dr. Ledyard be correct, could not Philip
change again? It is still the full moon, and the wind still
blows strong on the mill."

"That will not happen. Dr. Ledyard has guessed a part
of the truth, but as Philip Alderton's fiancée, you must
understand everything. It is not pleasant. Tell me, my dear,
did you know anything of Philip's health, or the health
of his family, before you came here?"

"Philip's health was always robust. You have seen how
quickly he recuperates from injury. But of his family,

I know little. I assumed that they all enjoyed good health."

"They did," interrupted James Ledyard. "Charles Alderton was a good age when he died, and had good health prior to his fatal seizure."

"Very well." Darwin cut a piece of Caerphilly cheese. "So let us begin only with facts, unencumbered by any theories. You examined the wounds of Philip Alderton, Dr. Ledyard, and you also examined the body of Tom Barton. I believe you drew certain conclusions from those examinations. Would you tell me what they were."

"They made me very uneasy," replied Ledyard. "Philip's wounds had been inflicted by an animal of some sort, that could not have been otherwise from their nature. But Barton's wounds were different. There were cuts and tears in his skin, but they were not the cause of his death. His skull had been crushed by some terrible impact. I was uneasy when I saw that, and wondered if somehow he and Philip could have fought each other in the pit."

"Which would reduce the mystery of the Immortal to a common assault," said Darwin. "I could see no reason for you to discourage my medical examination, unless you suspected your own conclusions and thought to shield someone else from grief and scandal. I think I know whom you hoped to protect. But you missed something. You did not also examine the bodies of the hounds."

"Of Cambyses and Berengaria?" Ledyard looked puzzled. "Why should I?"

"Why indeed?" said Pole. "Dammit, Erasmus, I told you you'd get nothing poking around inside a couple of dead dogs. It was the messiest business I've ever seen."

"A trifle smelly, I suppose," said Darwin cheerfully. "That is something to which any doctor quickly becomes accustomed." He cut a thick slice of roast beef and happily began to apply mustard with a lavish hand. "But it was informative. Now, another fact. Alice, my dear, those hounds were part of the household. Who looked after their care and feeding? I feel sure that it was not Philip."

"Barton looked after all the dogs," said Alice. "It was part of his duties. And I suspect that it was his idea to take them along to the mill."

"Which Philip Alderton readily agreed to," said Darwin. "That should rule out your notion, Dr. Ledyard, that Alderton had any prior intention to attack Barton using the story of the Immortal as a cover. He would never have permitted the dogs in such a case." He picked up a thick pie, sniffed at it closely, and laid it again on the table. "Well, what then of the hounds' wounds? They were like Barton's, not like Philip Alderton's. Brains beat out against a hard surface—such as the wall of the pit. When I saw that, the conclusion was clear. Alderton did attack Barton, as you had surmised. The hounds defended Barton, and then themselves. Alderton somehow killed all three, but not without extensive wounds inflicted by the desperate hounds. I'm sorry, my dear," he added, as Alice gave a low exclamation of horror. "That seemed to be the only explanation. Even with his great strength, it was hard to imagine how he could have done it. But had he done so, his wounds were inflicted by the dogs, not by the Lambeth Immortal. That was my thought, after examining men and hounds."

"But you raise more questions than you answer," protested Ledyard. "Charles Alderton also died in the pit, alone. And there has been a legend about the Beast that dwells there for hundreds of years."

"I know," said Darwin. "That was a real problem. As I told Jacob, the idea of an immortal being, or one with a vast lifetime, is anathema to me. It would be contrary to the survival of that species. So, I turned the question around. Accept that there had been strange events in the Alderton Pit for hundreds of years. What could it be, that could endure for five or more generations?"

The other three were silent. "Some kind of spirit?" ventured Alice.

"No spirits. For me, that would be the court of last resort, and contrary to all that I believe about the natural world. Is there anything else that could persist so long? I can think of one thing."

He turned to Ledyard. "Doctor, forget the pit, the Immortal, and all the talk of supernatural events. Imagine that you had just entered the room tonight for the first time. You went to the pit, I know, to protect Alice from what you had come to fear as a werewolf. You may be comforted to know that I believe your attack on Philip Alderton truly saved Alice's life. But suppose all that had not been in your mind. As a doctor, what would you have diagnosed in Philip Alderton, when he rose from that chair?"

Ledyard stared thoughtfully at the table for a few seconds. He looked up quickly, dark eyes full of surmise. "With those symptoms? They could well have been the onset of *grand mal*."

Darwin clapped his hands together. "Exactly. They could indeed have been caused by an epileptic seizure, a convulsive fit. Now that, as we well know, can be carried for many generations. It is a disease with a strong tendency to perpetuate itself through a family line. Charles Alderton, as you had already told me, died of a seizure. He had been alone in the pit when it happened. A severe convulsion, with no medical help nearby, could well be fatal to one of advancing years, who was already in failing health. The strain to the system is great in a case of *grand mal*."

"But Philip is not an epileptic," cried Alice. "His health has always been good. I have known him for over a year, and he has never been sick in all that time."

"And what does the pit have to do with all this?" objected Ledyard. "If Alderton were to suffer a seizure, why should it be only when he was in a hole in the ground?"

Darwin had picked up the same meat pie and was again sniffing at it suspiciously. "I hope that the cook has not been foolish enough to omit the cloves from a squab pie," he said in a worried voice. "I can smell mutton, onions and apples—but where are the cloves? I must have a word with her tomorrow."

He again replaced the pie on the table. "Why in a hole in the ground? Yes, indeed. That was a most difficult question. Accept that Philip killed Barton and the hounds, when he had no control over his actions. Remember, too, his look of the Viking, and recall the berserker, who showed tremendous strength when the killing rage was on him in Norse battles. Recall that Philip's clothes showed that he had been in some desperate fray at the bottom of the pit. It still left the question: why in the pit? And what had Gerald Alderton's old warning about the moon, the wind and the mill to do with all this? That was when I decided that I had to look at this pit, when the conditions were right for the appearance of the Beast."

"I wish you had told me more of this at the time, Erasmus," grumbled Pole. "I don't know anything about your *grand mal*, but the idea of being down there with the Lambeth Immortal was quite a *grand* enough *mal* to frighten me. 'Wind strong on the Mill' was quite right— you could hear my bowels churning with it from twenty paces."

"You surprise me, Jacob," Darwin said. He smiled his gap-toothed smile. "Are you not the man who tells of the midnight ascent of a Shiraz temple, guarded by the spirits of a thousand years of dead priests? You told me that on that occasion you did not turn a hair."

"Nor did I." Pole sniffed. "But there were rubies promised at the end of that climb. And a collection of heathen spirits are not half so alarming as a giant hound, ready to rip my backside off while I'm trying to scramble out of the pit."

"There is a legend of gold near the pit, also," said Ledyard. "A Viking treasure that was buried somewhere near here."

"Now, you should never have said that." Darwin swore heartily. "I'll never get him away from here now. Jacob, I'm leaving the day after tomorrow, with or without you." He turned again to Ledyard. "Did you ever read any of the works of Fracastoro of Verona? It is no idle question," he added, seeing Ledyard's puzzled look.

Ledyard shook his head.

"You should do so," went on Darwin. "His book on the methods of infection, *De Contagione*, sets a new direction for the analysis of disease propagation. He was an acute observer, and an ingenious experimenter. I thought of him when we were in the pit the other night. In one of his works, there is a brief discussion of epilepsy. He asserted, without further comment, that seizures can in some cases be induced artificially in a patient. He talked of exposing the sufferer to a regular, flickering light, as might be accomplished by a rotating wheel that intercepts a beam of sunlight entering a darkened room."

The others looked again at the instrument that stood at the far end of the table, the fan motionless on its front.

"The sweeps of the mill," Alice said suddenly. "We saw them tonight, cutting across the moon's face."

Darwin nodded. "If James Ledyard had not come tonight, you might not now be a living woman. When you are at the bottom of the pit, the rising moon strikes behind the mill. A strong wind turns the sweeps at their highest rate. The latticework in the rotating arms makes that flickering pattern to the eyes. I noticed it, thought of Fracastoro's remarks, and tried to time the period of the light. That device"—he pointed along the table—"achieves the same effect, independent of mill, moon, and wind. I had to have a way of varying the pace, since I was not sure of the exact frequency that would affect Philip Alderton."

"And Charles Alderton was similarly affected?" asked Ledyard.

"And Gerald Alderton also." Darwin nodded. "Gerald somehow discovered the circumstances that led to his seizures, and he tried to warn his descendants, while not revealing the family's misfortune to the world. It is ironic to think that it was his message that lured Charles and Philip to the pit, and assured the new appearance of the Immortal."

Bretherton entered the room as Darwin was speaking. "Mister Philip is awake. He seems very tired, but otherwise in no discomfort. He is bewildered to again be in his bed, when his last memory was of sitting in the dining room. I have told him nothing."

Ledyard stood up. "I will go to him. He is still my patient, regardless of tonight's events."

Alice did not speak, but she rose to her feet and left the room with Ledyard and Bretherton.

"She's had a terrible shock," said Pole. He was looking at Darwin shrewdly. "Her fiancé is a murderer. How will she react to that?"

Darwin shook his head. "I cannot tell. Alderton is not a pleasant man, and he is overbearing and graceless with the servants. But he must be pitied."

"James Ledyard is very fond of Alice," probed Pole. "And I think that you are very well disposed toward Ledyard. Do you now propose to have Alderton arrested as a murderer, for the killing of Tom Barton?"

Darwin sighed. His grey, patient eyes were troubled and weary. "Don't bait me, Jacob. You know the answer to that question very well. I am a doctor. My task is to save life, not to take it."

"And you think that James Ledyard has the same view?"

"His feelings for Alice make his decision harder, but I think he will reach the same conclusion. Our concern must be only to make sure that nothing like this can happen again. The Alderton epilepsy is a rare form, apparently called forth only by that special stimulus of a flickering light. When Alderton finds out what he did, I hope that he will offer himself for treatment or restraint."

"And if he does not choose to do so?"

Darwin sighed, and shrugged his heavy shoulders. "Then he must be forced to accept medical help, or placed where he can do no further harm. Remember, he must not be blamed for the sickness itself. He cannot help that disease, any more than you are to be blamed for your malaria. But he must accept responsibility for its control. Gerald Alderton faced a similar problem, and when he found out the truth he gave his life to religious works. But he already had children. Philip may decide, faced with the facts, that the Alderton line must end with him. That is not our decision."

He looked across at the remains of the food. In an absentminded way, he had slowly disposed of most of it, even the despised cloveless squab pie. He pushed his chair away from the table.

"If that happens," he went on. "I feel sure that James Ledyard will be more than happy to comfort Alice—and even squire her around the tombs of Egypt, if she wishes it. Ledyard has a genuine flair for the interpretation of early history."

"And you still propose that we should be on our way tomorrow for Lichfield?" asked Pole. "You are really willing to let Philip Alderton, James Ledyard and Alice Milner resolve the rest of this matter between them?"

"I think so." Darwin yawned and rose heavily from the table. "It is no longer our business. Come on, Jacob. I want to take a look at Philip Alderton, and it's getting late. We've had a busy day. One way or another, we've ended a family line, removed a Beast from the pit, and killed an Immortal. Now I have to go and look at a patient."

THE SOLBORNE VAMPIRE

It was late afternoon on the shortest day of the year. An iron frost had lain since noon on the ground outside, and now it was settling on the flat roof of the square brick warehouse.

At nine o'clock of that same morning, the building roof had been comfortably warm. The temperature inside had been scorching hot, well over ninety degrees. The explosion of the boiler, at twenty-seven minutes before midday, had taken out every window and scattered fragments of glass and black iron a quarter mile in every direction. The inside heat had been bleeding away ever since. Wet towels were turning rigid, and soon once-boiling water in jugs and bowls would freeze.

The injured had been treated and the dead removed. The clean-up crew had done their best and were leaving. Shards of metal, embedded deep in solid brick walls, would have to wait, as would a thorough examination of the shattered relic in the middle of the room.

Just two people remained. The younger, a man of about

forty with a gloomy, introspective face, was pacing one wall. He would not look at the ruined steam engine.

"That's it," he said. "It's all over. I should never have left Glasgow. I'll not build another one, no matter how you and Matthew urge."

Erasmus Darwin had been picking up bloody rags and swabs and dropping them into a bucket. Now he straightened. He had worked through the previous night with a difficult delivery, and awakened to come to the Birmingham suburb after only three hours of sleep. His fat face was grey and he drooped with fatigue, but he permitted no sign of that to show in his voice.

"You won't build another tonight, Jimmy, that I will admit. But tomorrow? Wait and see. I'll wager you will see differently."

"You would lose. I'm finished with all of this. I'll go back to instrument making."

"You cannot do that." Darwin bent to pick up one last rag, grunted at his aching bones, and moved to where his medical chest stood on a work bench. Somehow, despite his weariness, the smile on his pockmarked face managed to be reassuring. "You must labor on, Jimmy. The world awaits the perfection of your ideas. The day will come when they"—he swept a hefty arm to take in the whole of the north of England—"will use your engines to drive a million spinning jennys. Your inventions will run the world. A hundred years from now, water power will be one with Nineveh and Babylon."

"Waterwheels at least do not kill and maim."

"One man died here—miracle enough, seeing the force of the explosion. And I gather that Ned Sumpton disobeyed your orders."

"I told him not to start without me, that I would be busy at the Soho works until noon." For the first time, the balding Scotsman glanced at the wreckage of the engine that reflected so much of his dreams and labor.

"Ned was so impatient. I said to him, time and time, steam is not a toy, it's a force of nature. You treat it lightly at your peril. And then to ignore the pressure, and never to check the safety valve . . ."

"Whatever he did, he paid for that and more." Darwin closed the brass clasps on his medical chest. "Jimmy Watt, if you have trouble handling your job, how would you deal with mine? You've seen just one death today. Do you realize that it's my second, and close to being my third? I was able to save the mother—I hope—but the baby died within two hours of delivery."

"I couldn't handle your job, Erasmus. I know it, and you know it. Even if I had your medical knowledge, I lack your fortitude."

"As I lack your skills as engineer. There is space in the world for many complementary talents. As for fortitude, that is not innate. It is acquired by practice." Erasmus Darwin glanced out of the nearest window, now a ragged square of emptiness in the whitewashed wall. "Jimmy, tonight I think I will have to throw myself on your hospitality. I do not see a trip home as feasible unless I abandon the sulky. Even then it would be difficult. The roads were bad coming, and now they'll be like iron."

"Of course." The other man roused himself. "I'm a barbarian. You must be exhausted and starving. And in any case, if I sent you off without his seeing you, Matthew would never forgive me. You can stay with me. Let's go and have dinner now—if you feel ready for it?"

"I can hardly wait." Darwin hefted his medical chest and braced it against his broad chest. "I am famished. Will we eat at your home, also?"

"Oh, I think not. I'm not much of a one for eating, the way that you are." Watt surveyed Darwin's ample stomach, and for the first time since the accident a glint of humor came to his eye. "I think we'll dine at

Matthew's. He has more money than both of us together, and he keeps a far better table. And he'll be agog to know what new ideas you've had since the last Lunar Society meeting."

"You mean I will have to sing for my supper? What makes you think I am ready for that?"

"If you're not, it will be the first time ever." Watt was leading the way through a battered warehouse door that hung crooked on its hinges. "Come on. A wash, a nap, and a good meal. I'll send word to Lichfield that you won't be home tonight."

As the first night of winter put its lock on the land, the chance of more visitors to Matthew Boulton's sprawling and battlemented house seemed small. The house turned inward, shutters barred and doors bolted. Outside, a light fall of snow had begun. It was too cold for large flakes. The tiny stinging crystals did not settle where they fell, but blew restlessly across the surface in response to variable breaths of wind too weak to move tree branches. Small drifts built up against the hedgerows. Badgers burrowed deeper in their sets, and foxes followed their noses across the frozen countryside in search of winter hares.

Within the house, all was snug and festive. Christmas was only four days away, and ivy, holly, and mistletoe hung above the fireplace of the great dining room. At the long table, dishes came and came: smoked eel, broiled turbot, veal and ham pie, quails stuffed with chestnuts, stargazy pie, capons stuffed with onions and oysters, a great smoking round of roast beef flanked by roast parsnips and potatoes and carrots, brandied plum pudding with candied peel and hard sauce, and finally a whole wheel of Stilton cheese. Boulton, owner of the finest metal works in Europe, knew his man. He offhandedly apologized for the absence of roast goose and suckling pig.

The staff had scheduled those closer to Christmas. If only he had known that Darwin would be here . . .

"You would have done no differently." Restored by an hour of sleep and a mountain of food, Darwin was in his element. An appreciative audience inspired him. Between mouthfuls of dried apricots he had been enlarging on Dr. Withering's extraordinary and recent success with the humble foxglove to alleviate or even cure cases of dropsy, and the potential of that new dried-leaf decoction to supplement Jesuit-bark, aloes, and guaiacum. Even Watt seemed, in his interest in the subject, to be forgetting the day's disaster—except at some deep inner level always present in the gloomy, self-doubting Scot.

"You are, Matthew," Darwin went on, "a person of *method*."

At that moment the iron knockers on the great double doors of the house sounded like the hammer of doom.

Watt and Darwin jerked upright. Boulton did not react at all.

"Happens every night of the year," he said cheerfully. "Creditors, or councilmen, or couriers. Seeing it's close to Christmas, maybe it's carollers. Musgrave will see to them. Go on, 'Rasmus. You were, I think, about to enlarge on the uses of tartar of vitriol."

Darwin was not listening; or rather, he listened to something else: voices resounding in the slate-floored and oak-panelled entrance hall.

"Another place setting, I think," he said, wiping his hands absentmindedly on the edge of the tablecloth. "If you will permit me to bring another guest to dinner."

"Bring twenty, if you wish." Boulton indicated with a wave of his hand one of many vacant spaces. "Right there. But I didn't know you were expecting visitors."

"No more was I." Darwin did not stand up, but pushed his chair away from the table to give more space for his belly. As the door was opened and another man ushered in, he nodded in satisfaction. "Jacob. I thought I recognized your bark. Jimmy Watt, may I introduce Colonel Jacob Pole of Radburn Hall, my friend and neighbor. Matthew, you and Jacob already know each other. What's it like outside?"

"Cold as Jack Frost's backside." Pole greeted the other two men formally, but added, " 'Rasmus talks so much about you, I feel I know you well."

"And what does he say about us?" Watt, unlike Darwin, had stood up when Pole entered.

"He says that James Watt is one of the great engineers of our time, and Matthew Boulton is this nation's leading innovator of new machines." Pole was tall and gaunt, so thin that his clothes hung loosely on him. He walked across to the fireplace and stood facing it. His complexion gleamed sallow in the firelight, and the trembling hands that he held out to be warmed told of other legacies of foreign travel.

"Then sit down, man." Boulton waved to an unused setting at the table. "Even if you have eaten, those words deserve a second meal."

"In a moment." Pole hesitated, glancing from one man to the next. "I find myself in a difficult position. I am not alone, but with the cousin of my own oldest friend. He is outside in the hall. He greatly desires to speak with Erasmus. But I cannot disturb your dinner."

"Of course you can. You already did." Boulton started forward, as though to head for the door. Pole's uplifted hand stopped him.

"Let me be more honest with you. I thought that I would meet Erasmus on his way home, and there would be a chance of private conversation. It was not until we were at the factory that I learned that he had come here. Now, I don't know what to do. You see, the man with me has a problem that he describes as both private and personal."

"A medical problem?" Darwin sat up straighter.

"I do not know."

"I see. Gentlemen?" Darwin glanced at Watt and Boulton.

"I don't know about his personal problem, or if he chooses to talk about it in front of us." Boulton once again moved to the door. "I do know that it's not right to leave a visitor cold and hungry and waiting in the hall. Sit down, Jacob. At the very least, have food and drink. Mulled wine will bring some warmth to your bones."

"And food will add flesh to them." Darwin gestured to the table. "That veal and ham pie is the best that I have tasted this year. Trust me."

Boulton was returning with a man so muffled against the elements that his build and features were hard to determine. Frost on his eyebrows, moustache, and full black beard was slowly melting and running down his face and cloak.

"Thomas Solborne," Boulton said, "who is from Dorset. A county, he tells me, that is a good deal warmer than this one."

"Which would not be difficult, tonight at least. Gentlemen." Solborne spoke with the soft accent of the English southwest. He swept off his hat, with its long peak and earflaps, and was revealed as a florid man of about thirty, wigless and with abundant black hair that curled down over his ears. He bowed from the waist, scanned the group, and addressed Darwin directly. "Dr. Darwin, I know that I am intruding. Take my word, it was not planned this way."

"What did Jacob say, look for the fat one?" Again Darwin gestured to a place at the table. "Please, Mr. Solborne, sit down. It was not planned, you say? *Nothing* of today's events seems planned. I had thought to sleep in my own bed tonight. Let me, without delay, tell you my own feelings. Jacob already intimated to us why you are here.

Everyone in this room, except of course for yourself, is an old and trusted friend of mine. I value and rely on their discretion. You have a problem, about which I so far know nothing save that it is a private concern. If you choose to describe it here and now, you will find sympathetic ears and close lips. If you wish to defer discussion until we are alone, that too will be quite acceptable. We will eat, drink, relax, and spend the evening in pleasant conversation."

Solborne was slowly shedding layers of clothing; woollen gloves, two cloaks, a long scarf, and a leather jacket. He was revealed as a man of medium and unathletic build, slightly overweight. "Eat, drink, and talk. Those I may accomplish; but it is two months and more since I could last relax. The purpose of my visit to these parts was to meet Jacob, and thereby seek access to you. Your reputation in the southern counties is unequalled. You are often said to be the last resort in difficult medical cases."

"I am flattered." Darwin did not sound surprised.

"And also in—certain other matters." For the first time, Solborne hesitated. "I face a problem which may be medical, but which, quite frankly, points beyond the natural. I know that you reject such explanations."

"That puts the matter too strongly. I will not admit a supernatural explanation when a natural one can be found. And I should add, in my experience that has always been the case."

"But in *this* case . . ." Solborne spread out his hands. They were neat, well-kept, and had clearly seen no manual labor. He had placed food on his plate at Matthew Boulton's urging, but not touched it. "I'm sorry. I do not know where to begin."

"At any point. We are not building a house here, where the foundation and walls must perforce be completed before the roof goes on." Darwin smiled his ruined smile.

"We can return as necessary, and fill in any missing elements. The whole evening is ours. The most important thing is to give full detail, and omit nothing. Detail is at the heart of diagnosis. Consider this as a medical task, whether or not it proves at length to be so."

"Very well." Solborne finally, almost reluctantly, took a draught of red wine. "As Mr. Boulton mentioned, I am from Dorset. In fact, I hail from the farthest southern point of that county, near the tip of the peninsula known as Portland Bill. The Bill juts out into the English Channel, and my home sits on the western cliffs a couple of miles above it—am I giving too much detail, of no consequence to the matter?"

"We have as yet no way of knowing what may be relevant. Please continue."

"My family is of old Dorset stock. We trace the Dorset Solbornes back almost to the Conquest. It is debated whether the family takes its name from the nearby village of Solborne, or the village its name from the family. In any case, my ancestors have lived there five hundred years and more." Thomas Solborne caught the impatient look on Watt's face, and grimaced ruefully. "I tell you this, Mr. Watt, not as presumed evidence of superiority, but rather as an admission of possible family defects. I have some knowledge of animal husbandry. I know the problems likely to arise from too close breeding."

Darwin leaned forward. "Physical problems?"

"In animals. In the case of my own family, I may be referring to mental problems. Please be assured, I do not find it easy to talk of these matters."

"I understand. And you should be assured that although you have our full sympathy, you will receive from me—from all of us—the most logical and dispassionate analysis that we are able to provide. Nothing, of course, will go beyond this room."

"Thank you. I will try to omit nothing, no matter how painful or personal. I am thirty-one years old. I have one sister, Helen, eight years younger than I. My parents died within six months of each other, three years ago. The family estate of course passed to me, but Helen is unmarried and she and I both live at Newlands. That is the family home, one hundred and seventy years old. It was badly in need of renovation, and Helen and I undertook to accomplish that when the property passed to me.

"We restored the crumbling mortar—"

"Excuse me." Darwin held up a pudgy hand. "You say, 'we restored.' I suspect that you did not perform the work yourself. Would you clearly distinguish between your own acts, and those accomplished by others?"

"If it helps. We brought in workmen who restored crumbling mortar and replaced lost brick—the whole of Newlands is brick-built, except for twin towers of stone, one on the north and one on the south side. We had much of the woodwork replaced, wherever we found dry rot. Do you need to know the cost of these actions?"

"Was it a significant drain on your finances?"

"Not really. We have land and revenues in other parts of Dorset. Both Helen and I are fortunate enough to possess substantial independent means."

"Then let us continue. If necessary we will return to consider finances."

"The rebuilding that I have described took a long time to accomplish, but six months ago we were ready to take the next step: refurbishing the interior. New drapes, carpets cleaned or replaced, re-upholstering of furniture, and so forth. In this area, we knew that Helen would receive little help from me. I am not, technically speaking, color-blind, but I am close enough to it for my color aesthetic to be worthless. She, on the other hand, possesses a strong artistic sense. We agreed that I would be involved in financial decisions, but all other choices would be hers.

"Naturally, selections could not be made while sitting at Newlands. Helen would have to travel to Dorchester, twenty miles north, or even as far as Bristol, seventy miles away, where a wide variety of materials and designs were available. I had no qualms about that. She has travelled before without me, even to the Continent, and Helen has always had considerable independence of spirit." Solborne paused and took a deep breath, giving the impression that there was a lot more to be said on the subject. The listeners waited patiently.

"For example," he said at last, "I do not know your views of either politics or foreign affairs, but as mark of Helen's independent views, let me say that while I greatly oppose last year's revolt of the American colonies, she rejoices in it."

Darwin glanced at Watt, Pole, and Boulton, before he replied. "We are of mixed opinions. Myself, I hope for the ultimate success of the breakaway colonies. The more troubling question is, will it lead to other revolutions, closer to home?"

Matthew Boulton nodded vigorously and leaned forward. "That is exactly what I tell Erasmus. We are all of us firm monarchists here—quiet, Jimmy." Watt had made a sound between a grunt and an asthmatic wheeze, and Boulton turned to him. "I know that you favor the Young Pretender, but still you crave a monarch, even if he does not happen to be King George. Mr. Solborne, I have travelled much in Europe since the revolt in the Americas. France is stirring. There is unrest and fear in the royal families of Bavaria and Bohemia. The Margrave of Brandenburg has formed a special guard to seek out revolutionaries. Where will it end? Where *should* it end?"

"We will certainly hold that debate—on another occasion." Darwin held an open palm out to Jacob Pole, who sat frowning and waiting for his turn to speak. "Peace, Jacob. The floor belongs to Mr. Solborne."

The visitor, unfamiliar with the digressive give-and-take of Lunar Society members, had been sitting bewildered. At Darwin's "If you please, continue," he nodded.

"As I was saying, despite her young age and strong opinions, Helen is familiar with the ways of the world. Or so I thought."

Solborne fell silent again, until Darwin coaxed him: "Tell us about her. What does she look like, what are her interests?"

"She is as fair as I am dark. Friends have told us, it is an astonishment that two so different in appearance could be born from a single womb. She is short in stature, even for a woman. Helen claims five feet, but I suspect the final inch. Dainty in features and form. Men apparently find her attractive, since she turns heads at every market, fair, or gala. They pursue her. She sheds them with ease."

"She lacks interest in men?"

"Say rather, that Helen is more interested in other things. I mentioned her artistic sense. That is secondary to her interest in philosophy and her gift for mathematics. Few men can tolerate more than five minutes of Euclid, Archimedes, Spinoza, and Newton. They come, they listen, and they leave shaking their heads. So when Helen made a visit to Bristol to examine brocades, and wrote to say that she had been given an opportunity to see the demonstration of an extraordinary mathematical device, I was not in the least astonished—not then, or when she extended her stay by three days to learn more of what she had seen. I was, however, much surprised one week later, when she returned to Newlands. She was not alone. She had with her Professor Anton Riker of Bordeaux, and his extraordinary calculating engine. Have you heard of it?"

The others turned to Darwin. His grey eyes were thoughtful, and in them stirred something that Jacob Pole at least had seen before: an overwhelming and insatiable curiosity. "I know of the calculator built by Monsieur Pascal over a century ago," he said slowly, "which performed addition and subtraction by mechanic device. I am familiar with the improved version constructed by Herr Gottfried Leibniz, a generation later, which also permitted multiplication and division. But the name of Professor Riker is new to me."

"As it was to me, and to Helen. She insisted that the professor, together with his machine, visit Newlands. Let me say that initially I was surprised by the appearance of a guest, but not disturbed. It was only later that my aversion to Professor Riker developed."

"His description, too, if you will."

"Above middle height, and thinner than Colonel Pole. According to Helen, his eyes are grey with a tawny center and he possesses a gaze of peculiar intensity, but I cannot speak to that myself since he has not once met my eye. He has an accent to his speech, something I think of Central Europe, but I do not have ear or experience enough to place it. He is courtly and charming in manner, but it seems the false charm of a dancing master or an actor."

"Seems to *you*."

"You are very perceptive, Dr. Darwin. Helen and I disagree strongly. She cannot see beyond his brilliance, which in truth appears to be very great. The performance of the Riker calculating engine defies description."

"I will nonetheless request that you attempt it."

"I knew you would. Here." Solborne reached into a pocket of his leather jacket and produced a folded sheet of paper, thick and the color of clotted cream. "This is not my drawing. It is Helen's."

Darwin unfolded the sheet and held it close to one of the candelabra, while the other four crowded around. The main line drawing was in green ink and filled half the sheet. An expanded detail of one part was shown above.

"I have seen it for myself," Solborne said. "This is accurate as to both layout and proportion. Here on the flat upper surface"—he touched the upper part of the sheet—"you see nine keys or levers. Here are nine more. Each lever has ten possible settings, for the numbers zero through nine. Thus it is possible to define two numbers, each with up to nine digits. This is an eight-way lever which controls the *operation* of the engine. Addition, subtraction, multiplication, division, and the extraction of roots up to fifth order. And here"—he touched the paper again—"is where a number of up to eighteen digits appears. It is contained on a strip of paper, and it is *printed*, as by controlled type."

"Are these dimensions accurate?" Darwin was crouched with his nose almost to the paper.

"They are. The whole engine, including its base, is two feet wide, three feet deep, and rather less than three feet high. It is also heavy, ten stone or more."

"Ah." Darwin leaned back, his face sad and oddly disappointed. "Then I am obliged to question the inventive genius of Professor Anton Riker. There was, eight years ago, on display in the court of Emperor Joseph of Austria—"

"The automaton chess player of Baron Wolfgang von Kempelen, which took the form of a seated Turk."

"You know of it."

"Certainly. It was no automaton, but relied upon a hidden accomplice. The device was otherwise impossible."

"I am not persuaded of that. Before von Kempelen's secret was revealed, Mr. Solborne, I wasted an inordinate amount of my time and foolscap seeking to define a possible mechanism. I was unable to prove that such a chess-playing machine is impossible *theoretically*; only that it would be prodigious complicated, and probably enormous in size."

"Those observations would be yet more true of this

'calculating engine.' Dr. Darwin, my first response was yours exactly. This new machine, like the chess automaton, must be operated by some confederate of Professor Riker.

"Helen soon convinced me otherwise. First, the machine stands alone, not on some specially constructed dais or platform able to conceal a man. It works in bright light, with everything visible, rather than in obscuring gloom. The von Kempelen device was operated using a system of balls and magnets, impossible in this case. Finally, and far more important, consider what the engine *does*: the printed output is the result of a difficult arithmetic calculation, and it normally appears within thirty seconds of the complete statement of the problem. The input numbers are provided not by Riker, but by the audience—I have done it myself. There is no way that an assistant could know the problems in advance. Even with the use of tables, it would be impossible to provide the cubic root or quartic root of a nine-figure number, or the product of two such numbers, so quickly."

"True enough." Darwin pouted his full lips. "So, we have a mystery."

He seemed ready to settle back into brooding silence, but Solborne would not allow it. He took the sheet from Darwin and returned it to his jacket pocket.

"A mystery, perhaps, but not *the* mystery. I would not travel so far afield, in winter, merely for the sake of some calculating device. My concern is with Helen, and Professor Riker. I already told you that I did not care for him, and I requested to Helen that his stay at Newlands not be an extended one. He and his machine departed three days after their arrival, during which time he offered me numerous demonstrations of the engine's power. Then he left—but he did not go far. He rented a small house along the cliff, less than half a mile from Newlands, where he lives alone. And from that day forward, I saw the decline in Helen."

"Melancholic?"

"Not at all. I saw—and see—physical decline. She has been losing weight, steadily. She was always fair, but now her skin seems almost translucent. Her eyes are set deeper in her head, and the skin beneath them appears to be almost purple, as though bruised."

"And her manner?"

"Febrile, intense, yet cheerful. She seems distant from me, in a way that I have never before experienced. When I ask concerning her health, she says only that she is feeling tired, and does not seem able to get enough sleep. That is certainly true. She will nod off during dinner, or as soon as she sits down in a chair. I wonder what is happening."

It was Darwin's turn to hesitate. "Mr. Solborne," he said at last. "It pains me to suggest this, but I assume that the obvious explanation has occurred to you?"

"That Helen and Riker are romantically engaged, and she spends her nights with him? Of course. It is not the case."

"How do you know?"

"By taking an action that was not strictly honorable. As I told you, the main body of Newlands, including parlors, guest bedrooms, living room, dining rooms, and servants' quarters, is of brick. However, there are two towers of stone, one to the north and one to the south side, rising from the main house. I have a suite of rooms, including my bedroom and study, in the north tower. Helen occupies the southern one, with her bedroom and parlor and sewing room. There are two entrances to each tower. One leads through to the main body of the house; the other, seldom used and originally built I suspect for use only in case of fire, leads directly outside, onto a path that runs along the cliff. It runs, in fact, to and past the house rented by Anton Riker. Suspecting Helen's actions, I did two things. First, I placed locks on the outside of the tower doors. No one could then enter or leave Newlands without passing through the main body of the house. The only window in the south tower that can be opened wide enough to admit a person is near the top, overlooking a forty-foot sheer drop to stony ground.

"Second, I moved Joan Rowland, one of the servants who happens to be an unusually light sleeper, to a bedroom next to the inner door of the south tower. She was instructed to tell me if she heard any comings and goings at night."

"And did she?"

"Not a one. She said that she heard Helen—or someone—moving around in the tower, often late at night when the rest of the house was asleep. But Helen never left her own quarters."

"A necessary condition for chastity, but not a sufficient one." Darwin stirred in his chair. "Mr. Solborne, when I was a student at Cambridge, it constantly baffled me that there was a rule forbidding the presence of ladies in college at night, while open access was permitted to any woman during the day. An odd assumption seemed at work: that improprieties take place only at night. What of your sister's movements during the *daylight* hours?"

"Dr. Darwin, Jacob Pole warned me of your prescience. You are a mind reader."

"Not at all. I merely seek to close logical loopholes. During the day?"

"At close of day, which in this season means between four and five o'clock, Helen leaves Newlands and walks south along the cliff."

"To the house rented by Professor Riker?"

"That was my original assumption, that there was some sort of assignation involved. But it is not the case. As she walks south, he walks north along the shingled cliff to meet her. They stand in full view and talk to each other for five or ten minutes as darkness approaches. They just talk. They do not touch. Before it is fully dark, they part, and she returns home."

"You have been spying on them?"

"I am very worried about my sister. Daily she has grown more pale and tense, more wan and bloodless."

"And now we have one more mystery to consider. Timing." Darwin did not elaborate, but leaned forward in his seat and thoughtfully cut a wedge of Stilton. The room fell silent, except for the sound of steady munching and the wheeze of James Watt's asthmatic breathing.

"You seem to anticipate everything else." Solborne finally broke the silence. "So perhaps you have some notion of my real concern—the one I find so improbable that I am reluctant to voice it. The fear that brought me to you."

"Surely." Darwin licked his fingers. "All the components are present, are they not? Put aside, for the moment, the question of the calculating engine. Then we have a young woman who encounters a mysterious man from the Continent, perhaps from the central regions of Europe. Rapidly she comes under his sway. They meet every day, but only when the sun has gone from the sky. Access to her quarters cannot be obtained at night except through a high window set in a vertical wall, inaccessible to mortal man. She never goes out after dark, yet every day she becomes weaker, until she is as pale as though the blood itself were draining from her veins. Every day her intensity of manner increases, but so does her indifference to ordinary events. To anyone with a knowledge of European folklore, especially Slavonic traditions, a possible inference is clear."

"I know. I have seen no puncture wounds on her skin, but Professor Riker is a—"

"An inference that is clear, yet is also total nonsense. Life on Earth admits a huge variety of forms, but everywhere there is a logic, whereby form follows function. I can no more believe in *Das Wampyr* than I can believe in Sinbad's roc, a bird so large that it feeds on elephants. By the simple law of proportions, such a creature could never lift itself from the ground. And such a being as *Nosferatu*, the vampire, hated by all men but totally helpless during the daytime, could never survive the centuries."

"But if Riker is *not* that—that *thing*—then what is he? And if not he, then what is doing this to my sister?"

"I do not know." Darwin placed his hands over his paunch. The fatigue of the late afternoon had vanished and again he was eyeing the dish of smoked eels. "At this moment, I honestly do not know. But I assure you, Thomas Solborne, that we will find out."

⬦⬦⬦   ⬦⬦⬦   ⬦⬦⬦

> *My dear Erasmus,*
> *I told you, did I not, that I was the wrong man for your job? And pox on it, I was right. Tom Solborne hasn't said one word, but I'm sure he thinks I'm about as much use here as tits on a bull. . . .*

Alone in the coach, Darwin tapped Jacob Pole's letter on his knee, leaned back, and allowed himself to rock back and forward with the sway of the steady movement.

The problem was, Jacob was right. He wasn't the first choice—or even the second. But what option had offered itself? Solborne had arrived at the height of the season for winter ailments, when Darwin's *locum tenens* was already pressed into service elsewhere. Jimmy Watt was deep in the wreckage of his engine, in that mood of solitary thought that made him seem scarcely human. Transported to Dorset, he would see only steam. As for Matthew Boulton, he ran the great Soho factory under his own absolute control and he could not be spared for a day, still less a week.

Darwin comforted himself with the thought that a fortnight was not much time for Jacob to hold the fort, no matter how long it might seem to him.

On the other hand, if Helen Solborne were to die . . .

Darwin longed for a report from a man with his own keen diagnostic eye for medical matters. Jacob had not been pressed into service, he had gone willingly enough, but he could no more read the *facies* of impending death or disease than he could swim unaided from Dorset to the coast of France. How sick *was* Helen Solborne?

> *She's an attractive little woman, and she said hello to me polite enough. But Solborne is right, a lot of the time she doesn't seem to be all there. And Lord knows what she's talking about the rest of the time. Two days ago she asked me if I knew of some Italian type called Fibonacci, and his successions. I asked her if he was that Italian general who'd fought against Austria in the War of the Polish Succession, and she laughed like I'd made the biggest joke in the world and said that Fibonacci had been a good deal earlier and a much greater man, and when she said successions she meant sequences. That was one of our better conversations. Afterwards, Tom said she'd been talking about her mathematics. God help the man who marries her. . . .*

Helen Solborne did not sound like an easy dupe—or an easy subject for her brother's control. Darwin glanced down to the letter sitting on his knee. He had read it often enough to be sure that the information he sought would not be found there. Jacob was too full of his own opinions and interests to serve as impartial observer.

*. . . looks of a starved Spaniard, or maybe a
Portugee, though his accent says Hungary or even
farther south and east. Either way, I'd bet money
that his original name isn't Riker. I followed him
into Dorchester and watched him wander until
he found a shop that suited him. He ordered a
ton of food and spices delivered to that house he
rents, most of it foreign muck as bad as any I've
seen in Egypt or the Indies. No wonder he's thin
as a rail. He probably eats like a cormorant, but
I'll wager the stuff goes right through him. And
the amount of it! You'd be hard pressed to put
away all he ordered, 'Rasmus, and you'd make
two of him in size.*

Two of him in size. Darwin leaned his head back on
the stuffed leather of the coach seat, eyes closed but deep
in thought. They were skirting the chalky slopes of the
Western Downs, rumbling down to Dorchester and
Weymouth. Portland was a couple of hours away. The
tempering effect of the English Channel could already be
felt in the milder air.

Darwin turned to another page of Pole's letter.

Jacob might not be the best judge of exotic foreign-
ers or of talented young women, but he had other
strengths. He evaluated terrain and landscape with the
practical eye of a soldier and the methodical approach
of a first-rate artillery engineer.

*The west side of the Portland peninsula, where
Newlands stands, is actually a continuation of
a curious feature of the mainland known as
Chesil Bank. The bank is a shingle beach that
runs offshore of the mainland all its length, eight
miles and more. A body of water called 'The
Fleet' runs between bank and mainland. On the*

peninsula, however, the bank comes ashore, rises higher, and is more than thirty feet above the sea by the time it reaches Newlands. And Newlands is built on top of that bank. Tom Solborne said that the high window of the south tower was forty feet up. But that's from ground level. Add in the height of the bank, and the window is more like seventy feet above the water. I checked the wall beneath. It has smooth facings of white freestone. The only way to get in that window would be to fly in, unless a man could run up the sheer wall like a human spider.

You can also dismiss the idea of Helen Solborne, like Rapunzel, lowering a rope down to a waiting lover. He would have to be sitting in a boat and he'd get only one grab—the tide runs fast along this part of the shore.

Next I examined the door locks. They are padlocks, simple enough for someone with experience. I, for my sins, had them open in a half a minute, without a key. However, the locks cannot be reached from inside the tower. The only other possibility would seem to be an accomplice, opening the lock from outside. In the next day or two I therefore propose an all-night vigil outside the south tower. It's not as cold here as in Birmingham or Derby, but there's a dampness that blows in from the sea. Bring plenty of your pills and nostrums with you—I'll likely need them for my creaking bones.

From habit, Darwin patted the medical chest at his side. He might indeed need the contents for Jacob Pole, using them to treat the colonel's agues from tropical service; he was more and more convinced that any standard pharmacopeia would be useless in dealing with Helen Solborne.

Thomas Solborne was waiting as the coach rattled up the Newlands gravel drive.

"Quickly now," he said, helping Darwin down the double step. "There will never be a better time. What delayed you?"

The sun was setting, and a thick fog was creeping in from the sea.

"Broken traces, just beyond Wyke Regis." Darwin was already surveying the house and shoreline. "Where is Colonel Pole?"

Solborne pointed to a narrow road leading to the left. "Helen went for her afternoon walk and rendezvous. Jacob again agreed to follow her—discreetly—while I waited for you."

"What is her condition?"

"Deteriorating, at least to my eye. But Helen is of indomitable will. She admits only to a slight fatigue. Let us hurry. We have perhaps twenty minutes."

He led the way through the double doors at the front of the house. The entrance hall was long and wide, furnished with massive oriental standing vases and gloomy suits of old armor.

Darwin peered down at the polished floor. "Purbeck marble? I have never seen it before except in churches."

"It is mined locally. It is beautiful, wears forever—and is diabolically cold in winter. Were it not for Helen's strong views and preferences, I would cover everything with carpets."

Solborne was walking to the left, where a long curved staircase led upward to the next level. Darwin, still motionless in the entrance, saw an identical stair at the other end. He was forming in his mind a picture of the house layout and dimensions. Beyond the stairs must lie another room, and then the towers.

"Newlands was built with a high degree of symmetry."

Solborne had turned, aware that Darwin was not following. "The north and south ends of the main building form
a matched pair. But it is better if you see the tower containing Helen's suite of rooms."

"It is best if I see *everything*." Darwin, moving after
the other man, ran his hand along the smooth curve of
the banister. It was polished and free of dust.

The staircase brought them to an antechamber with two
doors. One, open, led to a dining room, thirty-five feet
long and with a log fire blazing on the seaward side. A
huge table of gleaming mahogany and eighteen chairs
dominated the middle of the room. The other door of the
antechamber was closed. Solborne opened it without
knocking and went through.

"Joan Rowland's bedroom." He pointed to the left,
where still another door stood ajar. "Joan spends every
night here."

"What is her relationship to Helen?"

"I thought of that also. It is respectful, but not close.
There is no way that Joan would jeopardize her future
at Newlands by serving as Helen's accomplice." Solborne
was at a door in a blank wall of white stone, no more
than five feet away from Joan Rowland's room. "And this
provides the only inside entrance to the south tower."

Darwin examined the door as they passed through. It
was panelled and not particularly thick. It would not
muffle sounds from its other side. He bent low and looked
at the latch with special care, checking that it had no
lock.

Beyond lay a large chamber, its octagonal shape matching the outside figure of the stone tower. A tight spiral
staircase of iron filigree led down to the tower's outside
entrance. Darwin did not attempt a descent—with his bulk
it would have been a tight fit—but asked, "Is the outer
lock still in position?"

"In position, and according to Colonel Pole, untouched.

He inserted a dab of candle grease into the padlock. It remains undisturbed."

The two men began their ascent of the wider stair that followed the outer wall of the tower. One level brought them to Helen Solborne's sitting room and study, with its own fireplace and south-facing window. Darwin tried to open it, and grunted.

"As you see." Solborne came to his side, and pushed hard on the casement. "A couple of inches of travel, no more. Not an entrance or an exit."

"For a human." Darwin was lingering over the many books. Solborne gave him an uneasy glance, and dragged him away. Ten minutes had passed since the arrival of the coach.

The next floor was a plain bedroom, above it a sewing room. Packets of furniture covering materials sat on every available surface.

"One more." Solborne had noticed that Darwin was breathing heavily. "And the only one with a window that can open wide. Up we go."

Full-length mirrors stood on all walls of the last story, throwing multiple reflections of both men. "As you see, Helen's dressing room. The morning light is excellent, because the window faces southeast."

He went across and threw it open. The thick-curtained window looked out over the sea. The fog was thickening, and a curl of mist drifted in. Darwin joined him and leaned out over a sheer drop. After a few moments he leaned one shoulder out and turned to peer upward. A gutter ran around the top of the tower, about eight feet above his head. He craned to look to the right, but the roof of the house itself was hidden around the curve of the tower.

"Fifteen minutes," Solborne said nervously. "Do you see anything?"

"Enough."

"Then we'd best be getting down again." He led the way, only to have Darwin pause near the door and bend down to examine a pair of heavy brass oil lamps.

"For dressing here after dark." Solborne waited impatiently. "On the occasions when Helen can be persuaded to attend a social evening gathering—which is rare indeed."

He breathed more easily once they were out of the tower and in the long dining room. "Is there anything else you would wish to see in the house itself, before Helen returns?"

"The roof of this part of Newlands." And, when Solborne stared. "It would, I think, be impossible for mortal human to ascend that sheer stone face. But it might be easy indeed to *descend* it."

"Ah!" Solborne's face lit with sudden understanding. "From the tower top, with the assistance of a rope. There is roof access through the attic."

He was already running for the stairs, and by the time that Darwin had negotiated three flights and reached the attic level, Solborne had opened a dusty roof skylight. He stood outside, in approaching darkness.

One glance was sufficient for both men. Solborne turned to his visitor and shook his head. The tower top stood a full fifteen feet above them. There was no sign of a ladder, or anything else that might assist in scaling the tower.

"What now?"

"We think again." Darwin, if anything, seemed pleased, as though some less interesting alternative had been disposed of. He led the way back down. When they emerged into the dining room a middle-aged woman with a thin, tight-lipped face was waiting for them. She examined Darwin, grimy and covered with cobwebs, with plenty of curiosity, but spoke at once to Solborne.

"It's happened again, sir. We had eight gallons or more,

now we have less than two. Someone is pilfering—and it isn't me nor Joan nor Liza."

"I am sure it isn't. I trust all of you completely." Solborne frowned, and muttered as though to himself, "As if I did not have enough on my mind!" And then, to the indignant woman, "There's only one thing for it, Dolly. Have Walter carry the barrels inside, and set them in the scullery. That way no one can wander along the road and steal our oil."

He turned to Darwin. "Mineral oil is in short supply this year, and winter prices are high. But never before have I found it necessary to guard our house reserves."

In the few minutes that they had been up on the roof, the big lamps around the walls of the dining room had been lit and trimmed. On a low table a few feet from Darwin, loaded dishes had magically appeared. There were plates of boiled prawns, vinegared mussels and whelks, and hot sausage rolls, as well as a cold rhubarb tart, jugs of fresh milk, and a flagon of apple wine. Before Darwin could take a step in that direction, a cloaked figure entered through the door at the far end.

Solborne shot Darwin a look that said "Not a minute to spare!" and stood waiting. Helen Solborne sauntered toward them, eyeing Darwin with as much curiosity and interest as he regarded her.

He decided in the first moment of inspection that both Thomas Solborne and Jacob Pole were right. She was tiny, five feet at most, with skin so fine and pale that the lamplight seemed to shine right through her skull. Although her figure was swathed in a long cloak, it was clear from her face that she was thinner than fashion demanded. She blinked constantly as though the oil lamps were too bright, and dark shadows limned her blue eyes.

But those eyes were fiercely intelligent, and the jaw firm. She looked Darwin right in the eye, and the little curtsey she offered seemed like a private joke between the two of them.

"It is a great pleasure to meet you, Dr. Darwin. If even as many as one fourth of Colonel Pole's stories about you are true, I await dinner tonight more eagerly than I can say."

Darwin folded his hands across his belly and bowed in return. "I am no more than a provincial physician, with most of my life taken up by the common round of routine medical treatment. Extravagant advance billing of an entertainment, Miss Solborne, is perhaps the surest way of ensuring high disappointment."

"And extravagant modesty is perhaps the surest sign of high self-esteem." She smiled, to reveal white teeth with a slight overbite. "My anticipation is undiminished. If you will excuse me, I must change now or be late for dinner."

As she drifted away through the door to the south tower, Solborne could not wait a moment longer.

"Well? What can you tell me?"

"I can tell you that I fully understand why the would-be suitors flock around Helen. Your sister is a most attractive woman."

"I mean about her *health*."

"My remark was not irrelevant to that issue. Sickness, true and serious sickness, is inconsistent with normal animal attraction. At some level, by smell or the natural language of the body, we respond to another's state of health. However, you desire a more formal diagnosis. I am willing to provide one, although I have had no more than an opportunity for superficial observation of your sister."

"And?"

"She appears in good health. Her gait, her posture, her willingness to indulge in badinage—yes, even her *cheekiness* toward me—all deny major disease."

"But you never saw her before. I assure you, she is *different* than she was three months ago."

"I believe you. And on that subject I am not bereft of ideas. However, I need proof. Did you invite Professor Riker this evening, as I requested?"

"Naturally. I walked down to his house this morning and told him that, as a noted inventor from the Midlands, you would be devastated were you to visit Dorset and depart without an opportunity to see the famous calculating engine at work."

"Was there hesitation on his part?"

"Not the slightest. He told me that he will be very busy for the next two weeks, exhibiting the engine, but at the moment he has time to breathe. He will be delighted to come here tonight after dinner, when he will show you the machine at work and allow you to propound your own mathematical questions. We can expect him, and his machine, within the hour. I freely admit to you, I do not share his delight at the prospect of his visiting Newlands. I am still convinced that he is doing my sister some terrible harm."

"Whatever harm is being done here, I am not yet ready to blame Professor Riker."

"Harm? Harm?" Jacob Pole, bustling in with his fingers and the tip of his nose a rosy pink, headed for the fireplace. He lifted the tail of his long coat, allowing the warmth from the blazing logs to irradiate his buttocks and the backs of his legs. "Welcome to Dorset, 'Rasmus. It's a raw and foggy night out there. I'll tell you one thing, if anyone comes to *harm* from all this it will be me. Tom can vouch for it, I've been out in all hours and all weathers, chilblains on my fingers and now scorch marks on my backside. I'm glad to be in for the night."

Darwin glanced at Thomas Solborne and sat down at the side table for a predinner snack. It did not seem like the best moment to mention that Jacob, if Darwin's plans held good, was likely to be outside again before the evening was out.

The calculating engine corresponded exactly to Helen Solborne's drawing. Riker had requested that the demonstration begin as soon as possible after dinner, "Since I have business tonight in Abbotsbury that cannot easily be delayed."

Two of the male staff of Newlands had carried the heavy rectangular box into one end of the dining room, grunting with effort, while Anton Riker hovered over them and told them twenty times that the engine must not under any circumstances be dropped.

Once the machine was in position, Riker called his audience's attention to the main features. The top, two feet wide and three feet deep, was of smooth hardwood coated with black lacquer. Two separate sets of nine levers were hinged at the upper surface. One additional lever allowed the operator to define the desired operation. All the levers projected upwards to form handles, and also continued below the surface, where their articulated brass rods were visible through the transparent glass sides of the engine. Riker demonstrated the action, moving a lever to one of its ten possible settings. As he did so the corresponding brass arm, jointed in two places, pushed into the opaque base of the engine. The base was roughly one foot deep, and each arm penetrated smoothly into its own separate slit in its upper surface.

There was one more slit in the base of the engine. It was very narrow and about two inches wide, no more than six inches from the ground, and it held a strip of cardboard or stiff paper.

The operator stood, or sat on a low stool in front of the machine.

"For example, take this problem," Riker said, after he had pointed out the different settings. He set the right hand lever of the upper set to the digit 2, and the right hand lever of the lower set to the digit 3. Finally he moved the operations lever to the setting that indicated multiplication. The actions of his skeletally thin fingers were deft and precise, and he hardly seemed to look at what he was doing. After a pause of about twenty seconds, long enough for his audience to become restive, there was a clicking noise from the engine's base. The strip of cardboard advanced in its position from the side slot. Riker tore it off and held it out to the audience.

Jacob Pole took the stiff paper and stared at the single printed digit. "Six," he said. "Two times three. Hmph."

"Not impressed?" Riker raised dark eyebrows. "I agree. We could all do as well, could we not? But come here, please, and sit down."

Pole, somewhat reluctantly, was installed on the stool.

"Now, enter a number with these." Riker touched the upper row of levers. "Any number that you like, up to nine figures."

The colonel, after a moment's thought, moved the levers to indicate 4-3-2-1.

"Very good. And now, a number with the lower levers."

"One-two-three-four. Is that all right?"

"Quite suitable. Go ahead. And now, specify an operation."

"Multiply?"

"Certainly, if that is what you would like. Move the lever."

There was a sound of metal on metal as the operation lever engaged. This time the silence lasted less than ten seconds. A series of clicks sounded from the base, and another cardboard strip emerged from the slot.

Riker indicated the base, without touching anything. "Tear it off."

Pole did so, and frowned down at it.

"Read what it says, Colonel Pole."

"It says, five-three-three-two-one-one-four. But how the devil am I supposed to know if that's right?"

"It will be correct, Colonel, believe me." Riker showed total self-confidence. He turned to Darwin. "Doctor, would you perhaps like to perform your own experiments?"

Darwin had been hovering close, like a child forbidden to touch a new toy. He nodded at once.

Pole gave up his seat and retreated to a corner of the room, frowning over the cardboard strip that he held. Darwin took Pole's place, his broad rump overflowing the sides of the stool. He employed each feature of the engine systematically, one after another. He paid particular attention to the length of the pause that followed each problem, and he studied the printed output carefully as it emerged.

"It's right!" Pole returned from the corner, where he had been scribbling on the slip of stiff paper. "Damme, I checked the answer by hand, and every digit is just as it should be. Professor, it's amazing."

"Would it not be stranger, Colonel Pole, if most were right and one was wrong?"

"But how the devil does it do it?"

Riker smiled indulgently. "That, sir, must remain my secret. Let me say that no clock maker in Europe—no, in all the world—is able to construct its like." He turned to Darwin. "Your hosts have seen the engine in operation before, several times. Do you have questions?"

Darwin shook his head and hunched low on the stool.

"Then with your permission." Riker addressed the waiting menservants. "Take the engine and place it on my gig—and carefully." Then, to the Solbornes and their visitors, "I must be on my way to Abbotsbury, as soon as the calculating engine is safely housed. My apologies if I do not stay longer."

The heavy machine was hauled downstairs and loaded carefully on board Riker's waiting gig. The professor bade goodnight to Darwin, who had followed him downstairs, and drove off. Darwin frowned after the light carriage, listening to the fading sound of the horse's hooves on the gravel. The fog of early evening had cleared, giving way to a faint and eerie sea-mist that came and went at random.

Solborne was waiting anxiously when he went back upstairs.

"Well?"

"Where is your sister?"

"She has retired to her rooms, probably for the night. She pleads fatigue. But what of Riker?"

"I agree with you. He is not at all what he pretends to be."

"You mean, he is a—a—"

"I do not mean that he is a vampire. He is something much more ordinary, and possibly far more dangerous."

"But my sister—when he was here, did you not see the change in her? She gazed at him steadily, and she did not speak one word."

"It was not necessary. Everything was pre-arranged. Can you be at the front door, warmly clad, in five minutes?"

"Of course. But why?"

Darwin ignored the question. He went across to Jacob Pole, who sat smoking his pipe, spitting into the fire, and staring over and over again at the printed figures produced by Riker's calculating engine. "Jacob, stir yourself. Our work for the evening is not yet over."

"Eh?"

"You will see. Get your warmest clothes, and meet me by the front door in five minutes."

"*Eh?*"

"We are going to track down a vampire. What else?"

"We are going to *what*?" Pole jerked upright and dropped his pipe. "My pistols—"

"Will hardly help, I think." Darwin was already heading

down the stairs to the main hall, where his own cloak and broad-brimmed hat had been hung on an antlered stand. "What possible use could pistols be," he said cheerfully over his shoulder, "against a vampire?"

Newlands stood close to the edge of the high sea-bank, which at this point of its southern course was a steep cliff dropping away to the water. Beyond the big house the shoreline ran in a concave curve. By walking fifty yards south, the three men could achieve a good view of the high tower containing Helen's suite of rooms. Beyond it, almost invisible, stood the house's dim-lit central portion and the north tower.

Darwin brought them to a halt. Solborne gazed around at the dreary and silent horizon.

"What now? I don't see a thing."

"It may take a while. Keep your eyes there." Darwin's pudgy forefinger was pointing to the south tower, where the highest window was faintly visible as a dark outline in white stone.

Tom Solborne frowned, while Pole kept his hand on one of two pistols stuck in his belt. It was easy to imagine a dark shape, hovering outside the curtained window or creeping up the smooth wall. Even if legend said that a lead ball would not work, it was certainly worth a try.

The wait stretched into twenty minutes, while the air grew colder and the men shivered. Three minutes more, and a series of creaking sounds disturbed the breathless night. They came from the upper levels of the white tower.

"Very soon now," breathed Darwin.

"Where is it?" Solborne scanned the tower from top to bottom. "What is it? How does it get in?"

"Not in." A different sound was added to Darwin's words, the whir of cords on pulleys. "Not in. *Out.*"

Heavy curtains across the high window were suddenly drawn aside. A beam of light, faintly visible in the mist that still swirled along the shore, speared out over the sea. It shone for twenty seconds, then vanished behind closing curtains. Half a minute later the curtains opened and the light was visible again.

"Now." Darwin was already on the move. "While Helen is preoccupied. Quickly."

The others hurried after him into the main door of the house and on up the left-hand stairs. They passed Joan Rowland's room, where Darwin paused long enough to look in on the startled girl and place a finger to his lips.

"Softly, now." He was opening the door to the south tower, slowly and silently. "I checked earlier that there is no lock here, but any loud sound would reveal our presence. Keep to the wall."

The advice was necessary. They were ascending the curved staircase in near-total darkness. Up through the sitting room and study, up through the empty bedroom. Finally they were on the flight of stairs that led to the dressing room. With the other two right behind him Darwin paused at the closed door, then rapidly swung it wide.

The room beyond was a confusion of light and shadow, of bright vertical bars marking boundaries for solid rectangles of darkness. That changed when Darwin seized one of the dark oblongs and spun it around on its axis. It became a full-length mirror, one of a dozen carefully placed around the walls of the room. Their glass picked up the light of four massive oil lamps in the middle of the chamber and reflected it as a single beam.

Helen Solborne had been crouched low by the window. She swung around as the door opened, dropping the cord to the window drapes. Darwin strode forward, picked up the cord, and decisively pulled the heavy curtains closed.

Helen remained kneeling, her face pale and tense. She

did not speak, but shrank back at Jacob Pole's accusing shout.

"Wreckers, by God! You're a damned wrecker, setting up false lights to deceive mariners! If I hadn't seen this, I wouldn't have believed it."

"Do not believe it yet." Darwin snuffed the light of three of the lamps, leaving one to illuminate the room. He turned to Tom Solborne, standing openmouthed in the doorway. "So much for your missing oil. Have there been reports of ships lost off this coast in the past few months?"

Solborne shook his head and stared at his sister.

"So it is not wreckers, Jacob," Darwin went on. "And it is not vampires. It is something with the potential to be more dangerous than both. It is *signals*, lights amplified by means of reflecting surfaces. I compliment you, Miss Solborne, on your mastery of light propagation and collimation." He waved his hand toward the array of mirrors. "But now it is over. Shall we then, as the bard advises, *'sit upon the ground and tell sad stories of the death of kings'*?"

"That was never our intent!" The blue eyes opened wide. "But you know. How can you? You arrived only this afternoon. Who told you? *What* told you?"

"No one told me. I know not from a single major event, but from an accumulation of many small ones. Now it is necessary that your brother know, too." When she remained silent, Darwin continued, "Come, Helen Solborne. This will serve better coming from you."

She shook her head, and turned her eyes to her brother.

"No? Very well." Darwin pushed three tall mirrors out of the way and pulled forth the chairs that stood behind them. He gestured to the others to sit down. "Apparently I must begin. You, Miss Solborne, may correct me as necessary.

"Your brother came to see me concerned only for your

welfare. You had, he feared, fallen under some evil influence. I must admit, my own first instinct upon hearing the circumstances was no more valid than his speculations on the undying monsters of Transylvania. For I thought of Dr. Franz Mesmer, whose 'animal magnetism' has allowed him for the past few years to achieve amazing control over subjects and patients in Vienna." Darwin regarded Helen Solborne with a definite glint of humor in his eye. "That theory did not survive my first exposure to you and Professor Riker. I judge you more likely to dominate and control *him*, than vice-versa.

"Nonetheless, I was forced to take seriously your brother's concern that you were the slave of an evil circumstance. I suspect that he may think so still, when he knows all. But I knew from my first look that you were—and are—not possessed by any demons but your own. You are suffering from one malady recognized by medical science: great fatigue. You have the look of someone who has seen no rest for many weeks. Of a woman, in fact, who occupies her nights providing signals that ships offshore are able to interpret."

"Smugglers!" Pole exclaimed. "They are running goods along Chesil Bank, and into The Fleet."

"Very true, Jacob." Darwin had one eye still on Helen Solborne. "Smugglers, however, who carry an unusual cargo. The Solborne family, as we were told on that first evening in Birmingham, does not lack for wealth. Can you see the mistress of Newlands, a lady of 'substantial independent means,' dealing in rope tobacco, Nantz brandy, or Alençon lace, when she can easily purchase them with her own funds?"

"It was a cargo more precious than lace," Helen said abruptly. "More valuable than gold or rubies. Brother, I seldom ask for anything, but I beg you, do not take this to the Court. Promise me that, and I will tell you everything."

Solborne had not sat down. He stared at her in total confusion.

"He cannot promise what he does not understand," Darwin said mildly. "Tell first, Miss Helen, then make your request."

"I cannot." And then, under Darwin's steady gaze, "But I must." She took a deep breath. "Very well. I will.

"Tom, you cannot guess how it distressed when you thought me the devoted slave of that—that *mountebank*, Riker. He is nothing, merely an intermediary for others. What I am doing, I do because I choose, not because I am in any way *controlled*. And this did not begin two months ago, with my trip to Bristol. It began a full year earlier, with my visit to France. I saw poverty there beyond imagining, people downtrodden and hopeless and reduced to animal existence. But in Paris I also met a group of men and women, small in numbers yet dedicated, who seek in France what was recently achieved by the American colonies: *freedom*."

"A revolt!"

"No, brother, not a revolt. A *revolution*. They cannot speak openly—King Louis, ineffectual as he seems, has ministers and minions both suspicious and bloodthirsty. Plans must be made in secret; in the churches, in the Paris catacombs, in the open fields, by sunlight and moonlight and candlelight. And still there is risk. When exposure comes too close, there is only one chance: the suspect must quit France entirely, and fly to another country. I have helped those in peril to find sanctuary." Helen Solborne walked forward and took her brother by the hand. "Tom, I have deceived you for one reason only: I seek to save human lives."

"I believe you." But Solborne was not looking at her. "If the King found out—he already becomes demented at any mention of the American revolt—he would fear for the spread to England, men would say treason—"

"And women would say compassion. Tom, I had no choice. Don't you see that?"

"It must stop, Helen. Tonight was the last time."

"The secret is out now. I will agree—if you will not go to London, and betray them. A score or more are here in England, facing certain death on a return to France."

"I will—think about it." Solborne met his sister's eyes for the first time. He sat down on one of the straight-backed chairs. "If you can promise me that there is nothing else. Nothing more that you are concealing from me."

"Brother, I will answer every question that you ask, openly and honestly. But do not betray those whose lives have depended on me."

Darwin caught Jacob Pole's eye, and jerked his head toward the door. "This is no part of our business," he said softly, as they headed down the stairs. "It is between Tom and Helen Solborne."

"Will she persuade him?"

"She is his little sister. She will throw herself on his mercy, and he will be unable to resist her."

"But 'Rasmus, this could be—*treason.*" Pole hissed the word. "If anything like the Americas were to happen here . . ."

"It will not. King George is sane only north-northwest, but there is too much of a bottom of good sense in our people and parliament for revolution to be a danger. The Continent is different. You heard Matthew Boulton. France is stirring, there is unrest in Bavaria and Bohemia. The royal courts must look out for themselves. The problems in Europe run broad and deep."

They had reached the bottom of the stairs and were passing Joan Rowland's room. She was standing by her bed in a long flannel nightgown, round eyed and as far from sleep as anyone could be.

Darwin turned to Pole. "I feared as much. Jacob, will

you do me a favor? Will you calm her fears, and tell her that it is quite safe to go to bed?"

"Me? You are the one who knows all."

"I lack your talent to soothe a lady's worries."

"Rubbish! You *boast* of it. Oh, all right." Pole turned into the bedroom. "You owe me, 'Rasmus," he said over his shoulder. And then, in a confiding voice to Joan, which happened to be quite loud enough for Darwin to hear. "You see how it is, Joan Rowland, the great Dr. Darwin goes off to roll his fat in a cozy bed, and leaves others to do his work."

Darwin smiled to himself as he continued into the dining room. He remained only long enough to adjust his scarf and button his greatcoat. Then he headed downstairs for the entrance hall. He left Newlands, and took the dark path that led south along the cliff.

Now came the difficult part.

Darwin walked slowly, chin tucked in low on his chest, hardly aware of the rough shingle beneath his feet. His eyes from time to time sought the sea to his right. Somewhere out there would be a ship, hove to, its crew perplexed. They would wonder, why had the signal light been interrupted? Was it safe to go ashore?

The house rented by Anton Riker was tiny, hardly more than a one-room cottage. There was no sign of the pony and trap in front of its only door. True to his word, Riker had gone to Abbotsbury, a few miles farther along the coast. Darwin could guess what that business was. Riker would soon be as confused as the ship's crew.

The cottage door was closed. It was hard to see anything through the single grimy window. A flickering light gleamed from within.

Darwin took a deep breath, swung the door open, and passed through in a single movement.

The low-ceilinged room was lit by two tallow candles

in stone bowls, one at each end of a table of knotty elm. The Riker calculating engine was on the floor over by the wall, looking exactly as it had in the Newlands' dining room. A bed stood to the right on one side of the fireplace, and on the other side was a child's cot.

Food was set out on the table: a leg of cold mutton, a great dish of pickled onions, dark bread and a steaming cauliflower. A quart pewter mug stood by the single plate. Next to that plate sat a man. He had a knife in his hand, and was about to slice mutton from the joint.

The man's legs dangled from the tall chair, and the crown of his head was no more than twelve inches above the table top.

Darwin nodded to him casually, as though meeting a dwarf late at night was the most normal and pleasant thing in the world.

"Good evening. I was hoping to converse with Professor Riker."

To anyone less observant, the other's brief hesitation would have passed unnoticed. "The professor is away on business," he said. And, when Darwin did not respond, "I am—his manservant. My name is Elie Marée."

The dwarf spoke good English, though with a definite Normandy accent. He slid down from the chair, moved away from the table, and bowed to Darwin. Standing, he was at most three and a half feet tall. His arms and legs were short and stubby, but the large head was well formed. Alert brown eyes swept Darwin from head to foot.

Darwin smiled his toothless smile. "I wonder if I might wait here for the professor's return."

Again, the pause for thought was scarcely discernible, but Darwin had a sense of rapid evaluation and of a definite choice made.

"Certainly." Marée waved to a seat at the other side of the table. "I am about to dine. If you would care to join me . . ."

"Perhaps a bite or two." Darwin sat down, picked up a pickled onion, and crunched it with pleasure. He wiped vinegar from his lips with his sleeve. The other man put out two plates, carefully carved mutton, and waited.

"I saw the calculating engine demonstrated earlier this evening." Darwin nodded to the machine. "It is a wonderful invention."

"Professor Riker is a man of outstanding talent."

"I would go beyond that." Darwin stood up from his chair and walked across to the engine. "This machine displays genius. One might even say it *contains* genius. Do you know the names of Jedediah Buxton, or George Lambert Walker?"

"They are new to me."

"They should not be. You have much in common with them. But one thing about this engine puzzles me more than any other."

"Indeed?" Marée's tone was completely neutral, but he had stopped carving. "I am afraid that an explanation must await Professor Riker's return."

"I am not sure of that. You see, Monsieur Marée, my question has nothing to do with the interior workings of the engine. It is something far more mundane."

The other remained silent.

"It is simply this," Darwin continued. "When the engine was brought to Newlands, it needed two servants to carry it to and from the carriage. But when Professor Riker left the Solborne house to bring the machine here, he was alone. The professor is not a man of powerful build. I wondered how it was possible for him, single-handed, to unload an engine heavy enough to need the efforts of two strong young men."

"I helped him." Marée was totally still.

"I feel sure that you did. In more ways than one." Darwin took hold of one corner of the calculating engine and lifted. It raised easily from the floor. "You helped to carry it, but more than that: you diminished its weight, from a hundredweight and more to less than half of that. By the amount, in fact, of your own weight."

Again, Marée's eyes showed that rapid evaluation and decision was going on behind them. The final shrug of his shoulders suggested that he did not care any more. He raised the carving knife, but only to spear slices of mutton and drop them onto the two plates.

"How much do you know—*Dr. Darwin*? I think you will agree that it gives away nothing to admit that I realize who you are."

"Nothing at all. One might say, in some sense, we were introduced to each other earlier this evening. Would you do me the honor of showing me the inner working of your invention?—I assume that it is all yours."

"Totally. Design and fabrication. Anton Riker is a brave man, and a good actor, but nothing more." Elie Marée hopped off his chair and went to crouch by the calculating engine. He pressed a concealed stud in the base, and the lower section slid open across its whole length like a drawer. "As you see. The levers here, that can be read off below as they are moved above. The type here, to print answers."

"Just so. But the *provision* of those arithmetical answers, Monsieur?"

Marée did not speak, but tapped his forehead.

Darwin nodded. "As I thought. I did not mention Jedediah Buxton and George Walker for no reason. They, like you, are phenomenal calculators, capable of feats of mentation far beyond most men. Unlike you, they lack the power of original engineering design." He leaned forward, examining the cavity at the base of the engine. "It is padded, but most cramped. Long hours inside must be uncomfortable."

"Believe me, Dr. Darwin, I am used to discomfort. The life of a dwarf is not all pleasure." For the first time,

Marée's voice betrayed emotion. He gestured to the engine. "Do you wish to see how I lie inside? It is a tight fit—even for a little man."

"That is not necessary. Come, eat your dinner. You have more than deserved it."

"I am not sure that I have appetite." But Marée closed the drawer and returned to the table. "What now, Dr. Darwin? You know my secret. You can easily expose me, and destroy my livelihood. You will surely not permit our other activities in England to continue. Whatever happens, I have no future."

Rather than answering at once, Darwin reached for a slice of mutton and began to chew on it moodily.

"There are other mysteries," he said at last. "It is not my purpose to cause you pain, but I do not understand why you follow such a life. You have great gifts, that is obvious. You have used them, too, but for deception. And you are here, in a foreign land, living with discomfort and uncertainty and danger—for you must know the consequences if your role in assisting a revolt in France were to be discovered. Why not use your powers openly, to do what you do so well?"

Despite his stated lack of interest in food, Elie Marée had begun to eat. He was picking at the cauliflower, breaking off pieces with his fingers. "What would be easy for another is not easy for me. May I tell a story, Dr. Darwin?"

"Whatever you wish, sir."

"I am twenty-seven years old. The life span of one such as I is not long—perhaps forty years. I do not complain of that. Christ and Alexander had fewer years to accomplish their work. But with the knowledge of short life, I am perhaps too impatient. I have always had a talent for engineering invention. Two years ago I had what seemed like a most valuable idea. As you know, water power increasingly runs our spinning wheels and looms.

But there is a problem in controlling the machinery to operate at a constant speed when the water flow varies.

"I have solved that problem. I place spring-loaded weights on the perimeter of the driven wheel. They move outward under centrifugal force as the spin increases, return inward as it decreases. Their changing position adjusts the water flow, according as the weights are farther from or nearer to the center. In this way, we can precisely govern and make constant the speed of the wheel, without human intervention. Do you follow?"

"I do, completely. It is most ingenious, and must be of vast value."

"I thought so. In fact, I was so convinced of its worth that I sought an audience with his Majesty, King Louis. I was quite prepared to offer my invention, without personal reward, for the good of France. But I made a fatal mistake. I was sure that King and Court would immediately grasp the significance of what I had done—as you did. The king, after all, has a reputation as a skilled locksmith. I did not think that a large working model would be necessary. Now I realize that I ought to have controlled some giant wheel on the Seine or the Loire River, to demonstrate an impressive mastery over Nature.

"But I did not. Instead, I brought to the Palace of Versailles a small scale model, without the means to drive it. I cannot describe my excitement as I waited in the antechamber for my audience. I had rehearsed a thousand times what I would say to the king.

"It was all in vain. I was lost as soon as I entered the door of the royal chamber, my model in my arms. A score of people were with the king, men and women both. I heard them titter and giggle and remark to each other as I came forward." Marée's voice became bitter. "To them I was not an inventor, Dr. Darwin, seeking to serve France. I was not even a man. I was a freak, a walking joke, a parody of humanity carrying in his arms a child's toy.

"I began my explanation, stammering and lame-tongued. The king was not listening, he was too distracted by his jesting courtiers. One of the gowned women said, with no attempt to keep the words from my ears, 'How does he propose to drive the little wheel? Piss on it, with his teeny-weeny little thing?'

"I stopped. The king waved a hand. I was ushered out. It was over, the end of my great audience."

Darwin nodded slowly. "Monsieur Marée, I understand the magnitude of your tragedy too well to offer sympathy. So let me instead ask two questions. First, would your 'speed governor' work as well to regulate the flow of steam?"

Marée frowned at the sudden change of subject. "I do not see why not. But I know little about steam power, although here in England it is much talked about."

"It will define the future. My second question: what will you do now?"

"I told you. Nothing. Unlike steam, I have no future."

"That is not an acceptable answer. I can see why you hate bitterly the court of France. I would feel the same. But vengeance can never make a full life. I have a different suggestion, if you will hear me out."

"Do I have a choice?"

"No. I speak now both as physician and engineer. For your physical condition, I regret to say that I can do nothing. It is congenital. For the rest—" Darwin rummaged in the pocket of his greatcoat, and came up with Jacob Pole's letter. "Do you have pen and ink?"

"I will get it."

Darwin smoothed a page and turned to its blank back side. "This part of the country may not be safe for you. You must travel to Birmingham, well north of here. When can you leave?"

"Nothing holds me here. If necessary I can leave at once."

"Good. I am going to give you an introduction to a Mr. James Watt." Darwin took the goose quill, dipped it, and began to write. "He will, at my request, employ you in the Soho works. I propose to point out that your possible contributions are many in number, and he should attend most carefully to your ideas on speed governors and anything else."

"Attend—as the court of France attended? Dr. Darwin, I may be in England, but my height is no greater than in Paris. I will be taken no more seriously."

"Not so. You do not know good Jimmy Watt." Darwin was scribbling furiously. "Talk to him of engineering, you could be stark naked and painted indigo and he would not notice. He has said to me, many a time, a man is not measured by wealth or stature or family name, but by the ideas that lie inside his head. You and he will get along famously—take my word on it. He will teach you *steam*."

He sanded the ink, blew on it, and stood up.

"Come to Newlands, early tomorrow morning. You will travel with Colonel Pole. You heard him, no doubt, tonight, but he did not see you and you observed only one aspect of him. You will discover the rest *in transit*. Let me only say that you may trust him with your life, and you should allow him to handle any emergency. As for me, I must divert to London for three days. When I return to Birmingham I look forward to hearing of your progress there."

He took one last look at the calculating engine, then went across to where Elie Marée was standing staring at the letter of introduction. He leaned down and held out his hand. "I say this, sir, in all sincerity. It has been an honor and a privilege to make your acquaintance."

The other man stretched up to his full height as they

shook hands. "And to make yours, Dr. Darwin." Elie Marée's eyes were level with Darwin's ample midriff. He raised them to the other man's face, and added in a voice of new confidence and optimism, "It is as you say, sir, a man must not be judged by his stature—or his *girth*."

A freezing wind blew in Darwin's face as he walked the edge of the cliff, but he chuckled at Marée's remark. A joke was the best barometer of mental weather. Forget Elie Marée's size. The man was *tough*. He would survive, and for him the best years were yet to be. James Watt would welcome him like a brother, and between them they would light a torch to set the world ablaze.

And when that happened—Darwin's thoughts grew more somber—Elie Marée would have his revenge. The force of science was stirring in the world, and the old order of courts and emperors could not stand against it. This cold wind of midnight, blowing south into Europe, was for the old regimes. With America gone, who could say where lightning might strike next? The crowned heads of Europe had reason to rest uneasy on their robed shoulders.

Darwin opened the front door of Newlands quietly and went light-footed upstairs. He hesitated on the landing. Should he wake Jacob Pole, and tell him what had happened?

No. He proceeded to his own bedroom. Tonight his thoughts were too dark for any company but his own. Tomorrow would be soon enough for his old friend to make the acquaintance of a great man.

THE TREASURE OF ODIREX

"The fever will break at dawn. If she wakes before that, no food. Boiled water only, if she asks for drink. I will infuse a febrifuge now, that you can give in three hours time if she is awake and the fever has not abated."

Darwin rose heavily from the bedside and moved to the fireplace, where oil lamps illuminated the medical chest standing on the oak escritoire. It was past midnight, and he moved as though he was weary to the bone.

Jacob Pole had been standing motionless by the fire, his eyes fixed on the restless form of the young woman lying on the bed. Now he bit his lip and shook his head unhappily.

"I just wish that you could stay the night, Erasmus. It's late already. Are you sure that the fever will lessen?"

"As sure as a man can be, Jacob, when we deal with disease. I wish that I could stay, but there is a bad case of puerperal fever in Rugeley that I must see tonight. Already the ways are becoming foul, but you know as well as I do that sickness will not wait on convenience."

He looked ruefully down at his leather leggings, spattered with drying mud from the late November rain. "If
anything changes for the worse, send Prindle after me.
He knows the route well. And before I go I will leave
you materials for tisanes, and instructions to prepare them.
Do you have somebody reliable to help you with them?"

"I do. But these will be done with my own hands. I
will trust you with her, but no one else."

"Aye, I should have known that. I'm sorry, Jacob. Weariness has a hold on me. I'll wake when I have a few
breaths of the night air."

He began to select from the medical chest, while his
companion walked to the bedside and gazed unhappily
at his wife as she tossed in fevered sleep. His weariness
showed only in his reddened eyes, and the more pronounced trembling of his thin hands.

Erasmus Darwin looked at him sympathetically as he
sorted the drugs he needed, then took paper and quill
and prepared careful written instructions for their use.

"Attend now, Jacob," he said, as he handed him the
written sheets. "There is one preparation here that I would
normally insist on administering myself. These are dried
tubers of aconite, cut fine. You must make an infusion
for three hundred pulse beats, then let it cool before you
use it. It serves as a febrifuge, to reduce fever, and also
as a sudorific, to induce sweating. That is good for these
cases. If the fever should continue past dawn, here is
dried willow bark, for an infusion to lower body temperature."

"After dawn. Yes. And these two?" Jacob Pole held up
the other packets.

"Use them only in emergency. If there should be con-
vulsions, send for me at once, but give this as a tisane
until I arrive. It is dried celandine, together with dried
flowers of silverweed. And if there is persistent coughing,
make a decoction of these, dried flowers of speedwell."

He looked closely at the other man and nodded slightly to himself as he saw the faint hand tremor and yellowish eyes. He rummaged again in the medical chest.

"And here is one for you, Jacob." He raised his hand, stifling the other's protest. "Don't deny it. I saw the signs again when I first walked in here tonight. Malaria and Jacob Pole are old friends, are they not? Here is cinchona, Jesuit-bark, for your use. Be thankful that I have it with me—there's little enough call for it on my usual rounds. Rheumatism and breech babies, that's my fate."

During his description of the drugs and their use, his voice had been clear and unhesitating. Now, at the hint of humor, his usual stammer was creeping back in.

Jacob Pole was glad to hear it. It meant that the physician was confident enough to permit his usual optimistic outlook to reemerge.

"Come on, then, Erasmus," he said. "Your carriage should still be ready and waiting. I can't tell you how much I appreciate what you've done for us. First Emily, and now Elizabeth. One life can never repay for two, but you know I'm ready should you ever need help yourself."

The two men took a last look at the sleeping patient, then Jacob Pole picked up the medical chest and they left the room. As they did so, the housekeeper came in to maintain the vigil on Elizabeth Pole. They walked quietly past her, down the stairs and on to the front of the silent house. Outside, the night sky was clear, with a gibbous moon nearing the full. A hovering ground mist hid the fields, and the distant lights of Lichfield seemed diffuse and deceptively close. The sulky was waiting, the old horse standing patiently between the shafts and munching quietly at her nosebag.

"That's strange." Jacob Pole paused in his work of filling the mare's nosebag. He looked down the road to the south. "Do you hear it, Erasmus? Unless my ears are going, there's a horseman coming this way, along the low road."

"Coming here?"

"Must be. There's no other house between here and Kings Bromley. But I don't expect visitors at this hour. Did you promise to make any calls out that way?"

"Not tonight."

They stood in silence as the faint jingling of harness grew steadily louder. The rider who at last came into view seemed to be mounted on a legless horse, smoothly breasting the swirling ground mist. The Derbyshire clay, still slick and moist from the afternoon rain, muffled the sound of the hooves. The rider approached like a phantom. As he grew closer they could see him swaying a little in the saddle, as though half asleep. He cantered up to them and pulled aside the black face-cloth that covered his nose and mouth.

"I'm seeking Dr. Darwin. Dr. Erasmus Darwin." The voice was soft and weary, with the flat vowels of a northcountryman.

"Then you need seek no further." Jacob Pole stepped forward. "This is Dr. Darwin, and I am Colonel Pole. What brings you here so late?"

The other man stiffly dismounted, stretching his shoulders and bowing at the waist to relieve the cramped muscles of a long ride. He grunted in relief, then turned to Darwin.

"Your housekeeper finally agreed to tell me where you were, Doctor. My name is Thaxton, Richard Thaxton. I must talk to you."

"An urgent medical problem?"

Thaxton hesitated, looking warily at Jacob Pole. "Perhaps. Or worse." He rubbed at the black stubble on his long chin. " 'Canst thou not minister to a mind diseased?' "

"Better perhaps than Macbeth could." Erasmus Darwin stood for a moment, head hunched forward on his heavy shoulders. "Who suggested that you come to me?"

"Dr. Warren."

"Warren of London?" Darwin's voice quickened with interest. "I doubt that I can do anything for you that he cannot. Why did he not treat your problem himself?"

Again the other man hesitated. "If Dr. Warren is an old friend, I fear that I bring you bad news. He can no longer sustain his practice. His health is failing, and he confided in me his belief that he is consumptive."

"Then that is bad news indeed." Darwin shook his head sadly. "To my mind, Warren is the finest diagnostician in Europe. If he has diagnosed consumption in himself, the prospect is bleak indeed."

"He holds you to be his master, especially in diseases of the mind. Dr. Darwin, I have ridden nonstop from London, and I must get back to Durham as soon as possible. But I must talk with you. Dr. Warren offers you as my only hope."

Thaxton's hands were trembling with weariness as they held the bridle. Darwin scrutinized him closely, measuring the fatigue and the despair.

"We will talk, Mr. Thaxton, never fear. But I cannot stay to do it. There is an urgent case of childbed fever six miles west of here. It cannot wait." He gestured at the carriage. "However, if you would be willing to squeeze into the sulky with me, we could talk as we travel. And there is a hamper of food, that you look to be sorely in need of."

"What about my horse?"

"Leave that to me." Jacob Pole stepped forward. "I'll see he gets a rubdown and feed. Erasmus, I suggest that you come back here when you are done, and take some rest yourself. I can send one of the servants over to Lichfield, to tell your household that they can reach you here."

"Aye. It bids fair to be a long night. Say that I will be home before sunset tomorrow. This is a bad time of year for fevers and agues."

"No need to tell me that, Erasmus." Jacob Pole smiled ruefully and looked at his own shaking hand, as the other two men climbed into the carriage. As they moved off into the mist, he stirred himself with an effort and led the horse slowly to the stables at the rear of the house.

"It is a long and confusing story, Dr. Darwin. Bear with me if it seems at first as though I am meandering."

Food and brandy had restored Thaxton considerably. Both men had made good use of the hamper of food and drink balanced between them on their knees. Darwin wiped his greasy hands absentmindedly on his woollen shawl, and turned his head to face Richard Thaxton.

"Take your time. Detail is at the heart of diagnosis, and in the absence of the patient—since it is clear that you are not he—the more that you can tell me, the better."

"Not 'he,' Doctor. She. Three years ago my wife, Anna, went to see Dr. Warren. At that time we were living in the heart of London, hard by Saint Mary-le-Bow. She had been feeling lacking in strength, and was troubled by a racking cough."

"With bleeding?"

"Thank God, no. But Dr. Warren was worried that she might become phthisic. He recommended that we move away from the London style of life, to one with more of country ways and fresh air."

Darwin nodded approvingly. "Warren and I have seldom disagreed on diagnosis, and less still on treatment. You took his advice?"

"Of course. We moved back to my family home, Heartsease, near Milburn in Cumbria."

"I know the area. Up in the high fell country. Clean air, and clear sun. A good choice. But did it fail?"

"Not for my wife's general health, no. She became stronger and more robust. I could see the improvement, month by month. Then—about one year ago—there came another problem. She began to see visions."

Erasmus Darwin was silent for a long moment, while the carriage rolled steadily along the graveled roads. "I see," he said at last. "Invisible to others, I take it?"

"Invisible to all, save Anna. Our house stands north of Milburn, facing out across Cross Fell. Late at night, in our bedroom, when the Helm stands on the fell and the wind is strong from the north, she sees phantom lights moving on the fell slopes, and hears crying in the wind."

"You have looked for them yourself?"

"I, and others. I have brought our servants upstairs to look also. We see nothing, but Anna is persistent."

"I see." Darwin paused again, reflective, then shrugged. "Even so, it does not sound like a matter for serious concern. She believes that she can see what you cannot. What harm is there in a will-o'-the-wisp? It does not interfere with your life."

"It did not." Thaxton turned directly to Darwin, intense and troubled. "Until three months ago. Then Anna found a book in Durham telling of the early history of our part of the country. Cross Fell had another name, long ago. It was known as Fiends' Fell. According to legend, it was renamed Cross Fell when St. Augustine came with a cross to the fell and drove out the fiends. But Anna says that she has seen the fiends herself, on two occasions. By full moonlight, and only when the Helm is on the fell."

"Twice now you have mentioned the Helm. What is it?"

"Dense cloud, like a thunderhead. It sits as a bank, crouching over the top of Cross Fell. It does not move away, even when the wind sweeping from the top of the fell is strong enough in Milburn to overturn carts and uproot trees. Anna says that it is the source of the fiends."

Darwin nodded slowly. The two men rode on in silence for a while, both deep in thought.

"Nothing you have said so far suggests the usual mental diseases," Darwin said at last. "But the human mind is more complicated than we can guess. Tell me, has your wife any other fears or fancies? Any other fuel for her beliefs?"

"Only more legends." Thaxton shrugged apologetically. "There are other legends of the fell. According to the writings of Thomas of Appleby, in Roman times a great king, Odirex, or Odiris, lived in the high country of the fells. He acquired a great treasure. Somehow, he used it to banish the Romans from that part of the country, completely, so that they never returned."

"What was his treasure?"

"The legend does not tell. But according to Thomas of Appleby, Odirex hid his treasure on Cross Fell. Local folk say that it is there to this day, guarded by the fiends of the fell. Anna says that she has seen the guardians; that they are not of human form; and that they live on Cross Fell yet, and will sometime come down again."

Darwin had listened to this very closely, and was now sitting upright on the hard seat of the carriage. "A strange tale, indeed, and one that I have not heard before in all my reading of English myth and legend. Odirex, eh? A name to start trains of thought, if we will but remember our Latin. *Odii Rex*—the King of Hate. What else does Thomas of Appleby have to say about the King of Hate's Treasure?"

"Only that it was irresistible. But surely, Dr. Darwin, you are not taking these tales seriously? They are but the instruments that are turning my wife's mind away from sanity."

"Perhaps." Darwin relaxed and hunched low in his seat. "Perhaps. In any case, I would have to see your wife to make any real decision as to her condition."

"I can bring her here to see you, if you wish. But I must do it under some subterfuge, since she does not know that I am seeking assistance for her condition. As for money, I will pay any fee that you ask."

"No. Money is not an issue. Also, I want to see her at your home in Milburn." Darwin appeared to have made up his mind about something. "Look, I now have the responsibilities of my practice here, and as you can see they are considerable. However, I have reason to make a visit to York in a little more than two weeks' time. I will have another doctor, my *locum tenens*, working here in my absence. If you will meet me in York, at a time and place that we must arrange, we can go on together to Milburn. Then perhaps I can take a look at your Anna, and give you my best opinion on her—and on other matters, too."

Darwin held up his hand, to stem Thaxton's words. "Now, no thanks. We are almost arrived. You can show your appreciation in a more practical way. Have you ever assisted in country medicine, two hours after midnight? Here is your chance to try it."

"The roof of England, Jacob. Look there, to the east. We can see all the way to the sea."

Darwin was leaning out of the coach window, holding his wig on with one hand and drinking in the scenery, as they climbed slowly up the valley of the Tees, up from the eastern plain that they had followed north from the Vale of York. Jacob Pole shivered in the brisk east wind that blew through the inside of the coach, and huddled deeper into the leather greatcoat that hid everything up to his eyes.

"It's the roof, all right, blast it. Close that damn window. No man in his right mind wants to be out on the roof in the middle of December. I don't know what the devil I'm doing up here, when I could be home and warm in bed."

"Jacob, you insisted on coming, as you well know."

"Maybe. You can be the best doctor in Europe, Erasmus, and the leading inventor in the Lunar Society, but you still need a practical man to keep your feet on the ground."

Darwin grinned, intoxicated by the clear air of the fells. "Of course. The mention of treasure had nothing to do with it, did it? You came only to look after me."

"Hmph. Well, I wouldn't go quite so far as to say that. Damn it all, Erasmus, you know me. I've dived for pearls off the eastern Spice Islands; I've hunted over half the Americas for El Dorado; I've scrabbled after rubies in Persia and Baluchistan; and I've dug for diamonds all the way from Ceylon to Samarkand. And what have I got out of it? A permanent sunburn, a bum that's been bitten by all the fleas in Asia, and a steady dose of malaria three times a year. But I could no more resist coming here, when I heard Thaxton talk about Odirex's treasure, than you could stop . . . philosophizing."

Darwin laughed aloud. "Ah, you're missing the point, Jacob. Look out there." He waved a brawny arm at the Tees valley, ascending with the river before them. "There's a whole treasure right here, for the taking. If I knew how to use them, there are plants for a whole new medical pharmacopeia, waiting for our use. I'm a botanist, and I can't even name half of them. Hey, Mr. Thaxton." He leaned farther out of the coach, looking up to the driver's seat above and in front of him.

Richard Thaxton leaned perilously over the edge of the coach. "Yes, Dr. Darwin?"

"I'm seeing a hundred plants here that don't grow in the lowlands. If I describe them to you, can you arrange to get me samples of each?"

"Easily. But I should warn you, there are many others that you will not even see from the coach. Look." He stopped the carriage, swung easily down, and went off to a mossy patch a few yards to one side. When he came back, bareheaded, dark hair blowing in the breeze, he carried a small plant with broad leaves and a number of pale green tendrils with blunt, sticky ends. "There's one for your collection. Did you ever see or hear of anything like this?"

Darwin looked at it closely, smelled it, broke off a small piece of a leaf and chewed it thoughtfully. "Aye. I've not seen it for years, but I think I know what it is. Butterwort, isn't it? It rings a change on the usual order of things—animals eat plants, but this plant eats animals, or at least insects."

"That's right." Thaxton smiled. "Good thing it's only a few inches high. Imagine it ten feet tall, and you'd really have a 'Treasure of Odirex' that could have scared away the Romans."

"Good God." Jacob Pole was aghast. "You don't really think that there could be such a thing, do you—up on Cross Fell?"

"Of course not. It would have been found long ago—there are shepherds up there every day, you know. They'd have found it."

"Unless it found them," said Pole gloomily. He retreated even farther into his greatcoat, Thaxton climbed back into the driver's seat and they went on their way. The great expanse of the winter fells was spreading about them, a rolling sea of copper, sooty black and silver-grey. The land lay bleak, already in the grip of winter. At last, after three more hours of steady climbing, they came to Milburn. Thaxton leaned far over again, to shout into the interior of the coach. "Two more miles, and we'll be home."

The village of Milburn was small and windswept, a cluster of stone houses around the church and central common. Thaxton's coach seemed too big, out of scale with the mean buildings of the community. At the crossroads that led away to the neighboring village of Newbiggin, Thaxton halted the carriage and pointed to the great mass of Cross Fell, lying to the northeast. Darwin looked at it with interest, and even Jacob Pole, drawn by the sight of his potential treasure-ground, ventured out of his huddle of coats and shawls.

After a couple of minutes of silent inspection of the bleak prospect, rising crest upon crest to the distant, hidden summit, Thaxton shook the reins to drive on.

"Wait—don't go yet!" Darwin's sudden cry halted Thaxton just as he was about to start the coach forward.

"What is it, Dr. Darwin? Is something the matter?"

Darwin did not reply. Instead, he opened the carriage door, and despite his bulk swung easily to the ground. He walked rapidly across the common, to where a boy about ten years old was sitting by a stone milestone. The lad was deformed of feature, with a broad, flattened skull and deep-set eyes. He was lightly dressed in the cast-off rags of an adult, and he did not seem to feel the cold despite the biting breeze.

The child started up at Darwin's approach, but did not run away. He was less than four feet tall, heavy chested and bowlegged. Darwin stood before him and looked at him with a professional eye.

"What is it, Erasmus?" Jacob Pole had dismounted also and come hurrying after. "What's his disease?"

Darwin had placed a gentle hand on the boy's head and was slowly turning it from side to side. The child, puzzled but reassured by Darwin's calm manner and soft touch, permitted the examination without speaking.

"It is not disease, Jacob." Darwin shook his head thoughtfully. "At first I thought it must be, but the lad is quite healthy. Never in my medical experience have I seen such a peculiar physiognomy. Look at the strange bone structure of the skull, and the curious regression of the jaw. And see that odd curve, in the relation of the thoracic and cervical vertebrae." Darwin puffed out his full lips, and ran a gentle finger over the child's lumpy forehead. "Tell me, my boy, how old are you?"

The child did not reply. He looked at Darwin with soft, intelligent eyes, and made a strange, strangled noise high in his throat.

"You'll get no reply from Jimmy," said Thaxton, who had followed behind the other two men. "He's mute—bright enough, and he'll follow any instructions. But he can't speak."

Darwin nodded, and ran his hand lightly over the boy's throat and larynx. "Yes, there's something odd about the structure here, too. The hyoid bone is malformed, and the thyroid prominence is absent. Tell me, Mr. Thaxton, are the boy's parents from these parts of Cumbria?" Darwin smiled encouragingly at the lad, though his own lack of front teeth made that more frightening than reassuring. A piece of silver, pressed into the small hand, was more successful. The boy smiled back tentatively, and pointed upwards toward the fell.

"See, he understands you very well," said Thaxton. "His mother is up on Dufton Fell, he says." He turned away, drawing the other two men after him, before he continued in a low voice. "Jimmy's a sad case. His mother's a shepherdess, daft Molly Metcalf. She's a poor lass who doesn't have much in the way of wits. Just bright enough to tend the sheep, up on Dufton Fell and Cross Fell."

"And the father?" asked Darwin.

"God only knows. Some vagrant. Anyway, Jimmy's not much to look at, but his brain is all right. He'll never be much more than a dwarf, I fear, but there will always be work for him here in the village. He's trustworthy and obedient, and we've all grown used to the way he looks."

"He's certainly no beauty though," said Jacob Pole. "That's a strange deformity. You know what he reminds me of? When I was in the Spice Islands, there was a creature that the Dutch called the Orange-Lord, or Orang-

Laut, or some such name. It lived in the deep forest, and it was very shy; but I once saw a body that the natives brought in. The skull and bone structure reminded me of your Jimmy."

"It's a long way from the Spice Islands to Cross Fell, Colonel," said Thaxton. "And you can guess what Anna has been saying—that daft Molly was impregnated by a fiend of the fell, some diabolical incubus, and Jimmy is the devilish result. What do you think of that, Dr. Darwin?"

Erasmus Darwin had been listening absentmindedly, from time to time turning back for another look at the boy. "I don't know what to think yet, Mr. Thaxton," he finally replied. "But I can assure you of one thing. The only way that a human woman bears children is from impregnation by a human male. Your wife's chatter about an incubus is unscientific piffle."

"Impregnation is not always necessary, Doctor. Are you not forgetting the virgin birth of Our Lord, Jesus Christ?"

"Don't get him started on that," said Jacob Pole hastily, "or we'll be here all day. You may not know it, Mr. Thaxton, but this is Erasmus Darwin, the doctor, the inventor, the philosopher, the poet, the everything—except the Christian."

Thaxton smiled. "I had heard as much, to tell the truth, from Dr. Warren. 'If you are wise,' he said, 'you will not dispute religion with Dr. Darwin. If you are wiser yet, you will not dispute anything with him.' "

The men climbed back into the coach and drove slowly on through Milburn, to Thaxton's house north of the village. Before they went inside the big stone-built structure, they again took a long look at Cross Fell, rising vast to the northeast.

"It's clear today," said Thaxton. "That means that the Helm won't be on the fell, and Anna won't be seeing or hearing anything tonight. Dr. Darwin, I don't know what your diagnosis will be, but I swear to God that the next twenty-four hours will be the hardest for me of any that I can remember. Come in, now, and welcome to Heartsease."

Darwin did not speak, but he patted the other man sympathetically on the shoulder with a firm hand. They walked together to the front door of the house.

"They are taking an awfully long time." Richard Thaxton rose from his seat by the fire and began to pace the study, looking now and again at the ceiling.

"As they should be," said Jacob Pole reassuringly. "Richard, sit down and relax. I know Erasmus, and I've seen him work many times in the past. He has the greatest power of observation and invention of any man I ever met. He sees disease where others can see nothing—in the way a man walks, or talks, or stands, or even lies. And he is supremely thorough, and in the event of dire need, supremely innovative. I owe to him the lives of my wife, Elizabeth, and my daughter Emily. He will come down when he is satisfied, not before."

Thaxton did not reply. He stood at the window, looking out at the inscrutable bulk of Cross Fell. A strong northeast wind, harsh and gusting, bent the leafless boughs of the fruit trees in the kitchen garden outside the study window, and swirled around the isolated house.

"See up there," he said at last. "The Helm is growing. In another two hours the top of the fell will be invisible."

Pole rose also and joined him by the window. At the top of the fell, a solid bank of rolling cloud was forming, unmoved by the strengthening wind. As they watched, it grew and thickened, shrouding the higher slopes and slowly moving lower.

"Will it be there tonight?" asked Pole.

"Until dawn. Guarding the treasure. God, I'm beginning to talk like Anna. It's catching me, too."

"Has there ever been any real treasure on the fell? Gold, or silver?"

"I don't know. Lead, there surely is. It has been mined since Roman times, and there are mine workings all over this area. As for gold, I have heard much talk of it, but talk is easy. I have never seen nuggets, or even dust."

Jacob Pole rubbed his hands together. "That's meat and drink to me, Richard. Fiends or no fiends, there's nothing I'd like better than to spend a few days prospecting around Cross Fell. I've travelled a lot farther than this, to places a good deal more inhospitable, on much less evidence. Yes, and I've fought off a fair number of fiends, too—human ones."

"And you have found gold?"

Pole grimaced. "Pox on it, you would ask me that. Never, not a pinch big enough to cover a whore's modesty. But luck can change any time. This may be it."

Richard Thaxton pushed his fingers through his black, bushy hair, and smiled at Jacob Pole indulgently. "I've often wondered what would take a man to the top of Cross Fell in midwinter. I think I've found out. One thing I'll wager, you'll not get Dr. Darwin to go with you. He's carrying a bit too much weight for that sort of enterprise."

As he spoke, they heard the clump of footsteps on the stairs above them. Thaxton at once fell silent and his manner became tense and somber. When Erasmus Darwin entered, Thaxton raised his eyebrows questioningly but did not speak.

"Sane as I am," said Darwin at once, smiling. "And a good deal saner than Jacob."

"—or than you, Richard," added Anna Thaxton, coming in lightly behind Darwin. She was a thin, dark-haired woman, with high cheekbones and sparkling grey eyes. She crossed the room and put her arms around her husband. "As soon as Dr. Darwin had convinced himself that I was sane, he confessed to me that he was not really here to test me for a consumptive condition, but to determine my mental state. Now"—she smiled smugly—"he wants to do some tests on *you*, my love."

Richard Thaxton pressed his wife to him as though he meant to crack her ribs. Then her final words penetrated, and he looked at her in astonishment.

"Me! You're joking. I've seen no fiends."

"Exactly," said Darwin. He moved over to the table by the study window, where an array of food dishes had been laid out. "You saw nothing. For the past hour, I have been testing your wife's sight and hearing. Both are phenomenally acute, especially at low levels. Now I want to know about yours."

"But others were present when Anna saw her fiends. Surely we are not all blind and deaf."

"Certainly, all are not. But Anna tells me that when she saw and heard her mysteries on Cross Fell, it was night and you alone were with her upstairs. You saw and heard nothing. Then when you brought others, they also saw and heard nothing. But they came from lighted rooms downstairs. It takes many minutes for human eyes to acquire their full night vision—and it is hard for a room full of people, no matter how they try, to remain fully silent. So, I say again, how good are *your* eyes and ears?"

"I tell you, they are excellent!" exclaimed Thaxton.

"And I tell you, they are indifferently good!" replied Anna Thaxton. "Who cannot tell a rook from a blackbird at thirty paces, or count the sheep on Cross Fell?"

They still held each other close, arguing across each other's shoulder. Darwin looked on with amusement, quietly but systematically helping himself to fruit, clotted cream, Stilton cheese and West Indian sweetmeats from the side table. "Come, Mr. Thaxton," he said at last. "Surely you are not more prepared to believe that your wife is mad, than believe yourself a little myopic? Short-sightedness is no crime."

Thaxton shrugged. "All right. All right." He held his wife at arms' length, his hands on her shoulders. "Anna, I've never won an argument with you yet, and if Dr. Darwin is on your side I may as well surrender early. Do your tests. But if you are right, what does that mean?"

Darwin munched on a candied quince, and rubbed his hands together in satisfaction. "Why, then we no longer have a medical problem, but something much more intriguing and pleasant. You see, it means that Anna is *really* seeing something up on Cross Fell, when the Helm sits on the upland. And that is most interesting to me—be it fiends, fairies, hobgoblins, or simple human skullduggery. Come, my equipment for the tests is upstairs. It will take about an hour, and we should be finished well before dinner."

As they left, Jacob Pole went again to the window. The Helm had grown. It stood now like a great, grey animal, crouching at the top of Cross Fell and menacing the nearer lowlands. Pole sighed.

"Human skullduggery?" he said to Anna Thaxton. "I hope not. I'll take fiends, goblins and all—if the Treasure of Odirex is up there with them. Better ghouls and gold together, than neither one."

"Tonight? You must be joking!"

"And why not tonight, Mr. Thaxton? The Helm sits on the fell, the night is clear, and the moon is rising. What better time for Anna's nocturnal visitants?"

Richard Thaxton looked with concern at Darwin's bulk, uncertain how to phrase his thought. "Do you think it wise, for a man your age—"

"—forty-six," said Darwin.

"—your age, to undergo exertion on the fell, at night?

You are not so young, and the effort will be great. You are not—lissom; and it—"

"I'm fat," said Darwin. "I regard that as healthy. Good food wards off disease. This world has a simple rule: eat or be eaten. I am not thin, and less agile than a younger man, but I have a sound constitution, and no ailment but a persistent gout. Jacob and I will have no problem."

"Colonel Pole also?"

"Try and stop him. Right, Jacob? He's been lusting to get up on that fell, ever since he heard the magic word 'treasure,' back in Lichfield. Like a youth, ready to mount his first—er—horse."

"I've noticed that," said Anna Thaxton. She smiled at Darwin. "And thank you, Doctor, for tempering your simile for a lady's ears. Now, if your mind is set on Cross Fell tonight, you will need provisions. What should they be?"

Darwin bowed his head, and smiled his ruined smile. "I have always observed, Mrs. Thaxton, that in practical decision-making, men cannot compare with women. We will need food, shielded lamps, warm blankets, and tinder and flint."

"No weapons, or crucifix?" asked Richard Thaxton.

"Weapons, on Cross Fell at night, would offer more danger to us than to anyone else. As for the crucifix, it has been my experience that it has great influence—on those who are already convinced of its powers. Now, where on the fell should we take up our position?"

"If you are going," said Thaxton suddenly, "then I will go with you. I could not let you wander the fell, alone."

"No. You must stay here. I do not think that we will need help, but if I am wrong we rely on you to summon and lead it. Remain here with Anna. We will signal you—three lantern flashes from us will be a call for help, four a sign that all is well. Now, where should we position ourselves? Out of sight, but close to the lights you saw."

"Come to the window," said Anna Thaxton. "See where the spur juts out, like the beak of an eagle? That is your best waiting point. The lights show close there, when the fiends of the fell appear. They return there, before dawn. You will not be able to see the actual point of their appearance from the spur. Keep a watch on our bedroom. I will show a light there if the fiends appear. When that happens, skirt the spur, following westward. After a quarter of a mile or so the lights on the fell should be visible to you."

As she was speaking, the sound of the dinner gong rang through the house.

"I hope," she continued, "that you will be able to eat something, although I know you must be conscious of the labors and excitement of the coming night."

Erasmus Darwin regarded her with astonishment. "Something? Mrs. Thaxton, I have awaited the dinner bell for the past hour, with the liveliest anticipation. I am famished. Pray, lead the way. We can discuss our preparations further while we dine."

"We should have brought a timepiece with us, Erasmus. I wonder what the time is. We must have been here three or four hours already."

"A little after midnight, if the moon is keeping to her usual schedule. Are you warm enough?"

"Not too bad. Thank God for these blankets. It's colder than a witch's tit up here. How much longer? Suppose they don't put in an appearance at all? Or the weather changes! It's already beginning to cloud up a little."

"Then we'll have struggled up here and been half frozen for nothing. We could never track them with no moon. We'd kill ourselves, walking the fell blind."

The two men were squatted on the hillside, facing southwest toward Heartsease.

They were swaddled in heavy woollen blankets, and

their exhaled breath rose white before them. In the moonlight they could clearly see the village of Milburn, far below, etched in black and silver. The Thaxton house stood apart from the rest, lamps showing in the lower rooms but completely dark above. Between Darwin and Pole sat two shielded oil lanterns. Unless the side shutters were unhooked and opened, the lanterns were visible only from directly above.

"It's a good thing we can see the house without needing any sort of spyglass," said Pole, slipping his brass brandy flask back into his coat after a substantial swig. "Holding it steady for a long time when it's as cold as this would be no joke. If there are fiends living up here, they'll need a fair stock of Hell-fire with them, just to keep from freezing. Damn those clouds."

He looked up again at the moon, showing now through broken streaks of cover. As he did so, he felt Darwin's touch on his arm.

"There it is, Jacob!" he breathed. "In the bedroom. Now, watch for the signal."

They waited, tense and alert, as the light in the window dimmed, returned, and dimmed again. After a longer absence, it came back once more, then remained bright.

"In the usual place, where Anna hoped they might be," said Darwin. "Show our lantern, to let Thaxton know we've understood their signal. Then let's be off, while the moon lights the way."

The path skirting the tor was narrow and rocky, picked out precariously between steep screes and jagged outcroppings. Moving cautiously and quietly, they tried to watch both their footing and the fell ahead of them. Jacob Pole, leading the way, suddenly stopped.

"There they are," he said softly.

Three hundred yards ahead, where the rolling cloud bank of the Helm dipped lower to meet the broken slope of the scarp face, four yellow torches flickered and bobbed. Close to each one, bigger and more diffuse, moved a blue-green phosphorescent glow.

The two men edged closer. The blue-green glow gradually resolved itself to squat, misshapen forms, humanoid but strangely incomplete. "Erasmus," whispered Jacob. "They are headless!"

"I think not," came the soft answer. "Watch closely, when the torches are close to their bodies. You can see that the torch light reflects from their heads—but there is no blue light shining there. Their bodies alone are outlined by it." As he spoke, a despairing animal scream echoed over the fell. Jacob Pole gripped Darwin's arm fiercely.

"Sheep," said Darwin tersely. "Throat cut. That bubbling cry is blood in the windpipe. Keep moving toward them, Jacob. I want to get a good look at them."

After a moment's hesitation, Pole again began to move slowly forward. But now the lights were retreating steadily uphill, back toward the shrouding cloud bank of the Helm.

"Faster, Jacob. We've got to keep them in sight and be close to them before they go into the cloud. The light from their torches won't carry more than a few yards in that."

Darwin's weight was beginning to take its toll. He fell behind, puffing and grunting, as Pole's lanky figure loped rapidly ahead, around the tor and up the steep slope. He paused once and looked about him, then was off uphill again, into the moving fog at the edge of the Helm. Darwin, arriving at last at the same spot, could see no sign of him. Chest heaving, he stopped to catch his breath.

"It's no good." Pole's voice came like a disembodied spirit, over from the left of the hillside. A second later he suddenly emerged from the cloud bank. "They vanished into thin air, right about here. Just like that." He snapped his fingers. "I can't understand how they could have gone so fast. The cloud isn't so thick here. Maybe they can turn to air."

Darwin sat down heavily on a flat-topped rock. "More likely they snuffed their torches."

"But then I'd still have seen the body-glow."

"So let's risk the use of the lanterns, and have a good look around here. There should be some trace of them. It's a long way back to Heartsease, and I don't fancy this climb again tomorrow night."

They opened the shutters of the lanterns and moved cautiously about the hillside. Darwin knew that the Thaxtons would be watching from Heartsease, and puzzling over what they had seen. He interrupted his search long enough to send a signal: four lantern flashes—all goes well.

"Here's the answer." Jacob Pole had halted fifty feet away, in the very fringe of the Helm. "I ought to have guessed it, after the talk that Thaxton and I had earlier. He told me yesterday that there are old workings all over this area. Lead, this one, or maybe tin."

The mine shaft was set almost horizontally into the hillside, a rough-walled tunnel just tall enough for a crouching man. Darwin stooped to look at the rock fragments inside the entrance.

"It's lead," he said, holding the lantern low. "See, this is galena, and this is blue fluorspar—the same Blue John that we find back in Derbyshire. And here is a lump of what I take to be *barytes*—heavy spar. Feel the weight of it. There have been lead mines up here on the fells for two thousand years, since before the Romans came to Britain, but I thought they were all in disuse now. Most of them are miles north and east of this."

"I doubt that this one is being used for lead mining," replied Jacob Pole. "And I doubt if the creatures that we saw are lead miners. Maybe it's my malaria, playing up again because it's so cold here." He shivered all over. "But

I've got a feeling of evil when I look in that shaft. You know the old saying: iron bars are forged on Earth, gold bars are forged in Hell. That's the way to the treasure, in there. I know it."

"Jacob, you're too romantic. You see four poachers killing a sheep, and you have visions of a treasure trove. What makes you think that the Treasure of Odirex is gold?"

"It's the natural assumption. What else would it be?"

"I could speculate. But I will wager it is not gold. That wouldn't have served to get rid of the Romans, or any invader. Remember the Danegeld—that didn't work, did it?"

As he spoke, he was craning forward into the tunnel, the lantern held out ahead of him.

"No sign of them in here." He sniffed. "But this is the way they went. Smell the resin? That's from their torches. Well, I suppose that is all for tonight. Come on, we'd best begin the descent back to the house. It is a pity we cannot go farther now."

"Descent to the house? Of course we can follow them, Erasmus. That's what we came for, isn't it?"

"Surely. But on the surface of the fell, not through pit tunnels. We lack ropes and markers. But now that we know exactly where to begin, our task is easy. We can return here tomorrow with men and equipment, by daylight—perhaps we can even bring a tracking hound. All we need to do now is to leave a marker here, that can be seen easily when we come here again."

"I suppose you're right." Pole shrugged, and turned disconsolately for another look at the tunnel entrance. "Damn it, Erasmus, I'd like to go in there, evil or no evil. I hate to get this far and then turn tail."

"If the Treasure of Odirex is in there, it has waited for you for fifteen hundred years. It can wait another day. Let us begin the descent."

They retraced their steps, Jacob very reluctantly, to the downward path. In a few dozen paces they were clear of the fringes of the Helm. And there they stopped. While they had examined the entrance to the mine, the cloud cover had increased rapidly. Instead of seeing a moon shining strongly through light, broken clumps, they were limited to occasional fleeting glimpses through an almost continuous mass of clouds.

Jacob Pole shrugged, and looked slyly at Darwin. "This is bad, Erasmus. We can't go down in this light. It would be suicide. How long is it until dawn?"

"Nearly four hours, at a guess. It's bad luck, but we are only a week from winter solstice. There's nothing else for it, we must settle down here and make the best of it, until dawn comes and we have enough light to make a safe descent."

"Aye, you're right." Jacob Pole turned and looked thoughtfully back up the hill. "Since we're stuck here for hours, Erasmus, wouldn't it make sense to use the time, and take a quick look inside the entrance of the mine? After all, we do have the lanterns—and it may well be warmer inside."

"—or drier, or any other of fifty reasons you could find for me, eh?" Darwin held his lantern up to Pole's face, studying the eyes and the set of the mouth. He sighed. "I don't know if you're shivering with excitement or malaria, but you need warmth and rest. I wonder now about the wisdom of this excursion. All right. Let us go back up to the mine, on two conditions: we descend again to Heartsease at first light, and we take no risks of becoming lost in the mine."

"I've been in a hundred mines, all over the world, and I have yet to get lost in one. Let me go first. I know how to spot weak places in the supports."

"Aye. And if there's treasure to be found—which I doubt—I'd not be the one to deprive you of the first look."

Jacob Pole smiled. He placed one lantern on the ground, unshuttered. "Let this stay here, so Richard and Anna can see it. Remember, we promised to signal them every three hours that all is well. Now, let's go to it—fiends or no fiends." He turned to begin the climb back to the abandoned mine. As he did so, Darwin caught the expression on his face. He was nervous and pale, but in his eyes was the look of a small child approaching the door of a toy shop.

On a second inspection, made this time with the knowledge that they would be entering and exploring it, the mine tunnel looked much narrower and the walls less secure. Jacob, lantern partially shuttered to send a narrow beam forward, led the way. They went cautiously into the interior of the shaft. After a slight initial upward slant, the tunnel began to curve down, into the heart of the hill. The walls and roof were damp to the touch, and every few yards small rivulets of water ran steadily down the walls, glistening like a layer of ice in the light of the lantern.

Thirty paces on, they came to a branch in the tunnel. Jacob Pole bent low and studied the uneven floor.

"Left, I think," he whispered. "What will we do if we meet the things that live here?"

"You should have asked that question before we set out," replied Darwin softly. "As for me, that is exactly what I am here for. I am less interested in any treasure."

Jacob Pole stopped, and turned in the narrow tunnel. "Erasmus, you never cease to amaze me. I know what drives *me* on, what makes me willing to come into a place like this at the devil's dancing-hour. And I know that I'm in a cold sweat of fear and anticipation. But why aren't *you* terrified? Don't you think a meeting with the fiends would carry great danger for us?"

"Less danger than you fear. I assume that these

creatures, like ourselves, are of natural origin. If I am wrong on *that*, my whole view of the world is wrong. Now, these fiends hide on the fell, and they come out only at night. There are no tales that say they kill people, or capture them. So I believe that *they* fear *us*—far more than we fear them."

"Speak for yourself," muttered Pole.

"Remember," Darwin swept on, "when there is a struggle for living space, the stronger and fiercer animals drive out the weaker and more gentle—who then must perforce inhabit a less desirable habitat if they are to survive. For example, look at the history of the tribes that conquered Britain. In each case—"

"Sweet Christ!" Jacob Pole looked round him nervously. "Not a lecture, Erasmus. This isn't the time or the place for it. And not so loud! I'll take the history lesson some other time."

He turned his back and led the way into the left branch of the tunnel. Darwin sniffed, then followed. He was almost fat enough to block the tunnel completely, and had to walk very carefully. After a few steps he stopped again and looked closely at a part of the tunnel wall that had been shored up with rough timbers.

"Jacob, bring the light back for a moment, would you? This working has been used recently—new wood in some of the braces. And look at this."

"Sheep wool, caught on the splintered wood here. It's still dry. We're on the correct path all right. Keep going."

"Aye. But what now?"

Pole pointed the beam from the lantern ahead, to where the tunnel broadened into a domed chamber with a smooth floor. They walked forward together. At the other side of the chamber was a deep crevasse. Across it, leading to a dark opening on the other side, ran a bridge of rope guides and wooden planks, secured by heavy timbers buttressed between floor and ceiling. Pole shone his lantern across the gap, into the tunnel on the other side, but there was nothing to be seen there. They walked together to the edge.

"It looks sturdy enough. What do you think, Erasmus?"

"I think we have gone far enough. It would be fool-hardy to risk a crossing. What lies below?"

Pole swung the lantern to throw the beam downward. The pit was steep sided. About eight feet below the brink lay black, silent water, its surface smooth and unrippled. To right and left, the drowned chasm continued as far as the lantern beam would carry. Pole swung the light back to the bridge, inspecting the timbers and support-ing ropes.

"Seems solid to me. Why don't I take a quick look at the other side, while you hold the lantern."

Darwin did not reply at once. He was staring down into the crevasse, a puzzled frown on his heavy face.

"Jacob, cover the lantern for a moment. I think I can see something down there, like a faint shining."

"Like gold?" The voice was hopeful. Pole shuttered the lantern and they stared in silence into the darkness. After a few moments, it became more visible to them. An eerie, blue-green glow lit the pit below, beginning about three feet below the lip and continuing to the water beneath. As their eyes adjusted, they began to see a faint pattern to the light.

"Jacob, it's growing there. It must be a moss, or a fungus. Or am I going blind?"

"It's a growth. But how can a living thing glow like that?"

"Some fungi shine in the dark, and so do some ani-mals—glowworms, and fireflies. But I never heard of anything like this growth. It's in regular lines—as though it had been set out purposely, to provide light at the bridge. Jacob, I must have a sample of that!"

In the excited tone of voice, Pole recognized echoes of

of his own feelings when he thought about hunting for treasure. Darwin knelt on the rocky floor, then laboriously lowered himself at full length by the side of the chasm.

"Here, let me do that, Erasmus. You're not built for it."

"No. I can get it. You know, this is the same glow that we saw on the creatures on Cross Fell."

He reached over the edge. His groping fingers were ten inches short of the highest growth. Grunting with the effort, Darwin took hold of the loose end of a trailing rope from the bridge, and levered himself farther over the edge.

"Erasmus, don't be a fool. Wait until we can come back here tomorrow, with the others."

Darwin grunted again, this time in triumph. "Got it!"

The victory was short-lived. As he spoke the hemp of the rope, rotted by many years of damp, disintegrated in his grasp. His body, off balance, tilted over the edge. With a startled oath and a titanic splash, Darwin plunged headfirst into the dark water beneath.

"Erasmus!" Jacob Pole swung around and groped futilely in the darkness for several seconds. He at last located the shuttered lantern, opened it and swung its beam onto the surface of the pool. There was no sign of Darwin. Pole ripped off his greatcoat and shoes. He stepped to the edge, hesitated for a moment, then took a deep breath and jumped feet-first into the unknown depths of the black, silent pool.

"More than three hours now. They should have signalled."

"Perhaps they did." Richard Thaxton squinted out of the window at the dark hillside.

"No. The lantern has been steady. I'm worried, Richard. See, they set it exactly where the lights of the fiends disappeared into the Helm." Anna shook her head unhappily. "It must be freezing up on Cross Fell tonight. I just can't believe that they would sit there for three hours without moving or signalling, unless they were in trouble."

"Nor can I." Thaxton opened the window and stuck his head out. He stared at the bleak hillside. "It's no good, Anna. Even when the moon was up I couldn't see a thing up there except for the lantern—and I can only just see that when you tell me where to look. Let's give it another half hour. If they don't signal, I'll go up after them."

"Richard, be reasonable. Wait until dawn. You'll have an accident yourself if you go up there in the dark—you know your eyes aren't good enough to let you be surefooted, even by full moonlight."

The freezing wind gusted in through the open window. Thaxton pulled it closed. "At dawn. I suppose you're right. I'd best check the supplies now. I'll take medicine and splints, but I hope to God we won't be needing them." He stood up. "I'll tell two of the gardeners that we may have to make a rescue trip on the fell at first light. Now, love, you try and get some sleep. You've been glued to that window most of the night."

"I will." Anna Thaxton smiled at her husband as he left the room. But she did not move from her vigil by the window, nor did her eyes move from the single point of light high on the bleak slopes of Cross Fell.

The first shock was the cold of the water, enfolding and piercing his body like an iron maiden. Jacob Pole gasped as the air was driven from his lungs, and flinched at the thought of total immersion. Then he realized that he was still standing, head clear of the surface. The pool was less than five feet deep.

He moved around in the water, feeling with his stockinged feet until he touched a soft object on the bottom. Bracing himself, he filled his lungs and submerged to grope beneath the surface. The cold was frightful. It numbed his hands instantly, but he grasped awkwardly at Darwin's arm and shoulder, and hoisted the body to the level of his own chest. Blinking water from his eyes, he turned the still form so that its head was clear of the surface. Then he stood there shuddering, filled with the awful conviction that he was supporting a corpse.

After a few seconds, Darwin began to cough and retch. Pole muttered a prayer of relief and hung on grimly until the spasms lessened.

"What happened?" Darwin's voice was weak and uncertain.

"You fell in headfirst. You must have banged your head on the bottom." Pole's reply came through chattering teeth. His arms and hands had lost all feeling.

"I'm sorry, Jacob." Darwin was racked by another spell of coughing. "I behaved like an absolute fool." He roused himself. "Look, I can stand now. We'd better get out of here before we freeze."

"Easier said than done. Look at the height of the edge. And I see no purchase on either side."

"We'll have to try it anyway. Climb on my shoulders and see if you can reach."

Scrabbling with frozen hands on the smooth rock face, Pole clambered laboriously to Darwin's shoulders, leaned against the side of the pit, and reached upwards. His straining fingertips were a foot short of the lip. He felt in vain for some hold on the rock. Finally he swore and slid back into the icy water.

"No good. Can't reach. We're stuck."

"We can't afford to be. An hour in here will kill us. This water must be snow-melt from the fell. It's close to freezing."

"I don't give a damn where it came from—and I'm well aware of its temperature. What now, Erasmus? The feeling is going out of my legs."

"If we can't go up, we must go along. Let's follow the pool to the left here."

"We'll be moving away from the lantern light up there."

"We can live without light, but not without heat. Come on, Jacob."

They set off, water up to their necks. After a few yards it was clear that the depth was increasing. They reversed their steps and moved in the other direction along the silent pool. The water level began to drop gradually as they went, to their chests, then to their waists. By the time it was down to their knees they had left the light of the lantern far behind and were wading on through total darkness. At last, Jacob Pole bent forward and touched his fingers to the ground.

"Erasmus, we're out of the water completely. It's quite dry underfoot. Can you see anything?"

"Not a glimmer. Stay close. We don't want to get separated here."

Pole shivered violently. "I thought that was the end. What a way to die—stand until our strength was gone, then drown, like trapped rats in a sewer pipe."

"Aye. I didn't care for the thought. 'O Lord, methought what pain it was to drown, what dreadful noise of waters in my ears, what sights of ugly death within my eyes.' At least poor Clarence smothered in a livelier liquid than black fell water. Jacob, do you have your brandy flask? Your hand is ice."

"Left it in my greatcoat, along with the tinder and flint. Erasmus, I can't go much farther. That water drained all my strength away."

"Pity there's not more flesh on your bones." Darwin halted and placed his hand on Pole's shoulder, feeling the shuddering tremors that were shaking the other's skinny frame. "Jacob, we have to keep moving. To halt now is to die, until our clothes become dry. Come, I will support you."

The two men stumbled blindly on, feeling their way along the walls. All sense of direction was quickly lost in the labyrinth of narrow, branching tunnels. As they walked, Darwin felt warmth and new life slowly begin to diffuse through his chilled body. But Pole's shivering continued, and soon he would have fallen without Darwin's arm to offer support.

After half an hour more of wandering through the interminable tunnels, Darwin stopped again and put his hand to Pole's forehead. It burned beneath his touch.

"I know, 'Rasmus, you don't need to tell me." Pole's voice was faint. "I've felt this fever before—but then I was safe in bed. I'm done for. No Peruvian-bark for me here on Cross Fell."

"Jacob, we must keep going. Bear up. I've got cinchona in my medical chest, back at the house. We'll find a way out of here before too long. Just hang on, and let's keep moving."

"Can't do it." Pole laughed. "Wish I could. I'm all ready for a full military funeral, by the sound of it. I can hear the fife and drum now, ready to play me out. They're whispering away there, inside my head. Let me lie down, and have some peace. I never warranted a military band for my exit, even if it's only a ghostly one."

"Hush, Jacob. Save your strength. Here, rest all your weight on me." Darwin bent to take Pole's arm across his shoulder, supported him about the waist, and began to move forward again. His mood was somber. Pole needed medical attention—promptly—or death would soon succeed delirium.

Twenty seconds later, Darwin stopped dead, mouth gaping and eyes staring into the darkness. He was beginning to hear it, too—a faint, fluting tone, thin and ethereal, punctuated by the harsh deeper tone of drums. He turned his head, seeking some direction for the sound, but it was too echoing and diffuse.

"Jacob—can you tell me where it seems to be coming from?"

The reply was muttered and unintelligible. Pole, his body fevered and shaken with ague, was not fully conscious. Darwin had no choice but to go forward again, feeling his way along the damp, slick walls with their occasional timber support beams. Little by little, the sound was growing. It was a primitive, energetic music, shrill panpipes backed by a taut, rhythmic drumbeat. At last Darwin also became aware of a faint reddish light, flickering far along the tunnel. He laid Pole's semiconscious body gently on the rocky floor. Then, light-footed for a man of his bulk, he walked silently toward the source of the light.

The man-made tunnel he was in emerged suddenly into a natural chimney in the rock, twenty yards across and of indefinite height. It narrowed as it went up and up, as far as the eye could follow. Twenty feet above, on the opposite side from Darwin, a broad, flat ledge projected from the chimney wall.

Darwin stepped clear of the tunnel and looked up. Two fires, fuelled with wood and peat, burned on the ledge and lit the chimney with an orange-red glow. Spreading columns of smoke, rising in a slight updraft, showed that the cleft in the rock served as a chimney in the other sense. Behind the fires, a group of dark figures moved on the ledge to the wild music that echoed from the sheer walls of rock.

Darwin watched in fascination the misshapen forms that provided a grotesque backdrop to the smoky, flickering fires. There was a curious sense of regularity, of hypnotic ritual, in their ordered movements. A man less firmly rooted in rational convictions would have seen the fiends of Hell, capering with diabolic intent, but Darwin looked on with an analytical eye. He longed for a closer view of an anatomy so oddly distorted from the familiar human form.

The dancers, squat and shaggy, averaged no more than four feet in height. They were long-bodied and long-armed, and naked except for skirts and headdresses. But their movements, seen through the curtain of smoke and firelight, were graceful and well coordinated. The musicians, set back beyond the range of the firelight, played on and the silent dance continued.

Darwin watched, until the urgency of the situation again bore in on him. Jacob had to have warmth and proper care. The dancers might be ferocious aggressors, even cannibals; but whatever they were, they had fire. Almost certainly, they would also have warm food and drink, and a place to rest. There was no choice—and, deep inside, there was also the old, overwhelming curiosity.

Darwin walked forward until he was about twenty feet from the base of the ledge. He planted his feet solidly, legs apart, tilted his head back and shouted up to the dancers.

"It's no good, Anna. Not a sign of them." Richard Thaxton slumped on the stone bench in the front yard, haggard and weary. "They must have gone up, into the Helm. There's not a thing we can do for them until it lifts."

Anna Thaxton looked at her husband with a worried frown. His face was pale and there were dark circles under his eyes. "Love, you did all you could. If they got lost on the fell, they'd be sensible enough to stay in one place until the Helm moves off the highlands. Where did you find the lantern—in the same place as I saw it last night?"

"The same place exactly. There." Thaxton pointed a long arm at the slope of Cross Fell. "The trouble is, that's right where the Helm begins. We couldn't see much of anything. I think it's thicker now than it was last night."

He stood up wearily and began to walk toward the house. His steps were heavy and dragging on the cobbled yard. "I'm all in. Let me get a hot bath and a few hours sleep, and if the fell clears by evening we'll go up again. Damn this weather." He rubbed his hand over his shoulder. "It leaches a man's bones to chalk."

Anna watched her husband go inside, then she stooped and began collecting the packages of food and medicine that Richard in his weariness had dropped carelessly to the floor. As she rose, arms full, she found a small figure by her side.

"What is it, Jimmy?" The deformed lad had been leaning by the wall of the house, silent as always, listening to their conversation.

He tugged at her sleeve, then pointed to the fell. As usual he was lightly dressed, but he seemed quite unaware of the cold and the light drizzle. His eyes were full of urgent meaning.

"You heard what Mr. Thaxton said to me?" asked Anna. Jimmy nodded. Again he tugged at her arm, pulling her toward the fell. Then he puffed out his cheeks and hunched his misshapen head down on his shoulders. Anna laughed. Despite Jimmy's grotesque appearance, he had somehow managed a credible impersonation of Erasmus Darwin.

"And you think you know where Dr. Darwin is?" said Anna.

The lad nodded once more, and tapped his chest. Again, he pointed to Cross Fell. Anna hesitated, looking back at the house. After the long climb and a frantic four-hour search, Richard was already exhausted. It would serve no purpose to interrupt his rest.

"Let me go inside and write a note for Mr. Thaxton," she said. "Here, you take the food and medicine. We may need them." She handed the packages to Jimmy. "And

I'll go and get warm clothing for both of us from the house. How about Colonel Pole?"

Jimmy smiled. He drew himself up to his full height of three feet nine inches. Anna laughed aloud. The size and build were wrong, but the angular set of the head and the slightly trembling hands were without question Jacob Pole.

"Give me five minutes," she said. "Then you can lead the way. I hope you are right—and I hope we are in time."

At Darwin's hail, the dancers froze. In a few seconds, pipe and drum fell silent. There was a moment of suspense, while the tableau on the ledge held a frieze of demons against the dark background of the cave wall. Then the scene melted to wild confusion. The dancers milled about, most hurrying back beyond the range of the firelight, a few others creeping forward to the edge to gaze on the unkempt figure below.

"Do you understand me?" called Darwin.

There was no reply. He cursed softly. How to ask for help, when a common language was lacking? After a few moments he turned, went rapidly back into the tunnel, and felt his way to where Jacob Pole lay. Lifting him gently, he went back to the fire-lit chamber and stood there silently, the body of his unconscious friend cradled in his arms.

There was a long pause. At last, one of the fiends came to the very edge of the ledge and stared intently at the two men. After a second of inspection he turned and clucked gently to his companions. Three of them hurried away into the darkness. When they returned, they bore a long coil of rope which they cast over the edge of the ledge. The first fiend clucked again. He swung himself over the edge and climbed nimbly down, prehensile toes gripping the rope.

At the base he halted. Darwin stood motionless. At last, the other cautiously approached. His face was a devil-mask, streaked with red ocher from mouth to ears—but the eyes were soft and dark, deep-socketed beneath the heavy brow.

Darwin held forward Pole's fevered body. "My friend is sick," he said. The other started back at his voice, then again came slowly closer.

"See, red-man," said Darwin. "He burns with fever." Again, he nodded at Pole's silent form.

The fiend came closer yet. He looked at Pole's face, then put a hesitant hand out to feel the forehead. He nodded, and muttered to himself. He felt for the pulse in Pole's scrawny neck and grunted unhappily.

Darwin looked at him with an approving eye. "Aye, doctor," he said quietly. "See the problem? If we don't get him back home, to where I can give him medicine and venesection, he'll be dead in a few hours. What can you do for us, red-man?"

The fiend showed no sign of understanding Darwin's speech, but he looked at the other with soft, intelligent eyes. Darwin, no Adonis at the best of times, was something to look at. His clothes, wrinkled and smeared, hung like damp rags on his corpulent body. He had lost hat and wig in his descent into the pool, and his face was grimed and filthy from their travels through the tunnels of the mine. On his left hand, a deep cut had left streaks of dried blood along wrist and sleeve.

Darwin stood there steadily, heedless of his appearance. The fiend finally completed his inspection. He took Darwin by the arm and led him to the foot of the ledge. After slipping the rope around Jacob Pole's body and making it fast, he called a liquid phrase to the group above. The fiends on the ledge hoisted Pole to the top and then—with considerably greater effort—did the same for Darwin. The red-smeared fiend shinned up lightly after them.

The others, taking the rope with them, quietly hurried away into the dark tunnel that led from the cave.

Together, Darwin and the fiend lifted Jacob Pole and laid him gently on a heap of sheepskins and rabbit furs. The red-man then also hurried away into the darkness. For the first time, Darwin was alone and could take a good look around him on the ledge.

The area was a communal meeting-place and eating-place. Two sheep carcasses, butchered and dressed, hung from a wooden tripod near one of the fires. Pole lay on his pile of furs about ten feet from the other fire, near enough for a comforting warmth to be cast on the sick man. Darwin walked over to the large black pot that nestled in the coals there. He bent over and sniffed it. Hot water. Useful, but not the source of the tantalizing smell that had filled his nostrils. He walked to the other fire, where an identical pot had been placed. He sniffed again. His stomach rumbled sympathetically. It was mutton broth. Darwin helped himself with the clay ladle and sipped appreciatively while he completed his inspection of the ledge.

Clay pots were stacked neatly along the nearer wall. Above them a series of murals had been painted in red and yellow ocher. The figures were stylized, with little attempt at realism in the portrayal of the fiends. Darwin was intrigued to see that many of them were set in forest backgrounds, showing boars and deer mingled with the distorted human figures. The animals, unlike the humanoids, were portrayed with full realism.

The other wall also bore markings, but they were more mysterious—a complex, intertwined network of lines and curves, drawn out in yellow ocher. At the foot of that wall lay a heap of jackets and leggings, made from crudely stitched rabbit skins. Darwin's eye would have passed by them, but he caught a faint bluish gleam from the ones farthest from the fire. He walked over to them and picked one up. It shone faintly, with the blue-green glow that they had seen moving on Cross Fell, and again near the rope bridge.

Darwin took a tuft of fur between finger and thumb, pulled it loose and slipped it into his damp coat pocket. As he did so, the red-man appeared from the tunnel, closely followed by a female fiend. She had a red-streaked face with similar markings, and was carrying a rough wooden box. Giving Darwin a wide berth, she set the box beside Jacob Pole. The red-man brought a clay pot from the heap by the wall, filled it with scalding water from the cauldron by the fire, and opened the wooden box. He seemed absorbed in his actions, completely oblivious to Darwin's presence.

"I see," said Darwin reflectively. "A medicine chest, no less. And what, I wonder, are the prescriptive resources available to the medical practitioner on Cross Fell?" He stooped to watch the red-man at his work.

"That one looks familiar enough. Dried bilberries— though I doubt their efficacy. And this is—what?—bog rosemary? And here is dried tormentil, and blue gentian. Sound enough." He picked up a petal and chewed on it thoughtfully. "Aye, and flowers of violet, and dried holly leaves. You have the right ideas, red-man—I've used those myself in emergency. But what the devil are these others?" He sniffed at the dried leaves. "This could be bog asphodel, and I think these may be tansy and spleenwort. But this?" He shook his head. "A fungus, surely— but surely not fly agaric!"

While he mused, the fiend was equally absorbed. He selected pinches of various dried materials from the chest and dropped them into the scalding water in the clay pot. He muttered quietly to himself as he did so, a soft stream of liquid syllables.

At last he seemed satisfied. Darwin leaned over and sniffed the infusion. He shook his head again.

"It worries me. I doubt that this is any better than prancing around Jacob to ward off evil spirits. But my judgment is worthless with those drugs. Do your best, red-man."

The other looked up at Darwin, peering from under his heavy brows. He smiled, and closed the box. The female fiend picked up the clay pot, while the red-man went to Jacob Pole and lifted him gently to a sitting position. Darwin came forward to help. Between them, they managed to get most of the hot liquid down Pole's throat.

Darwin had thought that the female was naked except for her short skirt. At close quarters, he was intrigued to see that she also wore an elaborately carved necklace. He bent forward for a closer look at it. Then his medical interests also asserted themselves, and he ran a gentle hand along her collarbone, noting the unfamiliar curvature as it bent toward her shoulder. The woman whimpered softly and shied away from his touch.

At this, the red-man looked up from his inspection of Jacob Pole and grunted his disapproval. He gently laid Pole back on the heap of skins. Then he patted the female reassuringly on the arm, removed her necklace, and handed it to Darwin. He pointed to the red streaks on her face. She turned and went back into the tunnel, and the red-man patted his own cheek and then followed her. Darwin, mystified, was alone again with Pole. The other fiends had shown no inclination to return.

Darwin looked thoughtfully at the remains of the infusion, and listened to Pole's deep, labored breathing. At last, he settled down on a second pile of skins, a few yards from the fire, and looked closely at the necklace he had been given. He finally put it into a pocket of his coat, and sat there, deep in speculation. One theory seemed to have been weakened by recent events.

When the red-streaked fiend returned, he had with him another female, slightly taller and heavier than the first.

He grunted in greeting to Darwin and pointed to the single line of yellow ocher on her cheek. Before Darwin could rise, he had turned and slipped swiftly away again into the recesses of the dark tunnel.

The female went over to Pole, felt his brow, and tucked sheepskins around him. She listened to his breathing, then, apparently satisfied, she came and squatted down on the pile of skins, opposite Darwin. Like the other, she wore a brief skirt of sewn rabbit skins and a similar necklace, less heavy and with simpler carving. For the first time, Darwin had the chance for a leisured assessment of fiend anatomy, with adequate illumination. He leaned forward and looked at the curious variations on the familiar human theme.

"You have about the same cranial capacity, I'd judge," he said to her quietly. She seemed reassured by his gentle voice. "But look at these supra-orbital arches—they're heavier than human. And you have less cartilage in your nose. Hm." He leaned forward, and ran his hand softly behind and under her ear. She shivered, but did not flinch. They sat, cross-legged, opposite each other on the piled skins.

"I don't feel any mastoid process behind the ear," Darwin continued. "And this jaw and cheek is odd—see the maxilla. Aye, and I know where I've seen that jawline recently. Splendid teeth. If only I had my Commonplace Book with me, I'd like sketches. Well, memory must suffice."

He looked at the shoulder and rib cage and moved his index finger along them, tracing their lines. Suddenly he leaned forward and plucked something tiny from the female's left breast. He peered at it closely with every evidence of satisfaction.

"*Pulex irritans*, if I'm any judge. Pity I don't have a magnifying glass with me. Anyway, that seems to complete the proof. You know what it shows, my dear?" He looked up at the female. She stared back impassively with soft, glowing eyes. Darwin leaned forward again.

"Now, with your leave I'd like a better look at this abdominal structure. Very heavy musculature here—see how well-developed the *rectus abdominis* is. Ah, thank you, that makes inspection a good deal easier." Darwin nodded absently as the female reached to her side and removed her brief skirt of rabbit skins. He traced the line of ribbed muscle tissue to the front of the pelvis. "Aye, and an odd pelvic structure, too. See this, the pubic ramus seems flattened, just at this point." He palpated it gently.

"Here! What the devil are you doing!" Darwin suddenly sat bolt upright. The female fiend sitting before him, naked except for her ornate necklace, had reached forward to him and signalled her intentions in unmistakable terms.

"No, my dear. You mustn't do that."

Darwin stood up. The female stood up also. He backed away from her hurriedly. She smiled playfully and pursued him, despite his protests, round and round the fire.

"There you go, Erasmus. I turn my back on you for one second, and you're playing ring-a-ring-a-rosy with a succubus." Pole's voice came from behind Darwin. It sounded cracked and rusty, like an unoiled hinge, but it was rational and humorous.

The female squeaked in surprise at the unexpected sound. She ran to the heap of furs, snatched up her skirt, and fled back into the dark opening in the wall of the ledge. Darwin, no less surprised, went over to the bed of furs where Pole lay.

"Jacob, I can't believe it. Only an hour ago, you were running a high fever and beginning to babble of green fields." He felt Pole's forehead. "Back down to normal, I judge. How do you feel?"

"Not bad. Damn sight better than I did when we got out of that water. And I'm hungry. I could dine on a dead Turk."

"We can do better than that. Just lie there." Darwin
went across to the other fire, filled a bowl with mutton
stew from the big pot, and carried it back. "Get this inside
you."

Pole sniffed it suspiciously. He grunted with pleasure
and began to sip at it. "Good. Needs salt, though. You
seem to be on surprisingly good terms with the fiends,
Erasmus. Taking their food like this, without so much as
a by-your-leave. And if I hadn't been awakened by your
cavorting, you'd be playing the two-backed beast this very
second with that young female."

"Nonsense." Darwin looked pained. "Jacob, she simply misunderstood what I was doing. And I fear the red-
man mistook the nature of my interest in the other female,
also. It should have been clear to you that I was examining her anatomy."

"And she yours." Pole smiled smugly. "A natural preliminary to swiving. Well, Erasmus, that will be a rare
tale for the members of the Lunar Society if we ever get
back to Lichfield."

"Jacob—" Darwin cut off his protest when he saw the
gleeful expression on Pole's face. "Drink your broth and
then rest. We have to get you strong enough to walk,
if we're ever to get out of this place. Not that we can
do much on that front. I've no idea how to find our way
back—we'll need the assistance of the fiends, if they will
agree to give it to us."

Pole lay back and closed his eyes. "Now this really feels
like a treasure hunt, Erasmus. It wouldn't be right without
the hardships. For thirty years I've been fly-bitten, sun-
baked, wind-scoured and snow-blind. I've eaten food that
the jackals turned their noses up at. I've drunk water that
smelled like old bat's-piss. And all for treasure. I tell you,
we're getting close. At least there are no crocodiles here.
I almost lost my arse to one, chasing emeralds on the
Ganges."

He roused himself briefly, and looked around him again. "Erasmus, where are the fiends? They're the key to the treasure. They guard it."

"Maybe they do," said Darwin soothingly. "You rest now. They'll be back. It must be as big a shock to them as it was to us—more, because they had no warning that we'd be here."

Darwin paused and shook his head. There was an annoying ringing in his ears, as though they were still filled with fell water from the underground pool.

"I'll keep watch for them, Jacob," he went on. "And if I can, I'll ask them about the treasure."

"Wake me before you do that," said Pole. He settled back and closed his eyes. Then he cracked one open again and peered at Darwin from under the lowered lid. "Remember, Erasmus—keep your hands off the fillies." He lay back with a contented smile.

Darwin bristled, then also smiled. Jacob was on the mend. He sat down again by the fire, ears still buzzing and singing, and began to look in more detail at the contents of the medical chest.

When the fiend returned he gave Darwin a look that was half smile and half reproach. It was easy to guess what the females must have said to him. Darwin felt embarrassed, and he was relieved when the fiend went at once to Pole and felt his pulse. He looked pleased with himself at the result, and lifted Pole's eyelid to look at the white. The empty bowl of stew sitting by Pole's side also seemed to meet with his approval. He pointed at the pot that had contained the infusion of medicaments, and smiled triumphantly at Darwin.

"I know," said Darwin. "And I'm mightily impressed, red-man. I want to know a lot more about that treatment, if we can manage to communicate with each other. I'll be happy to trade my knowledge of medicinal botany for yours, lowland for highland. No," he added, as he saw the other's actions. "That isn't necessary for me."

The fiend had filled another pot with hot water while Darwin had been talking, and dropped into it a handful of dried fungus. He was holding it forward to Darwin. When the latter refused it, he became more insistent. He placed the bowl on the ground and tapped his chest. While Darwin watched closely, he drew back his lips from his teeth, shivered violently all over, and held cupped hands to groin and armpit to indicate swellings there.

Darwin rubbed his aching eyes, and frowned. The fiend's mimicry was suggestive—but of something that seemed flatly impossible. Unless there was a danger, here on Cross Fell, of . . .

The insight was sudden, but clear. The legends, the King of Hate, the Treasure, the departure of the Romans from Cross Fell—at once all this made a coherent picture, and an alarming one. He blinked. The air around him suddenly seemed to swirl and teem with a hidden peril. He reached forward quickly and took the bowl.

"Perhaps I am wrong in my interpretation, red-man," he said. "I hope so, for my own sake. But now I must take a chance on your good intentions."

He lifted the bowl and drank, then puckered his lips with distaste. The contents were dark and bitter, strongly astringent and full of tannin. The red fiend smiled at him in satisfaction when he lowered the empty bowl.

"Now, red-man, to business," said Darwin. He picked up the medicine chest and walked with it over to the fire. He hunkered down where the light was best and gestured to the red fiend to join him. The other seemed to understand exactly what was on Darwin's mind. He opened the lid of the box, pulled out a packet wrapped in sheepgut, and held it up for Darwin's inspection.

How should one convey the use of a drug—assuming

that a use were known—without words? Darwin prepared for a difficult problem in communication. Both the symptoms and the treatment for specific diseases would have to be shown using mimicry and primitive verbal exchange. He shook off his fatigue and leaned forward eagerly to meet the challenge.

Three hours later, he looked away from the red fiend and rubbed his eyes. Progress was excellent—but something was very wrong. His head was aching, the blood pounding in his temples. The buzzing and singing in his ears had worsened, and was accompanied by a blurring of vision and a feeling of nausea. The complex pattern of lines on the cave wall seemed to be moving, to have become a writhing tangle of shifting yellow tendrils.

He looked back at the fiend. The other was smiling—but what had previously seemed to be a look of friendship could equally well be read as a grin of savage triumph. Had he badly misunderstood the meaning of the infusion he had drunk earlier?

Darwin put his hands to the floor and attempted to steady himself. He struggled to rise to his feet, but it was too late. The cave was spiralling around him, the murals dipping and weaving. His chest was constricted, his stomach churning.

The last thing he saw before he lost consciousness was the red-streaked mask of the fiend, bending toward him as he slipped senseless to the floor of the cave.

Seen through the soft but relentless drizzle, Cross Fell was a dismal place. Silver was muted to dreary grey, and sable and copper gleams were washed out in the pale afternoon light. Anna Thaxton followed Jimmy up the steep slopes, already doubting her wisdom in setting out. The Helm stood steady and forbidding, three hundred feet above them, and although she had looked closely in all directions as they climbed, she had seen no sign of Pole and Darwin. She halted.

"Jimmy, how much farther? I'm tired, and we'll soon be into the Helm."

The boy turned and smiled. He pointed to a rock a couple of hundred yards away, then turned and pointed upwards. Anna frowned, then nodded.

"All right, Jimmy. I can walk that far. But are you sure you know where to find them?"

The lad nodded, then shrugged.

"Not sure, but you think so, eh? All right. Let's keep going."

Anna followed him upwards. Two minutes later, she stopped and peered at a scorched patch of heather.

"There's been a lantern set down here, Jimmy—and recently. We must be on the right track."

They were at the very brink of the Helm. Jimmy paused for a moment, as though taking accurate bearings, then moved up again into the heavy mist. Anna followed close behind him. Inside the Helm, visibility dropped to a few yards.

Jimmy stopped again and motioned Anna to his side. He pointed to a dark opening in the side of the hill.

"In here, Jimmy? You think they may have gone in, following the fiends?"

The boy nodded and led the way confidently forward into the tunnel. After a moment of hesitation, Anna followed him. The darkness inside quickly became impenetrable. She was forced to catch hold of the shawl that she had given Jimmy to wear, and dog his heels closely. He made his way steadily through the narrow tunnels, with no sign of uncertainty or confusion. At last he paused and drew Anna alongside him. They had reached a rough wooden bridge across a deep chasm, lit faintly from below by a ghostly gleaming on the walls. Far below, the light reflected from the surface of a dark and silent pool.

Jimmy pointed to a group of objects near the edge: a lantern, shoes and a greatcoat. Anna went to them and picked up the coat.

"Colonel Pole's." She looked down at the unruffled water below. "Jimmy, do you know what happened to them?"

The boy looked uncomfortable. He went to examine the frayed end of the trailing rope that hung from the bridge, then shook his head. He set out across the bridge, and Anna again took hold of the shawl. Soon they were again in total darkness. This time they seemed to grope their way along for an eternity. The path twisted and branched, moving upward and downward in the depths of the fell.

At last they made a final turn and emerged without warning into a broad clear area, full of people and lit by flickering firelight. Anna, dazzled after long minutes in total darkness, looked about her in confusion. As her eyes adjusted to the light, she realized with horror that the figures in front of her were not men and women— they were fiends, powerfully built and misshapen. She looked at the fires, and shivered at what she saw. Stretched out on piles of rough skins lay Erasmus Darwin and Jacob Pole, unconscious or dead. Two fiends, their faces red-daubed and hideous, crouched over Darwin's body.

Anna did not cry out. She turned, twisted herself loose of Jimmy's attempt to restrain her, and ran blindly back along the tunnel. She went at top speed, though she had no idea where her steps might lead her, or how she might escape from the fiends. When it came, the collision of her head with the timber roof brace was so quick and unexpected that she had no awareness of the contact before she fell unconscious to the rocky floor. She was spared the sound of the footsteps that pursued her steadily along the dark tunnel.

Richard Thaxton surfaced from an uneasy sleep. The taste of exhaustion was still in his mouth. He sat up on the bed, looked out at the sky, and tried to orient himself. He frowned. He had asked Anna to waken him at three o'clock for another search of Cross Fell, but outside the window the twilight was already far advanced. It must be well past four, on the grey December afternoon. Could it be that Darwin and Pole had returned, and Anna had simply decided to let him sleep to a natural waking, before she told him the news?

He stood up, went to the dresser, and splashed cold water on his face from the jug there. Rubbing his eyes, he went to the window. Outside the weather had changed again. The light drizzle of the forenoon had been replaced by a thick fog. He could scarcely see the tops of the trees in the kitchen garden, a faint tangle of dark lines bedewed with water droplets.

The first floor of the house was cold and silent. He thought of going down to the servants' quarters, then changed his mind and went through to the study. The log fire there had been banked high by one of the maids. He picked up Anna's note from the table, and went to read it by the fireside. At the first words, his concern for Darwin and Pole was overwhelmed by fear for Anna's safety. In winter, in a dense Cumbrian fog, Cross Fell could be a death trap unless a man knew every inch of its sudden slopes and treacherous, shifting screes.

Thaxton put on his warmest clothing and hurried out into the gathering darkness. In this weather, the safest way up to the fell would be from the north, where the paths were wider—but the southern approach, although steeper and more treacherous, was a good deal more direct. He hesitated, then began to climb the southern slope, moving at top speed on the rough path that had been worn over the years by men and animals. On all sides, the world ended five yards from him in a wall of mist. The wind had dropped completely, and he felt like a man climbing forever in a small, silent bowl of grey fog. After ten minutes, he was forced to stop and catch his breath. He looked around. The folly of his actions was suddenly clear to him. He should now be on his way to Milburn, to organize a full-scale search party, rather than scrambling over Cross Fell, alone and unprepared. Should he turn now, and go back down? That would surely be the wiser course.

His thoughts were interrupted by a low, fluting whistle, sounding through the fog. It seemed to come from his left, and a good distance below him. The mist made distance and direction difficult to judge. He held his breath and stood motionless, listening intently. After a few seconds it came again, a breathy call that the fog swallowed up without an echo.

Leaving the path, he moved down and to the left, stumbling over the sodden tussocks of grass and clumps of heather, and peering ahead into the darkness. Twice, he almost fell, and finally he stopped again. It was no good, he could not negotiate the side of Cross Fell in the darkness and mist. Exploration would have to wait until conditions were better, despite his desperate anxiety. The only thing to do now was to return to the house. He would rest there as best he could, and be fit for another ascent, with assistance, when weather and light permitted it. Whatever had happened to Anna, it would not help her if he were to suffer injury now, up on the fell. He began a cautious descent.

At last he saw the light in the upper bedroom of the house shining faintly through the mist below him. Down at ground level, on the left side of the house, he fancied that he could see a group of dim lights, moving in the kitchen garden. That was surprising. He halted, and peered again through the darkness. While he watched, another low whistle behind him was answered, close to the house. The lights grew dimmer.

He was gripped by a sudden, unreasoning fear. Heedless of possible falls, he began to plunge full-tilt down the hillside.

The house and garden seemed quiet and normal, the grounds empty. He made his way into the kitchen garden, where he had seen the moving lights. It too seemed deserted, but along the wall of the house he could dimly see three oblong mounds. He walked over to them, and was suddenly close enough to see them clearly. He gasped. Side by side, bound firmly to rough stretchers of wood and leather, lay the bodies of Darwin, Pole and Anna, all well wrapped in sheepskins. Anna's cold forehead was heavily bandaged, with a strip torn from her linen blouse. Thaxton dropped to his knee and put his ear to her chest, full of foreboding.

Before he could hear the heartbeat, he heard Darwin's voice behind him.

"We're here, are we?" it said. "About time, too. I must have dropped off to sleep again. Now, Richard, give me a hand to undo myself, will you. I'm better off than Anna and Jacob, but we're all as sick as dogs. Myself, I don't seem to have the strength of a gnat."

"What a sight. Reminds me of the field hospital after a Pathan skirmish." Jacob Pole looked round him with gloomy satisfaction. The study at Heartsease had been converted into a temporary sickroom, and Darwin, Anna Thaxton and Pole himself were all sitting in armchairs by the fire, swaddled in blankets.

Richard Thaxton stood facing them, leaning on the mantelpiece. "So what happened to Jimmy?" he said.

"I don't know," said Darwin. He had broken one of his own rules, and was drinking a mug of hot mulled wine. "He started out with us, leading the way down while the rest of them carried the stretchers. Then I fell asleep, and I don't know what happened to him. I suspect you'll find him over in Milburn, wherever he usually lives there. He did his job, getting us back here, so he's earned a rest."

"He's earned more than a rest," said Thaxton. "I don't know how he did it. I was up on the fell myself in that fog, and you couldn't see your hand in front of your face."

"He knows the fell from top to bottom, Jimmy does," said Anna. "He was almost raised there." She was looking pale, with a livid bruise and a long gash marring her smooth forehead. She shivered. "Richard, you've no idea what it was like, following him through the dark in that tunnel, then suddenly coming across the fiends. It was like a scene out of hell—the smoke, and the shapes. I felt sure they had killed the Colonel and Dr. Darwin."

"They hardly needed to," said Pole wryly. "We came damned close to doing that for ourselves. Erasmus nearly drowned, and I caught the worst fever that I've had since the time that I was in Madagascar, looking for star sapphires. Never found one. I had to settle for a handful of garnets and a dose of dysentery. Story of my life, that. Good thing that Erasmus could give me the medicine, up on the fell."

"And that was no thanks to me," said Darwin. "The fiends saved you, not me. They seem to have their own substitute for cinchona. I'll have to try that when we get back home."

"Aye," said Pole. "And we'll have to stop calling them fiends. Though they aren't human, and look a bit on the fiendish side—if appearances bother you. Anyway, they did right by me."

Richard Thaxton dropped another log on the fire, and pushed a second tray of meat pasties and mince pies closer to Darwin. "But at least there *are* fiends on Cross Fell," he remarked. "Anna was right and I was wrong. It was a hard way to prove it, though, with the three of you all sick. What I find hardest to believe is that they've been there in the mines for fifteen hundred years or more, and we've not known it. Think, our history means nothing to them. The Norman Conquest, the Spanish Armada—they mean no more to them than last year's rebellion in the American Colonies. It all passed them by."

Darwin swallowed a mouthful of pie and shook his head. "You're both wrong."

"Wrong? About what?" asked Thaxton.

"Jacob is wrong when he says they are not human, and you are wrong when you say they've been up in the mines for fifteen hundred years."

There was an immediate outcry from the other three. "Of course they're not human," said Pole.

Darwin sighed, and regretfully put down the rest of his pie, back on the dish. "All right, if you want evidence, I suppose I'll have to give it to you. First, and in my opinion the weakest proof, consider their anatomy. It's different from ours, but only in detail—in small ways. There are many fewer differences between us and the fiends than there are between us and, say, a monkey or a great ape. More like the difference between us and a Moor, or a Chinee.

"That's the first point. The second one is more subtle. The flea."

"You'd better have some proof more substantial than that, Erasmus," said Pole. "You can't build a very big case around a flea."

"You can, if you are a doctor. I found a flea on one of the young females—you saw her yourself, Jacob."

"If she's the one you were hoping to roger, Erasmus, I certainly did. But I didn't see any flea. Of course, I didn't have the privilege of getting as close as you apparently did."

"All the same, although you didn't see it, I found a flea on her—our old friend, *Pulex irritans*, if I'm a reliable judge. Now, you scholars of diabolism and the world of demons. When did you ever hear of any demon that had fleas—and the same sort of fleas that plague us?"

The other three looked at each other, while Darwin took advantage of the brief silence to poke around one of his back teeth for a piece of gristle that had lodged there.

"All right," said Anna at last. "A fiend had a flea. It's still poor evidence that fiends are *human*. Dogs have fleas, too. Are you suggesting *they* should be called human? There's more to humanity than fleas."

"There is," agreed Darwin. "In fact, there's one final test for humanity, the only one I know that never fails."

The room was silent for a moment. "You mean, possession of an immortal soul?" asked Richard Thaxton at last, in a hushed voice.

Jacob Pole winced, and looked at Darwin in alarm.

"I won't get off on the issue of religious beliefs," said Darwin calmly. "The proof that I have in mind is much more tangible, and much more easily tested. It is this: a being is human if and only if it can mate with a known human, and produce offspring. Now, having seen the fiends, isn't it obvious to you, Jacob, and to you, Anna, that Jimmy was sired by one of them? One of them impregnated daft Molly Metcalf, up on the fell."

Anna Thaxton and Jacob Pole looked at each other. Jacob nodded, and Anna bit her lip. "He's quite right, Richard," she said. "Now I think about it, Jimmy looks just like a cross of a human with a fiend. Not only that, he knows his way perfectly through all the tunnels, and seems quite comfortable there."

"So, my first point is made," said Darwin. "The fiends are basically human, though they are a variation on our usual human form—more different, perhaps, than a Chinaman, but not much more so."

"But how could they exist?" asked Thaxton. "Unless they were created as one of the original races of man?"

"I don't know if there really were any 'original races of man.' To my mind, all animal forms develop and change, as their needs change. There is a continuous succession of small changes, produced I know not how—perhaps by the changes to their surroundings. The beasts we finally see are the result of this long succession—and that includes Man."

Darwin sat back and picked up his pie for a second attack. Pole, who had heard much the same thing several times before, seemed unmoved, but Anna and Richard were clearly uncomfortable with Darwin's statements.

"You realize," said Thaxton cautiously, "that your statements are at variance with all the teachings of the Church—and with the words of the Bible?"

"I do," said Darwin indistinctly, through a mouth crammed full of pie. He held out his mug for a refill of the spiced wine.

"But what of your other assertion, Erasmus?" said Pole. "If the fiends were not on Cross Fell for the past fifteen hundred years, then where the devil were they? And what were they doing?"

Darwin sighed. He was torn between his love of food and his fondness for exposition. "You didn't listen to me properly, Jacob. I never said they weren't about Cross Fell. I said they weren't living in the mine tunnels for fifteen hundred years."

"Then where were they?" asked Anna.

"Why, living on the surface—mainly, I suspect, in the woods. Their murals showed many forest scenes. Perhaps they were in Milburn Forest, southeast of Cross Fell. Think, now, there have been legends of wood-folk in England as long as history has records. Puck, Robin Goodfellow, the dryads—the stories have many forms, and they are very widespread."

"But if they lived in the woods," said Anna, "why would they move to the mine tunnels? And when did they do it?"

"When? I don't know exactly," said Darwin. "But I would imagine that it was when we began to clear the forests of England, just a few hundred years ago. We began to destroy their homes."

"Wouldn't they have resisted, if that were true?" asked Pole.

"If they were really fiends, they might—or if they were like us. But I believe that they are a very peaceful people. You saw how gentle they were with us, how they cared for us when we were sick—even though we must have frightened them at least as much as they disturbed us. *We* were the aggressors. We drove them to live in the disused mines."

"Surely they do not propose to live there forever?" asked Anna. "Should they not be helped, and brought forth to live normally?"

Darwin shook his head. "Beware the missionary spirit, my dear. They want to be allowed to live their own lives. In any case, I do not believe they would survive if they tried to mingle with us. They are already a losing race, dwindling in numbers."

"How do you know?" asked Pole.

Darwin shrugged. "Partly guesswork, I must admit. But if they could not compete with us before, they will inevitably lose again in the battle for living space. I told you on the fell, Jacob, in all of Nature the weaker dwindle in number, and the strong flourish. There is some kind of selection of the strongest, that goes on all the time."

"But that cannot be so," said Thaxton. "There has not been enough time since the world began, for the process you describe to significantly alter the balance of the natural proportions of animals. According to Bishop Ussher, this world began only four thousand and four years before the birth of Our Lord."

Darwin sighed. "Aye, I'm familiar with the bishop's theory. But if he'd ever lifted his head for a moment, and looked at Nature, he'd have realized that he was talking through his episcopal hat. Why, man, you have only to go and look at the waterfall at High Force, not thirty miles from here, and you will realize that it must have taken tens of thousands of years, at the very least, to carve its course through the rock. The earth we live on is old—despite the good bishop's pronouncement."

Anna struggled to her feet and went over to look out of the window. It was still foggy and bleak, and the fell was barely visible through the mist. "So they are humans, out there," she said. "I hope, then, that they have some happiness in life, living in the cold and the dark."

"I think they do," said Darwin. "They were dancing when first we saw them, and they did not appear unhappy. And they do come out, at night, when the fell is shrouded in mist—to steal a few sheep of yours, I'm afraid. They always return before first light. They fear the aggressive instincts of the rest of us, in the world outside."

"What should we do about them?" asked Anna.

"Leave them alone, to live their own lives," replied Darwin. "I already made that promise to the red fiend, when we began to exchange medical information. He wanted an assurance from us that we would not trouble them, and I gave it. In return, he gave me a treasure-house of botanical facts about the plants that grow on the high fells—if I can but remember it here, until I have opportunity to write it down." He tapped his head.

Anna returned from the window. She sat down again and sighed. "They deserve their peace," she said. "From now on, if there are lights and cries on the fell at night,

I will have the sense to ignore them. If they want peace, they will have it."

"So, Erasmus, I've been away again chasing another false scent. Damn it, I wish that Thomas of Appleby were alive and here, so I could choke him. All that nonsense about the Treasure of Odirex—and we found nothing."

Pole and Darwin were sitting in the coach, warmly wrapped against the cold. Outside, a light snow was falling as they wound their way slowly down the Tees valley, heading east for the coastal plains that would take them south again to Lichfield. It was three days before Christmas, and Anna Thaxton had packed them an enormous hamper of food and drink to sustain them on their journey. Darwin had opened it, and was happily exploring the contents.

"I could have told you from the beginning," he said, "that the treasure would have to be something special to please Odirex. Ask yourself, what sort of treasure would please the King of Hate? Why was he *called* the King of Hate?"

"Damned if I know. All I care about is that there was nothing there. If there ever was a treasure, it must have been rifled years ago."

Darwin paused, a chicken in one hand and a Christmas pudding in the other. He looked from one to the other, unable to make up his mind.

"You're wrong, Jacob," he said. "The treasure was there. You saw it for yourself, and I had even closer contact with it. Don't you see, *the fiends themselves are the Treasure of Odirex*. Or rather, it is what they bear with them that is the Treasure."

"Bear with them? Sheepskins?"

"Not something you could see, Jacob. *Disease*. The fiends are carriers of plague. That's what Odirex discovered, when he discovered them. Don't ask me how he escaped the effects himself. That's what he used to drive away the Romans. If you look back in history, you'll find there was a big outbreak of plague in Europe, back about the year four hundred and thirty—soon after the Romans left Britain. People have assumed that it was bubonic plague, just like in the Black Death in the fourteenth century, or the Great Plague here a hundred years ago. Now, I am sure that it was not the same."

"Wait a minute, Erasmus. If the fiends carry plague, why aren't all the folk near Cross Fell dead?"

"Because we have been building up immunity, by exposure, for many hundreds of years. It is the process of selection again. People who can resist the plague can survive, the others die. I was struck down myself, but thanks to our improved natural resistance, and thanks also to the potion that the red fiend made me drink, all I had was a very bad day. If I'd been exposed for the first time, as the Romans were, I'd be dead by now."

"And why do you assert that it was not bubonic plague? Would you not be immune to that?"

"I don't know. But I became sick only a few *hours* after first exposure to the fiends—that is much too quick for bubonic plague."

"Aye," said Pole. "It is, and I knew that for myself if I thought about it. So Odirex used his 'treasure' against the Romans. Can you imagine the effect on them?"

"You didn't see me," said Darwin, "and I only had the merest touch of the disease. Odirex could appear with the fiends, contaminate the Roman equipment—touching it might be enough, unless personal contact were necessary. That wouldn't be too difficult to arrange, either. Then, within twelve hours, the agony and deaths would begin. Do you wonder that they called him *Odii Rex*, the King of Hate? Or that they so feared his treasure that they fled this part of the country completely? But by then it was too late. They took the disease with them, back into Europe."

Pole looked out at the snow, now beginning to settle on the side of the road. He shivered. "So the fiends really are fiends, after all. They may not intend to do it, but they have killed, just as much as if they were straight from Hell."

"They have indeed," said Darwin. "More surely than sword or musket, more secretly than noose or poison. And all by accident, as far as they are concerned. They must have developed their own immunity many thousands of years ago, perhaps soon after they branched off from our kind of humanity."

Jacob Pole reached into the hamper and pulled out a bottle of claret. "I'd better start work on the food and drink, too, Erasmus," he said morosely. "Otherwise you'll demolish the lot. Don't bother to pass me food. The wine will do nicely. I've had another disappointment, and I want to wash it down. Damn it, I wish that once in my lifetime—just once—I could find a treasure that didn't turn to vapor under my shovel."

He opened the bottle, settled back into the corner of the coach seat, and closed his eyes. Darwin looked at him unhappily. Jacob had saved his life in the mine, without a doubt. In return, all that Pole had received was a bitter letdown.

Darwin hunched down in his seat and thought of all that he had omitted to say, to Jacob and to the Thaxtons. In his pocket, the necklace from the female fiend seemed to burn, red-hot, like the bright red gold from which it was made. Somewhere in their explorations of the tunnels under Cross Fell, the fiends had discovered the gold mine that had so long eluded the other searchers. And it was plentiful enough, so that any fiend was free to wear as much of the heavy gold as he chose.

Darwin looked across at his friend. Jacob Pole was a sick man, and they both knew it. He had perhaps two or three more years, before the accumulated ailments from a lifetime of exploration came to take him. Now it was in Darwin's power to satisfy a life's ambition, and reveal to Jacob a true treasure trove, up there on Cross Fell. But Darwin also remembered the look in the red fiend's eyes, when he had asked for peace for his people as the price for his medical secrets. More disturbance would break that promise.

Outside the coach, the snow was falling heavier on the Tees valley. Without doubt, it would be a white Christmas. Darwin looked out at the tranquil scene, but his mind was elsewhere and he felt no peace. Jacob Pole, or the red fiend? Very soon, he knew that he would have to make a difficult decision.

Appendix: Erasmus Darwin, Fact and Fiction

The facts about the life of the man who was arguably the greatest Englishman of the eighteenth century are straightforward enough.

Erasmus Darwin, the grandfather of Charles Darwin, was born on December 12th, 1731. He spent his childhood in Nottinghamshire, went up to St. John's College, Cambridge, in 1750, and took his BA degree in 1754. Next he moved to Edinburgh and studied medicine there for two years. Following a very brief attempt to set up a practice in Nottingham, Darwin after only two months moved to Lichfield, a town about fifteen miles north of Birmingham. There he gradually built up a huge reputation as a physician, which followed him to Derby when he moved to that town in the 1780s.

He married twice: in 1757 to Mary Howard, who bore him five children and died in 1770; and in 1781 to Elizabeth Pole, the widow of Colonel Pole of Radburn Hall in Derby (more on this later) who bore him seven children. Between his two marriages he consoled himself with the company of a lady who may or may not have been called Parker. At any rate, she bore him two children who were known as the Misses Parker and who when adult ran a boarding school for girls in Derbyshire.

Through the 1780s and 1790s Darwin became steadily more and more famous, to the point where he endured constant persuasion to move to London from his would-be patients—including King George III, who would gladly have appointed Darwin as Court Physician. He resisted all attempts, and at age 70 died in Derby on April 18th, 1802.

So far this seems like the typical life of a middle-class English gentleman, more successful than most in his chosen career but certainly not the stuff of legends. It is only when we look closer that Darwin begins to surprise us. He was the most famous doctor of his day and the last resort for difficult cases, particularly where mental problems were involved. His treatments were original, sometimes daring, and throughout his career he had a very high proportion of "miracle" cures.

In addition to his main profession, Darwin was also a best-selling poet. In that field he attempted and succeeded in the apparently impossible: the complete exposition of contemporary ideas in geology, botany, biology, technology, and the history of the natural world—in rhymed couplets. His two major poetic works were lengthy, *The Botanic Garden* and *The Temple of Nature*, and in the latter he presented his own theory of evolution. Two generations before Charles Darwin, Erasmus understood perfectly well the idea of the survival of the fittest, and he knew the importance of mutations in modifying a species. However, he also believed that acquired characteristics might be inherited, a discredited idea that found its most famous expression in the nineteenth century work of Lamarck.

Samuel Johnson, 21 years older than Erasmus Darwin,

was also born in Lichfield but chose to make his home in London. Perhaps that was just as well. Like Dr. Johnson he did not welcome rivals, and Lichfield was scarcely big enough for both of them. If we suspect that the intellectual company and competition in the English Midlands was less than in London, we must also note that Darwin founded the Lunar Society, which drew into it an incredible array of talented people—albeit more concerned generally with the sciences than the arts.

The Lunar Society met once a month, on the night of the full moon so that members could ride home by moonlight. Its attendees, most of them regulars, sound like a catalog of the most influential figures of the time:

—James Watt, the key figure in the development of steam power;

—Josiah Wedgewood, whose pottery in the second half of the eighteenth century became world-famous, a reputation it enjoys to this day;

—Matthew Boulton, England's leading industrialist of the time, whose metal works at Soho near Birmingham were also world-famous;

—Joseph Priestley, one of the founders of modern chemistry, whose move away from Birmingham upset him more for the loss of his colleagues at the Lunar Society than for any other reason;

—Samuel Galton, another wealthy industrialist whose grandson was Francis Galton, the pioneer of genetics and statistics;

—John Baskerville, the printer and typographer who created the wonderful Baskerville Bibles;

—Thomas Day, the author of the famous (but unspeakably sermonizing) *The History of Sandford and Merton*, a book which was still being inflicted on English youth as school prizes a hundred years later;

—William Murdock, the inventor of coal gas generation, gas lighting, and steam locomotives.

And of course there was Darwin himself. This whole group of men enjoyed fame in their own time, and helped to launch the Industrial Revolution in England.

Darwin was more than a founder, organizer, and stimulant to the Lunar Society. He was mechanically ingenious and a prolific inventor, scribbling out his endless stream of ideas as his carriage bore him on the extended medical rounds of Derbyshire. He had an original approach to everything, from the mechanics of human speech to windmills to water closets to a hydrogen/oxygen rocket motor. He wrote extensively on medicine, biology, physics, technology, gardening, agriculture, and the education of the young.

On the personal side, Darwin's appearance—even as told by his friends—does not sound too attractive. He became very fat by early middle age, to the point where by 1776 a semicircular section had been removed from his dinner table to make room for his belly. His face was badly marked by early smallpox, and he lost his front teeth while still a young man. The defense of his appearance by his good friend Anna Seward tells us more perhaps than it intended. Even though Darwin had lost his teeth, she says, and he did look like a butcher, it was untrue to claim, as others had done, that his tongue hung out like a dog's when he walked.

Looks aside, Darwin generally enjoyed good health and had an excellent appetite ("Eat or be eaten" was one of his mottoes). He suffered somewhat from gout, which he treated himself by abstinence from alcohol. He broke his kneecap in 1768, when he was thrown out of a carriage of his own design, and was after that always slightly lame. That he was able at the age of fifty to woo and win a rich and attractive widow, against the competition of handsome young rivals, suggests that Darwin's appearance was no hindrance to his enjoyment of life.

There are six biographies of Darwin that I suggest as good reading: Anna Seward's contemporary account, published in 1804; Charles Darwin's account of his grandfather's life, drawn mainly from family documents and published in 1887; Hesketh Pearson's 1930 biography; Maureen McNeil's 1987 book, *Under the Banner of Science*, which sets Darwin in the context of the politics and science of his time; and two highly readable biographies by Desmond King-Hele, *Erasmus Darwin* (1964) and *Doctor of Revolution* (1977), which offer the most rounded picture of the whole man. In drawing from these and other sources, I have tried to provide a fictional picture of Darwin that is consistent with the real man, in both his habits and his attitudes. For example, Darwin was not religious, and also not afraid to say so—something not common in his time. But his attitude to his fellow humans was always one of unusual benevolence and sympathy, regardless of differences in viewpoint.

Having followed the facts with Darwin in these stories, I must now say that the other characters presented here are largely fabrication. Darwin did know a Colonel Pole (Sacheverel, not Jacob), and following the Colonel's death married his widow; but there is no evidence that the two men were good friends—and some evidence to the contrary. Since the actions of these stories takes place in the second half of the 1770s I also found it convenient to transport Pole's house at Derby over to Lichfield, so as to make him a closer neighbor to Darwin. There is no evidence at all that the good colonel was an inveterate treasure hunter.

If most of the people other than Darwin and the members of the Lunar Society are inventions, the backgrounds to the stories are not.

The Devil of Malkirk

After the Rebellion of 1745–46 in Scotland, and the defeat at Culloden of Bonnie Prince Charlie (Prince Charles Edward, the Young Pretender), the Scots were forbidden by the Disarming Act to carry weapons. A first offense carried a fine of fifteen pounds sterling, a second offense meant transportation. The Scots were also forbidden to wear the kilt and other Highland dress until that ban was lifted in 1782.

Prince Charles Edward supposedly died in Rome in January 1788, still in exile. However, there had been in the 1750s and 1760s many rumors of his visits to England and to Scotland, in disguise and perhaps with a double to front for him in Europe. If the Prince had suffered a fatal accident while in Scotland, would the double have continued the royal imposture? I am willing to admit that possibility, and I assumed it in "The Devil of Malkirk."

The Heart of Ahura Mazda

Given the universally inquisitive and worldly nature of both men, it is hardly surprising that Erasmus Darwin and Benjamin Franklin would also be good friends. Darwin was twenty-five years younger, and admired the older man enormously both as scientist and politician. They met sometime before 1760, probably in 1758, and kept in touch up to Franklin's death in 1790. Naturally, Darwin followed closely Franklin's researches into electricity, which stands him in good stead in unraveling the mystery of "The Heart of Ahura Mazda."

The "lost rivers" of London, which the men follow in this story, are accurate both as to names and locations. The character of Joseph Faulkner resembles Franklin in age, nationality, and appearance, all the way to the bald head and fur hat. However, it seemed better to restrict the allusion to physical resemblance; just like Erasmus Darwin and Samuel Johnson in a single city, Darwin and Franklin would offer each other too much competition to be the lead character in a single story.

The Phantom of Dunwell Cove

"The Phantom of Dunwell Cove" invented little. Joseph Priestley was working with dephlogisticated air—his name for oxygen—in the 1770s, and Darwin would indeed have been keen to attend the Lunar Society meeting and hear of the latest progress. The influence of the Gulf Stream in tempering the climate of Devon and Cornwall was well known, and many an Englishman looked forward to an early spring journey to England's southwestern peninsula. The only explicit change to history is in timing. Humphry Davy learned of the anesthetic properties of nitrous oxide only in 1799. He reported becoming "absolutely intoxicated" after breathing sixteen quarts of it. Richard Dunwell is presumed to have discovered and used the gas twenty-some years earlier. That is unlikely, but certainly not impossible in an age of reduced communication.

The Lambeth Immortal

Although the general setting of this story is real, Lambeth is an invented village. It lies near the north coast of Norfolk, midway between The Wash and Cromer. Since the villages of Blakeney and Stiffkey are still there to this day, the interested reader can locate Alderton Manor with fair precision. "The Blues," cockles from Stiffkey, used to be famous, and the locals around Cromer still tell the story of Black Shuck, the giant hound who haunts the seacoast.

It would be quite plausible for Darwin to visit Norwich Hospital. As one of the first hospitals to be built outside London, it had been opened only in the early 1770s. At the time Norwich was the third largest city in the country, inferior in size only to London and to Bristol.

The lack of hospitals may have been a good thing since the death rate in them was terrifyingly high. As Darwin remarked to Ledyard in "The Lambeth Immortal," a book, *De Contagione*, by Girolamo Fracastoro had as early as 1546 proposed a germ theory of disease, but the hospital authorities remained blissfully ignorant of any such ideas; or of simpler ones, such as cleanliness. Sir John Floyer wrote a book, *Inquiry into the Right Use of the Hot, Cold and Temperate Baths*, which ran to six editions between 1697 and 1722. It does not mention anywhere the idea of bathing for the sake of cleanliness.

The Solborne Vampire

"The Solborne Vampire" mingles three important themes of Darwin's life. James Watt and Matthew Boulton excited Darwin's interests as engineer, though he probably recognized Watt as his eternal superior in that field. No one, however, was Darwin's superior when it came to medical diagnosis, or the skeptical evaluation of "supernatural" phenomena. Darwin was an ardent believer in the freedom of mankind, and welcomed both the American Revolution, and, in its less bloody phase, the French Revolution.

On the question of dates: the "chess automaton" of Baron Wolfgang von Kempelen was first exhibited in 1769. Emperor Joseph II of Austria, Empress Catherine of Russia, and Napoleon Bonaparte were all taken in by it, and persuaded that it was a real automaton. The centrifugal governor, which uses the speed of rotation of a steam engine to control the steam input, is attributed to James Watt and was produced around 1784. The relationship between Darwin and James Watt, the father of the steam engine, is neither invented nor exaggerated. They were close friends for 25 years. Watt said, after Darwin's death, "It will be my pride, while I live, that I have enjoyed the friendship of such a man."

The Treasure of Odirex

This story called for little background invention or supposition. Cross Fell is real. It is the highest point of the Pennines, the chain of hills that runs from the English Midlands to the Scottish Border. At one time Cross Fell was indeed known as Fiend's Fell, and according to legend St. Augustine drove the fiends away with a cross. Since then it has been called Cross Fell. Lead mines abound there, and have since Roman times.

The Helm is also real. It is a bank of cloud that sits on or just above the summit of Cross Fell when the "helm wind" is blowing. As a natural but a puzzling meteorological phenomenon, the Helm has attracted a good deal of scientific attention. The reasons for the existence and persistence of the Helm are discussed in Manley's book *Climate and the British Scene*, published in 1952.

As for the botany, the medications used by Darwin are pretty much those available to the practitioner of eighteenth-century medicine. The plants used by the red fiend are consistent with the botany of the high fells, but so far as I know the medical value of most of them has not been established.

The eighteenth century is hard to see through twenty-first-century eyes, and when we meet someone who thinks with a modern mind it is surprising. Like Franklin, Darwin was centuries ahead of his time. If in these stories I have emphasized his more colorful and flamboyant side, that should not obscure the real man. The true Darwin is not to be judged by his pockmarked face or his overweight body. He is to be judged by his mind, and on that basis he carries off the highest honors.

The man to remember is the one described in *The Torch Bearers*, by Alfred Noyes:

> . . . that eager mind, whom fools deride
>   For laced and periwigged verses on his
>   flowers;
>   Forgetting how he strode before his age,
>   And how his grandson caught from his
>   right hand
>   A fire that lit the world.

Erasmus Darwin makes us look around and ask a question: Who, two hundred years from now, will serve as an emblem for the best of our own times?